J.D. LINTON

The Last Storm

Copyright © 2022 by J.D. Linton

All rights reserved. No part of this publication may be reproduced, stored or transmitted in any form or by any means, electronic, mechanical, photocopying, recording, scanning, or otherwise without written permission from the publisher. It is illegal to copy this book, post it to a website, or distribute it by any other means without permission.

This novel is entirely a work of fiction. The names, characters and incidents portrayed in it are the work of the author's imagination. Any resemblance to actual persons, living or dead, events or localities is entirely coincidental.

First edition

Cover art by MoonPress Design | Moonpress.co
Proofreading by The Fiction Fix

This book was professionally typeset on Reedsy. Find out more at reedsy.com

Contents

Preface	v
Acknowledgement	vii
Chapter One	1
Chapter Two	7
Chapter Three	15
Chapter Four	23
Chapter Five	33
Chapter Six	39
Chapter Seven	48
Chapter Eight	60
Chapter Nine	69
Chapter Ten	79
Chapter Eleven	88
Chapter Twelve	100
Chapter Thirteen	111
Chapter Fourteen	123
Chapter Fifteen	137
Chapter Sixteen	148
Chapter Seventeen	159
Chapter Eighteen	173
Chapter Nineteen	185
Chapter Twenty	201
Chapter Twenty One	219
Chapter Twenty Two	232

Chapter Twenty Three	245
Chapter Twenty Four	264
Chapter Twenty Five	281
Chapter Twenty Six	296
Chapter Twenty Seven	308
Chapter Twenty Eight	327
Chapter Twenty Nine	340
Chapter Thirty	354
Chapter Thirty One	374
A Letter	381
About the Author	382

Preface

CONTENT WARNING

The Last Storm is a fantasy romance based in a fictional realm and while fun, the story contains elements that may not be suitable for some readers — Explicit sexual content, anxiety, panic attacks, profanity, kidnapping, physical and mental abuse from a parent (in the form of flashbacks), loss of a loved one, and violence (blood, war, death).

Readers who may be sensitive to these elements, please take note.

Pronunciation Guide
  Ara Starrin: Ar-ah Star-in
  Evander Starrin: Eh-van-der Star-in
  Elora: Eh-lor-ah
  Adon: Ay-din
  Rogue Draki: Row-g Drah-key
  Adrastus: Ah-drah-stus
  Doran: Door-in
  Thana: Than-ah
  Alden: All-din
  Iaso: Eye-ah-so
  Delphia: Dell-fee-uh
  Ewan: Eh-win
  Vaelor: Vah-ler

Adonis: Ah-dawn-is
Pyric: Pyre-rick

Acknowledgement

I have so many people that deserve thanks—

Jo, I feel I should thank you first and foremost. You were the first person I told that I wanted to write a book and your response was so supportive. Your belief in me sent me down a rabbit hole and it's thanks to you that I found my passion. I will forever be grateful for you, for this and so many other reasons. I love you, sis.

Hav, thank you for reading every version of this book (even the shitty first draft) and telling me how amazing it was and that I needed to keep going. I know that first draft was ROUGH, but you never failed to make me feel good about it. You have been such an incredible friend and alpha reader. I loved going to AU so much, but my favorite thing I gained was you as a friend.

To my hubbie, you've always been supportive of everything I've wanted to do and this was no exception. From helping me set up a writing desk to surprising me with a typing keyboard for mother's day to just really, genuinely believing in me, you've been an amazing partner and hand to hold. Thank you and I love you. Always.

To JN, Brittany, Jessica, and Taygan— my sweet, sweet beta readers, THANK YOU. Your help has been invaluable to me and you were all *so* incredibly helpful. I appreciate you all so much, and I would be nothing without y'all.

KC & Ky, thank you for being there for me during this whole indie publishing journey. It's been messy and chaotic and wonderful and life-changing. I am SO thankful that booktok brought you two to me and I can't wait to meet you two in person next year. It's going to be epic, I know it.

And to anyone I missed, just know I appreciate you. Every supportive person, every kind word, was a little push in the right direction and I mean it when I say, I would be NOTHING without y'all.

Chapter One

Ara

"Hurry up, now, Ara. Your father will be waiting." Suppressing a groan, I stuck my head in the doorway. "Almost ready."

It was the night of yet another dinner—one at which my father hosted several important figures, including King Adon. They occurred every other month or so, and I hated everything about them: the expectations, the shallow conversations, the extravagant, wasteful display of wealth and status.

I tugged at the corset sucking the breath from my chest.

And the dresses. I hated the dresses.

The sound of guests arriving caught my attention, and I glanced back at the mirror, wincing at my reflection. With my hair pulled back and pink dusting my eyelids and cheeks, I looked every bit the image my father wished me to be. Soft. Agreeable. Marriageable.

My father had been ready to marry me off for years. When my twenty-sixth birthday came and went, he started to push harder, insisting I settle down, and I consistently refused. I couldn't imagine settling down here, in this village, with the same people, the same scenery, the same...

Taking a deep breath, I pushed down the rising panic and turned to find my mother standing in the doorway.

"You're so beautiful, Ara," she whispered, clasping her hands together.

"So are you, Mother," I replied, taking her elbow and leading us to the staircase. From this angle, we could see each person as they arrived, and every pair of eyes found us in return as we crested the top step, setting my cheeks aflame.

Descending the marble staircase, I found Father first. He was talking in hushed whispers with Marcus, his next in command.

As the top general for King Adon of Auryna, the human kingdom, he was constantly engaged in conversation with his men, as the king relied heavily on him for border security. After almost twenty years of service, he had become hyper-vigilant, demanding to be kept in the loop about any and all activity, no matter what time of day. Because of this, our estate grounds were constantly patrolled.

Tonight was no exception. In every corner of the room stood a guard, trained and silent, blending into the background.

Resisting the urge to eavesdrop on their conversation, I scanned the room, looking for Finley just as King Adon entered the room.

He was lean and tall enough to constantly look down his nose at people, his chin high with self-importance. His skin was pale, his dark hair hanging in short curls over light brown eyes. While he was attractive enough to have women falling at his feet, he never entertained them or took a wife—he never entertained anyone outside of this room, actually. He was extremely private, never leaving his castle except for my father's dinners. Most of his own people had never even laid eyes on him.

As every guest flocked to his side, I turned, locking eyes with Finn. His face lit up, a grin stretching ear to ear. Sidestepping the other guests, he closed the distance between us, running a hand through his coppery hair.

"Aren't you a sight for sore eyes?" he teased, dropping his gaze down the length of my body before bringing it back up to meet my eyes.

"It's nice to see you too, Finn. Although, I saw you just yesterday..." I replied, a little shocked by the way his eyes devoured me.

Finley was my only childhood friend; our parents had been friends since before we were born. Since we were the same age, we essentially grew up together. At some level, I knew he had feelings for me, but he also knew I had no intention of marrying. I craved adventure, passion, something more, and as guilty as it made me to admit it, he was decidedly not that. He was safe, which made him a great friend, but I couldn't bring myself to feel differently—the way I knew he did.

He knew that, had respected it in the past, and yet...

"I could see your face every day and never tire of it," he whispered, stepping closer to tuck a stray hair behind my ear. My eyebrows furrowed at his boldness and I stepped back, studying his face.

"I should go join my mother," I said quickly, glancing about the room and backing away. "I'll see you in a bit."

Feeling his gaze on my back, I joined Mother and accompanied her to the dining room.

As with every other part of the house, my father had spared no expense with the dining room. The chamber was large and open with emerald-green walls, covered in antique mirrors of various sizes and ages, all framed in gold. The warm shimmer of hundreds of lit candles danced and swayed around us, lining the center of the long, mahogany dining table.

As I took my seat, Finley sat to my left, and I gave him a tight smile before greeting the woman to my right.

The meal was elaborate, consisting of several types of meats and vegetables, followed by a lavish menu of desserts and wines. It was all a display, a not-so-subtle brag, and as usual, it ground my nerves.

As dinner finally concluded and the servants cleared the table, I waited for my dismissal, but it never came. Instead, my father stood, clearing his throat.

"Thank you all for joining us tonight. While you have all dined with us before, tonight is a particularly special occasion," he said, scanning the table to make eye contact with each of his guests. I looked from him to my mother and she gave me a faint smile that didn't quite reach her eyes. When I looked back at my father, I found his eyes on me, and my mouth went dry.

"Ara, please stand. Let them see how beautiful my daughter is." He beamed, and I hesitated. Father gestured, raising his hand in a command to stand. I scooted the chair back, rising. "Finley, please join her."

My heart leapt into my throat, and I whipped my head to him.

No.

He winked at me, grinning with satisfaction.

No, this was not happening.

CHAPTER ONE

My cheeks flushed, my stomach in knots, as I slowly looked back at my father.

"Finley and Ara have been friends for as long as they have been alive. Before that, his parents, Marcus and Leia, were our dearest friends," he said, gesturing to Mother. "Over the years, our families were tied together by friendship and mutual respect, but we have decided a more permanent bond is in order. With great pride and love, we are happy to announce the engagement of our daughter, Ara, to their son, Finley."

Every thought in my head came to a screeching halt, and my skin went cold, frozen on the spot.

"Please raise your glass in a toast to the happy couple," he announced, raising his goblet to the room. "May they be as fortunate as we have been. May they have a long fruitful marriage, blessed with many children, and the privilege of growing old in each other's arms. To Ara and Finley," he said, raising his glass again and downing the contents.

Many children.

Growing old.

The room cheered, every face radiating with joy as if they all expected this. The room swayed under my feet.

Tearing my gaze from my father, I slowly turned to my mother. While she bore a smile, it was sad, apologetic. She took a small sip of wine, dropping her gaze to the table like she couldn't bear to look at me.

My vision blurred as my thoughts spiraled and a cold sweat broke out along my spine.

My father had just announced, to every family friend and the king himself, that I was engaged and without any interjection… I was.

Finn's fingers intertwined with mine, turning me to him.

He was overwhelmingly happy with no concern for the turmoil playing out behind my eyes. Maybe he didn't see it. Maybe….

Maybe he knew.

Maybe he wanted this, even though he knew I didn't.

Maybe he didn't care.

My face heated.

Before I could even ask, he grabbed either side of my face, bringing his mouth down to mine in a sudden, awkward kiss.

In front of the entire table.

They clapped and cheered, ecstatic.

Oblivious.

My face was on fire.

Chapter Two

Ara

I paced incessantly in my room.
I cannot marry Finn. I cannot.
He was a fine enough man—from a good family, kind, and he'd been my friend for years, but I didn't want a slow life. *Many children*, as my father had said, and Finn did.

We were simply cut from two different cloths and trying to stitch us together would only end in disaster, either his or mine... Ours.

Sighing, my feet slowed. I plopped down onto the mattress, bringing my face to my hands.

In actuality, it seemed everyone was cut from one cloth, and I was cut from an entirely different one. For my entire life, I had never quite fit in with the people surrounding me. It was as if I was watching through a window, understanding their wishes and desires to an extent, watching them settle, have children, build houses... But while they were content to live happily ever after here, I was not.

I couldn't possibly imagine living in the confines of this small village for the rest of my life, but I was so close to doing exactly that, teetering just on the edge of permanence.

This exact reason was why I read, to escape into stories of adventure and lust and soul-consuming passion—everything lacking in my real life. I lived through books, and they mended me for a time, but once they were finished, the hole in my soul returned, the emptiness in my chest that comes with crashing back to reality, reminded of duty and responsibility, rules and confinement.

In my heart of hearts, I knew no book would ever fill the ache that so constantly plagued me. It felt as if everything I desired was just out of reach, just barely out of sight, taunting me but never revealing itself, and I was desperately chasing it in every book I devoured.

They were just a patch, holding me together for the time being, but I was always left waiting, wanting for something, anything. Just more.

This feeling—this trapped, no end in sight, suffocating feeling—is what led me to the local pub for the first time years ago.

On a whim of rebellion and bravery, I had snuck out of my window and down the vine, escaping into town. It had been so late that night, the pub was the only thing still open, so I'd slipped in and never turned back. It became my place of peace, where I could just be normal. Free. Where I could just *breathe*.

And it was where I needed to go now.

Jerking to my feet, I ripped the pins from my hair and tossed them on the bureau. My hair fell around me in loose waves as I scratched at my aching scalp. Reaching around, I quickly untied my corset strings and yanked it overhead, dropping it to the floor, the ballgown quickly following.

CHAPTER TWO

Kicking out of the dress, I scooped it all up and hurled it into the bathing chamber where the maids would whisk it away in the morning—hopefully to never be seen again.

Rushing back into the room in only my undergarments, I stopped dead in my tracks. My mother was sitting on the bed with her hands in her lap, face downcast.

"I'm sorry I couldn't do more. Believe me when I say I tried, my love. I did," she said, her voice wavering. "I don't want you to think I wished this for you—"

She stopped mid-sentence when I dropped to my knees before her, taking her hands in mine.

"I would never think that, Mother," I replied.

She glanced up with misty eyes, throwing her arms around my neck.

"I want you to have love. Real, true love, Ara." She hugged me tighter. "I wanted that for you."

Wanted. Past tense.

My heart cracked a little at her words, but I squeezed her all the same before releasing her to sit beside her.

"I wanted that too," I whispered and we both just stared at the floor, unable to conjure the right words.

Of course, there was nothing to be said. When it came to my father, it was like arguing with a wall. His mind was decided, and it would not be changed except of his own accord.

It was done the moment he announced it.

"No… No. I will talk to him again. I know you don't want…" She gestured around the room, but I knew exactly what she meant. She meant everything. This house, this town, this life. "This."

Placing her dainty hand on my arm, she met my eyes, and I could see the sadness lingering behind them.

"But you know, and hear me out, Finn… He could be a kind husband and his family is well off. He could provide you with a life of ease if you could live with that," she said.

I bit my tongue as she spoke. *I could survive with it, but could I live? Would it be considered living?*

She continued before I had a chance to respond. "And just so you know, it is possible to live with a marriage of just friendship." She released a deep sigh. "It is that way with your father, for me at least. With friendship comes love, and just because I don't love him *that* way doesn't mean my life has been miserable. It has given me you and you are the best thing I could've ever asked for."

I sat up straighter, confusion and heartache welling in my chest.

"You don't love Father? I didn't know that," I uttered. "Either way, you know as well as I that Finn deserves more… more than I could give him. He deserves someone who would love to live that life with him, someone who would take pride in being his wife and mother to his children. That would not be me."

She nodded, her eyebrows furrowing.

"I know that's not what you want, Ara. I know," she said. "I will talk to Evander again. I will change his mind."

With that, she rose to her feet, placing her hand on mine for a moment before taking her leave.

I stared after her, long after the door had clicked shut again, unable to pull my eyes away. While I loved her for trying, I knew nothing would come from that conversation, and the thought alone was gut-wrenching.

My father had set me down a path I would never veer from. Taking a deep breath, I slowly shifted my gaze to the window, just as the moon peeked over the horizon. It was full and bright, casting my room in a pale glow like it was watching me in return. The more I stared, the sadder it looked, and eventually, gray clouds swelled, rippling and enlarging until they engulfed the moon, saving me from my distant onlooker.

The breeze drifted in through my open window, bringing with it the scent of blooms on the vine, and it snapped me out of my stupor.

Jumping to my feet and ripping open the doors to the armoire, I reached in to grab my classics: black trousers, a blue tunic, and my black fleece cape. Pulling the clothes on, I threw the cape over my shoulders, clasped it at my collarbone, and tugged my boots on, lacing them tightly. Reaching to the back of the cabinet, I grabbed my favorite dagger and slid it into my right boot.

I ran to the window, spared a quick glance below, and swung my leg over, finding traction on the vine. Climbing over the windowsill, I grabbed the thick vine with both hands and descended quickly. Once near the ground, I released, landing with a thud, and sprinted to the tree line to trot along the pathway just out of view.

As I came upon the pub, the moon revealed itself again, illuminating the clearing. The pub was a small brown building with a straw roof, no windows, and grass sprouting at every corner, surrounded by a grove of mangled trees growing up and out in every direction. A few yards behind it sat a small pond, rippling with the breeze.

As I stepped from the treeline, the door opened, washing the stoop in a warm glow. A couple tumbled out, clearly intoxicated, giggling and holding hands as they disappeared down the path.

People were happy here. The mead was good, but the company was always better.

Smiling to myself, I strolled to the door. Even from outside, I could hear the usual hum of chatter and laughter. The bell jingled overhead as I pulled the door open. Just as I stepped over the threshold, something tugged at me, demanding my attention. I glanced up and locked eyes with a devastatingly handsome stranger.

While I had never seen him here before, he seemed relaxed, reclining in the back corner with an ankle thrown over one knee, his arm outstretched over the chair beside him. I couldn't look away, even as he stared back at me. Examining every inch of his face, I knew in my bones I would never forget it as it burned itself into my memory.

His hair was black as night, hanging in loose waves to his shoulders. It surrounded a tanned, chiseled face, his eyes a dark red-brown.

Mesmerizing.

Tilting my head, I noticed a scar just under his left ear, thick and jagged, that continued down his neck, disappearing beneath his black, unbuttoned tunic, and I suddenly found myself desperately wanting to follow it lower, lower, lower...

Someone tapped me on the shoulder, wanting to exit through the door I was blocking, and I jumped, snapping out of the spell this stranger had seemingly placed over me.

Forcing myself to look away, I made a beeline for the bar where Livvy, the barmaid, was pouring drinks. I sat on an old stool, and it creaked under my weight as I waved my hand to her, nodding in greeting.

The skin on the back of my neck prickled with awareness.

CHAPTER TWO

He was watching me.

Normally, it would be alarming, terrifying even, to have a stranger staring so blatantly, but in all honesty, I struggled not to do the same. Something about him was so enticing, tempting.

Biting my lip, I relented, peeking over my shoulder. Just as I expected, his gaze was locked on me, his expression confused but intrigued.

Snapping back towards the bar, I was met with Livvy as she set the largest mug in front of me, full to the brim with mead.

"You look like you could use it," she said, shrugging. Looking past me, her eyebrows furrowed and she leaned forward, resting her elbows on the bar. "You know that man over there is staring at you, right?"

I nodded. "I know. I'm trying to avoid any more awkward eye contact with him." I raised the mug to my lips, easily downing its contents.

She lifted an eyebrow at me.

"Are you all right? You look like you've been through the wringer today," she asked. Concern pressed between her brows before she relaxed again, rolling her eyes. "Did you have to suffer through another delicious dinner with your parents and their friends?"

She didn't understand why I hated them so much, and I understood why she felt that way. Not everyone gets to indulge in a warm meal so regularly. From her perspective, maybe it seemed as if I was just ungrateful—and maybe I was—but it wasn't the food I hated.

"Well, yes, but that's not what brought me here today." I chuckled weakly, setting the mug down before I held my hand out to her. On my third finger was my mother's ring, given to me just after the announcement—a dainty, light blue diamond, bound with a silver band. Her mouth fell open at the sight. "It would seem I am engaged..." A shocked smile pulled at her lips. "To Finley. I was completely unaware until tonight, when my father announced it to me *and* every other guest, including the king."

The blood drained from her face, the smile disappearing as quickly as it came. She reached out, placing a hand on mine.

"Oh, hun..."

I shook my head to clear the rising tears, pulling my hand from hers.

"That's why I'm here. To forget that any of... *that* happened. I don't want to talk or think about it," I said, giving her a quick nod. "So please, can I have another?" I asked, lifting the empty mug.

With pity etched into her every feature, she obliged, leaving the pitcher with me as she reluctantly tended to the rest of the bar.

Chapter Three

Rogue

I hated being on this side of the border.
Not only did I have to hide my wings behind glamour, I was also among humans.

Auryna had been ravaging my kingdom for years, as long as I could remember. Three years ago, they had managed to kill my father, the king of Ravaryn, and effectively ended the Ten-Year War. Since then, they had continued raiding and pillaging our border towns, destroying homes and livelihoods as they encroached on our land, but we didn't have the numbers to fight back. After ten years at war, my people were too tired, depleted, and disheartened. We had lost too many.

That was why I was here—to find secrets, weaknesses, anything to hold over Adon's head.

It was at his command, or rather his general's, that my father was murdered. One of my own kind, a Fae, had infiltrated my father's court as a mere servant, giving them easy access to his bed chambers, where he was assassinated in his sleep.

Of course, there would have been no other way to kill a dragon.

My father was a Draig, a dragon shifter, the last of his kind, and he had been ferocious. Cruel and unforgiving. Merciless. Attempting to murder him while he was awake would have been a fool's errand, a suicide, and while I wasn't entirely devastated by his death, the fact that he was murdered so easily in our own home enraged me.

Sighing, I stood from my perch in the shadows.

This had been a complete waste. I'd been here for three days, sulking in the outer corners of the castle courtyard, hoping to overhear any useful bits of conversation. I'd learned nothing so far. Adon was extremely private, hidden deep within his castle, guarded at all times. I hadn't come across a single person who had actually met or even spoken with him, much less knew him and his secrets.

Clenching my jaw, I stalked out of the courtyard, shouldering a man when he got in the way. Frustration boiled in my gut.

I hated the humans. They were greedy. Selfish. *Mindless.* They just wanted to marry, rut, have a few children, and grow old without ever seeing the world. To make it worse, they didn't even have the ability to find their true mate, so they spent their entire lives with the wrong person. It was disgusting.

The sun was setting when I stepped onto the worn dirt path, and I decided to make a last-ditch effort at the local pub, where guards, servants, and maids tended to frequent.

No one knew more secrets than a castle worker, and no one talked more than a person drunk on mead.

Walking up to the door, I pulled the handle, and as soon as

CHAPTER THREE

I stepped inside, I felt the stares.

They must not get many newcomers here.

Scanning the room, I found it quaint, with dirty off-white walls and a long, wooden bar on one side with several mismatched bar stools. On the other was an arrangement of tables filled with patrons, half of them already drunk. In the back corner, a game of cards was being played.

I stifled a smile. There was my in.

The men scowled at me with distrust as I strolled to their table.

Definitely no newcomers.

"Hey, no harm here," I said, holding my hands in front of me. "I was just coming to ask if I could join your game." I pulled out a sack, giving it a shake so they could hear the jingle of coins inside. "Next round on me?"

Glancing at each other, they shrugged, scooting the chairs around to accommodate another, unknowingly accepting a snake into their coop.

A few hours passed as I feigned ignorance in the game, allowing them to win several hands and buying another round of mead with each loss, gaining their trust and loosening their lips.

As it turned out, they were a group of guards from General Starrin's estate, and with this much alcohol in their systems, they were more than happy to complain—the long working hours, the lack of sleep, even mentioning the shift change schedule.

"Now, not only do we have to keep intruders out, we have to worry about keeping his unruly daughter in," grumbled one of the guards.

I silently leaned forward at his words. *The general has a*

daughter?

"She may be unruly, but it doesn't bother me much having to watch her," another guard winked, taking a sloppy drink. "Especially when she's training with her weapons. She has the stamina of a sturdy woman and the body of a well-paid whore," he snickered, and the group howled with laughter.

My lip twitched in disgust at the way they talked about women, but I didn't dare breathe a word as they continued.

"No, I think she is determined to get herself killed or, better yet, one of us," one whined. "She is *constantly* trying to sneak into town. She would be better suited staying put and doing womanly duties, like her mother."

The group grumbled in agreement.

She sneaks out, does she?

My mouth quirked up in a grin. My plan was coming together before my eyes.

I remained in the corner as the guards finally got up to leave. This trip had, in fact, not been a waste. Leaning back, I stretched out an arm, resting it on the now-empty chair beside me, and crossed my ankle over my knee.

Sighing with satisfaction, I let the tension roll off my shoulders as I watched a drunken couple stumble out the door, laughing.

As soon as the door closed, it opened again. I froze as a woman entered. When she glanced up, she looked straight at me and I felt everything at once. The pull. The lust. The blinding, overwhelming *need*.

The bond.

I was staring at the most beautiful woman I had ever seen, and she was my mate. I knew it in my soul as we locked eyes.

Her long, dark hair was hidden in her cloak—as if that could hide anything about her. She stood out like stars against the night sky, commanding attention. Her eyes were a piercing storm gray, the same color as her blue-gray tunic, her lips full and red, begging for my kiss.

My fingers itched to touch her as I felt her gaze roam over me, and then...

She looked away, walking to the bar.

Did she not feel this?

I gaped at her as she waved at the blonde bartender. They clearly knew each other.

What is she doing here of all places? If they knew each other, she must have been here before. What was a Fae doing in Auryna?

My gaze locked on her as I lost myself in thought. When she peeked over her shoulder at me and found me still staring after her, she immediately jerked back to the bar.

Clearly, she felt it, at least, but why would she ignore it? Does she not realize what this is?

* * *

I sat in the corner as she spent the night chatting with her barmaid friend at the bar. Several people came and went, stopping by to speak with her for a few minutes before moving on. She was clearly a regular here.

As the night came to an end and people started to clear out, I stood, easing my way to a closer table. I slumped down into the chair, resting my chin on my hand, my elbow on the table, and my back facing the bar—close enough to overhear her but not enough to be obvious.

"I think I might need to go home soon. I do believe if I have one more, I won't be able to walk back, much less climb," she

said to the barmaid with a chuckle.
Climb?
The barmaid laughed lightly, almost sadly.
"Are you sure you'll be okay, Ara? If you can wait until we're closed, I can walk you as far as I can, so you don't have to go alone," she offered.
Ara, I whispered under my breath.
"No, I'll be fine," she replied, sighing. "I don't know what I'll do come tomorrow, but at least my last night of freedom was nice. Thank you, Livvy. How much do I owe you?"
"Oh no, hun. Tonight was on the house," she whispered, coming around the bar to hug Ara.
Last night of freedom? None of this made any sense.
Peeking over my shoulder, I watched as Ara strolled to the door, swaying from whatever she'd had to drink, and exited without another word. I waited a few seconds so as not to stir suspicion before I followed her out the door. Outside, I glanced down the path both ways—nothing—but just as I thought she'd vanished, a twig snapped to my left. I squinted toward the sound, finding her silhouette barely visible from the tree line as she stumbled through the forest.
So strange.
I prowled behind her, just far enough that she wouldn't hear me. Based on how much drink she'd had, though, I don't think she'd notice me if I walked directly down the path in broad moonlight.
We continued for about a mile before she stepped up to the edge of the tree line, glanced right and left, and stepped out into a grassy clearing.
My breath caught in my throat.
A crisp breeze blew by as she looked up to the sky, gazing

CHAPTER THREE

at the full moon sinking on the horizon. It illuminated her skin, her eyes reflecting the same brilliance.

She is mine.

My heart thundered in my chest. I ached to touch her, fill her, claim her. The bond was drowning me in lust, commanding me forward. I started to take a step toward her when she closed her eyes but hesitated, wanting to see what she would do next. She took a deep breath, her chest rising and falling slowly, as anguish sunk into her features.

My heart sank. The look on her face was gut-wrenching.

The fire inside me raged, consumed by her anguish and fueled by the mate bond. As a tear slid down her cheek, past her quivering lip, the ground singed at my feet and the smell of burning grass drifted up to meet my nose.

Taking another breath, she took off, jogging forward to the towering estate, stopping at the base of a thick vine with small purple flowers. My mouth fell open as she reached up, latched on, and climbed to the second-floor window with ease. She unlocked the latch and climbed in, disappearing from sight.

I stared at the window in disbelief, unable to close my mouth, when two figures strolled around the corner of the building, garbed in brown leather armor with a sword strapped to each hip.

No...

"He said there was a disturbance along the border. Apparently, some Fae attacked the looking tower at the northern tip and burned everything. None of the soldiers survived and all of their bodies were...charred. Everything was still smoldering when they arrived," a guard whispered nervously, his eyes darting to his companion. Even from my hiding spot,

I could see the sweat dripping down his forehead, his face scrunched in panic. "You don't think the creature would try to come to the Capitol, do you?"

The other guard ogled at him and I couldn't tear my eyes away as I inched closer to hear his response.

"Of course not. The Capitol houses the largest army in Auryna, not to mention the General offers housing to the most highly-trained men and assassins of the entire realm on these grounds," he said, waving a hand in dismissal. "No, it would be a fool to come here."

I froze, my fire sputtering out.

These grounds.

General Starrin hosts men on *these* grounds.

My mind flashed to the conversation from the pub, overwhelming me all at once. The general's daughter refused to stay on the estate grounds.

My eyes darted to her window, her silhouette black against the warm light in her room.

Everything clicked into place: the sneaking, the sadness, the lack of freedom.

My mate… I swallowed hard as she unclasped her cloak, tossing it onto her bed.

My mate was General Starrin's daughter.

Human.

She was human.

Chapter Four

Ara

A soft breeze blew in from the open window, pulling me from my dream. I stirred awake, visions of red eyes lingering as the smell of rain permeated the air. Opening my eyes, I grimaced as my head pounded.

Definitely too much mead last night.

And that stranger. He'd never been there before, not that I'd seen, and I doubted he would be back. The only newcomers in the tavern were those passing through, so I'd most likely missed my chance. Not that anything would've come from it, anyway.

I was engaged.

My heart sank and I brushed it off with a sigh.

Easing up, I let the covers fall to my lap. The room spun as nausea rolled in my gut. Resting my head on my hand to steady myself, I took a deep breath and turned to the window. Just as I'd hoped, the sky was dark and promising a formidable storm. The evergreen trees were blowing in the distance and the sky rumbled with thunder. Miles away, thick, white mist hung low, clinging to the mountains.

My favorite kind of weather.

Tossing the covers aside, I swung my legs over the side of the bed. They were lean from years of training, courtesy of my mother who demanded I learn to defend myself. My entire body was sinewy and strong enough to wield a sword for hours at a time, which I was extremely thankful for.

To be honest, my training was the only reason I was brave enough to wander the woods alone.

When I was thirteen, a war broke out between Auryna and Ravaryn. With my father being the general, he was called to duty, and for ten years, it raged. The Ten Year War was gruesome and bloody. Humans died by the thousands trying to push the Fae back to their land, but the Fae were incredibly vicious, cursed with terrifying magic, and the war gave them every opportunity to use it.

I still had vivid nightmares of the damage they caused.

Unlike most generals, my father thought it best to bring my mother and me along, not trusting anyone enough to safeguard us. He hid us in the medical tents during every battle, ensuring we were never truly separated from him. Still, no matter how far the tents were from the scene of battle, bits and pieces always reached us. The sound of swords clashing, men screaming and moaning in agony, the roar of creatures I never wished to see. The smell of burning flesh, the musk of men and filth, the metallic scent of blood.

So much blood.

It pooled in the fields, flowing into nearby creeks, which always ran red afterward.

Residing with the healers also allowed us to see the injuries firsthand. One particular image of a man was burned into my memory, haunting me at night. It looked as though a thorn bush had sprouted from the ground into his feet, weaving up his legs, torso, arms, and even his face, just under the skin. Thorns protruded from every visible surface.

I would forever remember his agonizing, tortured screams before a healer slit his throat to end his suffering.

The sound haunted me to this day, the smell of blood still triggering flashbacks, but I had given up trying to escape the war a long time ago. Now I just dealt with the fear and panic as best I could, desperately hoping each attack would be my last.

Looking back, my expectations of the Fae were not anything like the reality. I had always imagined they would be peaceful and beautiful. Poetic, even. One with nature, since she responded to their touch and will, unlike with humans.

When I did finally lay eyes on them, however, that was not what I saw. I saw death and rage and it instilled a fear in me I would never forget. They knew no mercy. Once the war finally ended with the assassination of King Adrastus, I vowed to never go back to that side of the continent.

If I never saw another Fae again, it would still be too soon.

With the reminder of why I needed to train, I leapt off the bed, stretched, and cracked my neck. At the armoire, I donned my black trousers and tunic, tugged on my boots, and slid my knife into the right one. Giving myself a once over in the mirror, I braided my hair away from my face and rushed out of the room, descending the stairs, and into the breakfast room where my father sat.

His breakfast was mostly eaten, only crumbs remaining. He stared at his cup of coffee, his expression tired, before sighing and acknowledging my presence.

"I will not argue about it. It is decided. You will marry

Finley and solidify the alliance between our families," he declared as I sat at the table, my appetite gone.

Staring at my empty plate, I had nothing to say. There was nothing I could say.

"I have several matters to deal with today. It seems there was a disturbance along the northern border. I will be with King Adon, discussing our response to this act of war," he said as he rose from his chair and headed out, pausing in the doorway. "Do not leave the grounds today, under any circumstances."

I didn't expect a heartfelt apology or even a simple explanation, but he was colder than I expected. I stared at the table for a few moments, numb, before gulping down a cup of coffee and grabbing a piece of toast, eating it on the way out the door.

With Father busy, training fell to Gus. He was large and lethal, but kind and patient with me. When I was younger, he had taken his time teaching me how to wield a small blade, ensuring I knew how to defend myself. I had respected him ever since.

When I arrived at our sparring circle, he was already waiting by the weaponry rack. Nodding in greeting, he gestured to the weapons. "What will it be today?"

* * *

We went round after round. I picked the swords, needing to feel the burn of tired muscles, the sweat of hard work, an outlet for the emotion churning inside me.

I hadn't realized how much pent-up anger was brewing until we began to spar.

CHAPTER FOUR

With each time he deflected, I grew more irritated, clenching my teeth, grunting, moving faster, harder.

Just as we clashed swords, the sound rang out across the clearing and he kicked a leg out, swiping my feet from beneath me.

Letting out a frustrated breath, I tossed the sword, letting it land a few feet away. I sat back on my hands, breathing heavily, my tunic soaked with sweat.

"All right, we're done for today." I glanced up at him to argue, but he held a hand up to stop me. "I can tell you're distracted and I am sure it has something to do with your new engagement."

I scoffed in response.

He was right, of course. I was distracted, and this session had done nothing to dampen it. Still, there was pity in his eyes, and it grated on my nerves. Gus was like a brother, so I knew he didn't want this for me, but I had no desire to see the sympathy on his face and even less so to talk about it.

I stood without a word and dusted off my trousers before striding to the sword. I swiped it off the ground, sheathed it, and placed it back on the rack.

"I'll see you tomorrow," he shouted from the circle as I jogged back to the estate, waving in acknowledgment without looking back.

Once inside my bed chamber, I shut the door behind me and slid down the wood, bringing my knees to my chest as I sat on the floor.

I was buzzing with anger and frustration. Anger at my father for this engagement, anger at the Goddess for dropping that stranger in my life only *after* the announcement of said engagement, anger at myself for not even speaking with him when I had the chance.

I clenched my fists, pulling my knees closer.

Anger at myself for not sticking up for myself, for letting everyone around me plan *my* fate as if I'm not even here, as if I am just an object to be passed around.

Clenching my eyes against the tears threatening to form, I stood, opening them to see thick clouds roll by my window. While I couldn't see the sun, I knew it had to be roughly noon.

Shift change time.

I ripped the drenched clothing off and pulled dry ones on. Jogging to the window, I glanced down to check for guards. When I spied none, I kicked a leg over the windowsill and descended the vine, landing with a thud and darting to the tree line.

My father might be able to force my hand, but he could not confine me to the estate grounds when he wasn't here.

On days like this, when my heart was heavy and my mind clouded, I resorted to books—to escape, to forget, to find freedom where I had none. While our town library was small, it had become my safe haven, and that was where I was headed. It was farther than the pub, nearly three miles, but I didn't mind the walk. It gave me a small semblance of independence.

As I walked under an open space in the tree canopy, a single drop hit my cheek, and I glanced toward the sky, breathing in the scent of coming rain and damp moss. More drops fell, and before I took another step, it was a downpour.

Pausing, I held my face upwards and let the cool rain soak through my hair and clothes. It washed away everything—the sadness, anger, anxiety, fear.

Stretching my arms out, palms up, I offered myself to the storm. Thunder rumbled in the distance, and the sky

CHAPTER FOUR

exploded with brilliant lightning in a heavy crack.

I took another deep breath. When I released it, every emotion of the last day or two left with it. Inhaling, I accepted everything the storm offered me. Strength. Peace. Renewal.

I gathered myself, smiling faintly, and continued to the library. At the door, I was met by Asha, the town librarian, who stopped me in my tracks.

"Absolutely not," she said, ushering me back out the door. "Wait here."

I stood under the overhang, waiting, as she grabbed something to dry me off with—not that I blamed her. My clothes were soaked. She came back with a large rag and I quickly dried off. Once inside, the smell of books and coffee surrounded me. Next to the smell of rain, this was my favorite. It always promised an exciting story, a new life to live, if only for a little while.

"Thank you, Asha," I replied, heading straight for the romance section.

"Goddess knows why anyone would come to a library during a torrential downpour, but if it was anyone, it would be you," she huffed. She didn't like when I tracked water into her library, but she always accepted me, understanding why I needed to be here.

I roamed the shelves, searching for the most devastating, gripping story I could find, and settled on a forbidden love story before strolling to my favorite chair. It was made of worn, brown leather and so large that it swallowed me when I sat in it. I grabbed the blanket I hid behind the chair and plopped down. Tucked away in the back corner of the library, I relished in my privacy, and the window that sat above it let in enough light to read most hours of the day.

Curling up and settling in, I devoured the book with hungry eyes, letting it whisk me away.

* * *

I woke several hours later to Finn lightly tapping my shoulder, whispering my name. Starting, I tossed the book on a nearby table and searched his face for any sign that he didn't know of the engagement, that he didn't knowingly agree to this, but there was none.

"Ara, hey, wait," he said as I turned away, tossing the blanket behind the chair, preparing to leave. "I'm sorry for not warning you about last night. Your father came to me, telling me of his wishes to marry us sooner rather than later, and well…" He rubbed the back of his neck, a blush creeping into his cheeks. "Let's be honest, you've always known how I felt for you. I *want* to marry you. I can provide for you. We can be happy," he pleaded. "I already have a nice house with plenty of room. You could even add a library and read all day long."

I almost felt pity for him. He didn't understand. He never had. He never would.

Our friendship had always been simple, and that's what I had enjoyed about it. He didn't push me for deep conversation or ask prying questions about my family. We just enjoyed our time, strolling through the woods, riding horses, sparring occasionally. He had even taught me to use a bow when we were younger.

I had always appreciated our friendship for what it was: a distraction and a few moments free from my father's grasp. He trusted Finley enough to allow me to leave with him, and I took any chance I could to escape the grounds.

Looking into his pleading eyes, it pained me to know I couldn't give him the life he so desperately longed for. If I were to marry him, my face would always be turned to the window, searching for more, and if not that, I would be a shell of the person I was now.

I couldn't be who I wished to be and the woman he wanted me to be.

"Finn, I meant it when I said I never wished to marry," I said, peeking up at him. Hurt flashed across his face, and I dropped my gaze to the floor. "It's not you. It's anybody, everybody. I've been locked away in his estate my entire life. I've never tasted true freedom, never been given the choice to decide anything for myself. My father would never allow me that, and now, he has taken away even my choice in who and when I marry," I said, gaining confidence as I went on.

I needed him to understand. As I forced myself to look up, my heart sank. Rejection was written into his every feature.

Hadn't he known this was how I would react?

A second passed as every emotion played out behind his eyes—confusion, hurt, denial, anger. His face hardened, his head cocking to the side as he leaned closer.

"Did it really never occur to you that your father allowing you to leave the grounds with me, so casually and so often, these past few months was unusual? You seem so utterly surprised that he's given your hand, but how many times has he been so casual about you leaving? Who else are you allowed to leave the grounds with?"

I gawked at him, my mouth falling open.

"We had hoped you'd wish to marry me on your own by now, but he's decided it's time, and I agree. I've cherished my days with you so far, and I will cherish every day we have to come. You were promised to me, Ara. I will have you," he declared.

I couldn't do anything but stare at him, aghast, as an angry blush crept up my cheeks.

"You will learn to love me, in time, and I'm a patient man. I will be waiting for that day," he said, looking at me with sureness and a twisted sense of compassion as if he was doing me a favor.

He paused as if waiting for a reply and when I didn't give one, he resolved to glide past me toward the door, leaving me in my shock.

Embarrassment flooded my body as my heart thundered in my ears.

I had been so worried that when I'd told him the truth, it would break his heart and ruin our friendship, somehow convincing myself that he'd been a pawn, just like me. A willing pawn, but a pawn all the same.

He wasn't.

He was an accomplice, a catalyst, aiming for control.

It was a slap to the face. Our entire lives, I had known him to be nothing but kind and respectful, but now…. Now, I was questioning every conversation, every experience we'd ever had.

The room spun around me.

How is this happening?

How can every man in my life be this determined to control me? Determining where I go, what I do, who I marry, when I marry?

Grinding my teeth, I inhaled deeply, exhaling to calm my pounding heart.

My patience was wearing thin.

Chapter Five

Ara

I grabbed the novel and gave Asha a quick goodbye before stepping out of the library.

The sky had cleared, and the setting sun left a blazing red-orange haze in its wake. All the land to the west was cast in its warm glow, and I suddenly found myself jealous of the sun. It got to see the entire realm every day, every exciting event and person, settling in each night with a peaceful embrace by the land.

Swallowing hard, I looked away, remembering sunset also meant my father would be home soon—just in time to discover me missing.

Rushing to the tree line, I willed my legs to go as fast as they could carry me, darting under branches and hopping over roots. It wasn't long before I neared the estate and slowed to a jog to catch my breath. Trotting along the outskirts of the main trail, I reached the clearing outside my window, glanced left and right, and froze when a guard rounded the corner.

It was later than I thought.

The shift change had already happened, and they'd be

setting the table for dinner, if not already seated. I waited, tapping my fingers on my thigh, as the guard strolled through the clearing—clearly not expecting any unwanted visitors as he walked right past me without a second glance. As he disappeared, I sprinted to the vine and climbed faster than I ever had, flipping myself over the windowsill before the next guard rounded the corner.

Once inside, I ripped the sweaty clothes off and threw them into my bathing chamber. After years of training outside come rain or shine, the maids were no strangers to finding disgusting clothing on my floors, so they would think nothing of it.

Grabbing a rag, I wiped off as much filth as I could, stepping in front of the mirror to examine my face. Thankfully, unruly hair and flushed cheeks were my only signs of exertion. Grabbing the small, wooden comb, I untangled my locks and smoothed it down, tucking the front strands behind my ears.

Staring at my reflection, I saw so much of my mother looking back at me: the dark hair and eyebrows, soft cheekbones, large eyes. Unlike her bright blue eyes, however, mine were gray, and my mother adored them. I would sometimes catch her staring as if lost in thought, and when I would nudge her, she would just remind me of how beautiful they were. Leaning closer, I studied the traces of lighter gray and pale blue streaking my irises, the same subdued color of storm clouds.

Maybe that's why I like rain so much, I chuckled to myself as I found my father's favorite dress, just in case he beat me to the table.

It was a simple, loose-fitting periwinkle dress with petal

CHAPTER FIVE

sleeves. He had always loved this dress because it reminded him of the flowers that bloomed in spring. When I was a child, he used to take me to play in the wildflower fields. We would run through the meadows, laughing and playing games. At the end of the day, we would share a treat as he told stories from his own childhood.

We used to be so much closer before the war, but something had changed in him, and our relationship changed with it.

I left as soon as I pulled the dress on, rushing to the dining room. As I turned the corner, I was met with the knowing eyes of my mother, sitting alone at the table with an abundance of food in front of her. Her plate was still empty, waiting.

"Hello, Mother."

"Hello, darling. I noticed you weren't in your bedchamber earlier," she replied. "Where have you been?" she whispered, glancing at the doorway.

I quickly sat in the chair, leaning over the table to whisper back.

"I was at the library with Asha, and I was completely safe. Nobody else was there; I just fell asleep reading a book," I explained in a rush.

"So, you didn't see Finn, then? He came by looking for you, which is why I checked your rooms. I told him you might be at the library—against your father's wishes, I might add—and he promised he would find you and send you home," she said, tilting her head, eyeing me. "If he were to mention anything about you being at the library to your father…"

Send me home? We weren't even married yet, and he already thought he could command me.

"I know, I know." I waved my hand through the air. "Yes, I

35

did see him. He found me sleeping and we talked briefly. I rushed home afterward hoping…"

She sighed, rolling her eyes.

"That you would beat your father to the table," she finished for me and I nodded. "Did you smooth things over with Finn, at least?"

The question set my blood boiling again.

"Goddess, no. If anything, it's worse. He helped Father plan this entire thing. He helped him spring it on me, or at least, he knew he was going to."

Her eyebrows furrowed with sympathy.

"I'm—"

She stopped mid-sentence as Father walked in, his expression weary and shoulders slumped. He looked exhausted as he walked around the table, gave my mother a kiss on the head, and took his seat.

"Hi, dear," she said.

"Sorry I'm late. It was a long day with King Adon," he said, filling his plate.

"Is everything all right? What will be done about the disturbance at the border?" I asked.

He glanced at me before returning to his food.

"Well, I don't normally like to involve you two in these types of matters, but I feel it needs to be said, for your safety. It seems a rather powerful Fae crossed the border and has remained here, undetected," he declared. "A small encampment of Fae soldiers sits north of the border, but all will be fine. There isn't much of the Fae army left, and we'll decimate the small force stationed there. It is nothing to worry about, Ara. However, until we discover this foolish creature, it is best for you to stay put. Both of you. Completely. Do not leave the walls of this estate. Not with anyone, not even Finley. Do you understand me?" He gestured to us both, eyeing me.

I nodded, but icy fear crawled up my spine. Not for the random Fae roaming Auryna, although that was terrifying, but for the chains tightening around my chest, suffocating me slowly. Numbness and hysteria settled over me simultaneously, warring with the other for prominence. It took everything I had not to panic.

His dark eyes peeked up at me again, and he smiled lightly when he noticed the dress.

"Ah, I do love that color. It brings back such happy memories of when things were so…simple. Now, here we are, my little girl, engaged," he sighed contentedly, dismissing the gravity of everything he just said.

Sadness overwhelmed me as I stared at him, looking but not seeing.

He was so sure of himself, so sure that I would perish the moment I got any semblance of freedom. He was so convinced that I would fulfill my purpose with Finn that it blinded him to the sorrow and desperation clinging to me.

I couldn't stand it, seeing him so pleased by what was tearing me apart.

After excusing myself with shaky hands, I returned to my room and softly closed the door behind me. I took one choked breath and collapsed onto the bed as sob after sob broke free.

I couldn't stop the tears that fell, couldn't breathe through the hopelessness.

I will be married to Finn.

The tears didn't stop until I fell into a dreamless sleep, exhausted.

* * *

Not an hour later, something pulled me from my sleep. I glanced through the window, realizing the moon had only risen to half peak, so it wasn't too late. As I woke fully, the conversations from dinner returned. Hysteria gripped me by the throat, tightening like a noose and choking off my breath. I brought a hand to my neck as overwhelming panic burned through my chest, and I did the only thing I could think of to stifle it.

I rose from the bed, quickly changing into trousers and a tunic. After tugging my boots on, I tucked my dagger in the right and climbed out of the window, descending the vine with a renewed sense of purpose. I needed to be as far away from this house as possible, as fast as possible.

Once I neared the pub, I allowed myself to breathe. The air of the woods always grounded me. As the smell of the needle-covered path, damp tree trunks, and forest flowers met my nose, a wave of calm settled over my soul.

Staring at the entrance, I knew tonight would be different. Expectation hung heavy in the air around me as I pulled the door open, embracing the honeyed scent of mead and Livvy's warm smile.

Tonight, I am free, and I will be free for as long as I have left.

Chapter Six

Rogue

Fate had been cruel my entire life, but this was by far the worst hand she had ever dealt me.

My mate was human.

The thought set off a whirlwind of conflicting emotions within me; every inch of my body still ached for her, but my mind was utterly repulsed by it. It could never happen. I would never stoop so low as to be with a human.

I would not.

As soon as I realized who she was—*what* she was—I dropped the glamour, thrust myself into the sky, and flew as fast as my wings would carry me back to the encampment.

Flying had always given me the space to think, and as I glided over the never-ending sea of evergreens, my mind returned to the plan I'd concocted in the pub.

Fuck.

Evander having a daughter was the only insightful information I had learned over the border, and I had been there for days. My general and his commanders were expecting something, anything, from my trip. I could not return empty-handed.

Years ago, when Auryna began ravaging the villages north of the border, our armies were already decimated, our people overworked and exhausted. Auryna's armies greatly outnumbered ours, and we couldn't manage to hold them off or defend their homes. We had to move our people farther inland for their safety, and they left everything behind—their homes, livelihoods, family lands, leaving them with nothing but their memories and devastation.

After a year of attempting to convince the council, they finally relented, agreeing we needed to cross the border again.

What finally convinced them, however, had nothing to do with me and everything to do with the endless suffering of our people at the hands of human armies.

A platoon of human soldiers had attacked a small village in the dead of night, murdering everyone—men, women, children. They pulled them half-asleep from their beds, dragged them outside into the freezing cold, and nailed them to their homes. We found their bodies days later, terror and screams frozen into their features.

I swallowed hard against the bile rising in my throat at the memory.

We needed leverage. There was no other choice. We were running out of time, and our people needed help.

I pored over every word I'd heard the past few days, just to be sure I hadn't missed a single detail, silently pleading for anything t0 overshadow this, to provide a viable opportunity elsewhere, hashing and rehashing every conversation, but there was none.

This was it. The frail human girl.

I released an exasperated laugh. At least by taking his only

CHAPTER SIX

daughter, one he had been hiding her entire life, I would cut Evander deep. To make it even sweeter, this was probably the exact reason she was hidden and under guard—yet, I had found her so easily, completely by accident.

Maybe I would kill her, too, to exact revenge for every Fae we'd lost at her father's command. An eye for an eye. I would love to see the look on his face when I dropped her lifeless body from the sky, letting it land at his feet. A dark grin pulled at my lips, even as a small, small part of me was sickened by the idea.

The sun was just peeking over the horizon as I landed gracefully and quietly back at the encampment, dimly lit with the yellow haze of sunrise. Feeling slightly more confident now that I had a rough plan, I headed for the general's tent, stalking down the muddy pathway lined with dozens of dirty tents on either side. Straight ahead was Doran's tent, candlelight pouring out from the open flap, indicating they were already awake and meeting.

Entering through the flap door, I found General Doran and all five of his commanders surrounding a rectangular table, overlooking a map of the continent. They were motioning to various points along the border, discussing weak spots. At my entrance, every face snapped to me with surprise.

"My King, we didn't expect you back so soon. Have you gathered the information we need? What have you learned?" Questions bombarded me all at once. As I held my hand up, they stopped immediately, awaiting my reply.

"The first three days were a complete waste. I learned nothing from the humans at court," I explained and their faces fell. "However, just a few hours ago, I learned that General Evander has a daughter, one he is extremely partial to, taking great measures to keep her hidden in his estate. Before tonight, I didn't even know he was married, much less had a child..." I paused, leaning over the map to find his estate, hidden just south of the king's castle in a discreet village.

"How does this help us, sire? Surely, she is kept under lock and key. It would be impossible to get to her," one commander challenged. Under normal circumstances, he would be right, but I shook my head.

"I know how to get her. By random luck, she appeared at the pub this evening, and I followed her home," I explained, carefully leaving out *why* I'd followed her. "It seems his daughter has a taste for breaking the rules. I watched her climb up a vine outside her window, so I know exactly which room is hers and how to get inside.

"I plan to use her as leverage to bribe the general, force him to lay down arms, and evacuate Ravaryn. Based on the extensive lengths he's gone to keep her safe thus far, I assume he'd do just about anything to get her back in one piece. I'm positive he'll be able to subdue Adon long enough for our people to rest," I said, silently pleading for it to be true. "*And* for us to gather forces.

"Once we take her, we'll have roughly a day before the general realizes she's missing. I believe he'll search the immediate towns first. With her history, I'm betting they'll think she just snuck out. Once they realize she's not there, they'll come after us hard and fast. So, we must be prepared to move as soon as I return with her."

They nodded in agreement, hurrying about to begin readying plans. One commander didn't move, though, a look of hesitation plain on his face.

I sighed inwardly. "What is it, Lee?"

"How do we know he won't immediately attack Ravaryn with a vengeance? To get her back, I mean."

I paused at the question. It wasn't something I'd considered. Not that I'd had the time to, but the answer was in the forefront of my mind, and I hated it with every bone in my body.

I couldn't believe I was about to divulge this information. "Unfortunately, the human is my mate."

There was a collective gasp, accompanied by looks ranging from pity to outrage.

"How is that possible? You cannot mate with a human!" an elder commander shouted. I shot him a glare, stopping him in his tracks. "My apologies. I am just stunned, as we all are. This has never happened before, to my knowledge."

"I have never heard of it either…" Doran said, peering at me curiously. "However, we can't worry about that right now. How will that help us?"

I nodded. "I'm going to claim her, mark her, and then I'll be able to find her anywhere. He'll never be able to hide her from me. If he ever attempts to go against his word, I'll find her and slit her throat. I'll make it abundantly clear that I will not give him a second chance."

There was complete silence in the tent as they all stared at me. Doran stepped closer, meeting my gaze with hesitation.

"Rogue… You cannot mark her and give her back. You will have essentially…given yourself to her. You know that. You will never be with anyone else. *Every* part of you will belong to her," Doran whispered.

I had known that—everyone did—but I still inwardly winced at his words.

"It's what's best for Ravaryn. We don't have another choice. I will sacrifice this for the good of our people," I affirmed, and he stepped back, giving a swift nod of his head. "I will take her tonight. Have the encampment packed and the soldiers ready to move when I return."

Turning on my heel without waiting for a response, I strode out of the tent before I took a deep breath, snapped my wings out, and thrust into the sky, letting the weightlessness and wind envelop me.

* * *

Returning to the estate, I hovered in front of her window, peeking through, only to find she wasn't in her chambers. I landed at the treeline, but just as I turned to leave and search the surrounding town, a young man exited through the front door.

A spike of jealousy shot through me.

He was clearly not related to the general, considering Evander was dark-complected and this man was red-headed and pale. He was too young to be a higher up in the general's ranks, so not one of his close working men, and I highly doubted Evander's wife would take a lover so openly.

He must be attempting to court Ara or at least one of her friends.

He walked with purpose, so I followed. We continued for about three miles, stopping outside a small building with a dainty metal sign hanging above the door: *Asha's Library*. As he closed the door behind him, I crept up to one of the few windows.

Sitting in a worn, oversized chair was Ara. She was slumped

to one side, her head resting on the inside of one elbow, her legs tucked in a blanket, and an open book dropped in her lap. She looked at peace, content—completely unlike how I had last seen her.

The man walked up and lightly tapped her shoulder. His touch was so casual, so sure. They must be close.

My lip twitched, my heart racing.

Ara startled awake, looking at him with searching eyes before her face solidified with anger. He muttered something I couldn't quite hear as she moved to leave. I inched closer to the window, sitting just under it to better hear their conversation.

"Let's be honest, you've always known how I felt for you. I want to marry you. I can *provide* for you. We can be happy. I already have a nice house with plenty of room. You could even add a library and read all day long."

My fists clenched, my knuckles cracking with the force. He wasn't just courting my mate; he expected to marry her.

"Finn, I meant it when I said I never wished to marry. It's not you. It's anybody, everybody. I've been locked away in our estate my entire life. I've never tasted true freedom, never been given the choice to decide anything for myself. My father would never allow me that, and now, he has taken away even my choice in who and when I marry."

Relaxing slightly, my heart ached for her, understanding the lack of freedom all too well.

"Did it really never occur to you that your father allowing you to leave the grounds with me, so casually and so often these past few months, was unusual? You seem so utterly surprised that he's given your hand, but how many times has he been so casual about you leaving? Who else are you permitted to leave the grounds with?"

He paused, and I held my breath, waiting for his next words, every muscle in my body tense.

"We had hoped you'd wish to marry me on your own terms by now, but he's decided it's time, and I agree. I've cherished my days with you so far and I will cherish every day we have to come. You were promised to me, Ara. I will have you."

Rage blinded me. It took everything I had to not barge in there and grab him by the throat, just to choke off whatever nonsense he was about to spew.

"You will learn to love me, in time, and I am a patient man. I will be waiting for that day."

Red hot fury enveloped me as smoke drifted from my palms.

She is mine.

My mate.

I knew it was the bond causing this reaction, but the knowledge did nothing to dampen my temper.

Finn stepped out of the library, clearly frustrated, and I couldn't control my feet as they followed after him. We trekked through the town until we arrived at, what I assumed, was his manor—no doubt bought with his father's money, considering his enormous sense of entitlement.

Surrounding the house were acres and acres of farmland, stretching out in every direction, covered with every type of vegetation: potatoes, barley, corn, cotton, flowers. Clearly, agriculture was his main source of income.

Studying the large house, heat flushed through me as I was reminded of his promise to "provide" for her, my mate. Before I could stop myself, fire sparked at my fingertips.

Willing it forward, the flames rapidly crossed the land,

racing toward the crops and scorching the ground in its wake. My mouth twisted into a vicious grin as the fire devoured everything with an insatiable hunger, razing every crop, leaving nothing but ash and char behind.

The flames edged toward the house, licking up the brick walls, growing higher until it latched onto the wooden roof and engulfed it in a roaring blaze. In mere seconds, the entire house ignited.

Every human inside raced out the door and away from the house, turning with mouths agape as they watched the manor go up in flames and smoke.

Let's see how well you can provide now, Finn.

I turned without a second glance, leaving to hunt down Ara once again.

Chapter Seven

Ara

I plopped down on a tall wooden stool and rested my elbows on the smooth bar before peeking around the room.

He wasn't here, the one I was secretly hoping to see; if there was one person who could've given me some small form of liberation, it was him—even if just for the night.

Of course, he wasn't here.

Fate would never allow me to be so lucky.

Turning back to the bar, Livvy strolled over to me with a mug.

"If anything about my life was ever lucky, it would be making friends with you, the best barmaid in Auryna," I said humorously, smiling over my mug as I brought it to my mouth.

"And don't you forget it." She winked and leaned forward on the bar, propping up on her elbows. "How's your night going so far? Mine's been full of sweaty men and crude comments, so surely, it's going better than that." Her sentence drifted off as she studied me. "But considering you're here

CHAPTER SEVEN

with me, maybe not."

I set the mug down, watching the liquid ripple.

"It's going about as well as last night. You know, I thought Finn and I had an understanding. I *thought* he understood that I had no intention of marrying him, or anyone, for that matter. At least, not until I was ready, but it doesn't seem that way. Or maybe he just doesn't care. He worked *with* my father. They decided, *together*, that it was time for me to marry," I said, chuckling under my breath. "I feel like such a fool. I should've seen it coming," I managed through a choked breath, my eyes burning.

She reached over, placing her hand on mine to give it a light squeeze.

"Oh, hun, I'm so sorry to hear that. I've spoken with Finley several times over the years, and I never would've expected him to do that. Hear me when I say this, you cannot blame yourself for not seeing it sooner. You can only judge the actions and words they show you. You cannot expect yourself to know what goes on behind closed doors," she whispered, squeezing my hand again.

I quickly wiped the tear escaping my eye as I nodded.

"All right, I think this calls for something a little stronger," she declared as she reached under the bar, pulling out two tiny glasses and an embellished decanter. She popped the cork out, the scent of strong, expensive whiskey wafting into the air. I scrunched my face at the bitter smell as she set the glasses down with a clank, pouring two shots. She downed one, and I the other.

The burning liquid slid down my throat, and I erupted in a coughing fit that had Livvy laughing heartily. As I was caught halfway between a cough and a laugh, the chime above the door jingled, and I turned just in time to lock eyes with my stranger.

My cheeks heated, and I abruptly stopped laughing, attempting to stifle my last cough. I jerked back to the bar, and Livvy eyed me curiously, arching one eyebrow.

"Don't say it," I warned, giving her my best glare.

She leaned over the bar to close the gap between us.

"Now, what are the odds that you would make steamy eye contact with that god of a man two nights in a row? Especially considering this is only the second time I've ever seen him here," she teased, shifting her gaze towards him as he found a table across the room. "If you don't leave with him tonight, I might."

Unwarranted jealousy bit at me, catching me off guard. I blinked rapidly, shaking my head to try and erase the feeling as she pushed away from the bar, winked, and returned to pouring drinks.

An hour later, I still hadn't gained the nerve to approach him. In my defense, he hadn't either, so there we sat—together but apart, separated by a mere ten feet.

Livvy came by regularly, refilling my mug and nudging me in encouragement, but the longer I sat there, the more convinced I became that maybe I was just meant for a monotonous life of early nights and dull sex... with Finley.

I groaned, cringing. Sleeping with Finn hadn't even crossed my mind, but now, fueled by mead, I couldn't stop picturing it.

With that thought running rampant, I glanced over my shoulder for the thousandth time, only to find he wasn't there. The bell above the door jingled, and my head jerked around as my breath left me in a whoosh, watching as it closed behind him. He slipped through my fingers. Again.

I tapped my fingers on the bar, staring at the door.

No, not again.

Reaching across, I grabbed the decanter and poured two more shots. I downed one right after the other, making eye contact with Livvy as I swallowed the second. She gave me a quick, knowing smile, nodding at the door.

I hopped off the stool and jogged to the door, pausing to take a breath before stepping out. Feeling the whiskey blur my senses, I looked left and right, seeing no one. I snuck around the pub and glanced around the back; there was still no sign of him.

A heavy wave of disappointment flooded me.

"Looking for me?"

My breath hitched as he stepped out of the shadows by a small pond. The soft gleam of moonlight bounced off the rippling water, illuminating his black silhouette.

"Let's say I was. Then what?" I challenged with a false sense of bravado, desire ripping through me at the sound of his voice.

"Well, then I'd have to admit… I was rather hoping you'd follow me out," he purred as he crept forward, moving towards me like a predator to his prey.

Steeling myself, I took the last step between us to close the distance and reached up, grabbing both sides of his face to pull him down to me. His mouth crashed to mine and the smell of smoke and evergreen spice engulfed me, followed by intense, overwhelming need.

He enveloped me—his mouth, his hands, his scent.

Him.

I pulled back, just for a moment, just to see his face, and

he leaned forward, following me. When he opened his eyes, there was a heat behind them, restraint in every muscle of his body. As I gazed at him, though, the look in his eyes changed to satisfaction, an arrogant smirk curving his lips. I stepped back in confusion.

Suddenly, a shimmer started behind his shoulders, a black shadow emerging from it. My eyes followed as the shimmer continued, stretching out from his body, leaving a dark, webbed skin in its wake. My heart thundered in my chest as enormous, leathery wings unfurled from his shoulder blades, snapping them out to full length.

My gaze slowly inched back to his face, snagging on his now-pointed ears before reaching his eyes. He tilted his head, grinning, reveling in my reaction.

A scream crawled up my throat as terror iced through my veins.

He was Fae—*the* Fae that burned down the entire lookout tower, the one who killed those men and had been sneaking through Auryna undetected.

How could I be so foolish? My father had warned me.

I turned to run, but he quickly wrapped a thick, muscular arm around my waist, snatching me back to him and pulling my back flush with his chest.

Every part of me was flush against him, and I could feel him pressing into my backside.

"Oh, no you don't," he growled in my ear as he leaned down, towering over me. I could feel his breath along my neck, and goosebumps spread like wildfire, flaming the lust still filling me.

I kicked and thrashed against him, attempting to free myself, but he only chuckled darkly against my ear.

CHAPTER SEVEN

"Yes, keep writhing against me like that and see how far you get," he whispered.

Gritting my teeth, I bent over to snatch the knife from my boot. I quickly unsheathed it from its hiding spot and stabbed it into his calf behind mine. He released me with an angry huff, and I stumbled forward.

He ripped the knife out of his leg with a grunt, tossing it into the pond. I turned in a panic to retrieve it, but he grabbed my arm and yanked me back to him, glaring into my eyes with a mixture of lust and rage.

"You shouldn't have done that." His other arm wrapped tightly around my waist, and in one powerful stroke of his wings, we shot into the sky. A scream escaped my throat just before the world went black.

* * *

As I stirred awake, the sound of bustling men and horses met my ears. I sat up straight, furs falling into my lap. My eyes darted about the unfamiliar room—no, not a room, a tent, with the bed I was lying atop the only thing in it besides a small fire in the center.

Hazy sunlight peeked through the closed flap door, and the night before came crashing back. My chest tightened with the memories, my heart pounding, fear tensing my muscles.

If a Fae kidnapped me, then the sounds coming from outside the tent...

My hands shook as I slowly pulled the blanket back and rose from the bed, my bare feet hitting the ground. Glancing down, I realized I was still in my clothing with my boots at the door, but my mother's ring was gone—surely stolen for its worth.

I took a deep breath against the rising panic as I tugged my boots on and pulled the flap door open, peeking my head out. My breath left me in a harsh gasp and I jerked back inside, my hands flying to either side of my head as the world swayed around me.

Fae.

Fae everywhere.

They looked mostly human with pointed ears, but I knew what lurked beneath the surface.

I stumbled away from the door, my chest tightening as my vision tunneled. I couldn't breathe.

Swords clashed in the distance, mixing with the shouts of men and the huffing of horses. The noise filled the tent, just as they had in the healers' tents all those years ago, and flashbacks of the war bombarded me.

All I could see was blood.

Death.

Fear consumed me as I retreated into the tent, closing in on myself as my back hit the wall. Sliding down the tarp, I hit the ground and curled into a tight ball, putting my head between my knees in an attempt to slow my breathing.

Breathe.

I forced my eyes open, looking for anything to ground me, anything calmer than I was. The bed. It was here. I was here. Not there.

Breathe.

A yellow haze poured through the door flaps. The sunrise promised light and warmth. It was here and I was here with it. Not there.

Breathe.

CHAPTER SEVEN

I inhaled deeply, breathing in the scent of damp earth. It pulled me back down, returning me to the ground, to the present. I slid my hands out beside me, feeling the cool dirt between my fingers as I laid my head back on the tarp.

I closed my eyes, willing my heart to settle. Sweat rolled down my forehead, and I wiped it away with the back of my hand, taking another deep breath.

My eyes snapped open at the sound of the door flap moving, and my stranger walked in.

I silently watched as he grabbed everything out of the tent—the blanket, the bed pieces, the lantern. He was dressed in black leather trousers and a black, flowing tunic with the buttons opened at the sternum, revealing sun-kissed skin over lean chest muscles. His wings were tucked at his back, the tips lightly dragging along the floor.

In the morning light, they weren't black, but a deep wine red.

His black waves were tied back into a knot at the base of his neck, loose tendrils falling around his face, a stubble having grown along his jaw. As he bent over, I noticed the scar again—thick and jagged, starting at his ear and disappearing underneath his shirt. That wound should have been fatal.

He glanced over at me, his eyes redder than they were before. They weren't brown at all, but a dark maroon red that reminded me of the darkest roses.

His gaze dropped, noting my position.

"Good morning," he said quickly, returning to his work. "Get a move on. We are leaving in five."

He walked out of the tent, carrying all the supplies. Before I had the chance to stand, another soldier walked in, and I froze, eyeing him warily.

He looked seemingly human-like, tall with pale, sharp features, pointed ears, and hair so blond, it was almost white. His eyes were an icy blue, although his gaze was warm and empathetic.

"Hello, Ara, my name is Doran," he said as he stepped closer, crouching down to my level. "We have your horse ready for you just outside, if you're ready."

He paused, slowly extending a hand to me, and I stared at it for a moment before reluctantly placing my hand in his. He smiled, pulling me to my feet.

He led me to the door, and as he held the flap open, I hesitated, my pulse skyrocketed again.

"It's all right; just stay close to me. No one will hurt you," he said, dipping his chin.

I almost wanted to believe him.

He stepped from the tent, and I followed after him, hoping I could stifle the fear from showing on my face. My nerves were frayed as we waded through seas of men, and I slowly realized just how many Fae surrounded me.

I focused on Doran's back as we continued, refusing to look at the rest of the Fae, even as I felt their eyes on me. After a few very long minutes, we made it to a gray-dappled horse with a black saddle lined with fleece. He turned as if to help me up, but I glided past him, disregarding his outstretched hand. Placing one foot in the stirrup and gripping the horn, I hoisted myself up and settled in the seat.

Giving an impressed smile, he nodded and turned to leave.

"Thank you, Doran," I said quickly and he stopped, looking back at me with a sad smile.

"You're welcome," he replied before he left, disappearing into the crowd.

CHAPTER SEVEN

I glanced over to my right to find my stranger was on a black horse next to me, and I groaned, turning forward again.

"Careful, or I might think you're not happy to see me."

I scoffed, my eyes whipping back to him, baring my teeth at his audacity.

"You kidnapped me, you fucking asshole. Who are you, anyway?" The brazenness of my tone shocked even me, sounding much braver than I felt. "Why am I here?"

His mouth fell open, clearly stunned, before he howled with laughter.

"For someone who was kidnapped, awoken by Fae, and has no idea where she is or where she's headed, you're pretty plucky. I'll give you that," he said as he caught his breath. "Truly, given the circumstances, would you want to ride with anyone else?"

"Quite literally anyone else. Doran, maybe?" I deadpanned.

His grin solidified, twisting into a smirk. "Like Doran, do you?"

My cheeks flushed as I held his gaze.

"Maybe." My eyes dropped down the length of his body and back up. "More than you, anyway."

The grin slid from his face, and he released a breathy chuckle.

"Careful, Ara," he warned, facing forward. He kicked his horse, clicking his tongue, and it trotted along and the horde moved forward with him.

My eyebrows furrowed as I glanced around and nudged my own horse forward.

"How do you know my name? Who are you?" I asked cautiously, catching up to his side.

Without looking in my direction, he answered, "Rogue."

Every snarky thought left me at once, my blood icing in my veins.

Rogue... Only one man went by that name.

I stared forward, my eyes out of focus, when he peeked over at me and laughed.

"So you've heard of me, then."

"You are..." I whispered, "The King of Ravaryn, then? Son of Adrastus, the draig?"

"Yes."

I nodded slightly, not sure how to react—if I *should* react—as we rode in silence. Dread took root in my gut, and I tensed my muscles, determined to keep me atop the horse, even as my thoughts spiraled.

Suddenly, his words from the night before rang through me.

I was rather hoping you'd follow me out here.

My cheeks flamed as embarrassment flooded my veins, and a sad, silent chuckle escaped me.

I had thought he'd wanted me like I had him, and...

Goddess, I'd kissed him. The King of Ravaryn. The son of Adrastus. The vicious counterpart to his father.

He let me kiss him. Kissed me back, even.

The embarrassment washed away as rage took its place, and I gripped the reins tighter.

"Why have you taken me?" I asked, but he didn't answer. "Because of my father, I'm assuming?"

Wait...

I whipped my head to him; he was already smirking, not even bothering to glance in my direction as he waited for me to piece it together myself.

"How did you... You followed me home that first night,

didn't you?" My mouth fell open in disgust and mortification.

"Honestly, it was very thoughtful of you to be there that night. You presented our salvation on a silver platter."

His words settled over me. He was right.

I did this.

Guilt dug its ugly claws in, and I kept my eyes forward, body numb, as everything my father had ever warned me about came crashing back.

Chapter Eight

Ara

We rode along the same trail for hours. It was a simple dirt path, well-worn by years of travelers, lined with luscious, green grass that continued over rolling hills for miles. The sky was clear as the sun peaked, and thick, fluffy clouds drifted in the breeze.

If given the chance, I would be able to find my way back to the border. The trail was simple enough, and we hadn't passed through any towns. Escaping the horde in such an open field, however, would be challenging. I would have to wait until we stopped, hopefully for the night, to slip out while they were sleeping. There would be no other way to leave undetected.

Lost in my plan, I didn't notice our surroundings changing.

The trail had narrowed, and the grass was no longer thick and green, but brown and wilted. There were no flowers, no vegetation of any kind besides dead grass and the trees up ahead—if they could be called that.

The air became stale and the horses uneasy as we neared the forest. These trees were unlike any I had ever seen. The

CHAPTER EIGHT

trunks were black and too smooth, almost as if oiled, and the leaves were unnaturally dark, almost blending in with the black bark and casting the forest floor in a suffocating shadow where nothing could grow.

"This is the Cursed Wood," Rogue whispered loud enough for only me to hear. "Just stay within the horde, and you'll be fine. We've crossed through several times before with no problems. As long as we keep quiet, we shouldn't attract any unwanted attention, and we'll make it through in less than three hours."

Unwanted attention?

"Does anything live in these woods?" I asked, carefully scanning the trees for movement.

"There are a few creatures, but not many, and we haven't come across them in years. Like I said, as long as we stick to the trail and remain as quiet as possible, they tend not to notice us," he whispered again, keeping his eyes locked on the trail.

As we entered, the Fae were silent. Tense. On guard.

If they were afraid, what were we walking into?

* * *

I kept an eye on the sun through the canopy as much as I could to track the time. If I was correct, we only had about an hour before we were in the clear. We hadn't seen a single creature, only trees as far as the eye could see. Exhaling slowly, I released my grip on the reins, relaxing slightly.

We're almost there.

But then, a small bird leapt onto the trail ahead of us.

About a foot in height, it had sleek black, iridescent feathers and skinny legs it used to bounce around on. From the side, the vibrant red skin surrounding its black beady eye was visible and its beak was long and slender, curving downwards into a sharp point. It stopped and curiously cocked its head towards us, turning and hopping in our direction.

I looked at Rogue in utter confusion and slight fear. Other than his chest heaving with rapid breaths, he was completely still, his gaze locked on the bird.

"When I tell you to run, you run. Go as fast as you can until you clear the woods and do not return, no matter what you hear. Wait for us there," Rogue muttered under his breath.

"Why? It looks harmless. It's so small and..." I uttered slowly, my sentence trailing off as hundreds more emerged from the trees, squawking as their beady eyes darted in every direction, bouncing mindlessly.

My heart sank as I realized they were inching closer with every hop. The horses pranced and pawed, snorting with anxiety as they pulled at their bits.

"These are slicers. Their bills are razor sharp and they travel in packs, taking down and devouring their prey in less than a minute. They are incredibly vicious," he whispered quickly, his eyes never leaving the bird in front of him.

My heart raced and I could feel the nervous sweat breaking out along my forehead. The bird directly ahead in the trail chirped again, bristling its feathers, before hopping once more towards Rogue.

"Run!"

The birds launched themselves into the air in one, swift movement, screeching before they swarmed. Talons protruded from their feet, slicing at Fae and horses alike.

The soldier closest to me fell from his horse, landing with

a thud, as a bird clawed at his eyes. Dozens of birds attacked him at once, slicing with claws and bills in a starved frenzy, shredding his skin. At his screams, I jerked away, scrunching my eyes, trying to stifle the flashbacks.

The screaming.

The blood.

It yanked me back to the war, and I bolted, my horse's own self-preservation carrying us at a gallop.

Even from this distance, Rogue's voice rang out over the commotion, and my hands yanked on the reins on instinct, halting the horse.

No, he told me to run...

I clicked at my horse to continue forward. He took a few steps before I pulled him to a stop again, debating.

He told me to run, but leaving them there... A sick thought reared its ugly head. *I could let the birds devour them. Save me from my kidnapper.*

Another shout—distinctly Rogue's—and something deep tugged me back, insisting I return. Groaning and swallowing the fear as best I could, I turned the horse and raced back.

Nearing the scene, fallen Fae and horses lay about the forest floor, slicers perched atop them, ravaging their bodies. A few feet away, Rogue, Doran, and several other soldiers were fighting off a dozen birds in a tight circle, their backs pressed to each other.

I hopped off my horse, picked up a sword from a fallen soldier, and stalked forward, my feet squelching in the muck and blood.

Three slicers noticed as I moved through the wreckage and launched simultaneously. I swung, slicing the head off one and cutting the other in two straight through the abdomen in one, rapid movement. The last bird, however, latched onto my side, slicing through my shirt and sinking its hooked claws into my skin. Feeling the blood trickle down my side, I grabbed the creature by the throat and ripped it off me. Prickles of blood oozed as the bird angrily pecked at my hand before I snapped its neck, dropping its lifeless body to the ground, eyes locked on the group ahead.

By the time I made it to them, most of the birds were dead at their feet. Rogue glanced up and his face lit with anger when he noticed me, taking a step in my direction.

Over his shoulder, a slicer surged at him, seemingly unnoticed, and I brought the sword back overhead with both hands as Rogue froze, eyeing me. In one swift motion, I hurled it past him, hitting the slicer dead in its heart, flinging it back several feet. Rogue's head whipped around as it bolted past him, narrowly missing his left wing. When he turned back to me, his lips parted in shock, his eyes wide.

Soon, the rest of the birds were either dead or fleeing.

Several moments passed in silence as the remaining Fae caught their breath and surveyed the damage. At least a dozen Fae had died, and all the horses were gone, either lost or killed—save Rogue's.

Leaving his commanders, Rogue marched over, grabbed my arm, and tugged me away from the group.

"What was *that*?" he demanded, his face tight with anger.

I recoiled back from him, staring incredulously.

"What? Saving your life? Sorry. Next time, I won't," I spat back, tugging my arm as I turned to walk away. His grip tightened, unyielding, as he lowered his face to mine.

"No, I mean coming back here," he said, glaring. "I told you to run."

CHAPTER EIGHT

I yanked my arm from his hand, buzzing with anger, and turned to face him completely.

"Yeah? Well, I don't take orders from you. You may be a king, but you're not *my* king."

His eyes went wide with rage.

"While you're in my kingdom, I am," he said, before his gaze dropped to my side, eyeing the growing red stain of blood on my torn shirt. A muscle ticked in his jaw. "Come on, we have to treat that before you bleed out."

He gripped my arm again, tugging me to his horse and grabbing supplies before leading me to a nearby tree.

"Take off your shirt," he commanded.

"No," I said, crossing my arms over my chest. I was *not* taking my shirt off in front of him, in front of all of them.

"Take off. Your shirt," he repeated as he stepped closer, towering over me.

"No." I tilted my face up to his, just inches above mine.

"You're insufferable," he seethed.

"And you're the only reason I'm here."

He inhaled deeply, his nostrils flaring.

"If you don't take it off, I can't treat your wounds, and if you don't die from bleeding out, you'll die from infection. Wounds from their talons tend to fester when left untreated. Then what good would you be to me?" he said with a smirk.

Irritation pricked at me as my eyes darted to the rest of the men. He followed my line of sight and huffed in annoyance.

He walked us behind a group of trees, and I pulled the shirt off with a harsh sigh, keeping my arms over my chest. His lips parted as his eyes found the wound. My brows furrowed as I looked down; four, deep gashes spread from the bottom of my right breast down to my hip bone, still leaking blood. At the sight, pain flared, and a hiss escaped my clenched teeth.

"All right, yeah," I conceded, sitting at the base of a tree as he knelt beside me.

The closeness brought with it the smell of smoke and evergreen spice. Resisting the urge to lean in and inhale, I watched as he unscrewed the lid off a small jar and dipped two fingers into the ointment.

"What is that?" I asked, pulling away as he neared my skin.

"It's a healing salve made from a plant that grows at Draig Hearth. When cultivated and harvested correctly, it can be made into an ointment that will heal any wound," he explained, applying it to the top of a laceration. Another hiss escaped my lips, and his eyes peeked up at me. "I know, it burns like fire."

Oh, it did. It took everything in me to sit still as he applied it painstakingly slowly.

To distract myself from the flames licking at my skin, I let my gaze roam over his features, following up the slope of his jaw. My eyes snagged on a pointed ear, then the scar right beneath it. This must have been the salve that healed the wound. Nothing else would have.

Dropping my eyes back to his hands, he continued applying the salve, inching farther and farther down my abdomen. When his fingers reached just above my hip bone, he stilled, resting them on my bare skin, his eyes glued to the curve of my body. He began to run his hand along my hip, leaving a blazing trail in its wake, decidedly different from that of the salve.

I grabbed his wrist, and his hand jerked back as his eyes snapped to my face with surprise. Embarrassment flushed my cheeks as he stood, clearing his throat and wiping his

CHAPTER EIGHT

hands on his trousers.

"There you go," he said, averting his gaze as I pulled my shirt back on.

"Thanks," I uttered curtly before I stood. As Rogue stepped over to join his men, all eyes went to him, their conversation ceasing immediately.

"Let's just get out of here before we make any plans. The smell of blood will attract other creatures." He didn't wait for a response as he grabbed the reins of his horse and walked him over to me. "Get on."

I started to argue, but I thought better of it and stopped, wincing as I hoisted myself onto the saddle, too tired to walk the last few miles. Based on the soreness of these wounds, I didn't want to.

We cleared the forest with no other issues. Once we were a good half mile from the trees, Rogue left to give his men an order before returning and hoisting himself up, settling onto the saddle behind me, his wings resting lightly on either side of the horse.

My body went rigid.

"What are you doing?" I yelped, whipping my head back to ogle at him.

Our faces were just inches from each other, and I jerked back, nearly falling from the horse. He quickly threw an arm around my waist and snatched me back against him.

"Well, seeing as you're riding my horse, I think it's perfectly reasonable for me to ride as well," he said, clicking for the horse to proceed.

We trotted forward, his arm firmly in place around my waist.

"We still have a full day's ride, maybe more, before we reach the castle. Normally, I would fly back, but I don't want to gain any unwarranted attention by carrying a human across my entire kingdom, and considering my horse was the only one spared, we're going to continue ahead of the group."

"Alone?" I asked, stifling the hope from my voice.

"Yes, Ara. Alone."

Just us... Facing away from him, I didn't even bother hiding my smile.

Running from just one Fae would be so much easier.

Chapter Nine

Rogue

A few hours into the journey, Ara had slumped against me, asleep. The fact that anyone, especially a kidnapped human, could relax enough to sleep around me was astounding. I didn't know if it made her impressive or foolish.

I glanced down at the human in front of me; she looked peaceful, much like she did in the library chair, her shirt still torn and stained red. The wound would be closed by now with the help of the salve, but the stain remained.

The moment I laid eyes on her in the woods, I was enraged at her audacity to disobey a king, disobey *me*, by returning against orders. No one defied me. Ever.

Except this infuriatingly reckless creature.

At the sight of that growing stain, though, panic struck me, and it irritated me beyond words. The mate bond made me unwillingly protective of her, the need to safeguard her almost overwhelming every other thought, distracting me from what was really at stake.

She was serving as payment, a bargaining chip—nothing

more. She would never be anything more than a means to an end.

She stirred and pressed further into me.

Tearing my eyes away from her form, I shifted uncomfortably, suddenly aware of her nearness. With the breeze, the scent of wildflowers and rain wafted from her hair, and my body tensed. With her backside pressing into me, the outline of her breasts was visible—taunting me—and I forced my eyes to remain forward.

I knew it was the bond fueling the lust—bringing the two people together who would produce the strongest offspring—but knowing that did nothing to tamper the resentment I felt. At the bond, at Ara, at the Goddess.

I did not need a mate, not at a time like this, and definitely not a human. It was wrong. The way my body reacted to her was wrong.

She doesn't even have magic. How could we possibly produce a powerful offspring?

My grip tightened on the reins.

Wrong. It's all wrong.

My jaw ached from how hard I was clenching my teeth when Blackburn came into view. Relief flooded through me at the sight, and I suddenly felt like I could breathe again.

Blackburn was an intimate village, conveniently located between the border and Draig Hearth. We rode along the dirt road, worn by thousands, leading to the heart of the village—a street lined with shops, apothecaries, and other family businesses. At the far end was a pub that doubled as an inn, which was exactly where we were headed.

Before we entered, I settled the glamour over my wings and eyes to dull my appearance and hopefully prevent us

CHAPTER NINE

from being noticed. Without the rest of my men and with a human captive in tow, it was best not to draw attention. Pulling her cloak from the saddlebag, I wrapped it around Ara's shoulders, careful not to wake her as I pulled the hood up, covering her rounded ears.

Fae were not kind to humans in any part of Ravaryn, but especially not here. This town was the first to accept refugees when the attacks began, offering them shelter and hearing their stories. Blackburn was home to Ravaryn's warriors, as well as the birthplace of pyric magic—the ability to wield the flames—and the people here were true to their magic's sake. They were fiery and fiercely loyal to the realm, ready to defend her with their lives against any who would seek to harm it. Right now, that was Auryna.

They demanded war when the attacks started, but we couldn't sacrifice the rest of our people to the endless army of King Adon. It would be pointless. They always had another head to replace the last, but we didn't. My refusal to engage angered them beyond words, and my return would only spark that rage again; hence, why we needed to lie low.

I slowed as we entered the village. While I might not be the most welcomed guest of Blackburn, the village still had its charms.

Street lamps lit with candles enchanted to never melt lined the road, illuminating the shadows of twilight and casting a soft, flickering glow on the people strolling by. They were smiling, at ease, and the sound of laughter drifted on the breeze with the smell of warm bread and smoke.

I nudged Ara, and she stirred, bringing a hand to the hood on her head. She glanced up at me with furrowed brows, and I smiled, leaning down to nuzzle my face in the crook of her neck to appear as lovers. She tensed, moving to pull away, but I wrapped an arm around her waist to hold her close, feeling how rapid her breaths were.

"We're in Blackburn," I whispered. "The people here will not take kindly to a human in their midst so I covered your ears. We need to stop and rest at the inn just ahead. Let me do the talking; just follow my lead."

She nodded before sitting up straighter, fully alert now.

Stopping at the hitching post, I dismounted with ease, turning to offer my hand in assistance. She glanced at my hand before swinging herself off, landing with a thud. I rolled my eyes and tied the reins to the post.

As I turned and headed to the inn, she jogged to my side, pulling the hood tighter around her face as she looped an arm through mine.

"Where are your wings?" she whispered, tilting her face to mine.

"I hid them with glamour. Nobody else in the kingdom has wings like mine and it would be too obvious who I was. It'll be safer if they don't suspect who I am… who you are," I replied quietly, tilting my head down to hers, keeping my gaze forward.

She nodded and released my arm, resuming the space between us as I discreetly pulled a dagger from its sheath.

"If the way you wielded a sword was any indication, I'm assuming you know how to use this if the need arises?"

She nodded again and swiped the blade, sliding it into her right boot without missing a step.

The door of the inn creaked as I pulled it open, the smell of cooked meat and mead pouring out to greet us. I sidestepped, gesturing for her to enter. As the door closed behind us, no one batted an eye besides the barmaid serving tables. She gave a quick nod as she passed by with a tray of pork and potatoes.

Ara's eyes followed as the barmaid set the tray down, her stomach growling loudly, and I suppressed a smile at the growing blush on her cheeks.

"We haven't eaten all day," she said, shrugging her shoulders.

"I'm hungry too, believe me."

We quickly took the closest table, sitting with our backs to the wall so we could survey the room during our meal. The waitress came by to ask if we were here for food or drink, and I quickly responded "both" before she took off to the kitchen.

"This place doesn't seem so bad," Ara muttered, her eyes locked on a father and daughter. They laughed loudly, coaxing smiles from those around them, but when the father reached over to clap his daughter on the back, he accidentally knocked over a mug of mead. They paused as they glanced at each other before erupting in laughter once again and grabbing rags to mop up the mess.

Jealousy hung heavy in my gut as I stared.

Growing up with my father, effortless love was never something I experienced. For most of my childhood, I was left alone, only occasionally joined by a servant or maid. I think they mostly pitied me, knowing disappointment and abhorrence were the only emotions my father ever offered me, but as the son of such a king, no one risked their life, or Goddess forbid their child's, by allowing them to talk to me, much less play, so I never had the chance to truly enjoy someone's presence—especially not with a parent.

Taking a forced breath, I tore my eyes away and allowed the numbness to return, washing away the memory.

"No, it's not. The people are happy here, as long as you're Fae," I explained. "The Ten Year War and the continuing attacks have hurt a lot of people, ruined a lot of lives, and they are not quick to forgive."

She whipped her face to me, her gray eyes narrowing with suspicion.

"What attacks?"

Releasing a low laugh, my fists clenched under the table, my knuckles cracking. *Of course.*

"In the three years since the war, several of our border towns have fallen to Auryna. Most were attacked in the dead of night while they slept. It always comes unexpectedly, and anyone unlucky enough to be found is always brutally murdered. Always," I declared, anger burning in my chest, reminding me of my hatred for humans, of why this woman could never be my true mate.

I inched away from her, leaning on my elbow, needing to distance myself from her. She glanced at me, noting my movement before turning back to the people around us, as if they would reveal the truth in my words.

"Half the people in this town are refugees, attempting to restart their lives after their homes were burned to the ground. It is no longer safe for Fae to live along the borders, which is why we didn't run into any on the road here," I continued.

Uncertainty set deep into her features, creasing between her eyebrows.

"I've never heard anything about this, and my father is the general. He would never order such barbaric attacks." She turned her eyes to me, studying my face. "Why would I believe anything you say?"

CHAPTER NINE

"Ask anybody here. They won't hesitate to tell their story," I challenged, motioning my hands to the room. "I'm not lying. Not about this."

A muscle ticked in her jaw as her gaze bounced around the room, landing on the small children chasing each other between tables. The crease between her eyebrows deepened, and I could almost see the gears turning, trying to gauge whether to believe me or not.

"That's why I've taken you: to bribe your father into ceasing his relentless attacks," I whispered.

Her eyes dropped to the table.

Clenching my jaw, I turned just as the waitress brought our food.

* * *

Thank the Goddess, the inn had two rooms available, so we didn't have to share close quarters. Ara was the personification of complicated and any breath I could take away from her was a welcomed one.

Sitting in a decrepit leather chair across from the fireplace, I watched the flames dance. Mesmerized by the music of crackling logs, my thoughts returned to General Evander. He would know she was missing by now, potentially would have already searched the local town, and he would soon be turning to Ravaryn.

My gut twisted at the thought.

He would look to the burned tower first, finding the remnants of our camp a few miles north, but he wouldn't find any Fae, not for at least a few hours in any direction. After I left the encampment, my men hastily cleared the remaining

Fae from the area, but fear still gripped me—fear that my people would get caught in the crossfire, fear that he would somehow catch up to us or my men before we could reach my castle.

Taking a deep breath, my hand dropped to my bouncing knee. From here, Draig Hearth was only a few hours' ride; we should reach it by midday tomorrow if we left early enough.

Once there, I would be able to breathe again. The castle was an impenetrable fortress, specifically designed for Draigs over a millennium ago. It sat atop a steep hill at the very northern tip of the continent, a cliff at its back that dropped off into an angry ocean, and only one road in, constantly policed by guards and archers. Its design made it easy for Draigs to come and go as they pleased while still rendering it nearly impossible to attack. Once there, she would be lost to him unless I deemed otherwise.

As the flames fizzled out to embers and a crisp settled in the air, I rose with a sigh, sauntering to the bed and bracing myself for another sleepless night.

Creak.

My head swiveled to the door, listening intently. Another creak sounded outside my door, and anger boiled in my chest.

Striding to the door, I yanked it open and reached my hand into the darkness, snatching Ara's neck as she attempted to sneak past my door.

Squeezing just enough to lessen her air supply, I led her into my room and quietly closed the door behind us, her eyes wide and furious as I backed her into the wall.

"I'm still not sure if you're brave or just plain foolish," I ground out inches from her face, my hand still locked around her throat.

CHAPTER NINE

She made no attempt to remove it as she glared at me through her lashes. Feeling her pulse beneath my palm, my grip tightened, and her lips twitched with restraint, unwilling to beg for mercy. I smirked, admiring her will, before my gaze dropped to her lips, still red and full even as they turned down with rage.

After a moment, I relented, lessening my grip, and she gasped for air as I led her to the bed. When she realized, she pulled away, and my grip tightened again as I faced her.

"Don't worry. I would never stoop so low," I said and she scowled, her pulse thundering beneath my fingers. "Now, sit."

Releasing her with a shove, she stumbled backward to the bed before quickly glancing at the door.

"Go ahead, try again," I said with a laugh, sliding my belt off. Quickly snatching one arm, I wrapped the belt around her wrist, securing her to the bedpost.

"Do not—"

"Too late."

She tugged at the belt, grimacing when it didn't budge.

"If you're not going to stay willingly, then you'll stay like a prisoner."

"I can't stand you," she seethed between clenched teeth as I strolled to the chair, pulling the extra blanket from the back.

"Good. The feeling is mutual." Walking around the bed, I laid on the floor between the bed and door, flattening and stretching out my wings beneath me. Folding my hands behind my head and crossing my feet, I sighed loudly as she tugged on the post; it rattled but held.

"Go to sleep, Ara. We have another long day tomorrow."

She yanked her arm a few more times, to no avail. "Ugh!"

She resigned from her efforts, throwing herself onto the bed without another word.

Staring at the ceiling, I listened, waiting for her breaths to even out, and drifted off to sleep after her, dreaming of spring storms.

* * *

The sounds of her muffled cries and thrashing pulled me from my sleep before the sun had even risen. Panic sank its ugly claws in, and I jerked up in a daze.

I rushed to her bedside, sure she was being attacked, but instead, found her still asleep, slick with sweat and struggling against whatever had taken hold of her dreams.

Hesitantly, I reached a hand over her shoulder, but before I had the chance to wake her, her eyes snapped open. She inhaled sharply, sitting straight up, as if electrified by some unseen force. I snatched my hand away and staggered back a few steps.

We stared at each other for a moment, confused and half asleep, before she dropped her head to her free hand, slowing her breathing.

"Goddess, you scared me," she mumbled.

"Scared you? *You* woke *me* with all your groaning and thrashing," I replied, waving a hand and grabbing the blanket from the floor. "I thought someone was attacking you."

She remained silent, her forehead still resting on her hand.

"It was a... nightmare. Nothing more," she said, tossing the blanket off and jerking at her restraint. "Well, I'm not going anywhere with my arm still tied, am I? Care to undo it now?"

Chapter Ten

Ara

It was a little before midday when I caught sight of the castle for the first time, pulling an audible gasp from my mouth.

"Welcome to Draig Hearth," Rogue announced.

The castle was magnificent, dramatic, a towering structure that sat atop a steep incline, several spires reaching to the sky. One tower rose higher than the rest, swallowed by the low-hanging clouds. Along the south side of the castle, a dark red vine crept its way up, consuming the castle, giving it the appearance of being engulfed in maroon flames.

As we neared it, the sound of raging waves and seagulls greeted us, even over the wind furiously whipping my hair. The north side of the castle backed against a cliff that dropped off into an ocean, and the smell of brine hung in the air, thick with humidity.

As we followed the only road to the entrance, more guards appeared, making themselves known. They patrolled the path with swords strapped to each hip, dressed in blood-red tunics. While their shining black helmets hid their faces, I could feel their disdainful gazes glued to me as we passed. My eyes stayed locked on the gate ahead, but my pulse sped up with each step closer.

The only road in.

Glancing around, I realized there was no other gate in or out. This singular road was it, the other side a cliff. Fear crawled up my spine, pulling me straighter, suddenly aware.

Once through these gates, I can never leave. Not without Rogue's approval.

Rogue shifted behind me, shattering my bubble of thought and reminding me he was there, touching me, leading me to my new cage.

It started with fidgeting, my fingers tapping on my thigh, but as we neared the steel gates, panic washed over me, drowning me in fear.

I snatched the reins up, halting the horse and yanking to the side in an attempt to turn him, but Rogue quickly wrapped his hand around mine, regaining control.

"What are you doing?" he shouted, tightening an arm around my waist, and the walls of my cage closed in, narrowing down to his touch.

I jerked against him—in an attempt to dismount the horse or dislodge myself from his touch, I didn't know—but it did nothing. He held me against him in a grip of steel, and my mouth went dry as my breath escaped me.

"What is wrong with you?" he said, stopping the horse and grabbing my chin to turn me to him. As he saw my expression and glanced at the gates, I watched as understanding dawned on him. "Look at me."

My eyes darted about, noticing every guard surrounding us as they inched closer to their king, gauging the situation.

CHAPTER TEN

"Look at *me*, Ara. Not my guards." His grip tightened on my chin as he tilted my face up, forcing me to look into his eyes.

"I cannot go in there," I whispered harshly, my voice shaking. "I cannot willingly go into another keep, another tower, another cage. I cannot—"

"Stop. I will not lock you in the tower," he said, his voice stern and deliberate. I stared into his eyes, studying him, trying to gauge his intentions; he seemed genuine enough—or perhaps I was that desperate to believe him. Either way, I took a trembling breath, nodding lightly as he released my chin.

Sitting forward, we continued through the gates. He steered us into the bailey before dismounting and handing the reins to a stable boy, not bothering to offer his hand this time. I hopped off, following him up the grand entrance where two guards pulled the large, wooden doors open before him.

Walking into the entryway was like entering another world, another time.

It was ancient and lavish with floors made of black stone. Along every wall sat dozens of golden candelabras of every shape and size, lit with tall, white candles, bathing the room in a hazy, flickering glow.

Straight ahead was a grand staircase with dark, wooden handrails that merged with the wall and continued upwards, forming an arch above the staircase. Every inch of the wood was carved with intricate designs I couldn't place. In a daze, I stepped closer, needing a better look at the one calling my attention.

It was a dragon, sailing through clear skies, the sun large above him and the earth far below. I traced its wings delicately with my fingertips, leaving a trail through the dust, the wood smooth and cool beneath my touch.

Rogue cleared his throat, and I jerked my hand back with a start, turning as he glided past me, ascending the stairs.

"My guards will escort you to your chamber," he said without looking back, waving his hand at two guards. They stalked towards me as Rogue turned the corner at the top of the stairs, leaving me at their mercy. My mouth fell open, my breath leaving in a whoosh, as I stared after him until the guards roughly grabbed my arms, dragging me to the staircase.

"Rogue!" I pulled my arm, and their grip tightened to the point of pain. "That hurts," I snapped at the guard to my right, but he only scowled, squeezing tighter. I gasped, jerking my arm. "Rogue! You said—You said I wouldn't be locked in there."

"Quiet, human, before we give you a reason to scream," the guard to my left said with a cruel smirk.

My heart sank as nausea rolled in my gut.

Betrayal.

As they dragged me up the stairs, bruising my arms, I felt nothing but betrayal.

My cheeks flamed with anger and embarrassment as we rounded the top step and took a left around the corner. They pulled me down a long, empty hallway, leading me to a single door at the far end, nearly indistinguishable from the rest of the wall.

A guard pulled a key ring from his pocket, unlocked the door, and shoved me through, following behind me as I stumbled to a stop in front of yet another staircase.

My body was frozen, my eyes shifting higher, higher,

CHAPTER TEN

higher, continuing up the spiraling stairs into darkness...into the keep. Large hands shoved at me again, and I started the climb with my heart in my throat, eyes burning with unshed tears.

At the top of the staircase was another door, already open, revealing my chambers. It was a simple room with a wooden bed, an already-lit fireplace, and a leather chair facing the window overlooking the sea.

With one more shove, I fell forward, my knees cracking hard against the stone. My eyes scrunched, watering at the sharp pain radiating through my legs.

"Don't leave until told otherwise," a guard ordered as they left, closing the door behind them.

My throat tightened at the click of a lock and I dropped my face to my hands with a sob. Closing in on myself, I gave myself five minutes.

Just five minutes. The same small amount of time it took me to follow Rogue out of the tavern. The same amount of time it took me to believe him. The same amount of time it took me to climb those infernal stairs.

Just five minutes, and then I inhaled deeply, steeling my nerves, and checked my boot. I released a breath of relief at the feel of Rogue's dagger in my palm. In a castle of Fae, at least I had a weapon. Pulling it from my boot, I shoved it under the pillow before tugging the boots off and placing them by the fireplace.

Turning the chair, I plopped down, mesmerized as I watched the flames dance. My eyes followed their movement, their warmth, letting it carry me away as the rage set in. Rogue said a few simple words, promising to not lock me in the keep, and I foolishly believed him.

How had I gone from being confined to my father's estate, safe, in Auryna, to quite literally trapped in enemy territory not even two days later? All because I stupidly followed what I thought was my one chance at freedom.

What a cruel sense of irony fate has.

* * *

A few hours passed before I realized the fire never dulled or diminished. Sitting up, I turned my ear to the fire, listening for the distinct sound of burning wood, which was still audible. I crouched down, peeking into the fire. The logs were there, blackened, but otherwise untouched, crackling as usual.

It must be enchanted.

With fascination, I glanced about the room, looking for anything else that might be enchanted, and paused at the window. There were no glass panes, and yet, even though it was raining, no water fell on the stone floor, not even a breeze blew through.

Strolling over, I slowly reached my hand out through the opening. About six inches out from the windowsill, I hit a solid, invisible wall. Cautiously, I slid my hand up and around, exploring for gaps, but it connected to the wall on all sides and remained solid as stone, no matter how hard I pushed.

I guess they don't want anyone throwing themselves from the window.

Standing on my tiptoes, I peeked over the edge, just enough to see the waves crashing on jagged rocks below.

Just then, my door opened, and I whipped around, only to be met with a small woman, clearly Fae. My body tensed as

CHAPTER TEN

my eyes darted to the dagger under my pillow.

She was short, with pointed ears and deep violet hair. Walking with her head hanging low, she carried a tray of food to the bed, gently sitting it on the edge with trembling hands before turning to me without raising her eyes.

"My name is Thana," she said. "I'm assigned to be your lady's maid."

A lady's maid?

"My name is Ara," I replied, momentarily stunned.

"I was told to bring you food, as you haven't eaten today," she said meekly. "I was also ordered to give you a message from the king."

She placed a small, folded note on the tray before turning to leave, dashing from the room as quickly as she came. As she disappeared down the staircase, I rushed to the bed, eagerly picking up the parchment.

> *You are free to roam the castle as you please, but <u>do not</u> try to escape.*
> *Rogue*

A rush of relief eased the tension in my chest, and I inhaled a shaky breath. While I may be confined to this castle, I wasn't confined to this room, and that had to be enough—for now.

Mustering a burst of courage, I pulled on my boots, then grabbed the dagger and slid it into my boot. Jogging to the door, I continued down the stairs two at a time before I could lose my nerve and turned around. Once I reached the bottom, however, my feet stopped, unsure of where to go from here. I stared down the dimly lit hallway and decided to simply go forward, following it until it opened into another elaborate archway, leading to a library.

My steps slowed as I entered, and the smell of old books engulfed me. Tears pricked my eyes as I took it in, the magnitude, the history, and an overwhelming sense of awe filled me. There were shelves upon shelves in every direction, several levels, and sliding ladders reaching all the way to the ceiling. There must be hundreds, if not thousands, of books.

I strolled to the closest bookcase, examining the spines along the shelf at eye level. The entire row was full of thick tomes, heavy with dust and cracking leather, indicating age. Pulling one particularly thick one from the shelf, I flipped it open. Blowing the dust from the page, I read the title aloud under my breath: *The Long and Thorough History of Healers.*

Closing and replacing it on the shelf, I reached for another, *Draigs and Their Wyverns of Old,* when a raspy voice spoke behind me.

"Hello. Can I help you?"

He was a tall, elderly man, slumped at the shoulders, with thick, white hair hanging down past his waist and pale gray eyes. I met his stare, and his lips parted as shock registered on his face.

He must realize I'm the human. My heart thundered in my chest, and I tensed, prepared to reach for my dagger, but his expression relaxed, returning to one of curiosity.

"I see you've found the history section of the library. Do you like to read?" he asked genuinely with a smile.

I settled some, giving a quick nod.

"Well then, if I may make a suggestion…" He stepped over to the shelf, grazing the titles before pulling out a large tome bound in black leather. "This is a full history of Ravaryn's royalty. Seeing as you're in this kingdom now, it may be helpful, or at least interesting, to read about our royalty and customs."

He handed me the book with an outstretched arm and took a step back; it dawned on me then that he was being careful to not invade my space. While his consideration surprised me, I was extremely grateful for it.

"Thank you. We don't have access to such works in Auryna," I said quietly, walking to a nearby table to take a seat.

"My name is Alden, by the way." He ambled over to the table, his hands clasped together in front of him. "I've been the librarian here since Rogue became king."

I glanced up at him to find his eyes were kind, wise. *Trustworthy*, I thought.

"My name is Ara," I replied.

Alden's smile deepened. "Well, it's very nice to meet you, Ara."

Chapter Eleven

Ara

I spent the rest of the evening in the library, strolling through the aisles and reading through the tome Alden gave me.

Because it was so large, I decided to start at the end and work my way forward. Opening the book with a thud, I flipped through the pages. The movement sent a cloud of dust into the air, and I coughed, waving my hand in front of my face. I leafed through the last few pages, noting Rogue's most recent predecessors—Vaelor and Adrastus—and stopped on the current king of Ravaryn.

Under his name was a detailed sketch of Rogue's upper half, including his wings, drawn in the same deep shade of red as his eyes. His hair was shorter, black and curled, but his face was the same, unaged. I ran a finger along the sketch, the page smooth save for the small marks made with pencil. My finger slid over a wing and down to his neck where the thick scar should be but wasn't.

Under the sketch, it read:

CHAPTER ELEVEN

> *Rogue Draki*
> *243rd King of Ravaryn*
> *Son of Adrastus Draki and Edana of village Blackburn*
> *Ability: Pyric, fly (did not present ability to shift like father)*

Hmm. I had known the previous king of Ravaryn was a Draig, but it hadn't occurred to me that Rogue may also be one. Although, if this book was to be believed, I guess he wasn't. For him to have pyric magic, his mother must have been a flame worker—that wasn't an ability typically possessed by draigs.

Flipping a few pages forward, I stopped when I found Adrastus.

The resemblance was there, but he was older, his eyes a lighter shade of red, angrier, more vibrant. His hair was just as black as Rogue's but cropped short, his expression severe, almost a scowl. Something about the way he was drawn aligned with everything I'd ever heard of him, rendering him just as harsh as legend claimed he was.

"He was brutal," Rogue's voice sounded from behind me.

I jumped violently, my heart racing. He walked around the table and sat across from me uninvited, leaning back in the chair, legs spread.

His eyes dropped to my arm, narrowing, and I followed his line of sight. In this tunic, a hand print bruise around my bicep was visible, already purpling. He sat forward as his gaze shifted to my other arm, eyeing the matching mark.

"I'll kill them," he seethed, deathly still, before jerking to his feet and striding to the door, leaving a trail of swirling smoke in his wake.

"Hey—" Jumping to my feet, I jogged after him. I grabbed his wrist, and he whipped around, eyes wide as he looked at my hand on his arm. "*You* ordered them to take me," I said, releasing him. His eyes snapped to mine with furrowed brows.

Our faces were so close, I could almost feel his breath on my cheek, and my feet instinctually took a step back. With a tight jaw, he nodded once, averting his gaze, and I took another step back, returning to the table. Surprisingly, he followed suit, sitting in the chair across from me once again.

"Alden recommended it to me," I said, suddenly feeling as if I was trespassing.

"You met Alden, did you?" he asked, raising an eyebrow, and I nodded. "Well, if anyone would befriend the human, it would be him, I suppose."

He tilted his head to stare at the sketch of Adrastus, his hand lifting to his throat where his fingers found his scar absentmindedly.

"Did he do that to you?" The question fell from my mouth before I had a chance to stop it, and I stilled, feeling heat seep into my cheeks.

Dropping his hand, anger flashed behind his eyes. His mouth fell open, then snapped shut.

"That's a bit personal, don't you think? Or do you just not have simple fucking manners where you're from?" My cheeks flushed furiously at each word. "I guess I shouldn't be surprised, considering how barbaric Auryna is."

I released a breathy laugh, my embarrassment morphing

into indignant.

"Funny coming from the creature who quite literally *kidnapped* me and is holding me hostage. If anyone was raised without manners, I would say it's you."

We glared at each other for a tense few moments, and a muscle ticked in his jaw. Without looking away, he took a deep breath, rising to his feet.

"You should return to your chambers, Ara. It's getting late."

I scowled after him as he strode to the door.

"Oh, and consider them dead," he said over his shoulder.

My fists clenched on the table as I attempted to calm myself. Taking a forced breath, I closed the tome and searched the shelves for another book. Grabbing a seemingly interesting one, I plopped down into a large leather reading chair, and there I remained until the early hours before dawn, solely to spite him and his infuriating commands.

* * *

The sound of the door clicking open pulled me from my sleep the following morning. My hand flew to the dagger, gripping the handle under my pillow. As Thana entered the room, I released it, sliding my hand from the pillow. She pushed the door open with her shoulder, hands occupied with a breakfast tray.

"Good morning," I said as she set the tray on my bed, glancing at the one from the night before, still left untouched.

"Good morning," she replied quickly as she picked up last night's tray before hurrying to the door. "Oh, the king asks that you to meet him in the courtyard. He has a sparring circle prepared."

"A sparring circle? What for?" I asked, baffled.

"I do not know," she said, looking at me properly for the first time. Her eyes were the color of amethyst, matching her hair.

"Well, thank you," I said, offering a light smile. She returned it, nodding goodbye before descending out of sight.

Catching a whiff of bread and honey, my stomach growled, and I devoured the food on the tray, along with the cup of tea.

As I finished, I glanced down at my clothes and grimaced. I had been wearing the same clothes for days. Hopping up, I strolled to the small dresser, not expecting much, as I pulled the knob on the top drawer.

My mouth fell open. Inside was an exact copy of what I was already wearing and nothing else. Yanking the other drawers open, they were all empty. I lifted the garments, and they seemed to be my size.

Tossing them on the bed, I jogged back to the dresser, thought of my cloak, and pulled the top one back open.

Inside was my cloak, the same one I'd worn for years.

Another enchantment.

With excitement, I closed it again, picturing my lost dagger, and opened it. Nothing. It was empty. Disappointment flooded me, and I pushed it closed, turning away.

I quickly changed into the clean clothes and grabbed the dagger, sliding it into my boot as anxiety bubbled in my chest.

Once outside, I spotted Rogue standing near an elaborate weaponry rack, holding every weapon I could possibly imagine. He was clad in all black, as usual, his tunic sleeveless with a deep V in the center. His hair was tied half up, away from his face, but a few tendrils fell forward as he leaned over

CHAPTER ELEVEN

the rack, grabbed a sword, and swung it in a tight circle.

When he noticed me, he gave me a wicked grin and motioned me over. I swallowed hard as I descended the entryway steps and crossed the courtyard.

"I figured with how well you handled a sword, you may want to spar, even just to land a few blows on me. And well… I have nothing planned for today, so I'd like to see just how good you really are," he taunted, spinning the sword in his hand. Giving me another smirk, he quickly closed the space between us and swung.

"Hey!" I ducked, lurching towards the weapon rack and picking up the first sword I touched. Turning, I thrust it up just in time to meet his sword with a loud clang.

Adrenaline rushed through me.

"Don't worry," he said in a low voice, his face too close for comfort. "The swords are spelled. They won't do any more damage than a wooden training sword."

His face was smug, and it ground at my nerves.

He took a small step back, and I lunged forward, swinging low. He blocked, so I spun and swung again at his opposite side. My sword connected with his ribs, and he twisted with a huff, chuckling with amusement as I gritted my teeth.

He's taking it easy on me.

I swung the blade again, but blow after blow, he blocked. Frustrated, my swings got faster, harder. We continued this way for longer than I anticipated before he swung back at me, catching me in the thigh, and my knee buckled. A hiss escaped my clenched teeth as I hit the ground hard on one knee.

He knocked the sword from my hand, and I swiftly pulled the dagger from my boot, hurling it at him. It spun end over end before he stepped to the side and caught the blade between his thumb and his forefinger, just inches from his face.

What in the hell?

He laughed and kicked out his foot, sweeping my other leg out from under me. I fell to the ground, scowling, growing more irritated by the minute.

"Good, yes. Great? I'm not so sure." He leered, extending a hand.

I took it, yanking him down. He yelped in surprise as he fell directly on top of me, landing with his hands firmly planted on either side of my face. His eyes were wide with shock and a strange intensity, and for a moment, my heart stuttered.

I'm not sure why I did it, but I brought my hand up hesitantly and paused before my fingertips skimmed the scar on his neck. He closed his eyes, tensing beneath my touch, as I slid my fingers over his shoulder, down his back, and along the base of one wing. His breath hitched, and my eyes snapped back to his. They were wide with lust and failing restraint, darting from my eyes to my lips, just before his mouth crashed to mine in a bruising kiss.

One hand firmly gripped my chin, angling my mouth to his, and he devoured me as if he had longed for this, wanted this. His tongue probed my lips, seeking entrance, and a hunger for him burned through me, almost blurring my thoughts. *Almost.*

My hand slid further down his back, along his waist, teasingly along his belt line when I felt it.

Ripping the dagger from its sheath, I stabbed it into his side and rolled him off me, jerking to my feet. He grunted, one hand flying to his side as he looked at me with bewilderment

CHAPTER ELEVEN

that quickly shifted to understanding. Releasing a low laugh, he slowly pulled the knife from his side and tossed it to the ground.

"You wicked little thing," he purred, heat pounding behind his eyes.

"I'm just using every asset at my disposal." I smirked. "Men are so easily distracted."

"Do you kiss every man you spar with, then?" he asked, prowling closer.

"No." My cheeks reddened as I held his gaze. "It worked well enough on you, though."

He was standing directly in front of me, his face a solid foot above mine.

Suddenly, he gripped my hair, wrapping the strands around his fist, and ripped my head back, exposing my neck. I froze, barely daring to breathe, as he brought his face down and leisurely ran his lips along my neck. "Yes, I guess it did."

He paused at the connection between my neck and shoulder, biting it lightly. My breathing stopped, waiting—for what, I didn't know. It felt as if time stood still with us as we stood there, locked in this embrace, my skin on fire wherever he touched me. His lips on my neck, his teeth. His hand in my hair, another on my waist, pulling me into him. His solid chest pressed into mine.

He released me with a small shove, and time resumed, moving fast enough to make my head spin.

"Don't do it again."

With that, he swiveled on his heel and strode away. My only movement was that of my heaving chest as I desperately tried to catch my breath and watched him stalk back to the castle, his fists clenched at his sides.

*　*　*

Irritation bit at me as I climbed the spiral staircase, exhausted and rubbing my sore thigh.

Rogue got under my skin in a way no one else ever had and that alone vexed me to no end. He frustrated me, infuriated me, perplexed me… intrigued me. Something about him pulled me in, like a moth to a flame, and it felt as if I was simply waiting for the inevitable burn that came with flying too close to the fire.

As I crossed the top step, Thana stood and greeted me with a hesitant smile, dragging me from my thoughts. Next to her was a large tub of steaming water that filled the room with the scent of lavender.

I sucked in a ragged breath, extremely grateful.

"Is this your doing?" I asked, and she nodded sheepishly. "Oh, you are Goddess sent, Thana. Thank you."

Crossing the room, I ripped my sweaty clothes off, stepped over the edge, and sank in up to my neck, reclining my head. The warmth swallowed me, easing the ache in my tired muscles.

With my eyes closed, I hadn't noticed Thana moving, so when she lifted my arm to scrub it with a sponge, I jumped, snatching my arm back out of instinct. She gasped, eyes wide with surprise.

"Sorry, I just… You don't have to do that. I can wash myself," I said, cheeks flushing, but she lightly grabbed my arm again, resuming.

Without lifting her eyes from her work, she spoke. "I have always been a lady's maid, and as odd as it may seem, I enjoy the mundane tasks. It gives me a sense of…purpose, caring for someone else. I actually find it quite cathartic, and it has been a long time since I've had another female to care for."

My mind snagged on her words, wondering who the last female may have been. Surely one of Rogue's lovers. A small pit of jealousy formed in my gut and the irritation returned in full force.

"Edana was the last woman I was a lady's maid for. She was incredibly sweet and kind to me, even as Adrastus held her against her will."

Edana...

"Edana? Rogue's mother?"

"Yes. You know, many refer to Adrastus as the Cruel King, but cruel is not a strong enough word to describe him. He was vicious, without a heart or soul. After he kidnapped Edana from her village, he thought she'd bend to his will since they were fated mates, but when she didn't, he locked her away." Her hands stilled. "She never left. Not until she died."

The sorrow from her voice seeped into my bones, a painful empathy taking root. "How did she die?"

She glanced up at me, as if deciding what she should say, if she should say anything at all.

"She died giving birth to Rogue."

My heart broke. For her, for him. Without his mother, Rogue was left to Adrastus—just a child at the mercy of the man they deemed worse than cruel.

"Did he... Is he why Rogue has that scar?" I whispered, motioning to my neck.

She set the sponge down, nodding slowly. "When he was thirteen."

My hand flew up to cover my mouth in horror.

"On his thirteenth birthday, Rogue... He should've been

able to shift like his father, but for some reason, he couldn't." She flinched, closing her eyes. "I was there that day, watching from a window inside the castle. It was only about six months after Adrastus usurped the throne, and things were still unstable with the sudden transition of power. He expected Rogue to show the realm another powerful Draig, the first of his kind to also wield the flames. He was to be a demonstration of undeniable strength, the continuation of the Draki line."

My chest clenched in anticipation of what was coming, desperately not wanting to hear but feeling like I needed to.

"When he couldn't, Adrastus exploded in a rage, shifting enough that his claws extended to the length of fingers. He... He sliced him, through him. That scar, you only see the tip of it at his neck," she uttered, shaking her head, her gaze unfocused. "Adrastus sliced him from his ear down to the opposite hip. From the window, it looked as if he had cleaved him in two. There was so much blood, and his screams... It still haunts me to this day."

The blood iced in my veins, my stomach twisting with nausea. I knew the weight of carrying what she saw, what she heard, but our scars... They were nothing like the one Rogue carried, visible to the world, to scrutiny, a testimony of his father's own hatred.

Tears pricked my eyes for the young, thirteen-year-old boy who had to bear that wound and the man still carrying it now.

"He should've died, and I'm sure that was Adrastus' intent, but our healer, Iaso, healed him... barely. It took her weeks, months maybe, and when he finally did recover, Adrastus said nothing. He didn't care."

We sat in silence, her words hanging heavy in the air

between us, as I was unable to conjure an adequate response.

With a deep breath, she picked up the sponge again, resuming her work, and my thoughts clung to Rogue in a way they hadn't before.

Chapter Twelve

Rogue

My blood boiled with frustration as I marched through the castle.

She was right. She had easily distracted me, and I fell right into her pretty little trap.

The more I dwelled on it, the more it irked me. The damned bond was clouding my judgment.

Smoke drifted from my palms. My eyes darted to it, glaring as the smoke rolled off in heavy waves. It had been decades since I'd lost control, and this was the third time in a week my magic seemed to have a mind of its own.

Scoffing, I clenched my fists, jerking them down to my sides as I continued to the library. Once there, I found Alden pouring over a thick tome laid openly on a stand. Hearing my footsteps, he closed his book, turning to face me with his hands clasped behind his back.

"How are you today, Rogue?"

Alden had been the librarian and a close advisor since my father died. He had served King Vaelor, the one who ruled Ravaryn for two hundred years before my father assassinated him; he was extremely well-versed in kingdom politics, and I valued him dearly for it.

When I took the crown, he returned to Draig Hearth, offering his services. I thought to deny him at first, finding it impossible to believe that a friend of Vaelor would serve under me, but Iaso vouched for him. She believed his heart to be genuine, so I accepted him into my inner circle. Over the years, he had proved to be one of my closest and most trusted allies.

"I'm fine," I sighed, sitting in a chair. "I sent correspondence to General Starrin a full day ago. He should have received it by now, correct?"

"I would assume so. Did you list the terms for Ara's return?" he asked, and I eyed him.

"Yes, of course. Lay down arms, convince Adon to stop the attacks by any means necessary, and evacuate the villages that rightly belong to Ravaryn," I stated, just as I had the day before. He knew the terms.

"And in exchange, you'll return Ara to him? Safely?"

I sat up straighter, turning to face him fully, as his use of her first name, so nonchalantly, was starting to irritate me.

"Alden, you know this. What's going on?"

He wrung his hands in front of him.

"Alden."

"You cannot just give her back," he said, raising his chin and meeting my eyes. "She does not belong in Auryna."

"What do you mean?"

"Ara…" His head shook slowly, holding my gaze with a serious intensity. "She is not human. Not entirely."

My breath left me in a whoosh, confusion muddling my thoughts, and my palms started to smoke again.

Alden looked at me with a seriousness that, even for him, was unusual. "She is the lost daughter of King Vaelor."

My heart thundered in my ears. I watched his mouth move, heard his words, but couldn't fully process what he was saying.

"No... He didn't..."

"Yes, Rogue. He did. He had a human lover, whom he intended to marry before he was killed...by Adrastus. She fled to Auryna immediately after his death, fearing for her own life, for the life of their baby," he explained slowly, as if scared I would explode at any minute—which, considering how panicked I was becoming, was not entirely irrational reaction.

The fire beneath my skin burned hotter with each passing second, heating the air around me, and Alden took a step back, wiping sweat from his brow.

He would not lie to me, which meant... My mind cleared all at once, and razor-sharp focus tunneled onto one thing, one person.

Ara.

Not only was she the daughter of the previous king of Ravaryn, but my father had murdered hers and threatened her mother's life.

My chest felt tight.

He threatened *her* life.

"How is this possible? She shows no signs of Fae blood. How can you be sure?"

"Her gray eyes. I would know them anywhere. They are undoubtedly King Vaelor's," he said with unwavering sureness. "As for how this is possible, the human would've had to have a powerful Fae place a spell over her womb while she was pregnant. It would've suppressed any Fae characteristics from ever revealing, even down to the pointed ears. That spell, however... It's typically used as a curse. It will prevent Ara from ever accessing her power, if she even has any. She will never feel the Fae half of her," he whispered quietly, sadly.

My heart physically ached for her.

To lose half of herself, her soul, her very existence... Even as a half-Fae, not being one with your magic is painful, in a deep, devastating kind of way, the kind of pain that comes from never being truly content, from endlessly searching for something that could fill what's lacking—but she would never find it as it was cursed to never reveal itself.

A curse that leaves you always longing for more.

"Do not breathe a word of this. To anyone. Do not tell her," I ordered. She may never access her other half, but I could spare her the heartbreak of realizing what she could never have.

"Rogue..." He started, and I cut him off.

"Do not. Tell her." I glared at him with all the kingly power I could muster, even as it felt flat, hollow.

With hesitation, he nodded, conceding, and I turned on my heel, leaving the library as quickly as possible.

* * *

Back in my chambers, my feet paced incessantly. My fire had already burned a track into the old carpet, filling the room with the scent of singed fabric and hazy smoke.

How ironic that my mate would be the daughter of the man my father killed *and* half-human. I released a sad laugh. *The*

Goddess must really hate me.

At least it explained the ability to have a mate bond with her. *An irritatingly inconvenient bond.*

"What am I supposed to do with this information?" I thought aloud as frustration bit at me, my pacing stopping mid-step as it struck me. "It cannot change anything."

For the good of my people, she had to be returned to Starrin when the general agreed to the terms, and he would. I couldn't keep her here, even if I wanted to, or he would double down on his efforts to destroy Ravaryn.

He already hated the Fae. This would just give him a reason to unleash his hatred and rage upon my people. If he knew...

Another thought hit me like a ton of bricks.

He doesn't know she's not his.

There was no way he would allow her to survive, much less live in his estate as his own, had he known. He must not know about her mother's past at all.

The realization only reinforced my decision—no one else could know.

No matter how much he loved her before, he wouldn't when he realized what she was. For this plan to work, he could never find out.

Starrin was known for being ruthless when it came to Fae. He led the charge during the Ten Year War, and he was still organizing the merciless attacks along the border. While he may have hidden it well, his abhorrence was laid clear in his battle strategy.

If he were to find out before the deal was struck, he wouldn't take the bribe, and my kingdom would be on the verge of falling to Auryna. If he found out after the exchange...

CHAPTER TWELVE

Anxiety stole the breath from my lungs and on instinct, I left my room in search of Iaso.

Iaso was the castle healer and had served several monarchs before me. She was one of the oldest people in Ravaryn, and due to her sway over plants, she was definitely the best healer in the entire realm. She could bend them to will, to an extent, and this included encouraging them to be more potent—in healing or poisoning. She could heal almost any wound, so long as there was still a heartbeat, while also being able to poison someone without a trace.

It made her the best ally in the realm, as well as the most dangerous.

She was also the only reason I was still alive. Without her, I would've died the day my father sliced me—not that he would've minded.

Hurt washed over me at the memory, stinging the skin along my scar, but I ground my teeth and pushed it down as I always did, letting the numbness return.

As Iaso was one of the oldest, she also had the most advice to give. I desperately hoped she would be able to give me something, reassurance maybe, and settle my rising panic.

Rapping a light knock on the ancient, wooden door, I slowly pushed it open, the hinges squeaking as it moved.

"Iaso?"

"Well, hello there. Long time, no see," she answered as her head peeked out from behind another wall. The sunlight flowing from her greenhouse windows illuminated her umber skin as she greeted me with a warm smile. She glided across the room and threw her arms around me in a tight embrace.

While she was one of my best advisors, she'd also become

my safe haven after we moved into Draig Hearth, taking me under her wing as she healed me.

I wrapped my arms around her and stood there for a moment, letting the smell of honey and herbs settle my nerves.

"How are you, my son?" she asked, pulling back. Her golden eyes roamed over my face and body, checking for damage of any kind.

"I'm all right. I actually have something I wanted to discuss with you," I said in a hushed whisper.

She guided me to the table and chairs near the window overlooking her extensive greenhouse. The greenhouse, as well as the surgery, was built specifically for her—an incentive to be the castle healer when Draig Hearth was first built a millennium ago. Here she had remained, by choice, serving every monarch since.

"What is it, Rogue?" she asked, pulling my attention back to her.

"Alden has briefed you on everything regarding Auryna, correct?"

She nodded.

"Has he spoken to you of the human girl I kidnapped?"

"Yes, the daughter of General Starrin. You plan to use her as leverage," she replied simply.

I sighed, steeling myself to speak the words. "He has just informed me that he believes she is the lost daughter of King Vaelor."

She froze, averting her gaze for a moment.

"Elora's daughter?" she asked.

"Elora?" My heart leapt into my throat.

"Elora was Vaelor's human lover," she uttered, dropping

her gaze to her greenery. "I remember her."

"So you knew?" I demanded, rising to my feet. "You knew a child of Vaelor was out there, and you never told me?"

Anger burned in my chest. The two people I trusted most knew of this secret and they both withheld it. A fierce wave of betrayal ripped through me.

"Sit down, Rogue," she ordered calmly, bringing her gaze back to me. "Let me explain."

I sat reluctantly, needing to hear her explanation.

"After your father murdered Vaelor, she came to me, completely distraught. She came here, sobbing helplessly, and told me of his death. She was hiding in his chambers when Adrastus stormed the castle in search of him, and she hid as he sliced Vaelor's throat with his claws," she explained, her gaze distant.

My hand found my scar on instinct, shame tightening around my throat as it often did when I heard the stories of his cruelty.

"After he left, she rushed to Vaelor and tried to stop the bleeding, but it was too late. She found me then, still covered in his blood. She told me of her pregnancy and begged me to help. She knew if anyone ever found out, if your father found out, he would kill her and the baby… So, I placed a spell over her womb to suppress the Fae blood in the child. It was the only way to keep her safe."

Ara. Not just some child. He would've killed Ara.

Sweat broke out along my spine as my thoughts spiraled.

My father.

If Ara ever found out, she would blame me. She would know my father was the reason she lost half of herself and her true father. She would know he was the reason her mother had to flee in fear for her life and quickly marry Starrin, forcing her to grow up in Auryna, completely unaware of her true identity.

She would hate me.

I don't know why I even cared at all. I shouldn't, and yet, the thought of her hating me more than she already did sent a spike of panic through my chest.

Looking at Iaso, I couldn't blame her. If she hadn't placed the spell, there was no doubt Ara would be dead right now, murdered by either my father or Starrin.

"I don't know what to do, Iaso. Do I give her back and let her go on with her life, forever in the dark? Or do I tell her?" My thoughts tumbled out of my mouth. "What would telling her even do, besides giving her more reason to despise me? I have to give her back. She is the only leverage we have, and this plan is the only hope for Ravaryn. And if her father—Starrin, I mean—found out before the exchange, would he still want her back?" I asked, but I knew the answer.

"No," I continued, "He would sooner let Ravaryn and all its people burn to the ground before he traded his blood lust for a Fae, even one who was once his daughter... Hell, he would be the one to light the match."

She listened to my rambling with sympathy in her eyes.

"And if he found out after, would he even allow her to live?" I took a deep breath. "She's my mate, Iaso."

I watched as tears gathered in her eyes. She had always wanted a mate for me, or at least someone to make me happy, and she had never been shy in saying so. Although, I'm sure this isn't exactly what she had in mind.

"I cannot answer that for you, Rogue. I can't tell you what to do. I myself put that spell on her mother's womb. At the

CHAPTER TWELVE

time, it was what was safest, but now... Is it time for the truth to be revealed? Would she be safe if it was known? Is it even your place to decide that for her?" she asked. When I didn't respond, she continued, "Would you want to know in her situation?"

"I don't know," I answered honestly, resting my head in my hands.

"I'll leave it at this: do you think she deserves to know?"

Of course, she does, but I'm not ready to see the look on her face when she finds out.

Guilt mixed with self-contempt sank in my gut, weighing me down to the chair.

* * *

Fury took hold of me as I left Iaso's chambers, heading for the front door of the castle. As soon as I exited, I snapped out my wings and thrust up into the sky.

My fucking father. Of course, this is his fault. It always is.

I slammed into the ground at my father's burial site, dust and earth flying up around me. My fire raged, thrashing beneath my skin. For once, I released it entirely, unable to hold it back any longer. The grass surrounding my feet immediately went up in flames, and the fire followed behind me as I marched to his monument, scorching footprints into the marble steps.

"Why? Why were you such a fucking tyrant? A *plague* to Ravaryn. What did I do to deserve you?" I shouted at his statue, flames licking up his feet. "A terrible king. A terrible mate... A terrible father."

The flames rose, engulfing him, as they should have when

he was alive.

My only regret stared me in the face: that I didn't burn him to ash when I had the chance.

"How can you be dead and *still* have such an effect on my life? It wasn't enough for you to ruin me, *torture* me, my entire life. You had to dig your grimy claws into me in the afterlife too, didn't you?" My throat burned, my eyes hot. "Ruining my mate bond... Is this your revenge for me killing Mother? An eye for an eye as you always said?"

I chuckled darkly as tears ran freely down my cheeks.

I didn't want the mate bond. But now? Now, he'd taken it from me before I even had a chance, just as he had done my entire life, ensuring I never had a taste of happiness.

The overwhelming hurt in my chest was cracking me in two. My fire exploded, incinerating everything around me, including my clothes. It returned to his statue, his monument, and I glared, willing it to burn hotter, more intensely, to devour everything in its wake. The granite cracked, pieces tumbling to the ground at my feet.

I roared in rage, in agony, in hatred, and the ground shook, birds taking flight in the nearby forest. The fire flared, burning blue before the entire monument exploded, tossing me back several feet.

I hit the ground with a thud, choking on a sob as the monument and surrounding forest burned to the ground.

Chapter Thirteen

Ara

It had been days since I'd seen Rogue. Actually, the only person I'd seen was Thana.

She had warmed up to me since our first meeting and I to her. She no longer seemed scared of my presence; we even chatted when she visited, bonding over our mutual love for reading. After that, she started bringing her recommendations from the library with her when she came, and we would trade books.

Surprisingly, her favorite genre was romance—not that I minded, as it was also mine—but the romance novels in Ravaryn were much different than those in Auryna. They were detailed, with sex laced into almost every story, and I loved it. I devoured book after book.

However, reading these books only brought my thoughts back to Rogue. His red eyes, his Goddess-forsaken wings, the ease with which he handled a sword, the smoke and evergreen spice scent that seemed to follow him. It was intoxicating.

Then, irritation would inevitably prick at me. He was the vicious king of Ravaryn and my kidnapper, holding me captive as a prisoner of war, a thing to be ransomed. That in and of itself should have turned me off, disgusted me, terrified me, but my body didn't seem to care. I was constantly having to remind myself of how much I should hate him.

I even dreamed of his touch. It felt so real; even now, I could almost feel his hand sliding up my leg, gripping my hip, before gliding his hand down to my...

No.

My chest tightened with unease, and I stood from the leather chair, clenching my jaw.

On instinct, I headed for the library, to the books that would grant me a distraction, an escape.

Crossing the hallway, I passed Doran as a look of worry bit into his features.

"Doran, hi," I said a little too loudly, happy to see a familiar face. Any face, really.

"Ara, it's nice to see you again," he said with a soft smile.

"Have there been any updates in the correspondence with my father?"

He averted his gaze.

"It's not really my place to speak of such matters with you," he replied, and my heart sank. Giving a sharp nod, I started to turn away when he continued. "However, I guess it wouldn't do much harm. No, there hasn't been, at least not to my knowledge, but that is to be expected. I would assume he's with King Adon right now, attempting to convince him there is no other way."

That gave me pause. If my father had to convince King Adon of anything to get me back... Nausea rolled in my stomach, and I suppressed it from showing on my face.

If my father had to convince King Adon of anything, it

CHAPTER THIRTEEN

would be to cease the attacks, which meant they were, in fact, attacking. Murdering women and children. In their homes. If they weren't, there would have been no reason to kidnap me in the first place. They needed leverage, just as Rogue had said.

My chest ached.

"Thank you for letting me know," I replied weakly, turning to the library, my eyes unfocused.

My mind kept picturing the people in Blackburn. They were Fae, yes, but they seemed normal enough. Children played in the street as we left, just like any human child would. Women gossiped and laughed as their children ran amok; no one was evil or vicious like I remembered from the war...

The Ten Year Wear.

Had we started that? Were we the aggressors, then?

Lightheaded, I stopped, closing my eyes as I braced an arm on the wall. Taking a deep breath, I continued to the library and paused in the doorway, glancing around before heading to the history section.

Grazing the shelves, I picked up a book with *Blackburn and its People* written on the spine and walked to a nearby chair, sitting slowly as I opened to the first page. I didn't look up again until I'd finished the entire book.

Blackburn was the birthplace of pyric magic, hence the name. It made sense that Edana hailed from there, being a fire worker herself. Blackburn was also one of the oldest cities in Ravaryn, with a long history of loyal patriots. They raised the strongest warriors, men and women alike, and were an incredibly proud people.

That would also explain why Rogue had covered my ears when we arrived.

Replacing the book, I stared at the endless rows of shelves, at the stories and elaborate histories of the Fae. The people of Ravaryn. The terrified people who were seeking safe haven from my father.

Suddenly overwhelmed, I hurried out of the library and down a hallway I didn't recognize, losing myself in an entirely different world.

The walls were made of gray stone, like the castles of old. I ran my fingers along the wall, the stone cold, in direct contrast to the warm, springtime air filling the hallway.

I ambled down the hall, my hand dragging along the wall behind me when I came across a small window. Peeking through, I caught sight of a long greenhouse completely encased in glass, condensation clinging to the panes and creating a rainbow blur from the vegetation inside. I poked my head through the open window to find the entrance, and my eyes followed it to the castle wall. It must be connected to the room straight ahead.

Walking up to the old wooden door, I knocked lightly. Anxiety bubbled in my chest as I waited to see who or what might open the door. Rogue said I was free to roam, and that invitation hopefully extended to this room.

When the door opened, however, my breath caught as a devastatingly beautiful woman smiled in greeting.

This must be Rogue's lover. He was bound to have one somewhere in the castle.

She looked to be about my age with smooth, rich brown skin and translucent golden eyes that reminded me of amber. Strands matching her eyes spiraled through her curly hair, shimmering as she moved. She was clothed in an earthy green dress that hung off her shoulders, and along her upper arms

CHAPTER THIRTEEN

were golden bands, encrusted with emeralds, her fingers decorated with similar gold and green jewelry.

The smell of honey and herbs met my nose, bringing a sense of ease with it.

"Hello there. How may I help you?" she asked, but her eyes found the curve of my ear before I could answer. Her smile deepened, revealing a dimple in one cheek. "Ah, you must be the human I've heard so much about." She stepped aside to hold the door open and waved an arm to motion me in. "Come in."

I hesitated before entering but then noticed the entire back wall of the chamber was made entirely of glass, overlooking the greenhouse. Gasping, I couldn't look away as my feet led me toward it.

"Ah, yes, my greenery. I'm the healer, Iaso."

Iaso. The one who healed Rogue. Not a lover, then. I glanced back at her, only to find her staring lovingly out the window. The sunlight peeked in, illuminating her in a beautiful yellow hue, her skin and eyes glowing with the light.

"My name is Ara and yes, I'm the human."

"It's nice to meet you, Ara. Come. Have a seat and let me look you over." She motioned to the chair.

I shook my head, holding my hands up in front me. "I'm all right, honestly. I just came seeking entrance to the greenhouse. Rogue said I was free to roam and I haven't seen anyone besides my lady's maid in days, so I've been out… roaming," I said sheepishly, a blush creeping into my cheeks. "I hope I haven't disturbed you."

She looked at me curiously.

"Oh no, child, not at all. So, you haven't seen Rogue since sparring then?" she asked, cocking her head to the side.

How did she know about that?
"No, I haven't," I replied.
"Well, I'm sure he's just busy, running a kingdom and all," she dismissed, waving her hand. "I do see the bruise on your arm, though; is that tender at all?"
I glanced down, having forgotten it was there.
"A little, but it doesn't bother me."
"Oh, none of that now," she said, grabbing a jar of salve. "Here, this will help."
She rubbed the ointment into my arm, and my mouth fell open as her eyes quite literally glowed. She peeked up at me with a grin, noticing my stare.
"There, all done." She stepped back, admiring her work. I pulled my gaze away from her metallic irises to glance down at my arm, my lips parting in awe as the bruise started to fade. "It'll be completely gone by the end of the day. Now, did you still want to see the greenhouse?"
I nodded, and she looped her arm through mine, tugging me forward.
"Well, there's no one better to give the tour than me."
A genuine smile pulled at my lips as she guided me to the door.

* * *

Back in my chambers, I was feeling somewhat better after having met someone new, someone kind and welcoming. She reminded me of my mother in that way—kind to everyone.

Iaso had led me through the greenhouse, explaining the different uses of each plant. It was fascinating to hear her discuss her knowledge, even if I couldn't keep up as she spoke.

CHAPTER THIRTEEN

Afterward, we sat at her table, and she shared a tea she'd created. It was delicious, bringing a sense of calm over me that carried into the rest of the evening.

She had also explained how she had cared for Rogue after she healed him, seeing him as her own. As much as it bothered me to admit, hearing she wasn't with Rogue in *that* way brought a small bit of relief.

I couldn't stand him, and yet, I couldn't stand the thought of him with another woman.

Now, curled in the old chair in my chambers, I watched as the flames danced in the fireplace. Flickers of dim, orange light and dark shadows swayed throughout the room, bouncing off the walls.

Mesmerized and lost in thought, my mind returned to home, and a deep, suffocating sadness washed over me; my mother would be distraught by now. She was far too sweet, too tenderhearted, to be put through this. I would think my father, at least, would be desensitized to acts of war, but then again, my safety had always been his utmost priority... so maybe not.

His efforts to keep me safe had always seemed so excessive, but considering he knew Auryna was attacking the border towns, it made sense he would fear for my safety. I was sure he worried something exactly like this would happen as some form of retribution.

Shifting in the chair, I released a long, slow sigh. All the puzzle pieces that hadn't seemed to fit together were falling into place before my eyes.

He had always told us there was peace between the kingdoms. Everyone in our village, all of Auryna, thought so, and we had been none the wiser. His meetings with the king, were they ever truly about keeping our border safe? Or were they conspiring their next attack?

It made me physically ill to think about it.

Blackburn still hadn't left my mind, and that was only one town. There were hundreds along the border that I hadn't seen, all once filled with families and lives and history—all burned down and abandoned.

For the first time since I had arrived, I understood Rogue's plan. If this was what it took to stop the bloodshed, I would willingly be the pawn used to checkmate Evander.

There was still that lingering concern in the back of my mind, though. *What am I supposed to do when I return? I cannot go back as if I don't know what he's done.*

I refused to go back and roll over, bending to Father's will as I always had.

I would have a voice when I returned, and he would hear it. I would make him listen.

Taking a deep breath, I stood and walked to the bed, laying my head down. With my eyes locked on the fire, I drifted off into a deep, dreamless sleep.

* * *

After breakfast with Thana, I spent all day in the library, halfway hoping to see Alden or even Rogue, but no one had appeared.

Sighing, I stood from the reading chair, grabbing the novel I'd been halfheartedly thumbing through. Just as I turned to leave, Alden entered the library, and a minuscule amount of excitement bubbled in my chest at the sight of a friendly face.

"Oh, Alden, hi. It's nice to see you again," I said as I strolled

CHAPTER THIRTEEN

over to him and he jumped at my voice.

"Ara, how nice to see you. I'm actually very busy, so I must continue on my way, but good day to you," he replied in a hurry, and the smile slid from my lips. A look of regret passed over his face, and he paused as if to speak again before apparently thinking better of it and disappearing behind the shelves.

Disappointment flooded me.

I am just the human, the leverage, I reminded myself. They already treated me better than I ever could have expected, better than any prisoner could ask for. It was foolish of me to expect conversation as well. Still, the thought did nothing to quell the disheartening loneliness that had rooted itself in my chest.

It seemed loneliness would follow me, no matter where I went.

Taking a deep breath, I continued out of the library in silence, then into the hallway to my chambers. Looking around, I didn't recognize a single face, and no one bothered to glance in my direction.

Of course not.

A beam of sunlight caught my attention as someone opened and closed the front door. I paused for a moment, the tempting possibility lingering in front of me, practically offering itself to me as the guards walked away, distracted with their trivial chit-chat. With a sudden burst of courage, I jogged down the stairs, strode through the foyer, and threw the door open. Sunlight flooded the entryway, and I held my face to it, welcoming the warmth.

I hadn't been outside since I sparred with Rogue, and even then, it had been cloudy. I hadn't felt the warmth of the sun in days, maybe weeks.

Hurrying down into the bailey, I noticed guards posted at the front gate, eyeing me, so I took a right, following the path. Around the corner was a steep, rocky incline I would have to climb to continue, but considering my only other options were to pass the guards or go back inside, I stalked forward with determination. Reaching up, I grabbed the rocky surface and began climbing.

Once I finally crested the tallest point, my mouth fell slack in awe. I was standing on a cliff edge, overlooking the ocean just as the sun began to set.

The sky to the west was painted a vibrant red and orange, reflecting off the rippling water like flaming art. The sky to the east was a dark navy blue, spotted with twinkling stars and a bright moon peeking over the horizon.

I had never been high enough to see the sky split like this, and it was breathtaking. Taking a seat on the ledge, I brought my knees to my chest, admiring the view.

I had never seen much of anything in Auryna, and I never truly expected to. Looking back, I knew I had silently accepted a fate of living through books, and once I was betrothed to Finley, my fate was solidified. I knew in my bones that I would live and die in that village, even as I tried to convince myself of broken dreams.

I may be a prisoner, but this was the most incredible thing I'd ever seen.

A wave of guilt washed over me. I shouldn't feel this way. It was wrong, so wrong, but I couldn't help it. I never expected to see any other part of the realm, much less any land in Ravaryn, and, sitting here, I couldn't *not* appreciate the beauty before my eyes. No description in any book would ever compare.

Hopelessness pulled at my heart as I thought about going home, quickly followed by shame as I realized I didn't want to, not really. I didn't want to stay here as a prisoner, but I also didn't want to be handed back to my father, to live firmly within his grasp once again. Or worse: Finn's.

Goddess, I cannot fathom going back after all of this and marrying that small-minded fool.

Inhaling deeply, slowly, I breathed in the warm, briny air, letting it settle my nerves.

I just want to...live, not merely survive.

Live.

I was lonely here, in enemy territory where I knew no one, but I had freedom, in a twisted sort of way. I felt like a person rather than just the daughter of General Evander Starrin—the protected, fragile, ignorant daughter.

At the very least, I had developed a voice, and that felt... good.

Tightening my arms around my legs, I rested my chin on my knees, sitting there on the rocks as the sun disappeared under the ocean, welcoming the moon to take its place.

Just as the world went dark, lit only by silver moonlight, the silhouette of a large creature appeared, flying through the sky toward the castle. Jumping to my feet, I rushed into the shadows, ready to retreat down the incline.

But it wasn't a creature.

It was Rogue.

I sat back, observing, as he coasted on the wind, angling his wings to descend toward the ground. It was graceful, calm, almost beautiful. Sneaking to the farthest corner of the castle, I peeked around as much as I could and watched as he stepped onto the ledge. He stood tall, relaxing his wings as he rolled his shoulders. His chest rose and fell with a deep breath, and his head snapped in my direction.

Gasping, I jerked back behind the castle, my eyes wide, my cheeks heating furiously. I paused for a second before running to where I had climbed up and descending quickly. As I landed on my feet, I turned and bumped straight into a warm, muscled chest.

Chapter Fourteen

Ara

"Oh, I'm—" I stopped mid-apology when I looked up, locking eyes with Rogue. His hair hung in loose, wind-blown waves, a cocky grin on his face.

"Like what you see?"

I quickly stepped back, realizing I was still pressed into his bare chest. My eyes dropped to my palms on his skin and locked on his scar. My mouth fell open, the blood draining from my face.

It stretched diagonally from the left side of his neck, over his chest, and down his abdomen, all the way to his right hip bone. It was thick and jagged as if it hadn't wanted to heal, like Iaso had forced it to close.

"Yes, yes, I know," he said, dismissing my look of shock, completely unlike our last conversation.

"Well, hearing about it and seeing it are two different things…" I replied quietly, reaching out a hand to run my finger along the scar absentmindedly. He froze but didn't stop me as I traced it from his chest down, stopping before I reached his hip bone.

"Heard about it, did you?"

I snatched my hand back, realizing what I'd done. "Oh, uh—Sorry."

As I started to sidestep around him, the breeze picked up, engulfing me in his scent, and I inhaled deeply. His scent was intoxicating. My heart pounded with lust, entranced by everything that was *him*, and my eyes snapped back up. His mouth ticked up in a smirk, and I took a step back from him.

Something about him was irresistible, tugging me toward him at every turn, and I couldn't stand it. I was compelled by him, enraptured, and for what? He was my kidnapper. He was Fae. He was cruel. Why must I constantly have to remind myself of that?

I had been so desperate for a conversation, but now, the only thing I wanted was to be far away from him and the sway he had over my body. I stepped around him, a look of confusion crossing his face as I hurried to the door.

"Hey, it's fine. If it bothered me, I would've stopped you," he said with a smirk.

Irritation flared in me. He was the enemy; yet, my body was singing for him.

This is wrong.

I continued walking without looking back, but he jogged up to my side, continuing beside me. My breath hitched as his arm brushed my shoulder, setting my skin on fire.

"And here I was, thinking you'd be excited to see me after so many days apart," he teased, glancing sidelong at me, and I forced myself to not look up.

"Oh, right, where are my manners? How nice of you to grace me with your presence. Would a simple thank you suffice, or would you like me to throw myself at your feet?"

CHAPTER FOURTEEN

"Well…" His smirk widened into a grin. "The thought of you on your knees before me *is* an intriguing thought."

I halted, glaring at him as my cheeks flamed.

"That is not what I meant," I snapped.

He dipped his head, stepping closer.

"I know exactly what you meant," he replied, closing the gap between us. He ran a hand along my side, pulling my hips against his body. My eyes dropped to his hand before darting back to his face and I jerked out of his grasp. With a mind of its own, my hand reached back and cracked across his cheek in a hard slap. His head snapped to the side, and he released a low, breathy laugh.

"Do *not* touch me."

His eyes darkened as he rubbed his cheek, and a red handprint began to show.

"That should not turn me on." A vicious grin pulled at his lips. "But fuck…it does."

I gaped at him for a heartbeat, torn on how to react, how I *wanted* to react, before turning on my heel. He let me go this time without another word.

Back in my chambers, I closed the door behind me, pausing to take a breath. As I leaned back on the door, I could still feel his palm on my hip, blazing a trail along my body. It was as though his touch had been burned into my memory.

I knew, without a doubt, I would dream of him again tonight.

* * *

After a few hours of restless sleep, I resolved to go to the library. At least there, I could entertain my mind instead of lying in bed, unwillingly dreaming of Rogue.

Sitting up, I took a deep breath, glancing out the window. The sky was dull blue with the yellow haze of sunrise, the tail end of stars fading out. The waves were calmer today, the breeze light, bringing with it the warmth of spring.

Strolling to the dresser, I cleared my mind to see what it would offer me and pulled the drawer open. Inside was deep, royal blue silk, the color of the sky just before dawn. Pulling the dress from the drawer, I held it up and decided to try it on.

Turning to the mirror, I gazed at myself, stunned at how different it was from anything I'd worn before. Unlike the corseted dresses in Auryna, this one was surprisingly comfortable, made of pure softness that shimmered and flowed as I moved. With thin straps and a scoop neck, it revealed my shoulders and cleavage, hanging loosely from my waist with a slit that reached my hip. It would allow perfect access to my dagger if I had a thigh strap...

Smiling, I rushed back to the dresser, silently asking for the strap and a pair of sturdy sandals. When I pulled the drawer open again, a black leather strap sat at the bottom, a dark sapphire encrusted in the center, next to a pair of matching sandals. I pulled them both on, sheathed the dagger to my exposed thigh, and faced the mirror.

The smile slid from my face.

The reflection looked...beautiful. My cheeks burned.

I felt ridiculous.

Why was I wearing something like this? Here, of all places.

Sighing, I returned to the dresser, picturing my normal clothes, and pulled it open. My heart skipped a beat; it was empty. I quickly closed and opened it again. Empty.

CHAPTER FOURTEEN

"Are you—" I scoffed, my eyes bulging. Taking a step back, I examined the dresser. "Are you messing with me?"

It obviously didn't answer, and I felt even more ridiculous. Trying the drawer one more time, I opened it to find it still empty, *and* the clothes on the floor were gone.

"All right then," I whispered to myself, glancing in the mirror one more time before steeling my nerves and walking down the stairs.

As I passed the staircase to the front entryway, I glanced down, and there stood Rogue, speaking with Doran and two guards. His mouth stopped moving as his eyes slowly raised to mine, and he stilled, his lips falling slack. My gaze dipped down his body, taking in every inch, and the room suddenly felt too warm, my skin flushing from the heat.

He was wearing black leather trousers, and my eyes widened when I realized his tunic was the same deep blue color as my dress. *That sneaky dresser.* His hair still hung loose around his face, though it was combed now, with his crimson wings on full display as usual. My fingers itched to touch them, to feel the smoothness on the underside, and they shifted under the weight of my gaze.

A burning hunger to feel *him,* every part of him, tore through me. I stood straighter, resisting the urge to descend the stairs.

His gaze was scorching, lazily sliding down my body, snagging on my exposed cleavage before returning to my eyes. His attention was locked on me, not even bothering to listen to his companions as I dipped into a faint curtsy before turning, feeling his eyes on my back as I walked out of view.

My heart was still racing when I made it to the library, pausing in the doorway to gather my thoughts.

"Hello, Ara," Alden said as he walked around a bookshelf. "Please, allow me to apologize for our last encounter. I had a great many things weighing on my mind, but that was no excuse."

"Oh, no. Please, no apology necessary," I replied, offering him a light smile and waving a hand in dismissal.

"Well, in that case, let us discuss books, as I am sure that is what you came for. Have you read any more of the book I suggested?" he asked with a thin smile, his eyes tight as he wrung his hands in front of him.

"No, I haven't, but I'll make sure to read through it today."

He strolled to the historical shelves and pulled out the thick tome, handing it to me with an encouraging look. "It can be a tricky subject, but an interesting one."

I nodded and walked to the nearby table, Alden following behind me. Flipping through the back pages, I passed over Rogue and Adrastus, stopping at King Vaelor.

The first thing I noticed was his gray eyes—a dark, stormy gray that almost felt familiar. His hair was brown and long, hanging past his shoulders.

> *Vaelor, the Last Storm Bringer*
> *241st King of Ravaryn*
> *Son of Alden and Ara of village Nautia*
> *Ability: Willing of storms, control of lightning, creation of electricity*
> *Death: Assassinated by Adrastus Draki*

My blood went cold as my eyes snapped to Alden.

"His father...Is that you?" I asked in absolute shock.

He nodded, leaning over to look at the sketch with furrowed brows.

"Yes, he was my son."

"How can you stay here, then? Working for Rogue?" I blurted, gaping at him.

"I don't work for him, Ara. I work *with* him. I came back to Draig Hearth to form my own opinions about him, and I stayed because he is not his father. This throne was thrust upon him rather quickly, and after a lifetime with Adrastus, he needed a helpful hand, a friend."

I stared at him for a moment, taken aback by his sincerity, before glancing back at the sketch and noting the similarities.

Uneasiness formed in my gut as I studied them both, like something was staring me in the face, but I couldn't quite see it. Alden tapped his finger on the page, and I noticed the note scribbled at the bottom, newer than the rest of the writing, scribbled in black ink.

> *Had a human lover who was with child at the time of his death. Neither she, nor the child, was ever found or identified.*

"Oh…"

It was understandable why they would go into hiding, but I didn't understand how they could've stayed hidden for so long. Surely, the child, being half-Fae and half-human, would've shown attributes of both.

"How could they hide in either Auryna or Ravaryn? The mother would have to remain in Auryna for her safety, but what about the child? They would have Fae characteristics.

She couldn't hide them there forever," I thought aloud.

I looked up to find Alden gazing down at me, his eyes full of sympathy, but he said nothing.

"What?"

"Does he not look familiar?" he urged gently, the crease between my eyebrows deepening at his insistence.

"Yes. He looks like you," I replied flatly.

"He looks like *you*, Ara."

I gaped at him, blinking rapidly, trying to process his implication.

"What are you talking about, Alden? That's not possible," I said weakly. "That's not..."

"The child went missing twenty-six years ago. You are twenty-six, are you not?"

My eyes widened as I stared at him, looking but not seeing.

Twenty-six. The same age as me, with a human mother.

Gray eyes... My eyes. The ones that matched no one else in the family. The ones my mother adored.

No. I am no one.

No one.

My mind flashed back to the last conversation with my mother. She said she wasn't in love with Evander... *Had she been in love with another?*

A cold sweat broke out along my spine as my heart thundered in my ears.

"We look similar, have the same eyes, because Vaelor was my son...and you are his daughter."

No. Evander is my father. Why would I believe him? I don't know this man.

My eyes darted to Alden's face. To his eyes. *My* eyes.

The room spun, and I grabbed the table to steady myself.

CHAPTER FOURTEEN

"Why would I believe you? You don't even know me."

"Your mother is Elora."

It wasn't a question. He wasn't asking. He already knew. I couldn't think straight as he pulled out a small journal from his robes.

"This was your mother's. She wrote in it while she lived here. I found it hidden in the library when I returned just a few years ago," he said softly, setting it on the table in front of me.

Hesitating, I stared at the journal for a moment before flipping it open, and a sketch slid out from between the pages, falling to the table. A gasp escaped me as a shaky hand flew to my mouth. I tilted my head to get a closer look, but there was no mistaking my mother's face, much younger than I had ever seen her. I swallowed hard against the alarm rising in my throat as I opened the book to the first page, releasing a choked sob when I recognized my mother's neat handwriting.

I snapped it closed, resting my hand on top while my other clutched at my chest, willing my heart to calm before it exploded in my chest.

"How is this possible? She never said anything even vaguely about this. My father... Evander, he would not keep this from me." I stilled as it dawned on me. "He doesn't know, does he?"

"No, he does not," Alden confirmed. "For your mother's safety, she had to flee Ravaryn and hide the pregnancy until she married another. Otherwise, Adrastus would have found her and killed you both."

My heart stopped. *Adrastus. Rogue. He cannot know. He would kill me before I ever made it back to Auryna.*

"Why? Why would you tell me this?" I stood, backing away

from the table. My eyes darted around the room, everywhere except to Alden's face.

My breaths were coming fast, too fast, but not bringing air.

"Ara, please try to remain calm. No one can know what I have revealed to you; I just needed to tell you. You deserved to know who you are." I looked into his pleading eyes, his hand outstretched to me. I took another step back, shaking my head, and he flinched. "I helped your mother, and I can help you too. Tell me what you need, and I will do my best."

What do I need?

I needed clarification. An explanation. Anything to make it make sense.

"Can you send a letter to my mother?"

He nodded quickly, rushing to his office. He returned with a small piece of paper, ink, and a quill. "Come with me."

I followed him to a private corner by a fireplace, already lit.

"Write what you must."

How do I even begin?

I stared at the paper for a long moment before scribbling down anything that came to mind, dumping every possible question I could conjure onto one letter. I needed answers for everything. She had lied to me for twenty-six years, and I needed to hear confirmation from her.

> *Mother,*
>
> *I'm well; do not worry about that. However, I just learned something, and I need to hear it from you directly. I'm not sure where to begin or how to ask this, so I'll just say it.*

CHAPTER FOURTEEN

> *Am I Evander's daughter, or am I Vaelor's?*
>
> *If not Evander's, how could you hide this from me? I understand hiding it from the world, but from me? Do I not deserve to know who my father is? Who I am? What I am?*
>
> *How did you hide the Fae blood? Why do I appear entirely human?*
>
> *Please, for once, tell me the truth. I need to know everything. I <u>deserve</u> to know everything.*
>
> *I will anxiously be awaiting your reply.*
>
> *-Ara*

By the time I'd finished, tears had dripped from my cheeks onto the page, freckling it with wet spots. I blew on it to dry the ink before folding it and handing it to Alden.

"How do we get it to her?"

He took it from me with a deep sigh. "I'll send it through the flames. Once it burns completely, it will appear wherever your mother feels safest, and no one else will be able to see it until after she finds it."

He tossed the note into the fire, whispering something under his breath until the paper burned and disappeared in a plume of smoke.

"Does she know how to do that? How to respond?" I asked, but I knew what he would say.

"Yes. This is how she and Vaelor communicated for a long time."

I didn't know my mother at all. My eyes fell to my feet, panic turning to a heavy stone of hurt in my gut. My throat burned, threatening to unleash every ugly emotion, and I clenched my jaw as I struggled to hold back sobs.

Bringing my trembling hands to my face, I sat down on the floor, pulling my knees to my chest as I had a thousand times before. As a sob wracked my body, I released everything, every overwhelming emotion, unable to hold it in any longer. Tears flooded my cheeks, and my body shook with the force of the wails stuck in my throat.

Alden squatted beside me, placing a steady hand on my back.

"I know there's nothing I can say to make this better, but you deserved to know the truth. You deserved to make the decision about what happens next."

The choice. He was offering me the choice of my own fate. I threw my arms around him, hugging him tightly as my tears wet his robe; he hesitated before wrapping his arms around me in return.

Without warning, the fire roared, and I jumped back as a folded note floated from the fireplace, landing in my lap. My stomach flipped as I stared at it, my hands unwilling to lift it just yet.

"There's your answer, Ara," Alden said quietly, standing to give me space.

I closed my eyes to take a breath, swallowing hard as I opened them again and unfolded the note slowly.

> *My dearest daughter,*
>
> Oh Goddess, I cannot even begin to describe how relieved I am to hear you are alive.
>
> Please believe me when I never meant for you to find out this way. I would've told you eventually, but it never

seemed like the right time, and then I blinked, and you were grown. I was so scared to tell you, that you would hate me for keeping it from you for so long; I could never get the words out.

It was wrong of me, I know, and I understand your anger. I just hope I can earn your forgiveness one day. I am so sorry, Ara.

As for your other question, you never presented any Fae characteristics because I had a healer named Iaso place a spell over my womb before I left Ravaryn. I'm sure you've met her if you are at Draig Hearth. It will suppress your Fae side forever, but I had to do it to keep you safe. After Vaelor's death, I did what was necessary to hide you from Adrastus. You were all I had left... I couldn't let him take you, too.

It broke my heart to take that part from you. You may never present any of your father's magic, but you are more like him with every passing day. You have his bravery, his kindness, his heart, and his longing for adventure. I see so much of him in you, especially in your eyes.

He would be so proud of you, Ara. He nearly burst with excitement when he found out I was with child. He even named you, choosing the name Ara after his mother.

He loved you so much, just as I do and always will.
Please try to understand.
With <u>all</u> my love,
Mother

My heart was broken, for my mother and myself, for what she had to endure in silence all this time. My whole life, I thought she was bending to Evander, but she wasn't.

She was wielding her hidden strength like a weapon.

I clutched her letter to my chest as I collapsed in on myself, my shoulders slumping forward as I cried hopelessly. The pain, the rage, the shock—it all clawed its way out, and I couldn't stop it.

She had to flee for fear she would be killed, along with me, and when Rogue found out... My tears stopped abruptly as icy terror filled me.

I whipped my head to Alden, wiping my cheeks.

"I have to leave. I have to get back to my mother. Please, you helped her escape, didn't you? Can you help me too?"

He nodded curtly before offering his hand.

Chapter Fifteen

Rogue

Seeing Ara this morning did something to me.

I could feel the mate bond pulling at every fiber of my being, even as I actively avoided her. Seeing her also craving my touch only solidified it. It took every ounce of strength I had not to bend her over the rail in front of every guard and claim her as mine the second we locked eyes.

And it wasn't one-sided. I could see the heat behind her eyes, the restraint in her muscles as she resisted the urge. She wasn't oblivious to the bond, even if she didn't understand what it was yet. She felt it all the same.

As soon as she disappeared out of sight, I marched out of the castle and took to the sky, needing space from her, needing my own air. Just her scent set my body on fire, and it was everywhere in the castle, taunting me, tempting me.

When she watched me land last night, I had caught her scent, and it had overwhelmed me enough that I let the bond drive me forward. I *had* to be closer to her. Touch her. Feel her.

If she hadn't slapped me, I would've taken her right there

in the courtyard. I would've shoved her against the wall and claimed her, biting the delicate spot at the base of her neck as I filled her, marking her as mine, marking me as hers. I would've made her scream my name so loud, every Fae in Ravaryn would know who she belonged to. Who *I* belonged to.

My cock hardened at the thought, and my jaw clenched painfully tight.

She had more control over my own body than I did, and she didn't even know it. She invaded my every thought, my every dream, my very being. It was maddening.

I knew the bond would only grow stronger with each passing day, pulling us together until it was impossible to resist, but knowing it and experiencing it were two entirely different things. Worse even, none of this mattered until I figured out how to tell her about Evander and Vaelor.

My stomach twisted at the thought, but I couldn't force the words from my mouth, knowing it would hurt her. Unfortunately, I also knew not telling her would hurt her more; thus, restarting the turmoil of warring thoughts.

Thunder boomed in the distance as a storm blew in, snapping me back to reality. Combined with the setting sun, the sky darkened quickly.

With gritted teeth, I returned to the castle.

As soon as I walked in through the doors, her scent consumed me, as if she had been here recently. An insatiable hunger ripped through me—a starvation only for her.

Making a beeline for her chambers, I climbed the steps two at a time. Smoke rolled off my skin in waves, heating the stairwell just like it had in the entryway this morning.

I threw open her door and stopped dead in my tracks. The

CHAPTER FIFTEEN

room was empty.

My heart beat faster, a sinking feeling in my gut.

I strode to the library, only to realize her scent was everywhere. She had been here today, all day.

Entering Alden's study, his face told me everything. He stood slowly, lifting his chin, and I slowed my pace, feeling anger rising in my chest.

"What did you do?" Each word grated out from between my teeth.

"She had a right to know, Rogue. She had the right to decide her fate."

My spine stiffened with betrayal, a scowl twisting my face. "Where is she?"

"She wanted to leave," he said simply, as if that one statement didn't hold enough weight to crush me, as if it didn't turn everything upside down—our plans included.

My chest ached, nearly sucking the breath from my lungs. He didn't waver as I stormed to him, accepting his fate. I grabbed him by the throat, lifting him into the air as smoke filled the room with a white haze.

I glared into his eyes, but he wasn't apologetic. He stood by his decision, wrenching the knife of betrayal deeper into my gut. Taking a deep breath to try and calm my thundering heart, I dropped him, and he fell to his knees, gasping.

Every emotion I'd suppressed came rushing back, the pain in my chest overwhelming, suffocating, as I backed away, bracing a hand on the doorway.

Alden had betrayed me.

She had wanted to leave, to leave me.

Of course, she did.

I shouldn't be surprised, and yet, it still somehow managed

to catch me off guard. I had kidnapped her; of course, she would run. So why did it feel like more than just a prisoner running from their captor? This deep, gut-wrenching ache threatened to swallow me whole.

It felt like a reminder. A reminder that my father didn't want me. That I killed my own mother. That my only friends were here out of obligation.

Still, even as the thoughts bombarded me, I couldn't stop my feet as I stormed out of the library to the front door and shot to the sky, surveying the land.

I had to find her, even if it made me every bit the monster my father was.

She couldn't have gotten far, and she would be heading the way we came. She wouldn't know any other way.

It had started raining since I'd returned, the storm soaking my hair and clothes as I flew over the forest leading to Blackburn. Lightning cracked in the distance, sporadically lighting the darkness.

Then, I spotted her.

Even with her hood pulled tight over her head, hiding her face and hair, I knew it was her. I would recognize that scent anywhere: rain and wildflowers.

I slammed into the ground in front of her, and she halted in her tracks as fear flashed across her eyes. Hurt flared again, quickly replaced by anger. She was not just fleeing from Ravaryn, but me. She was leaving me. Her mate.

"Let me go," she said, tightly gripping her dagger.

"You know I can't do that," I said, stepping closer. Her scent filled every corner of my mind, blurring everything else from existence. I needed her like my fire needed air, and my feet stepped closer of their own volition.

CHAPTER FIFTEEN

She hesitated as I edged closer, her lips parting. The same heat burned behind her silver eyes as her cheeks flushed with desire.

Her body sang for me, just as mine did for her.

I closed the final step between us and looked down at her, meeting her gaze. My heart raced, my breaths heavy, and her chest rose and fell just as quickly.

Gripping her chin, I raised her face to mine. Soaked hair clung to the sides of her face, water dripping off her eyelashes.

Every inch of me craved her.

My eyes dropped to her lips, red and soft, calling to me. They parted in a gasp and my self-control snapped. My mouth crashed to hers in a bruising, breathless kiss.

Right. This felt so, *so* right, even as my mind told me it was wrong.

She kissed back ferociously, bringing one hand to my face and pushing herself into me, as if she yearned for more. She ground her hips into me, and I felt myself harden, pressing into her. She gasped against my mouth at the feeling of me, and I grinned, sliding my hand down her hips, holding her against me.

She stilled, pausing for a moment, before burying her dagger into my stomach and taking off in a sprint.

Rage and lust burned through me as she ran, her cloak billowing behind her. She had fooled me *again*. I let out a roar of frustration, and she whipped her head back to me in fear before running harder, faster. I pulled the dagger out and dropped it to the ground.

"You can run, Ara, but it will do you no good."

Giving her a head start, I took to the sky, following behind her. I knew she was afraid, but it did nothing to stop me. It only fueled the deep, primal instinct she awoke in me—the prey to my hunt.

She ran for almost an hour, but she was tiring and still nowhere near Blackburn. Finally, as the rain shifted to a torrential downpour, I swooped down, landing directly in front of her yet again.

Standing tall, I glared down at her.

"Are you done?"

She shook her head slowly, her breathing heavy, her jaw clenched.

My little fighter.

Mine.

The bond was blinding me and I could see nothing but her.

Her.

Mine.

She reached down to her boot, to grab another dagger I assumed, but my fist knotted in her hair, pulling her back up painstakingly slowly. She eyed me furiously, her lip pulled back in a snarl. Once she was standing, I tipped her head back, exposing her throat. Lowering my face, I slid my lips along hers, down her chin, along the curve of her neck.

"I know you feel it, this hunger that's eating at us. My fire *burns* to be inside you, Ara," I said, and she inhaled sharply. Bringing my mouth towards her ear, I whispered, "You're mine, just as I am yours. The feeling pulling you towards me? That's our mate bond."

She jerked back, horror written into her face. I gripped her hair tighter, holding her in place, licking the curved shell of her ear. She shivered, melting into me ever so slightly.

So strong willed, my mate.

"Tell me you don't want this." I paused, waiting for her

response, but there was none. I pulled back and brought my gaze to hers, my hand still wound tightly in her hair.

An internal struggle played out behind her eyes, but it sat side-by-side with hunger. It warred with her restraint and hesitation, pulling her in opposite directions.

She swallowed hard.

"Get out of your head," I whispered, bringing my face closer to hers. "Tell me you don't want me as badly as I want you. Tell me, and I'll release you right now."

Even as the words tumbled from my mouth, I regretted them, sure she would take the opportunity, but her eyes darted to my mouth and back instead. My heart raced, a dark hope blooming in my chest. The seconds felt like years as the answer I so desperately craved danced along her lips.

A heartbeat later, the intensity shifted in her gaze as she made her decision and nodded. A grin tugged at the corner of my mouth.

"Say it. Tell me you want me, need me, deep inside you, filling you." *Where I was meant to be.*

"I want you," she rasped, her cheeks flaming.

"Want what, Ara?" I purred, smirking at how her cheeks flushed when I teased the words out of her, needing to hear her say them. When she hesitated, I started to release her hair.

"I want you...inside me."

I groaned, crashing my lips to hers. Walking her back to a nearby tree with one hand on her cheek, I kissed her fiercely, releasing my other one from her hair and sliding it down to her neck.

When her back hit the tree, she brought her hands to either side of my face, grinding her hips into me. My hand slid down her shoulder, her side, to her hip, slowly lifting her shirt and skimming the soft skin of her belly. She whimpered into my mouth, and I groaned at the sound.

I could only imagine how sweet her moans would be when my cock sank into her.

My fingers trailed up her torso to cup one breast, and she arched into my touch, making me harden almost to the point of pain. I brought a thumb to her nipple, circling it, and she moaned into my mouth—a sweet, honied moan that sent the rest of my self-control crumbling.

I tore my lips from hers, and her eyes snapped open in protest. Undoing the clasp of her soaked cloak, I dropped it to the ground before grabbing the hem of her shirt and pulling it over her head. Her long hair spilled over her naked form like a frame, a halo, and I stepped back to admire her, throbbing at the sight.

She was the most beautiful woman I had ever seen, to ever exist. Nothing, no one, had ever deserved to be worshiped more. All men should be made to kneel before her.

But she would have to settle for me.

Dropping to my knees, I slid my hands up her waist slowly, taking my time, scorching a trail up her body to her breasts. I cupped them both before bringing my mouth to one nipple, sucking hard as she moaned, pushing her chest into me, arching her back off the tree.

She wound her fingers in my hair as I moved to the other, flicking with my tongue before slipping my hands down. She lifted her hips for me as I slid her trousers down to the ground, lifting one foot and then the other as I pulled them off, flinging them to the side.

Sitting back on my heels, I raised one leg and placed it

CHAPTER FIFTEEN

over my shoulder, then the other, until I was supporting her weight with my arms wrapped around her backside, holding her to me. Lifting her, I propped her on the tree and shifted her hips, revealing her sex. *Fucking beautiful.*

The smell of her arousal nearly drove me feral, and I couldn't see straight through the strength of the mate bond. It demanded I continue—as if I could ever stop.

She jerked, screaming, as I ran my tongue across her center to her clit, and I groaned in approval.

Fuck. She tasted better than she smelled.

"You're already so wet for me," I growled, giving another long swipe with my tongue. "Such a good girl."

She whimpered as I slid two fingers in. I reveled in every shift of her hips, every sound she released. My fingers moved faster, matching pace with my tongue as I devoured her, curling against her sensitive spot mercilessly until she unraveled in my grasp.

"Rogue," she moaned as she tightened around my fingers, and I could've come in my trousers at the sound of my name on her breathless lips. I lowered her as she came down from her climax, placing one foot on the ground at a time before I slowly stood. Her eyes widened as I brought my soaked fingers to my mouth, licking the taste of her from them.

"Please. Now," she implored, her gaze smoldering, needing, begging, as if I would ever deny her.

But that was all I needed to hear. I pulled my shirt overhead and unbuttoned my trousers, dropping them to the ground with little ceremony as her eyes lowered to my cock, painfully hard for her. Wrapping my hands around her backside, I lifted her, and she quickly wrapped her legs around my waist as I leaned her against the tree, lining myself up at her entrance.

I paused as I looked directly into her eyes, expecting to see hesitation but finding none. "Are you sure?"

She nodded quickly, wrapping her arms around my neck and pulling me closer.

I eased into her, slowly sheathing myself as her head fell back against the tree, lips parting in a gasp. We groaned in unison at the tight fit, and I pulled out, slamming back into her.

Nothing had ever compared to this feeling, the bliss that was her, molded to me and breathless in my grasp.

"You are mine," I growled into her neck, pulling out slowly and sliding back in.

"Yours," she moaned.

Thrust.

"You are not leaving me."

Again.

Again.

Again.

I pulled out, and she whined at the loss as I flipped her around so her chest was flat against the tree. Gripping her hips, I lifted them to meet me and entered her again with a deep groan, my own head falling back before the need to *see* her pulled it forward again. With each pounding stroke, her moans grew louder, and I slid my hand down, finding her clit, circling, needing to hear the sound of her release again, feel it around my cock.

"More, Rogue. I need more," she panted.

I knew exactly what she needed because I desperately needed it too. The need to claim her was overwhelming every other sense, every thought.

CHAPTER FIFTEEN

A deep roar escaped me as I pounded into her one final time, filling her. My canines extended, and I skimmed them along the delicate skin of her neck. Taking a deep breath, I let her scent consume me as I bit into the connection at her shoulder. She screamed in pleasure, climaxing around me as my fire flowed through the wound, burning into her, binding me to her.

The world blurred.

There was no one else. There would never be anyone else. My entire existence shifted, shattering and rebuilding around her.

My mate.

She would never be free of me.

Mine.

The taste of her met my tongue as my scent merged with hers, forever branding her.

Mine.

I licked the wound.

Hers. Completely and utterly hers.

She stilled, and I paused. She jerked against me, gasping in pain. I stepped back, panic flaring in my chest as she staggered away from the tree and dropped her hands to her knees.

"Ara?" I said, stepping towards her.

She turned to me, her eyes wide with fear, every muscle in her body tense. I watched as her eyes suddenly seemed to glow.

No, not glow.

Lightning cracked across her irises.

Chapter Sixteen

Ara

I staggered away from the tree. *Something is wrong.*
 I could suddenly feel everything, everywhere, all at once. The electricity bouncing across the clouds from miles away. The buzzing at my fingertips. The pulse of Rogue's heart with each rapid beat.

My eyes and ears were stinging as if lit on fire. Reaching up with shaking hands, I found my ears and felt as they molded into a point.

"Ara?"

I turned to Rogue, and his face dropped.

Looking down, I watched in horror as blue, almost white, sparks flickered and sprang from my fingertips. My heart raced, pounding painfully, as the rain beat down harder. Faster.

Sparks. On my fingers. From my fingers.

My breath left me in a whoosh and refused to return. *I can't breathe. I can't—*

Thunder boomed overhead, and the sky lit up a brilliant white. I jumped at the sound, scrunching my eyes against the

CHAPTER SIXTEEN

searing pain. Panic washed over me like ice water, sucking any remaining air from my lungs.

Opening my eyes to Rogue, he didn't seem frightened, or even surprised. He wasn't surprised. *Why...*

My quivering lips went slack, my chest ripping open as it dawned on me.

"You knew." It wasn't a question. The look on his face told me everything. *He knew.* "Did you know this would happen to me when you did that? Bit me like a feral animal?"

He knew.

Hot, angry tears spilled from my eyes. I could feel the crackling electricity humming just underneath my skin, buzzing, begging to be released. I was lit with energy, almost to the point of pain, as it reached every possible inch of my body.

"No, I swear. I didn't know it would do this. Ara, please," he urged, stepping forward, reaching out a hand to me. I staggered back, shaking my head, and hurt flashed across his face.

"But you knew. About Vaelor. You knew. Were you ever going to tell me, or would you have just handed me back when I served my purpose?" I said, barely controlling the hysteria crawling up my throat.

Angry lightning cracked across the sky, and it called to me, demanding my attention. I lifted my face, feeling the energy hum across my irises, and the sky exploded again.

I am always just a thing to be possessed. Used for a purpose. Used.

My jaw clenched. Another crack of lightning.

Not anymore.

"You lied to me." My gaze returned to Rogue, and I watched

in numb horror as lightning struck the tree beside him. "And I gave myself—"

My body went cold.

I just gave myself to him, the King of Ravaryn.

The vicious monster who kidnapped me. Who lied to me.

Regret and hatred ripped through me. I leaned onto a tree with one arm as devastation spread like wildfire, catching and scorching every foolish feeling I had for him.

"Ara, you have to calm down. You're new to your power. It *will* drain you," he said slowly, stepping toward me.

My grip tightened, and the tree popped under my palm as power raced through it, burning it in every direction.

As I raised my face to him, lightning struck the ground by his feet, and he stopped where he was. It struck again, hitting another tree, again and again—fueled by rage, by hurt, by regret. I stepped toward him as the rain poured, sizzling as it combined with lightning and fire, steam and smoke swirling around us.

I couldn't control it as the furious sky laid ruin to everything around him, and he just stood there, watching me with sad eyes. As emotion and power overwhelmed me, a scream tore from my throat, and lightning exploded one final time, lighting the forest as bright as daylight before it went dark.

Completely exhausted, I swayed, stumbling, and landed in strong arms.

Tears trickled down my face as betrayal and grief settled in my bones.

How will I ever hide in Auryna now? What will become of my mother? My father?

"I will never forgive you," I mumbled, slurring my words.

"I know," he whispered, and it echoed through my mind as

CHAPTER SIXTEEN

I slipped into darkness.

* * *

A groan escaped me as I opened my eyes to cloudy daylight, my head pounding.

As I came to, I sat straight up, the blanket around me falling to my lap. I was in my bed in Draig Hearth.

The memories bombarded me, and I squeezed my eyes shut, dropping my head to my hands. Taking a deep breath, I opened my eyes to examine my hands for any traces of electricity or burns, but there were none. Reaching up hesitantly, my fingers were met with a point on each ear, and I choked back a sob, jerking my hands down.

How will I hide? What will happen to my mother? To Ravaryn?

My eyes blurred with tears as I glanced up, noticing Rogue asleep in the chair.

"Get out."

His eyes snapped open, his mouth falling slack as he popped up from the back of the chair. He rose to his feet, a look of relief on his face.

"Get. Out," I bit out through clenched teeth as a tear escaped my eye.

He stopped in his tracks, his gaze following the tear as it rolled down my cheek, his mouth set into a tight line. He stood there for a moment, clenching his fists, before he turned and left without a word.

Minutes later, Alden strode into the room, and I gasped. A thick ring of purple bruises circled around his neck, and my stomach dropped with a heavy stone of guilt. It wasn't my hand responsible for those bruises, but it was my fault.

"Alden, I am so sorry," I whispered as he neared the bed.

"There is no need to apologize. You didn't do this," he said, gesturing to his neck.

"Maybe not, but it is my fault all the same."

"No, it is I who must apologize to you. If I'd been able to hide your escape longer, maybe you would've made it far enough away..." His gaze shifted to the exposed wound on my neck, and I quickly covered it with my hand, dropping my eyes.

"Ara, you should know you've been asleep for two days. Rogue explained what happened... the mate mark, your magic, everything."

My heart stopped. *Two days? Mate—?*

Wait.

I audibly gasped. "Is that what this is? What does it mean?"

"Ara..."

My heart raced at his hesitation.

"Alden, what does it mean?" I asked again, harsher this time, and he finally met my gaze.

"You will... You will never leave here undetected. By claiming you, he will always know where you are. He'll be able to track you, no matter how far or fast you run."

The blood pounded in my ears, the room swaying around me. Jerking to my feet, I rushed from the room and down the spiral staircase.

"Ara! That's not every—"

I had no idea where I was going, but my feet propelled me forward, storming down the hallway past Iaso's chambers and stopping before a dark door with a dragon engraved on it and blackened wood along the bottom, burned from his fire.

CHAPTER SIXTEEN

This was his room. I knew it in my bones.

Heat flushed me as rage surged in my gut, and I threw open the door. It slammed into the wall as my eyes darted around the room, searching for my target and landing on Rogue's surprised face.

"Ara? What are you—"

I stalked over to him, and he opened his mouth to speak, but I reared my hand back, cracking across his cheek hard enough to whip his head to the side. My hand stung with the force.

I stepped back as he slowly turned his face to mine, rubbing his cheek, chuckling darkly.

"I take it Alden explained the bite?"

"You insufferable, arrogant, egotistical asshole!" I marched toward him again, my fingers sparking with anger.

He snatched me by the wrist and spun me around, tucking my arm behind me and wrapping his free arm around my waist. He lowered his head down to my neck as I attempted to jerk my arm free but to no avail. I elbowed him in the gut, and he grunted, releasing a low laugh as he tightened the hold on my arm.

A gasp escaped me as I arched forward.

"While I do love how fiery you are, there's no point in fighting me, Ara."

My fists clenched, nails biting into my palms, but I stilled in his hold.

"That's my good girl."

Embarrassment and fury lit my cheeks as my teeth gritted. He slowly slid his hand down from my waist and into the front of my trousers, sliding lower, lower... and I lost all semblance of cohesive thought.

"Do you not remember how good it felt?" he purred, his voice like dark red wine, smooth and sensual. Intoxicating. "Your body craves mine, just as mine does yours."

My head fell back onto his chest as he dipped two fingers into me, coaxing a moan from my throat. He pulled out, entering me again, and I bit back another moan, refusing to give him the satisfaction.

He lowered his head to the exposed side of my neck and lazily licked at the wound. My eyes snapped open wide, and the anger returned tenfold.

How had he distracted me so easily?

Energy cracked across my fingers where I gripped his arm, spreading under his skin, and he yelped as it seared him. As he released me, I jerked away, turning to face him. My eyes fell to his arm; black marks in the shape of lightning were burned into him, spreading out from where my palm had been.

Following my eyes, he looked down and examined his arm with fascination.

"Well, isn't that interesting?" he asked, his brows furrowing.

"Do not touch me again. Do not talk to me, or even look at me. You may have forced this claim upon me, but I will never be yours, not in any way that matters. I will never be your mate, Rogue."

His face was tight as smoke swirled around him.

"You would have to kill me first," I snapped, spinning on my heel. As I strode from the room, bright orange flames licked up the walls, clouds of black smoke spilling from the open door. I slammed it shut behind me.

Returning to my own chambers, I found Iaso seated on the bed, seemingly awaiting my return.

CHAPTER SIXTEEN

"Well, hello there. Rogue found me after he left your chambers and asked me to check on you. I'm happy to see you're finally awake." She turned to the window, watching as the storm ravaged the ocean, causing the waves to swell and crash along the shore. "Although, I'm not surprised to see it's raining again."

Hurt sank in my chest. "You knew."

"Oh, dear child, yes, I knew. I served your father long before Rogue. I may not look it, but you know I'm quite old." She hesitated. "I knew your mother, too. I must admit, I'm the one who placed the spell upon her womb."

"I know. She told me."

Even as they both confirmed it, I still couldn't wrap my mind around the fact that my mother not only fell in love with a Fae, but she'd lived here, trusted these people, made friends and memories.

I don't know her at all.

"You wrote to her, then?" I nodded, and she smiled softly. "Yes, her and Vaelor... They were so in love. I truly believed they would've changed this realm—and mind you, they would have." She gazed out the window again. "They were dear friends of mine, and it's been so long since I've been able to speak freely of them. You do look so much like your mother." She glanced back at me. "But those eyes... Those are Vaelor's."

My gaze dropped to my feet as my eyes stung with unshed tears.

"Well, come here. Let me have a look at you. That is what I came here for, after all."

I walked to the bedside, sitting as she stood. She closed her eyes as she placed a hand on either side of my face, and a warmth spread through my skin from her palms. We stayed this way for a brief moment before she opened her eyes, glowing softly. They immediately found the wound on my neck, before raising to meet mine, and she stepped back, giving me space.

"You seem right as rain," she laughed, and I just glared at her. "How do you feel?"

"I feel fine."

She studied my face, and I knew she knew I was lying.

"All right then. Although, you know, anger has a way of finding its way out if you hold onto it for too long. Don't let it fester, child." She strolled to the door, but paused, turning back to me. "Oh, has anyone explained the purpose of the mate bond to you?"

"Not yet," I uttered hesitantly.

She released a heavy sigh, pulling out a small bag of tea as she walked back to the bed. She grabbed my hand and placed it on my palm, closing my fingers around it.

"The mate bond chooses your partner based on biological compatibility. It...couples people based on how strong their offspring would be. That is its purpose. It fuels the lust that would create a powerful Fae."

My eyes bulged, never leaving her face as she spoke.

"This," she said, squeezing my hand, "is to ensure you don't produce a child from your mating. It will prevent a pregnancy. While Rogue asked me to give you this, it's entirely your choice."

"Thank you," I uttered, mortified but grateful—overwhelmingly grateful. Blinking rapidly, I turned away from her, placing the mesh bag in a small cup to pour heated water over it. We sat in silence as it brewed.

I wasn't entirely surprised that was the purpose of the

bond. Looking back, there were so many instances in which it was clear some external force was pulling me towards him, completely out of our control. It made sense, the lust. It was just the bond.

Just the bond. I shook my head to clear my thoughts as the liquid darkened, and I looped my fingers through the handle. Bringing it to my lips, I sipped it and turned back to Iaso.

She nodded, reaching out a hand to give my shoulder a light squeeze. With that, she stood and left without another word.

The gesture reminded me so much of Livvy. My eyes watered at the memory; she had been my only true friend back home.

I desperately hoped she didn't know of my current situation. She had encouraged me to follow Rogue out and then I never returned. I hoped she thought I went home and just hadn't had the chance to return. At least I knew my father wouldn't openly share the news of my kidnapping, so I highly doubted anyone in the village knew anything at all.

Strolling to the chair, I turned it to the window and sat, staring out as the rain fell. Lightning struck the ocean miles away, lighting the stormy darkness for a moment—beautiful in a way that sunshine could never be.

I had always felt a connection to the sky, to storms. They seemed to understand me, rain falling when I needed it most, and now, I guess I understood why.

Vaelor. My father by blood.

The past few days had been a whirlwind, and trying to process everything left me dizzy at the onslaught of information. Bringing my head down, I rested my forehead on my palm, begging it to steady my racing thoughts.

Everything I knew had been a lie. My father. My mother. Rogue, who was also apparently my mate, something I never thought possible. Alden, who was also my grandfather.

To top it all off, it seemed everyone knew except my father and me... Evander, I mean.

When he found out, he would be hurt, confused probably, but he loved me. He'd raised me, played with me, protected me. No matter whose blood I was, I was his daughter all the same.

When I do tell him...

A small beam of hope lit in my chest.

He wouldn't be so cruel to the Fae. He couldn't be, not when his only daughter was part Fae as well. He would stop the attacks on Ravaryn, if only for my sake.

He would understand, I thought, chewing my lip as lightning struck the sea again.

Chapter Seventeen

Ara

It had been almost a week since I'd seen Rogue.

I was grateful, hoping this feeling, this hurt, would diminish with time apart. But while I had no desire to see or speak to him, I still found myself holding my breath every time the door opened.

I hated it, the space he occupied in my mind, so freely, so unwanted. For the past week, I had secluded myself in my room, distracting myself with whichever book Thana brought that day and holding out hope that we would receive news from my father, but we hadn't. It had been weeks now and still nothing.

It only added to the anxiety building in my chest. Either King Adon agreed to the terms or he didn't. *What could possibly be taking so long?*

Bringing a hand up absentmindedly, my fingers found the marks on my skin. The wound had healed but left a small scar of teeth marks. Rogue's mark, a symbol of his permanent connection to me.

Embarrassment still flooded me every time I was reminded

of him, of that night, of what we did.

What was I thinking? I dropped my head to my hands.

It was a moot question, because I knew I hadn't been thinking at all. My mind had been so clouded with the overwhelming *need* for him. It was undeniable—I needed his touch like I needed air, like the earth needed rain. Not touching him, feeling him, being with him would have been like asking the sun not to rise.

The way his eyes burned into me, I knew he craved me just as badly. Once I surrendered, there was nothing else, no one else. I felt nothing but his touch and the voracious, insatiable hunger for *more*.

But now, I saw him clearly.

He's a liar, a manipulator, and the fact that I expected anything more from him made me a fool, I reminded myself. Again.

That was the root cause of the hurt blooming in my chest, stealing my breath: I expected more, wanted more.

Foolish. So foolish.

The doorknob turned without warning, startling me from my thoughts. Thana entered the room with tea, two cups, and two books, smiling as if everything was right in the world.

"Morning," she chirped as she set the tray on the bed. "All right, this one is a grand love story full of adventure and excitement," she said, handing me a thick book bound in blue leather with gold filigree. "I read it just yesterday, and it's quite good. I think you'll particularly enjoy certain scenes..." She winked.

"And this one?" I asked, reaching for the smaller one. It was older, bound with cracked brown leather.

"This one is a love story between a Fae and a human." She glanced up at me with a knowing look.

CHAPTER SEVENTEEN

"Is it—"

"No, it's not your parents' story. I just thought you might enjoy reading the tale, everything considered."

"Thank you, Thana."

She gave me a soft smile as she reached for the kettle, filling two cups.

"Iaso also sent me with tea. She said it's good for restoring mental clarity and rejuvenating the mind." She shrugged her shoulders.

Thank the Goddess for Iaso and Thana.

As she poured the steaming green liquid, I studied the kettle, so clearly Iaso's. It was off-white porcelain, with green leaves crawling up from the bottom, the handle a thick vine that looped up around the lid.

Thana held out a cup, and a sweet, floral scent filled the air. I sipped it, savoring the warmth as a wave of calm settled over me. The tea looked normal, just like any other, but the instant relief as my anxiety dissipated told me she must have spelled it or enhanced the leaves while they were still growing. The way she always knew what would be needed was astounding.

"She does always seem to know what everyone needs when they need it, doesn't she?" Thana asked as I visibly relaxed. She reached across to pick up the book from my nightstand and flipped through the pages. "Is this the one about the knight and the servant? I believe I've already read this one." She stood, strolling to the window.

"Still raining I see," she said softly. It was daytime now, but the heavy clouds still blocked the sun, casting the castle in darkness, just as they had when I woke days ago.

"I can't control it. I don't know how or why it's doing this, much less how to stop it." Guilt pricked at me and I averted my gaze.

"It's connected to your emotions," she said plainly.

My eyes snapped back to her. "What? How do you know?"

"All Fae magic works that way. Usually, the magic presents when you're very young, and you have years to learn to wield it and adapt before it develops to full strength. You, however—your magic was thrust upon you at full strength all at once." She turned to me. "It is completely understandable that you haven't mastered it yet. You will one day, though."

So many emotions bombarded me at once—guilt, disappointment, embarrassment. If I had been born and raised here with my biological father, I wouldn't be in this situation. I would've known how to control it.

"How will I ever learn?" I asked aloud, not really expecting an answer.

"You should speak with Alden. He did train King Vaelor, after all."

My mouth fell open as irritation bit at me.

"Why am I just now hearing of this? No one has explained anything," I said, exasperated.

"You never asked," she said, shrugging her shoulders, and I glared at her. "All right, seeing as you don't have a book for me this time, I'll leave you to yours." She walked to the door, looking back over her shoulder. "Do let me know what you think of those two when you get a chance," she said, continuing down the stairs.

I stared after her, my jaw still on the floor.

I never asked?

Rolling my eyes, I grabbed the small, brown book and flipped it open, attempting to distract myself, but it only

CHAPTER SEVENTEEN

lasted a few, irritating minutes. With a huff, I stood and raced down the stairs to the library.

"It's so nice to see you out and about, Ara. Welcome back," Alden said with a small smile. With his long hair braided behind his back, his neck was visible. The bruises were gone, but it did nothing to lessen the guilt; seeing him only reminded me of what Rogue had done because of me.

"Good morning, Alden. I was actually hoping to speak with you."

"Yes?" he asked, tilting his head with curiosity.

I took a deep breath, steeling my nerves. "Thana mentioned you may be able to help me with my magic…as you helped Vaelor."

A soft smile curved his lips. "Ah, I see. Is that something you desire? To learn to wield it?"

"Well, yes…" I said, my brows creasing with confusion. "I have to stop this rain."

"It will mean more than that, more than merely stopping rain. When you decide to connect with your magic, it will meld with you. It will become a part of you and you of it, as it always should've been. You must decide if that is something you truly want because it will not be easy," he explained, "and it cannot be undone."

Everything had happened so fast, I didn't have a minute to think about what I wanted, but that was something I loved about Alden: he always gave me the truth *and* the choice. He was the only one.

I turned to the large, open window, biting my lip as I considered his words. *Is that what I wanted?*

As I stared, the rain lightened, the clouds thinning slightly. Through a small gap, beams of yellow, hazy sunlight peeked through, bouncing off the sparkling waves below for the first time in days.

My lips parted as the sky answered for me.

My connection to the sky had only deepened since the awakening of my magic, and I felt it reaching out to me, weeping for me—*with* me. I hesitated, but the thought of melding with my magic, with the sky, suddenly felt undeniably right, like maybe I wouldn't feel so alone.

"Yes," I declared, turning back to Alden. "Yes, I want to learn."

He beamed, grinning ear to ear, something akin to pride shining in his eyes.

"Good. That is very good. I have much to do today, but be ready at sunset tomorrow. I have somewhere to take you." He nodded and patted me on the shoulder. "I must return to my work, but rest assured, I will see you soon."

* * *

The sun had dipped below the water, leaving a trail of burning orange and red in its wake, as I arrived at the library the following evening. Through the window, I watched as the stars slowly revealed themselves, twinkling against the inky darkness. It had been clear all day, without a drop of rain, and the relief I felt was like a small breath of fresh air.

"The library does have the best view," Alden said as he joined me, admiring the sky's artwork. When the sun had disappeared entirely, he spoke again, breaking the silence. "Come. I have somewhere special to show you."

I followed him as we exited the castle and entered the bailey. Large torches had been lit along the wall, casting the courtyard in ominous, flickering shadows and illuminating the dark, blood-red tunics of the guards. Alden strode towards the gate, and I slowed, noting the stares. He paused when I didn't follow, turning back to me to offer his elbow. Reluctantly, I looped my arm through his, and we strolled through the gate untouched.

Once outside and away from the light of the castle, my eyes quickly adjusted, the moon nearly bright as day. We walked for some time down the slope that led to Draig Hearth, staying close to the eastern border, and eventually made it to a small beach with soft waves lapping at the sandy shore. Just ahead, an old, wooden dock sat with a boat tied to it.

I glanced up at Alden, and he gave a soft smile.

He led me down the dock and gracefully stepped onto the boat before he turned to offer a hand. I took it, stepping aboard as the boat swayed beneath us. Releasing me, he untied the rope and grabbed the oar, using it to push off the dock.

"Where could we possibly be going in a boat?"

"You'll see." He dipped the oar into the water, paddling us out.

I stared out to the endless sea, trying to wrap my mind around the fact that it wasn't actually endless. I knew it had to end somewhere, crash on some distant shore, but looking out, it followed the horizon to the edge, meeting the sky in every direction.

"There. That's where we are going," Alden proclaimed, pointing past the front of the boat.

I squinted, and in the far distance was a small dot of land, barely distinguishable from the surrounding black waters.

Eventually, Alden stepped into the shallow water and pulled

the boat onto a beach that backed into a cliff edge. My eyes followed it to the top just as he extended a hand to me—jagged, solid stone all the way up. As I stepped onto the sand to follow him, I opened my mouth to speak, but it merely fell open as he disappeared behind the rock face.

I jogged over to peek around the ledge and found a set of hidden stairs, steep and climbing parallel to the cliff. Shaking my head, I began the climb, but it was much taller than it seemed. When I finally made it to the top, I braced my hands on my knees to catch my breath. *Good Goddess, I need to train more.*

Sucking in another deep breath, I stood to finally see the island in its entirety. There was a field atop the plateau, trees bordering the edges, blowing in the breeze, and the center was cleared, covered in grass and patches of wildflowers—except for a small circle made of rocks and dirt.

"It's beautiful," I said, amazed.

"Yes, it is. Vaelor used to bring your mother here for privacy."

Alden motioned to the ground, pointing to a stone with the letter E carved in it, and I dropped to my knees, running my hand over the stone, smooth from the elements.

E for Elora.

My heart ached, suddenly feeling heavy in my chest, and I sank to the ground as the weight seemed unbearable. Crossing my legs beneath me and flattening my hands on the cool grass, I took a deep breath and imagined my mother reminding me to breathe, to find the calm around me. I wish it was her speaking to me, rather than my own endless thoughts. I wasn't enough; I never had been. I had always needed her, needed her steadiness, her peace, her

CHAPTER SEVENTEEN

perseverance. *I miss you so much, it hurts.*

"They loved each other deeply," he said, sitting beside me. "I'd always hoped he would find someone kind, someone who would give him the love he deserved, and that was your mother. She loved him fiercely and stayed with him until his last breath."

"How did he die? I mean, I know Adrastus, he...but how?" I don't know why I felt the need to ask, but knowing my mother was there made me feel like I should know. I needed to understand what she went through, what she suffered with in silence all these years.

Alden took a breath, and I braced myself for the story.

"The day it happened, your mother had *just* told Vaelor she was with child. He was overjoyed, as we all knew he would be. He had prayed to the Goddess they would be blessed with a child." He glanced at me, a wistful smile on his lips. "He never held humans in lower regard than that of the Fae, you see. He wanted peace with Auryna, they both did, and their marriage was to be proof of that. You were to be proof that there could be peace, and even love.

"Then, Adrastus came. He stormed the castle in the dead of night, somehow finding their chambers. Vaelor knew something was happening, so he told Elora to hide in the closet. As soon he shut the closet door, Adrastus burst into the room... She was forced to watch as they fought, but Adrastus was a Draig. He was too strong, could shift on command, and he sliced Vaelor's throat before he even had a chance."

A tear slipped from my eye, rolling down my cheek.

"Your mother hid until Adrastus left. She tried to stop the bleeding, stayed with him until his last breath before she ran to Iaso's chambers for help. That's when Iaso placed the curse to protect you. It wasn't well known that Vaelor had a lover—thank the Goddess—so Adrastus didn't know of her existence, and she couldn't risk him learning that a child of Vaelor's lived, so she fled to Auryna and married Evander before she began to show."

Silent tears poured down my cheeks. Not only did she have to witness the brutal murder of her love, but she had to flee from the life she had built and dreamed of.

Rage at Rogue's family burned through my chest, and guilt consumed me so suddenly, so overwhelmingly, leaving no room for air, for reason, for anything. My chest was tight, my lungs on fire, but I forced several deep breaths and raised my face to the sky. My eyes followed as dark clouds blew in the breeze, the stars twinkling through the gaps. Eventually, my breathing steadied, but the feelings remained; I feared they might never leave.

With a heavy sigh, Alden stood to his feet. "This island is also where I taught your father, and it's where I will teach you."

He extended a hand and hoisted me up before leading me to the circle of stones. It was much larger than it appeared from a distance; massive boulders surrounded the sparring circle. At the head of the circle was a carving of what appeared to be lightning reaching down to meet the blade of a sword.

"Vaelor carved that when he felt he had finally mastered his magic. It was the symbol he chose for his kingdom, as he was the Storm Bringer."

My eyes narrowed on the carving, studying it intently. "I saw that title in the book of monarchs. What is a Storm Bringer?"

"Storm Bringer is the title given to those who possess a very rare form of magic. Your father is the only one to have existed in my lifetime. For Vaelor, it was created through my and his mother's combined magic, then blessed by the Goddess. I can wield electricity." He lifted his hand as a ball of crackling blue light floated above his palm. "Ara, my mate, had the ability to call the rain from the clouds, so together, they formed Vaelor's ability to *create* storms and control lightning."

"Is that why my emotions seem to affect the weather?"

He paused, as if unsure how to continue.

"As I said, the magic of a Storm Bringer is rare, and it is not something that has passed through a bloodline before. It's typically only gifted by the Goddess, but then again, she seems to favor you as much as she did Vaelor."

My brows furrowed. "I'm confused. We don't learn about magic in Auryna. You're going to have to break this down for me like you would a child."

Alden nodded, pausing for a moment as if to compose his thoughts. "For the most part, magical abilities are passed through bloodline: shifting, connections to the elements, the ability to change the weather—like my mate, Ara. Those are but a few, but they can be mixed or combined when a child is born to true mates, like Rogue's wings from his father and fire from his mother. Usually, the magic leans one way or the other, choosing either the mother's *or* the father's magic, with the child never more powerful than their parents. It's what we call familial magic. However, there are instances where the Goddess blesses her chosen ones, those she deems worthy, with more powerful magic."

He peeked over at me, shaking his head. "Ara, you should not have the abilities you have. Being half-Fae…"

"I should have half the normal ability," I finished for him.

"Yes, exactly, but you do not. You, at the very least, have the same strength as your father, and even he was unusually powerful. It can only mean that the Goddess has chosen you," he said confidently as if he truly believed that.

A shocked laugh escaped me. "That's impossible, Alden. Up until a few days ago, I didn't even know I was Fae at all. Why would she choose me of all beings?"

"That's a question only she can answer, but the spell Iaso cast should have prevented you from ever presenting any Fae characteristics at all. The simple fact that Rogue was able to break it so easily tells me the Goddess must have a hand in it. She wanted it to happen. You've truly had no signs or clues at all before Rogue claimed you?"

"No." The dream in Blackburn flashed through my mind, the one I'd dismissed as soon as we'd left the inn. "Well, I guess, in retrospect, some things do seem obvious, but at the time, I just brushed them off as coincidence."

"Like what?" His eyebrows creased together as his eyes searched my face.

"Well, I've always felt a connection to the sky. As if it knew what I was thinking, what I was feeling." He nodded as I spoke. "Then, while we were in Blackburn, I had a strange dream, and it felt so real."

"A dream?" He looked at me intently. "Tell me exactly."

"All I remember was standing in an open clearing..." I glanced around and my eyes widened as my heart rate spiked. "Much like this one. Exactly like this one, actually. The sky was dark, ominous, and a storm was blowing in. The wind was howling, and I... I knew the sky was trying to tell me something, urging me to understand *something*, but I didn't know what. That's when a bolt of lightning shot down to

CHAPTER SEVENTEEN

the ground, but it didn't flash and burn away. It stayed there, connected to the ground, sizzling and crackling, but I wasn't afraid. I felt... safe. Comforted. I reached my hand out to it, and when my hand entered the light, a warmth washed over me—a wave of what felt like recognition, maybe."

I turned to Alden, and he was frozen, his face blank.

"Alden?"

"You had that dream? In Blackburn, you say?"

I nodded wearily. "Why? What does it mean?"

"I'm not entirely sure, but I can tell you Vaelor had the exact same dream when he was young before his powers surfaced."

"The exact same dream?" I gaped at him, chills spreading across my skin.

"Yes. Exactly." He paused, bringing his thumb and forefinger to his chin. "I'll scour the library and speak with Iaso to see if she's ever heard of dreams repeating in a bloodline. I didn't think much of it when Vaelor came to me about it, but now..." He shook his head in a daze. "It must mean something."

After a moment, he cleared his throat.

"All right, enough history for today. Let's get to work. Accepting and working with your magic will be difficult, so we better start now while we still can."

"What do you mean?" I asked, my mind muddled.

"Well, at some point, Rogue is going to strike the bargain with Evander," he said slowly like he had to force the words from his mouth, "and you'll be headed back for Auryna, if that's what you should choose."

My gaze met his at the realization. I'd been on the edge of my seat, waiting for the correspondence from my father, but had somehow forgotten that I'd be returning permanently. I would never see Alden again. Or Thana. Or Iaso.

Or Rogue.

So many emotions hit me at once—sadness, fear, regret—but none of them mattered. My mother was still there, and she needed me.

More than that, all of Ravaryn needed this deal to work.

I blinked away the sting of tears and stepped into the circle, electricity sparking at my fingertips.

Chapter Eighteen

Rogue

I didn't know what was worse—the fact that I'd claimed her before she knew what it meant or that I'd known her true identity and hadn't told her.

You're no better than your father, a voice whispered in the back of my mind.

I knew it was true. I had shackled her to me, just as he had my mother.

She would never outrun my reach. I would always know where she was, for the rest of her life, and not only would her absence leave a gaping hole in my chest, but I would feel it every time she was sexually aroused, in my presence or not.

My teeth gritted against the spike of jealousy that shot through me.

She vowed to never be my mate, which meant she would find another, and I would be cursed to suffer as her pleasure was served by others.

Not that I didn't deserve it; I did. I deserved it all and more for the pain I caused her, but the thought still had bile rising in the back of my throat. The thought of any man touching her, her skin, her lips, her...

Smoke trailed behind me as I flew, my vision tinted red.

To think, this had been the plan the entire time. Bite her, strike the deal, and hand her back.

A low laugh escaped me at how overwhelmingly naive I had been, so incredibly ignorant. When the day came for the exchange—and it would—it would tear me in two to watch her leave with hatred still burning in her chest.

The look of betrayal in her eyes still haunted me, day and night.

I should've told her. I should've told her everything.

Regret had consumed me over the past few days as I carefully avoided her, just as she commanded.

"I will never be your mate, Rogue. You would have to kill me first." Her words echoed through my mind constantly. I hadn't even wanted a mate when she was thrust into my life. I hadn't wanted a mate when she arrived at the castle or tricked me with a kiss or touched my scar, but something shifted in me at some point.

I didn't know when it happened—when the disgust shifted to toleration, when just tolerating her shifted to...hope.

But that night, she *chose* to be with me, and after a lifetime of being hated, forgotten, and alone, in that moment, I had wanted it so badly. I wanted her. A life. A mate. To be chosen.

Wanted.

I wanted to be wanted.

I wanted *her* to want me.

And when I claimed her, it wasn't really my claim at all. It was my surrender.

That's the thing with the mate mark. While the urge to do it is nearly impossible to resist, it's not an absolute between

CHAPTER EIGHTEEN

mates. It's a choice.

My parents never marked each other, because to mark is to surrender. I didn't claim her in ownership. I claimed her as my one, devoted myself to one. With that mark, my body and soul were bound to her. I would never be with anyone else, emotionally or physically.

It would be her or no one, until my last breath, and she didn't want me.

My knuckles rubbed at my sternum, the ache returning to my chest as I flew over the sea, the castle visible in the distance. The sun was setting on the horizon, painting the ocean a fiery orange, and it suddenly dawned on me that I could see the sun.

The sun.

Today had been clear, free of the rain that Ara created in her turmoil, and for the first time in days, I felt like I could breathe. A very small breath.

As the sky darkened and stars twinkled to life, I neared the castle and spotted Alden and Ara strolling down the path that led out from Draig Hearth. My breath caught in my throat.

Why were they outside the gates? Adrenaline poured through my veins like liquid fire, my heart racing. *Surely Alden is not so foolish as to try and help her escape again.*

As much as it pained me, we needed her to save Ravaryn.

I followed behind them, hidden in the shadows, as they made their way down to the shore, loaded onto a boat, and paddled out.

Before long, they docked at a small island, and my eyebrows furrowed with confusion. There were several plateau islands scattered about the coast, but none were ever visited. Unless you had wings, it was nearly impossible to reach the top.

Every isle was enclosed in sheer cliffs that dropped off on all sides.

My eyes bulged as they disappeared into the rock.

I flew closer, just out of sight, only to see a small, hidden staircase, and my heart thundered. Landing at the top, I perched in a tree and waited.

They crested the top step within a few minutes, Ara behind Alden, and stopped, surveying the island.

"Vaelor used to bring your mother here for privacy."

My heart stilled. I suddenly felt wrong for eavesdropping as sadness pressed into her features, but I couldn't pull myself away. It had been days since I'd seen her face.

She sat on the ground and carefully reached out to a rounded stone, as if her mere touch would ruin it. Her fingers traced the E carved in it.

The ache in my chest wrenched as Alden spoke of Vaelor and Elora's love. Not only did my father deprive me of ever experiencing that, but he took it from Ara as well.

Did he say his son? My breath left me in a whoosh. *Alden... was Vaelor's father? I hadn't known that. How had I not known that?*

Then, Ara mentioned Adrastus, and my focus snapped back to her. She was asking about Vaelor's death. Surely she already knew my father killed him, but the story was gruesome and devastating.

My eyes never left her face as Alden told the story. Tear after tear slid down her cheeks as she listened in silence, and the wood under my palms cracked with the force of my restraint. Each tear was another blade through my chest, urging the fire within me to surge; I fought it back with every ounce of control I had, but I *wanted* to run to her. I wanted to hold her and wipe the tears from her cheeks. I wanted to do anything to staunch the pain she was feeling, but I didn't. I sat, watching, fighting against every screaming instinct.

After what felt like an eternity, Alden finished his story, and they sat in silence for a moment before they stood, strolling to the circle in the far corner of the island. I followed behind, skirting along the edge of the tree line. Once we neared the stones, my eyes immediately spotted King Vaelor's crest carved into the stone.

This must have been where he trained and developed his magic.

Scooting closer, I listened as Alden explained the symbol and what a Storm Bringer was. What he said afterward, however, caught me by surprise. I hadn't even considered the strength of her magic and what it meant for her to wield it as a half-Fae, but as he explained how the Goddess must favor her, it all made complete and total sense. She favored Ara.

I fell back into the tree behind me, my lips parting as my breath left me in a silent whoosh. That explained why I was able to break an unbreakable curse. The Goddess didn't want it there.

Why hadn't Alden spoken to me of any of this?

I didn't have time to consider the question before Ara began speaking of the dream she had in Blackburn. We hadn't discussed it after she woke, and I hadn't cared enough at the time to ask, but now, listening to its contents, there was no denying it was tied to her magic. If Vaelor had the same dream, it meant something. Nothing ever happened by coincidence.

Something nagged at me, and I dropped my eyes in thought. Everything that had happened to her, with us, the breaking of her curse...she was the same, but entirely different. She was human, but not.

My head whipped back to the ring, eyes quickly finding the sharp point of her ear, and it was as if the wool had been pulled from my eyes at that very moment.

I could not give her back. She would no longer pass for human. Evander would kill her the moment he saw her. Panic swarmed me, heating the air as she stepped into the circle and small blue sparks danced along her fingertips.

She did not belong in Auryna any longer.

* * *

They trained for hours. Alden had instructed her how to visualize and command her magic, but she hadn't made any progress thus far. She was visibly frustrated, sweat soaking through her tunic from the effort.

The moon sank on the western horizon, mere minutes before sunrise when Alden finally called it. "I think it's time we call it a night, yes?"

She nodded, wiping the sweat from her brow.

As they disappeared down the hidden staircase, I walked to the circle, examining it from the outside. As I stepped into it, the remnants of Vaelor's magic mingled with mine, but it wasn't threatening. Vaelor had always been known as the Kind King, and the magic left behind here echoed that. I strolled to the largest boulder where the crest was carved, running my fingers along the symbol.

I had always harbored a deep respect for Vaelor. I hadn't known him personally, but the stories of him were in such stark contrast from those of my father. Adrastus was hated and rightly so. He was barbaric, merciless, and bloodthirsty. Thus, when he took the throne, he single-handedly thrust Ravaryn into turmoil. The people were constantly afraid, and it led to unrest. There was never a moment of true peace during his reign.

Under Vaelor, however, Ravaryn *only* knew peace, within its borders and with Auryna. There were no wars, and our people were happy. Vaelor reigned with fairness and respect, and it showed in every corner of his kingdom. When he was murdered, all of Ravaryn mourned for years.

While I held still resentment toward the humans for everything they'd done, my father's murder was not entirely unwelcome. The fact that the humans were able to worm themselves into Draig Hearth, my home, made my blood boil, but the end of Adrastus signaled the end of a terrible monarch for Ravaryn and offered the chance for a new ruler. It offered hope.

Then, to my complete surprise, people had placed that hope in me. As much as I hated it, the abuse I suffered at his hands was common knowledge, and I'm fairly certain that was the only reason they have allowed me to reign. The crown remained mine at their mercy. They were waiting to see what I would do, who I would become. They were giving me a chance, and I decided a long time ago that I would not let them down. Hence, my need to secure the border and offer them the peace they so rightfully deserved.

I might not be trained in the inner workings of a kingdom yet, but I could offer them that much. I would save Ravaryn, rather than drive it into the ground like Adrastus would have.

"Please let me be better," I whispered aloud, to whom I didn't know, but thunder rumbled in the distance in response.

My head snapped to the sky, searching for the impending storm, but there was none.

I sighed, stepped back from the stone, and leapt into the sky.

A faint green haze glowed over the ocean as the sun slowly woke, and I took my time flying back to the castle, reveling in the sunrise, thankful for clear skies.

As I neared the castle, the green shifted to soft yellow and orange as light devoured the darkness. The sparse clouds hovering on the horizon reflected it, creating highlights of pink and purple.

Beautiful. Relieving.

In stark contrast to the twisted plan that had taken root in my mind, refusing to leave.

I stepped onto the ledge and continued into the side entrance, marching straight to Doran's chambers, opening the door without bothering to knock. Doran was still sound asleep, so I strolled over and plopped down beside him.

"Wake up."

He jerked straight up, startled from his sleep, and rubbed his eyes.

"Rogue. What have I said about barging in here?" He glared at me.

Doran was my general, but he was also my only friend. He was the only one brave enough to speak to me as a child, even if it was only once, and I never forgot it. Clinging to that hope of a friend, even one so distant, had pulled me through my darkest moments. As we got older, he quickly rose through the ranks of my father's army, and after his death, I named Doran my general, as we'd grown closer over the years.

I waved my hand in dismissal, scoffing.

CHAPTER EIGHTEEN

"Oh, come on. The day is wasting away. As my general, you should be awake by now anyway."

He glanced out the window and rolled his eyes when he realized it was barely past sunrise.

"Well, I'm up now." He threw the blanket off and stalked to his dresser, pulling out a shirt. "What is it?"

"I can't just come by to enjoy your cheerful disposition?" I offered him a smile as he glowered at me.

"Not this early. Have you even slept?" He studied my face. "From the look of those dark circles under your eyes, I would assume not. Is this about Ara, again?"

During my avoidance of her, I'd been checking in with everyone who came in contact with her—Doran, Iaso, Alden, and Thana. I may not have had *my* eyes on her, but I made sure everyone else did.

"Yes, but not exactly," I uttered, and he turned to face me, his brows pulling together. "I don't want to give her back. We can't, actually."

His eyes widened but before he could speak, I held my hand up.

"I've been considering this all night. You know Ravaryn's safety is my utmost concern." He nodded hesitantly. "I will ensure its safety, but I don't think handing Ara over will guarantee it anymore."

I met his eyes, and a heavy wave of seriousness settled over the room.

"I think I have a better course of action. I want to assassinate General Starrin."

His jaw fell slack.

"You cannot be serious," he whispered forcibly. "We already have a plan, a good one."

"Doran, admit it. Our plan was rushed and okay at best. When we took Ara, it was a last resort. We had no other choice but to use her as ransom, and it all depended on his love for his daughter—his *human* daughter—who is, in fact, not his daughter at all and has Fae blood coursing through her veins, which is made abundantly clear by her pointed ears and magic she can't exactly control yet. That plan will never work now."

His eyes were wide as he averted his gaze and brought his hand to his mouth in consideration.

"And this has nothing to do with your desire to keep Ara here?" He glanced back at me with suspicion.

Of course, some small part of me wanted her here.

"Even if it did, it doesn't matter. Evander won't release his grasp on Ravaryn once he discovers who she is, *what* she is. Even worse, I fear he'll blame us and attempt to retaliate. I've thought through every possibility, and this is the only solution I could come up with. If we assassinate him, Adon will lose his most valuable general. It will give us time to raise and train an army of our own, and when he inevitably replaces Evander, we'll be ready."

Doran slowly nodded his head.

"I'm guessing you already have a plan, then?"

"I'm going to send him one last letter, saying to meet in two days from now for the handover, or I will kill her. He's taken too long, and it's time to force his hand."

"What if he denies? You're going to kill her, then?"

He knew I wouldn't. It was an empty threat.

"He won't. From all accounts, he loves her more than anything else, and on top of that, us taking her was a huge hit to his pride. He will want her back just to soothe his ego, if for no other reason." *Hopefully.*

"So, you set up the meeting and what? Ambush him? He'll see that coming from a mile away. Besides, you know they're going to demand we meet at the Marsh."

The Marsh was a small area of land where magic couldn't be used, a place well-known to both Auryna and Ravaryn. The lack of magic had plagued philosophers for as long as it had existed. Some argued it was the birthplace of the realm; others claimed it was because the Goddess still resided there, blocking out all other magic besides her own.

"Not if we bring Delphia," I said hesitantly, and he whipped his head back to me in outrage, anger flushing his pale cheeks.

Delphia was Doran's twin sister. While Doran was gifted with brilliant battle strategy, his sister was given the ability to merge with her surroundings, essentially becoming invisible. It made her the perfect spy, but Doran was *extremely* protective of her. He had never even given her the chance to put her skills to good use.

"No, absolutely not. How could you even suggest that?" He stalked back to me, his spine rod straight.

"The Marsh isn't large enough to hold an entire human encampment, so they'll have to set up elsewhere. If she can sneak us into their camp, I can kill him while he sleeps, just as he's done to so many of our people. If we wait until the meeting, it will be hand-to-hand combat, and they'll outnumber us, you know that."

He stared at me, jaw clenched.

"She'll remain hidden the entire time, and I'll defend her with my life," I added genuinely.

"It will be her decision. I will not decide that for her."

"How soon can she be here? We will need to leave as soon

as possible."

"She can be here tomorrow morning," he said, turning to the window, concern pressing into his features.

"Thank you, Doran," I said, rising to my feet.

"You know she'll hate you, right?" he asked without another glance in my direction, and I paused, closing my eyes. "Ara, I mean."

The deep ache burrowed in my chest, and I rubbed my knuckles against my sternum.

"She already does."

Chapter Nineteen

Ara

"Wake up, lazy bones. You've almost slept the day away."

Groaning, I peeked one eye open to see Thana smiling down at me, holding coffee and honeyed bread. I sat up, the blanket falling into my lap as I glanced out the window. The sun was already lowering on the horizon.

"No kidding," I mumbled, rubbing my eyes with my palms. "I was working with Alden all night. He agreed to help me."

"Oh, that's great," she said, pouring a cup of steaming coffee and handing it to me. "Did you make any progress, then?"

"None. At all." The frustration from the night before bit at me, and I took a deep breath, stifling it. We had spent hours in the ring, and I hadn't wielded the electricity even once. It seemed to have a mind of its own, only responding to my emotions, not when I actually wanted it to.

Alden explained I should view my magic as another limb, an extension of myself, and I should be able to control it like so, but no matter how hard I focused, it didn't budge.

"I'm sure it will just take time. I don't have magic, but my mother always compared it to muscle—weak at first, but as you train, you become stronger over time. Just keep trying. I'm sure you will master it in no time," she reassured me, patting my leg.

"Thank you," I replied, although I wasn't sure I fully believed her.

We ate in silence after that, eating our fill.

"I just realized I've never even asked about your family. How rude of me," I apologized, wiping my mouth. "What are they like?"

She stilled, chewing her food slowly before her throat bobbed, her gaze falling to the floor. "I haven't seen them in many years. I lost contact with them after our village was attacked and destroyed."

"Oh," I breathed. "Thana, I'm so sorry."

"It wasn't your fault." She wrung her hands in her lap. I reached out to place my hand on top of hers, just as Livvy had done for me so many times, and she flinched. I jerked my hand back, dropping my gaze.

"Sorry," she whispered.

"No, don't be. *I'm* sorry, truly," I said.

She sighed, closing her eyes.

"Yes, me too," she uttered, clearing her throat as she rose to her feet. "I best return to my duties."

I was steeped in guilt at the horrific deeds of my father, and it was only exasperated by the pain on her face, in her features, her eyes. I bitterly regretted asking and resurfacing the memory. It was a miracle she could stand to be in the same room as me, much less be my friend.

"I-I didn't mean to cause you any pain. I'm sorry for bringing it up."

CHAPTER NINETEEN

A tight smile pulled at her lips.

"I know. You didn't know, and how could you? You're just as ignorant about the attacks as the rest of Auryna's people."

I flinched as though I had been slapped, but she was right. I had allowed myself to remain ignorant, blindly trusting whatever my father—Evander said.

"I won't be so clueless when I go back. He'll have to listen." I motioned to my ears. "His vendetta against the Fae cannot continue when his own daughter is one. I'll make him listen, Thana."

She looked at me doubtfully, before dipping her chin and exiting without another word.

I paused for a moment and walked to the window, lost in thought. A small part of me worried what my father would think, whispering doubtful thoughts.

Would he love me any differently? Or would things return to the same monotony, day in and day out? Would he still push for me to marry Finn?

No. He could push for whatever he wanted, but I would stand my ground.

For once, I will *stand my ground.*

Running my hand through my hair, my fingers grazed my ear, feeling its point.

A small chuckle escaped me as I realized Finn would never agree to marry me now, anyway. No human would agree to marry a Fae; the prejudice was too thick, too solid.

It was the exact opposite of what Vaelor and my mother wished for the realm. Sighing, I dropped my forehead to my palm, scrunching my eyes as the guilt returned like clockwork—an incessant reminder every day, every hour, every minute.

It seemed guilt was the only thing I was capable of feeling lately.

Vaelor and my mother had desperately hoped to harbor peace between Auryna and Ravaryn and now, there was more strife than ever, and the humans were so completely ignorant of it, so recklessly trusting. They had no idea of the devastation Auryna wrought.

There was so much wrong. It was all so wrong: the death, the war, the hate.

The Fae are not monsters. They are not.

I am not.

How naive I had been, spending years wishing for more—more adventure, more freedom. A sick laugh bubbled from my throat, and I jerked to my feet, tapping my fingers on my thigh as I paced, attempting to burn off the rising tension pouring through my veins. My chest tightened, breath by breath, step by step, thought by thought, as I fought for control against the panic—a vicious serpent carefully winding around my heart, constricting and preparing to feast upon whatever I allowed it to.

In a twisted game of fate, I got what I wanted. I wasn't in Auryna anymore, blissfully unaware of everything I knew now.

But would it be considered blissful, to be so ignorant of everything that must change?

No, it would be selfish. Weak. I had been weak. Cowardly.

The emotions swirling in me were spiraling, swelling, growing. The embarrassment that came with Rogue claiming me, for being attracted to him at all, for being so blind for so long. The crushing guilt on behalf of the man who raised me while simultaneously ordering the murder of Fae children.

CHAPTER NINETEEN

The sadness for my mother and her lost love, the fact that she had to grieve alone for so long. The anger that I wasn't who I thought was, but would never get to be who I was meant to be.

It was overwhelming, and I was suddenly drowning, the sea of torment sucking the remaining breath from my lungs. I turned to the window, silently begging the sky to calm me, to dull the burn in my chest, but as I braced my hand on the windowsill, my chest rose and fell too quickly, and with my lack of air came dark, heavy clouds.

"No," I sobbed under my breath.

The clouds billowed, growing and twisting until they swallowed the sun. I tried to breathe slowly, to calm myself and the storm developing before me, but no air would come. My chest was too heavy, too tight.

Lightning crackled across the sky, and a black, winged silhouette stood out against the brilliant white.

Panic struck me, the weight on my chest now crushing.

I was causing this, and Rogue was out there.

With the throat-tightening fear came the rain. All at once, it was a downpour, thunder rumbling in the distance, but moving closer—ever closer, louder, deafening as it followed the lightning racing across the sky.

Lightning cracked again, spearing down and striking the sea, now raging beneath Rogue. Veins of white raced across the thrashing waves, and a choked gasp escaped me. Lightning struck, again and again, feeding from my horror.

Rogue was narrowly missing each bolt as he rapidly flew closer to the castle.

Tears streamed down my cheeks. I couldn't control it. I couldn't stop it. I gripped the windowsill with both hands, my knuckles white with effort, silently urging him to fly faster.

The sounds of howling wind and roaring rain were the only things I could hear—not even my own sobbing met my ears, drowned out by the sky's unwanted answer to my hysteria. Thickening clouds blackened the sky as the rain fell in heavy sheets, and I could no longer see Rogue or even the ocean.

The lightning struck again, striking Rogue's silhouette, and a guttural scream ripped from my throat as he fell unconscious from the sky, tumbling end over end.

I sprinted to my door, ripping it open, and continued down the steps in a frenzy. Once in the hallway, several shocked guards turned to me from the entryway, and I rushed to them.

"Ro-Rogue. He was struck—" I couldn't breathe. I clutched my chest with shaking hands. "He was struck by lightning. He fell."

They immediately turned on their heels toward the front entrance. I trailed close behind but hesitated just before we reached the door. Instead of following them outside, I turned and ran in the opposite direction, back up the stairs. My muscles screamed as I willed my feet to go as fast as possible.

I pushed open Iaso's door, and it slammed against the wall.

"Iaso! Help!" Panicked tears soaked my cheeks as my chest burned. "Iaso!"

She rushed out of the greenhouse, eyes wide.

"It's Rogue. He was struck by lightning and-and he fell from the sky. It was my fault," I managed through choked sobs.

Her mouth fell open, and her eyes bulged. She quickly snatched some supplies, stuffed them in a satchel, threw it over her shoulder, and rushed past me out the door. I followed behind her and we ran out into the storm, my

CHAPTER NINETEEN

hysteria only urging it on.

We rounded the corner of the castle, and a shaky breath of relief escaped me.

He had managed to land on the ledge instead of in the choppy sea. Mere feet behind him, the waves crashed mercilessly against the rock, capped with white. They would have swallowed him whole and refused to ever give him back. Icy terror shot through me at the thought, creating a fresh wave of tears and panic, and I darted forward. My breath caught in my throat as we pushed the guards aside and saw Rogue sitting up, propped up on one hand.

I stammered on words that wouldn't form as I dropped to his side. The rain was torrential, soaking everyone to the bone, thunder rumbling overhead.

"I-I am so sorry. I didn't—" My eyes frantically searched him for any sign of injury. He leaned forward, placing his hands on either side of my face, turning my gaze to his.

"Breathe," he commanded, and I did. "I'm fine, Ara. It's all right."

I held his gaze, my breaths matching his, and the rain slowed to a drizzle.

"I'm sorry," I whispered. Another tear escaped my eye, and he wiped it away with his thumb.

"I'm sorry too," he said, his voice strained as he ran his thumb along my cheek again. "For everything."

His gaze was intense, sincere, and I nodded slightly in understanding. The rain stopped altogether, and we stilled, his eyes darting to my mouth as my lips parted, our breaths heavy.

"Oh, no, you don't," Iaso said.

I jumped, jerking from his grasp and to my feet. Turning

away from Rogue, I wiped the remaining tears from my cheeks as they flushed furiously.

"Drink this. *That* will have done some damage, even to you," she insisted, shoving a vial into his hand. He drank obediently, coughing and sputtering as he downed it.

"Hell, Iaso, what is that?" he said, wiping his mouth.

"You'll thank me when you live to see tomorrow." She winked at him and picked up her bag. "Now, go to your chambers and rest. That tea will knock you out soon enough." She glanced around, scowling at the guards.

"You're lucky Ara came to find me and didn't leave your life in the hands of these fools." She jerked her thumb at the guards surrounding him, still frozen in shock.

His eyes found me again, and my chest constricted under the weight of his gaze. My breath hitched audibly, and I swiveled, rushing back to the castle door, feeling Iaso on my heels.

"Ara, wait," she called as we entered. I paused, taking a breath before facing her.

"Iaso, I promise I didn't mean to do that. I was standing in my room, and I was… I was just overwhelmed with everything, and the next thing I knew, there was a storm…and then…and then it all happened so quickly."

I brought my hands to my forehead, swaying and trembling with exhaustion. Iaso reached an arm out to steady me, a comforting warmth drifting from her palm.

"Trust me, child. I know you didn't. Your magic is strong," she said, looking me over. "It's drained you, hasn't it?"

I nodded, and the room spun with the movement.

"All right, let's get you back to your chambers. You'll need the tea to help you rest and recover too." She guided me

CHAPTER NINETEEN

up the stairs and to the bed. After I laid down, she reached into her bag and pulled out a similar vial to the one she had given Rogue. As she handed it to me, her eyes glowed golden, illuminating her face.

"Just giving it a little extra oomph," she winked. I tipped it back and drank gratefully, desperately craving a release from the utter exhaustion. I knew it would at least grant me that.

As I downed the last bit, my eyelids became heavy, and I laid back, slipping into the darkness.

* * *

It was well past morning when I woke the following day. As I stirred, the tiredness in my muscles lingered, reminding me of the night before.

My mind wandered to Rogue, worry bubbling in my chest. *Iaso would be tending to him. He would be fine.* I stifled the rising emotion with a sigh and rose from the bed, walking to the window. It was still cloudy outside, but no rain, thankfully.

A knock at the door pulled my attention, and Thana entered.

"Did you just wake up? I checked in earlier, but you were still asleep. I'm so glad you and Rogue are all right."

"Yeah, I just woke up, and thank you. Me too," I said, gesturing to the chairs, but she hesitated. "Listen—"

"I wanted to apologize for my reaction yesterday," she said in a rush before I could finish.

"No, *I'm* sorry. I'm sorry for dredging up painful memories. I didn't mean to hurt you."

"You couldn't have known. It was an innocent question," she said, waving a hand in dismissal. "Enough of that. We have more exciting things to discuss." A smirk pulled at the corner of her mouth. "Notice I didn't bring breakfast?"

"Well, I hadn't, but I do now." Anticipation fluttered in my gut. "Why? What's going on?"

"It seems Rogue has requested you join him this morning. Apparently, he slept in as well." I started to protest when she walked to the dresser. "You know this was a gift from Adrastus to Edana. He had hoped pretty clothing would soothe her over. He was a fool, obviously."

Ah.

She hesitated before pulling the drawer open. Her smirk deepened into a grin, her eyes wide as she peeked over at me mischievously. My head was already shaking as she pulled out a gown of crimson silk.

"No," I protested, holding a hand up.

"Oh, yes," she giggled. "I had always heard of this dresser but never seen it in action. Come on, it'll be fun," she insisted, clutching the dress in her hands.

I paused, considering it. *I shouldn't care.* I shouldn't care what his reaction would be to that dress or that it's the exact shade of his eyes, but even as I thought it, my heart raced, and a thrill of excitement shot through me. I stifled a grin, rolling my eyes, and she squealed.

I'll be going home soon enough. He has to fulfill the bargain, so what harm could it do?

She rushed over to my side and pulled me to the mirror, holding the dress in front of me. Both of our heads tilted as we admired it.

"How did you get it to give you this?"

"I saw it in a shop once, and it just stuck with me," she said. "I'm glad it did because Rogue is going to burn up at the sight." She paused and laughed before adding, "Or burn all of us up—save you, of course. Whichever comes first."

Before I could protest, she urged me to undress, helping me pull the soft silk overhead. As it settled over me, her mouth fell open in awe before curling into a soft smile. She placed a hand on my shoulder, turning me to the mirror, and I stilled.

It was so unlike anything I'd ever worn before.

The silk was a deep maroon, accentuating the flush of my cheeks and lips. Its halter top came down into a deep V, exposing my cleavage and sternum, ending in a point at my waist. I turned to find the back was completely open, my entire back revealed. There were two slits on either side, exposing my legs all the way to my hips, and I knew it would flow as I walked.

My cheeks reddened. I had never exposed this much skin before.

"You look exquisite," she said proudly.

"Thank you," I whispered before turning to her. "Your turn."

She paused before grinning ear to ear. "Well, who am I to argue?"

As she rushed to the dresser, I glanced back in the mirror. My heart pounded at the thought of Rogue seeing me like this. Grabbing a comb, I attempted to control my bedhead before Thana grabbed it moments later.

"Here, let me." She brushed through it and pulled half of it up, twisting it into a small bun, leaving a few tendrils of hair framing my face. "Oh!"

She jogged to the dresser and pulled out a small container.

"I didn't know if it would give it to me, but it's lip rouge." She tilted my face to hers and rubbed the cream onto my lips. When she was finished, I glanced back at the mirror, and my lips were painted the same dark maroon as the dress.

"Thana... I don't know if I can leave the room like this," I said doubtfully. Embarrassment pricked at me, and I suddenly felt foolish.

"Oh, yes you are. You look too good to stay hidden up here." She turned, grabbing the lilac fabric from the bed, shades lighter than her hair. As she pulled it on, a smile tugged at my lips. It was beautiful, long and flowing, swooping down her back to reveal swirling purple tattoos extending the entire length of her spine.

"That looks incredible on you."

She turned, holding her hands out to her sides to show it off. It swooped in the front just as it had in the back, revealing her cleavage.

"All right, now I don't feel as bad about how much skin I'm showing," I gushed with a laugh.

She rolled her eyes as she took my elbow and led us to the doorway. "You should never feel ashamed showing your skin. It's just that: skin. Skin the Goddess gave you, no less. You should be proud."

Suddenly...I was. I felt beautiful, so while my heart thrummed with anticipation and excitement, I held my chin high as we descended the stairs.

As we exited the stairwell, I glimpsed Doran with a female who looked exactly like him in the foyer. She had the same white-blonde hair with the same icy eyes and pale skin. She was a little shorter than him, but she couldn't be much younger, if at all. They had to be related.

"Who is that?"

Thana followed my gaze and froze, a light tint of pink flushing her skin.

CHAPTER NINETEEN

"D?" she shouted.

The woman's eyes shot to us, her face lighting up. "Thana!" They ran to meet each other and embraced in a tight hug. Doran smiled as he watched their reunion. Pulling back from each other, they spoke in unison.

"How have you—"

"Oh, I have missed—"

They both laughed.

"How have you been? You look…" Thana's eyes did an up-down as her mouth tilted up in a warm smile. "Well. You look well."

"And you look ravishing," the woman said, and Thana's blush deepened. "I'm good. I was in Blackburn, actually. I had only been there a short while before Doran sent for me."

Thana cocked her to the side as her eyebrows pulled together. Doran's eyes darted to me, and he stepped forward, clearing his throat.

"Well, we have much to talk about, sister. Why don't we go to the library? I'm sure Alden would love to see you while we're here."

His sister, then.

She rolled her eyes at him and hugged Thana tightly again, peering over her shoulder. Her eyes widened as she spotted me, and she whipped her head back to Doran, one brow lifted. He gave a quick nod, and she released Thana, stepping around her as she strolled toward me.

"Hello, I'm Delphia, Doran's twin sister. You must be Ara. I've heard quite a lot about you."

"I can only imagine the things you've heard, but yes, I'm Ara," I replied.

She beamed at me with the same warm disposition as her

brother.

"Hopefully, Doran will give me a moment of free time during my stay." She looked over her shoulder, sticking her tongue out at Doran, and I stifled a laugh as he sneered. "I would love to sit with you sometime and get to know each other a little."

"Yes, I would love that," I said, and I meant it. She felt as warm and trustworthy as her brother.

Delphia nodded, grinning, and turned back to Doran as he stuck his elbow out to her.

"She seems sweet," I said as we continued to the breakfast room.

"Oh, she is. We've been friends for as long as I've known her."

"When did you two meet?"

"They came to the area when Adrastus was still very much alive. Doran had just joined the king's army, so she always stayed close by. One day, I slipped out to the market in a neighboring village, and well," she laughed, her eyes distant as she relived the memory, "I bumped into someone I couldn't see, and she materialized right in front of my eyes, apologizing profusely. She had been peeking around a tree, too nervous to enter alone, I guess, but we talked, I took her arm, and we went into the market together. We've been friends ever since."

"She was…invisible?" I asked, my eyes wide.

"Yes, invisible. That's her magic, to be able to blend into her surroundings."

"Oh, wow," I replied, making a mental note to be aware when she was near.

I hadn't been to the breakfast room before, but as we

CHAPTER NINETEEN

rounded the corner, my mouth fell open at the back wall—a wall of windows. It reminded me of our breakfast room at home, but where ours overlooked the border mountains, these looked over the ocean.

An image of my mother eating alone flashed in my mind and sadness threatened to crush me. Taking a forced breath, I stifled it, as I seemed to constantly be doing lately. *I would be home soon,* I reminded myself, but I didn't know if the thought was reassuring anymore.

As I stepped closer in a daze, aiming to get a better look, I realized it wasn't windows at all—rather, a large open wall, just as every other window space in the castle was, separating the room from the great vastness it overlooked with nothing more than a thin spell.

With a deep breath, I shifted my attention to the table. It was long and rectangular, set in the center of the room, with enough space to seat at least a dozen people. My eyes followed to one end where they found Rogue—his gaze already locked on me, his lips parted slightly.

He was wearing a black tunic, buttons open, and his usual black leather trousers. His hair was hanging in loose waves around his face, and his crimson wings were on full display, relaxed behind him. As my eyes met his, my heart raced, and heat filled me, craving his touch. I stood tall, resisting the urge to fling myself into his arms, even as my body longed for him.

His scent reached me then—smoke and evergreen—and I inhaled deeply, reveling in it. It was engraved in my senses by now.

Wetness pooled between my thighs, and I swallowed hard, my eyes never leaving his.

Suddenly, as if he could sense my reaction, he tensed. His eyes were dark as they slowly roamed down the length of my body, taking in every inch, lingering on my exposed hips. Under the heat of his gaze, the room felt warmer, my skin flushing, and Thana cleared her throat, as if she could feel it too.

"Enjoy your breakfast," she said quickly as she spun on her heel and strode through the door. I turned to reach for her, but she was already gone, the door clicking shut in her wake.

We were alone.

I closed my eyes for a split second, the blush deepening in my cheeks. When I opened them again, I regained whatever composure I could and took my seat across the table, avoiding his gaze.

Chapter Twenty

Ara

After I finished eating, he spoke, finally breaking the silence that hung between us the entire meal. "You're avoiding me."

"What do you mean? I'm right here."

"Look at me," he demanded, and I clenched my jaw, staring down at my plate. His chair screeched as he slid it back, and my eyes jerked up, my mouth falling open as he stalked around the table.

He pulled my chair out from the table and knelt in front of me, grabbing my chin with his thumb and forefinger, turning my face to his. I met his gaze, heart pounding in my chest.

"Do you still not want me?" I shook my head, and he released a low, breathy laugh. "Are you sure?"

His free hand slowly slid up my arm, and I closed my eyes. He inched his way to my shoulder, running his thumb along the bite mark. A bolt of white-hot desire shot through me, pulling a slight gasp from my lips, and his grip tightened on my chin.

"Look. At. Me," he demanded, and my eyes snapped open

to him. "I can feel it. Your desire for me. Your arousal." He rubbed his thumb along the bite mark again, and I moaned, leaning into his hand. "With this delicious little mark, I will always know when you are in need of me."

I should be shocked, disgusted…but it only flamed the raging fire that spread through me at his touch, at his words.

"Tell me to stop."

I paused, searching his face for something, anything, to snap me out of it, to remind me why this was wrong. Unfortunately, every thought I'd had for days dissipated in a flash at the intensity in his eyes, the sincerity.

He wanted me just as badly.

"I'm not agreeing to be your mate," I whispered, and he dropped his gaze, nodding.

He started to stand, but I reached my hand out to his face. As my fingertips grazed his cheek, he froze, closing his eyes. I slid my hand into his hair, knotting my hand in it.

His eyes snapped open, his gaze blistering.

My heart leapt into my throat, and I jerked him forward, crashing his mouth to mine before I could lose my nerve. He hesitated, just for a moment, before he deepened the kiss, groaning and placing a hand on either side of my face. The sound went straight to my core, reminding me of every delicious sound he'd made that night, and I moaned at the intensity of every feeling, every touch, every breath.

He slowly stood, pulling me with him, unwilling to part from my body. As soon as I was on my feet, he slid his hands down to my backside, pulling my hips into his. Without warning, he lifted me, and my legs wrapped around his waist on instinct.

Sitting me on the table, he broke the kiss, smirking as his

hands slid down my thighs to my knees, parting them wide. My cheeks flamed as the thin strip of my dress fell between my knees, the only thing covering my bare sex.

"I brought you here for breakfast. Now, it's my turn." His gaze sank to my core, and his smirk deepened into a devilish grin, his tongue clicking as he slid the fabric over, exposing me. "Oh, how thoughtful of you to dress for the occasion."

He slowly dropped to his knees before me, pulling me to the edge of the table before throwing both of my legs over his shoulders. "Lean back," he commanded, and I laid against the table, the surface cool beneath my heated skin.

He slid his flat tongue along my slit, slowly like he was savoring every inch. A loud moan escaped me, and my back arched, my hands grasping at the edge of the table. With a low chuckle, he planted a hand on my lower belly, holding me in place as he swiped and licked my clit.

Oh, Goddess.

This feeling was too good. It was blinding. It shouldn't be physically possible to feel *this* good.

"You are..." He licked long and slow, followed by two fingers sliding into me. "Delicious, Ara."

He pulled out, thrusting back in, and I gasped, overwhelmed by the feeling of it all. My fingers tightened on the table, my knuckles white, as I struggled to find something to hang onto, to ground me to reality.

"This"—he licked again, groaning into me—"is mine. No one will make you feel as good as I do." He picked up his pace, unraveling me by the very thread of my existence, intertwining it with his. "Ever," he growled, and I shattered.

"Rogue," I screamed, sparks clouding my blackening vision as my orgasm tore through me.

"Hmm," he groaned, increasing his pace, dragging out the overwhelming pleasure until I came down from the high. "I want to hear my name on your lips every time you come apart beneath me."

With his eyes locked on mine, he rose to his feet, his lips slick with my arousal. Slowly, he brought his fingers to his mouth again, as he had our first time. With a wicked grin, he licked the taste of me from them; every part of me flushed, but I couldn't tear my eyes away.

"You are, by far, my favorite meal." My breath hitched as he prowled closer. He leaned over me, bracing himself on one hand by my head while the other trailed down the curves of my body. "I would have you for breakfast every day you'd allow it," he whispered into my ear, sending goosebumps across my skin.

The sun poured through the window, illuminating us with beams of warm, morning sunlight. With a slow, deep inhale, he glanced out the window. A muscle ticked in his jaw before he lowered his gaze back to me. His eyes roamed over my face as he ran his thumb along the mate mark once more, and I stared at him in return, taking in every feature—he was beautiful, tragically beautiful.

Then, he pulled back and stood. I followed closely behind him, sitting up on the edge of the table, my brows pulling together.

"Unfortunately, I have to go." He gripped my chin again, tilting my face to his. "Try not to dream of me too much while I'm gone," he said with a smirk.

He tilted his head, gazing at me for a moment before his face fell slightly. Something I didn't recognize flashed behind his eyes, something sad, haunted, but it was gone as fast as it

CHAPTER TWENTY

had arrived.

He released me with a deep sigh, turning to the door.

"Wait, where are you going?"

"To resolve an issue," he replied. "Doran and I should be back in a few days. Maybe a week."

He glanced back over his shoulder at me, pausing for a heartbeat before stalking back to the table. He gripped my cheek and kissed me deeply, fiercely, branding the feel of him into my skin, as if I would never feel it again.

Releasing me, he turned, rubbing his chest as he left without another word.

* * *

My heart was still racing in the aftermath of what we had just done when rational thought returned and irritation bit at me. It wasn't what we'd done that bothered me, though; it was the fact that he'd avoided the question, just as Evander would've done.

Foolish. That entire... thing was foolish. I am so—

I huffed, bringing my palm to my forehead. The way he got under my skin, the way I allowed it, was dangerous. I knew it, and yet, I couldn't resist.

Ever the moth to his flame.

Dropping my hand, I turned to see the damage and grimaced. What was left of the food was pushed to one side of the table, a quarter of it on the floor. Hesitantly, I scooped it and awkwardly placed it back on the dishes, cleaning up as much as I could. Once I was satisfied, I stepped back, smoothed my hair, and took a deep breath before exiting the room.

Turning in the direction of the library, my feet stilled. Something tugged at me, pulling me in the opposite direction, and I peeked over my shoulder. The hallway was empty, dimly lit as if no one frequented this side of the castle. Biting my lip, I gave in to the curiosity, strolling down the abandoned hall.

Following it around the corner, I was met with a long, dusty hallway that led to a dead-end with a single black door, shrouded in shadows and worn with age. Slowly, I edged closer. The edges were splintered and a thick layer of dust clung to the top. Compelled forward, I tried the handle, and disappointment flooded me when it didn't budge.

Locked.

I stepped back, contemplating whether I should leave, but I hesitated, staring at the door.

Trying the handle one more time, I jiggled it. To my immense surprise, it clicked and turned, the door creaking as it opened. Adrenaline shot through me as I stepped across the threshold, and a fire lit on its own in the corner.

Just as I thought: an abandoned bed chamber.

Along the back wall was a window that overlooked the sea, but unlike every other window in the castle, it wasn't protected by a spell. This one had two old glass panes outlined in tarnished gold that clicked shut in the middle.

Cobwebs stretched across the upper corners of the room, and, like the rest of the hallway, a thick coat of dust had settled over the furniture and floors. In one corner, a large sheet had been thrown over the bed. I gently slid it off, coughing as the dust bombarded me and the sheet crumpled to the floor. Waving my hand to clear the air, my eyes immediately found the crest on the backboard.

CHAPTER TWENTY

My legs felt weak beneath me, my heart pounding in my ears as I gaped at it. With trembling hands, I reached up to run a finger along Vaelor's crest, a bolt of lightning racing down to meet a sword.

When I touched it, my skin pricked with goosebumps, and I jerked my hand back. Stumbling away from the bed, I backed into another piece of covered furniture, a table of some sort. I cautiously tugged the sheet off, revealing an old wooden desk. Tucked inside one of the drawers were old papers, notebooks, pens, vials of ink, and a sketch. My hands shook as I picked it up, already knowing who it would be.

Raising the picture, I was met with the soft smile of my mother. She was younger in the sketch, younger than I'd ever seen her, and it struck me how alike we looked. Gently laying it on the desk, I reached to the back of the drawer and pulled out a notebook. Turning, I tugged another sheet off a nearby chair and sat, flipping the book open to the first page. My breath hitched.

My dearest Elora...

I snapped the notebook closed, suddenly feeling like an intruder as tears pricked my eyes. Walking back to the desk, I picked up another book and returned to the chair. My mouth parted as I opened it, reading notes detailing Vaelor's own power. As I flipped through the pages, I found entry after entry detailing his experiences with his magic and his reign.

The pages stopped on a random entry.

> *My magic seems to have a mind of its own lately. When she is around, it loses all sense of control. I have no will over it, whether it be rain or lightning. Even the electricity at my fingertips sparks for her. I have no control, and it's maddening. This woman is maddening.*

My eyes blurred with tears, and I closed the book before they could dampen the pages. Lifting my eyes, I found a painting above the fireplace. My throat tightened, fighting off the tears as I stared. It was Vaelor and my mother, standing close to each other, my mother smiling at the artist while Vaelor smiled at her. Both of them beamed, and I could feel the warmth of the love they shared. It was written in their countenance: the way his arm wrapped around her waist, the way she laid her hand on his arm and leaned into his shoulder.

She loved him. They loved each other.

Silent tears streamed down my face as I studied the painting through blurred eyes.

I didn't know how long I sat, just staring, but when I glanced out the window, the sun was lowering in the sky and heavy clouds were rolling in to meet it. As I stood, stiffness popped in my joints, and I reached up in a stretch. I started to turn towards the door when my eyes caught on the closet.

The closet.

My heart stopped for a split second, and then it was thundering in my ears. My vision tunneled, and I couldn't look away.

My mother.
That closet.

CHAPTER TWENTY

I couldn't form full thoughts. The room swayed around me, and my eyes involuntarily dropped to the floor, searching for evidence, but there was nothing. The floor was bare, just cold, gray stone. No rugs. No blood.

No sign of the murder.

But the closet.

My eyes slowly raised back to it, and the thought of my mother hiding in there, watching helplessly as the man she loved was butchered, flashed in my mind over and over. My eyes found the painting again—the love, the happiness, *safety*.

Feeling dizzy as my chest tightened, I turned back to the closet. With shaky knees, I slowly stepped to the side, as if I could skirt around it and leave the memory hanging over the room undisturbed. I took another slow step before turning, snatching the journal, and darting out. I swung the door closed behind me and vaguely heard it click shut as I hurried down the hallway.

A cold sweat broke out along my spine, the thundering in my ears drowning out the sounds of my frenzied steps. As I passed Iaso's chambers, I jerked to a halt.

This journal, this day, was not something I wanted to dwell on right now. I needed something, anything, before the overwhelming emotion welling in my chest imploded, taking the castle with it.

I clenched and unclenched my fists, taking a deep breath before bringing a hand to the door. Hesitating for a moment, I knocked lightly and opened the door, peeking my head through.

"Iaso?"

"Over here, child," she hummed, stepping in from the greenhouse, smiling as she wiped her hands on her apron.

"I hope I didn't disturb you," I said, strolling to the table.

She glanced down at the book in my grasp, and her head slowly tilted to the side. "Enjoying some light reading?"

"Yes. Staying distracted." I tucked the book into my lap, covering it with my hands. "I actually came to ask if you had any tea that could help. I haven't been sleeping that well as of late."

"Oh, of course." She walked to a nearby shelf, and when she returned to the table, she poured varying amounts of tea leaves into a mesh bag and handed it to me. "This should help. I must warn you though, it can make dreams a little...intense."

* * *

His red eyes burned into me from between my legs, his arms wrapped around my hips while his hands firmly gripped my inner thighs, pulling them apart.

"Open wide for me," he commanded, his voice deep and gravelly.

I moaned at his words, relaxing as he spread my legs apart and swiped his tongue along the most sensitive part of me. My back arched, his name drifting from me in a pant, and he pulled back with a dark grin on his lips.

"Say it again."

"What—"

"Say my name again."

"Rogue, please." My breath hitched as he slid a finger in, pulling out before thrusting it back in.

"Eyes on me, little storm," he commanded. I brought my eyes to his, and he slowly leaned down. My pulse raced as I watched him run his flat tongue along me. "When you feel

CHAPTER TWENTY

pleasure like this, I want you to know who's giving it to you."

He curled his fingers inside me as his tongue swirled, and my eyes rolled back.

"Only I can make you feel like this."

I wound my fingers through his hair, and he hummed against me as he sucked, tearing a loud cry from my lips. He pulled his fingers from me, sliding them into my mouth as he crawled up the length of my body. I sucked them clean, and he chuckled darkly. He pulled his fingers from my lips, gripping my chin with his wet hand, and kissed me deeply, groaning into my mouth as he sheathed himself inside me. I gasped at the feel of him, and he smirked against my mouth.

"This is *mine*."

He lowered his mouth to the mate mark and bit it harshly, sending stars across my vision at the sensation.

He pounded into me mercilessly, using his thumb to circle my clit, threatening to send me over the edge. I slid my hand down to his shoulder, and my fingers grazed the base of one wing. He growled into my ear at the touch, increasing his pace, and an eruption of butterflies lit me from the inside.

So close.

So good.

"So fucking good." The words escaped me of their own volition, barely louder than a whisper.

I felt his grin against my skin before he bit the mark again, and a blinding orgasm ripped through me, obliterating everything in its path. My chest arched into him, and my nails dug into his back.

"That's my good girl," he whispered into my ear.

* * *

I jumped awake when Thana entered my chambers, gasping for air.

"Oh, are you all right? Did I just wake you?"

"I'm fine. Iaso gave me some sleeping tea yesterday." I dropped my eyes as my cheeks flushed. "My dreams were... vivid."

"Oh yeah, that tea is intense. I've had it a time or two." She strolled to the bed and set the tray down, revealing coffee, eggs, toast, and fruit. My stomach growled at the sight, and she laughed.

"Sounds like I'm right on time. Speaking of breakfast, how was yesterday with Rogue? I noticed the doors were kept... closed." She smirked, and the blush in my cheeks deepened. "Oh, I knew that dress would invoke a reaction. He can hardly stay away as it is."

My face tilted to her as my eyebrows scrunched. "What does that mean?"

"Hmm?" she asked casually as she continued eating.

"That he can hardly stay away?"

Her chewing slowed as she stared at her plate. She wiped her mouth, avoiding my gaze. "Oh, it's just..."

"Thana, what is it?"

"I—" She sighed, facing me. "He has us keep him updated... on you, on your well-being, what you do throughout the day. It's pretty well known throughout the castle that you ordered him to stay away, and he has been," she explained, and my eyes widened. "But it's obvious he cares for you, even if he would never admit it. This is the only way he can make sure you're...all right without seeing you himself."

My lips flattened as my hands gripped the arm of the chair, turning my knuckles white.

CHAPTER TWENTY

I should've known. This is his castle, his people, and he is his father's son. He'd kept Edana locked away, constantly under his thumb. Why would I assume Rogue wouldn't do the same?

Thana's eyes caught onto the tension in my jaw and stopped talking. She paused, as if to say something else, before turning back to her food and eating in silence. My face snapped to the window as the clouds swirled and darkened. This time, I hoped the thunderstorm found him, wherever he was, and soaked him to the bone.

Let him know who sent it, I silently urged the sky. *Let there be no doubt it was me.*

"I've lost my appetite," I said without turning away from the window. "I think I would like some time alone."

"Oh, are you sure? I brought—"

"Yes, please."

She nodded curtly, and guilt sank in my stomach at the tightness in her features. She started towards the door, leaving the tray behind.

"Thana, I'm sorry. I don't blame you. I know you didn't have a choice. My anger isn't at you. It's at him."

She nodded and continued, but just before she reached the steps, she spoke with her back to me.

"You shouldn't be angry with him, not really. Rogue... He's had a hard life that you know *nothing* about. Yes, he invaded your privacy, and that was wrong, but he didn't have the best example of how to approach things growing up. I would know. I was here."

I shrunk back in the chair at her words, my shoulders slumping.

"He's trying to give you the space you asked for, Ara. He's doing as you asked, and that action alone is the very opposite of what his father would have done. He cares for you, and he's trying his best to show it, in the ways he can."

My mouth fell open before snapping shut, and I bit my lip as she descended the stairs.

I'd known Adrastus was cruel to him—just as he was to the rest of his kingdom— but I hadn't considered that, with his mother gone and him isolated from the rest of Ravaryn, no one had been left to show him kindness.

Guilt tore the breath from my chest. I glanced at the window, grimacing as the rain slowed to a drizzle before stopping entirely. I hoped it never reached him in the first place.

Averting my gaze, it landed on Vaelor's journal. I quickly picked it up, flipping it open in need of a distraction.

> *Today, I received news that a Draig has emerged and is terrorizing a small village just south of Blackburn. It's frustrating and incredibly disappointing that a Fae would attack his own people. Innocents. According to the reports, the Draig destroyed several houses while raiding and pillaging, stealing the incomes of several families. I sent Ewan with supplies to rebuild their homes and enough food to replenish their stores, but this Draig needs to be taken care of. We cannot manage to rebuild another village if he were to attack again.*

My blood went cold. Not the distraction I was hoping for, but I continued to the next page.

CHAPTER TWENTY

> *Ewan found the Draig. It's Adrastus, son of Drakyth, and he's residing in an estate south of Blackburn. The information is not entirely surprising, considering the location of his attacks (and there have been many since my last entry), but why? Why now? I cannot fathom reason enough to do this to your own people. Is he running out of money? Is his ornery dragon form clouding his mind? I think once we determine his 'why,' we can learn how to stop him, or at least figure out his pattern.*
>
> *It pains me to think of raising arms against one of my own people.*

I closed my eyes, inhaling a shaky breath, and flipped to the next page.

> *He's looking for a mate.*
>
> *According to a servant from Adrastus' estate, he is looking for his mate. He must feel her close by for it to agitate his dragon so. My heart aches for the person he does find... but that is not the only information we received. If the servant is to be believed, it would seem Adrastus sired a child well before he began the attacks, about ten years before, but the boy had been born without wings, and when he saw it, he flew into a fit of rage, destroying the nursery and abandoning the boy and his mother.*
>
> *According to Father, for any shifting form to be passed down a generation, the child must be produced from the union of mates. Magic that strong cannot be inherited*

> *without their combined power, not without the help of the Goddess herself. Apparently, he's been searching for the past decade, but to no avail, and now he's getting frustrated, hence, the violence. He's trying to force her hand.*
>
> *I ordered Ewan and Father to speak of this to no one. For the safety of that child, no one must know who his father is and hopefully, for the child's sake, Adrastus will never find him. May he live a happy life, away from the cruelty he would surely face from his father.*

The journal shook in my grasp.

Adrastus fathered a child before Rogue. Rogue had a brother, and yet, no one knew except for Alden and a man named Ewan. Closing the journal, my eyes found the fire, letting the ebb and flow carry my thoughts.

I have to tell him—before I tell anyone else. If not, I'm no better than any person who withheld the truth from me. What good the information would do, I didn't know. I had no name or description, but it was not my place to keep it from him.

Hours passed as I watched the never-ending flames dance, lost in thought as my mind swirled around Rogue and his family. I couldn't help but wonder where he was now, what he was doing, imagining the look on his face when I told him of his lost sibling.

Just as the orange light of sunset peeked through the window, a light knock sounded from the door. Startled, I spun to see Thana peeking her head in.

I sat up straighter, motioning to the chair beside mine, and she swung the door open with an elbow to enter with a silver

CHAPTER TWENTY

tray, carrying a kettle and two cups.

"I wanted to apologize for my harshness earlier." She avoided my gaze as she crossed the room and set the tray on the side table. My stomach sank at her avoidance, and I reached out to place a hand on hers.

"Please, don't apologize. There is nothing to apologize for. Someone had to burst my self-righteous bubble, and if it was anyone, I would prefer it to be you," I said, and she released a shaky laugh. Her eyes glanced up to meet mine before dropping back to the tea tray.

"Well, I'm glad I could be that for you," she said, seeming to relax some and sitting in the chair opposite me. As she reached for the kettle, she accidentally knocked over a teacup, and it clattered to the ground, shattering. She jerked to her feet, and I jumped at the sudden movement. "Oh, I'm so sorry about that. I'm feeling a bit out of sorts this evening."

Concern creased between my eyebrows. "Are you all right? Are we…all right?"

"Yes, I'm fine. Don't worry about me," she muttered, leaning over to clean up the pieces.

I leaned over to help, placing the broken pieces on the tray. Once we finished, she sat up to pour the dark tea into the remaining cup.

"Well, at least I managed to pour that one," she said, chuckling softly. "Yes, of course, we're all right. I hate that we fought this morning, and I just…I had to come back to make sure you were okay, to reconcile things. You've become a dear friend of mine, even if I was terrified of you when you first arrived."

We laughed in unison, and I relaxed, taking the cup from her.

"I couldn't imagine anyone being scared of me."

She grinned. "Well, I couldn't imagine being scared of you now, either."

My mouth fell open in mock hurt.

"Hey, I do have magic now. Maybe you *should* be scared," I teased back, sending another round of laughter between us. "So, what tea is this?"

Bringing it to my nose, I inhaled the aroma. It was earthy with an undertone of something sweet—cherries, maybe?

"Oh, this is a special tea from Iaso. She said it's one for the heart of *confused lovers*," she said, enunciating the last two words.

"No, she did not," I said with a giggle, swatting her arm.

"Yes, she really did. Try it. She did say it was delicious, at least." I blew on the steam, and she watched as I took a tentative sip. It was sweeter than it smelled.

"Oh, it's really good," I said, taking another sip.

"Good." Her smile faltered slightly as she nodded, turning her gaze to the fire.

The sun was fully set now, perfectly framed by the windowsill as it cast the room in a golden glow. As the warm rays fell over us, a feeling of lightness settled over me.

Chapter Twenty One

Rogue

The Marsh was directly south of Draig Hearth, just a few miles inland from the coast, split in half by the border, deeming it the official meeting place between Ravaryn and Auryna for as long as anyone could remember.

Because it was just Doran, Delphia, and I, we decided to ride as close as possible to the border mountains. I would then fly them over one at a time, as navigating through the rocky foothills would add at least half a day to our journey.

It only took a little over an hour to fly over with one person in tow, but by the time I dropped Doran north of the Marsh, flew back to get Delphia, and returned, I was utterly exhausted. It took everything I had to not slam us into the ground upon landing.

We had a few hours before sunset and an entire night before their troops would arrive, so Doran and Delphia left to scope the area in the remaining hours of daylight. As they left, I staggered to a nearby tree and leaned against it, trying to catch my breath as my wings sagged behind me. Every muscle in my back was screaming, but the precious time we saved was worth it.

As my breaths slowed, I reached up to rub my sore shoulders, and my thoughts returned to Ara.

She would be safe in Draig Hearth, but the thought of her there, alone and without my protection, created a knot of unease in my gut. We needed to return as soon as possible, but the reason we were here weighed heavily on my mind.

She will not welcome my return.

My stomach churned as the irony dawned on me. I had spent my whole life trying to be the opposite of my father, and yet, here I was.

My father murdered her true father, and I'm here to murder the one she has.

I took a deep breath as my chest tightened and closed my eyes, letting my head fall back on the tree.

I am my father's son.

It hurt to know how desperately I didn't want to become someone—something—and yet, no matter how hard I tried, I couldn't outrun the monster nipping at my heels.

Releasing a defeated laugh, I pushed off the tree, surveying the small clearing we'd landed in. There was a large rock face to our back, the shoreline to the left, and the tree line to our front. I had chosen this spot so no one could sneak up on us unseen, but it also gave me a full view of the sky.

I knew her magic wouldn't reach this far, but it settled some deep part of me to see the sky was still clear.

The last storm she'd caused terrified me—not because I was stuck in it, but because I'd known in my bones it was her. Her anguish. Her disappointment. Her regret for what we were. The quickness in which it formed told me she was

CHAPTER TWENTY ONE

panicked, and when I'd looked toward Draig Hearth, I'd seen her silhouette standing in her window, watching. I tried to get back to her, but it was no use—then I heard her scream.

My heart shattered hearing the agony in her voice. When the lightning struck me, I knew it wasn't her fault, and to think she blamed herself pained me.

The look of relief on her face, when she saw me conscious, lit a tiny beacon of hope in my chest. I knew it was because she blamed herself, not because she cared for my well-being. I knew that, and yet, I still clung to that hope. Even now, as foolish as it was, a small part of me hoped my mission here wouldn't turn her away from me forever.

A fool's hope. She will hate me, just as my mother hated my father, I reminded myself. If there was one thing my father taught me, it was that nothing kills more than hope.

My jaw hardened and I slung the pack off my shoulder, pulling out my sleeping furs. We opted to forgo tents to avoid notice, but there was no way I was sleeping on the bare ground if I didn't have to.

Keeping my hands busy, I gathered firewood and began setting up the fire pit when they returned.

"How you're not already unconscious is beyond me," Doran said as they strolled into the clearing, dropping their packs by mine.

"Me and you both," I replied. The exhaustion swept through me again, down to my very bones, and I plopped down on my furs. It was dark now, the ground lit by nothing but the moonlight and the small fire.

Tucking my hands behind my head, I gazed at the night sky as the stars twinkled to life and eased my tension.

***

I jerked awake, already hard, the urge to find Ara blinding.

She was aroused but dreaming. I don't know how I knew, but I did.

Chuckling to myself, I laid back down as the memory of our last encounter flashed through my mind. *'Try not to dream of me too much.'*

I reached down, wrapping a hand around the base of my length, stroking it, reliving our last moments—the taste of her on my tongue. She was the best damned thing I'd ever tasted.

I would fly across these mountains a hundred times if I meant I could spend the rest of my days buried between her thighs.

I imagined sinking down between her legs and wrapping my arms around her hips, gripping and spreading her thighs as I tasted her again. She moaned my name in my grasp and the sound went straight to my cock.

"Say it again." She did. *"Eyes on me, little storm."* She followed my commands beautifully. I stared into her eyes as I licked her pretty cunt, and the thought alone nearly sent me over the edge. When she knotted her hands in my hair, I pulled my fingers from her and pushed them into her mouth. Blazing pride swelled in my chest as she sucked them clean, and I eased inside her, overwhelmed by the feeling of her.

"This is mine."

The fierce need to actually be with her, to satisfy her, for her to let me, to want me, burned so intensely that the air warmed around me as I pumped my hand faster.

I sunk my teeth into her mark. She cried out in pleasure,

CHAPTER TWENTY ONE

sinking her nails into my skin as she climaxed around my cock. The sight of her combined with the delicious sound of her moans coaxed my own from me, and I finished in my hand.

I collapsed back on the ground, breathing heavily as the sun's first rays peeked over the horizon, setting the sky on fire. Closing my eyes, I threw my arm over them, smiling faintly.

It was still clear.

* * *

Not even minutes after I'd closed my eyes, raindrops hit my skin. A few at first, but by the time I pulled my arm from my eyes, it was a downpour. Menacing clouds swelled, blocking the sun, and it darkened with every passing second. Doran and Delphia jumped awake as we were soaked, shouting in surprise.

This was too sudden to be natural. It was Ara. Adrenaline fueled by fear rushed through me, jerking me to my feet.

"Something is wrong," I whispered to myself, face turned to the sky.

"What is it?" Doran yelled over the howling wind, holding his hand up to shield his eyes.

"It has to be Ara, but I don't know why." A sinking feeling in my gut whispered that I knew why—her dream of me, of us. The anxiety in my chest shifted to hurt. Clenching my jaw, I marched past Doran to the tree line. "Let's take cover and hope it passes soon."

Just as we crossed into the forest, the rain slowed and stopped, the clouds clearing to reveal the sunrise once again.

Puddles and mud were the only signs it had stormed at all.

My hand ran through my hair, pulling the wet strands from my face as my brows pulled together in confusion. *I would give anything to know what you're thinking, Ara.*

Doran and Delphia looked at me as if I could explain, and I cleared my throat.

"Let's just find the encampment. No point in lying back down now."

They nodded, following me deeper into the forest.

It was mid-morning when we spied the camp from the tree line. They had arrived in the early hours, setting up their tents south of us.

The meeting was planned for this evening, an hour before sunset, so it gave us the entire day to survey the army. We sat in the trees, hidden, and used the invaluable time to study them—how they moved, where they went, how they prepared, paying special attention to the movement of higher ranks. As the sun peaked and began its descent, I realized their numbers were smaller than usual. Soldiers had stopped arriving hours ago.

Something tugged at me, a thought in the back of my mind, and I analyzed the layout of their camp again.

"Doran, there's no general's tent," I whispered. "And where's the rest of his men? He's never traveled with so few men before."

"What..." He squinted his eyes, searching the grounds, just as I'd done.

"Why would Starrin not stay in his own tent?"

"I'm not sure. That's unusual," he uttered. "As for the number of men, I would assume this whole ordeal has been a huge hit to his pride, so in his eyes, the fewer people who know, the better. Actually, now that I think about it, maybe he didn't want to alert anyone he was traveling here at all. Having the king's general leave so suddenly, to the Marsh of all places, would pique too much interest. It makes sense he would hide his presence by staying in an indistinguishable tent."

I nodded slowly, uneasiness curling in my gut. *Of course, he would make this even more difficult.*

"We'll just have to find his tent when we get down there." When Doran didn't reply, I faced him, hesitation plain on his face.

"That's not safe. We planned to find the tent first so the mission would be quick. In and out. If we have to search for his tent, that increases the chances of us being seen," Doran argued. "I cannot allow you to take Delphia into that trap."

I opened my mouth to speak when she interjected.

"Brother, I know you're only concerned for my safety, but I think this is a decision for me to make, not you." She looked at him with affection before turning her gaze to me. "This is the best plan, the *only* plan. We have to save Ravaryn…and Ara." She smirked at me, and before I could disagree, she continued, "It's my duty as Fae to do this. No one else can. Let me do what I was born to do, Doran."

Doran's mouth was tight, and Delphia patted his shoulder.

"We'll be fine," she insisted. "We should go now, though, before they expect us. The sun will set in a few hours."

I gave a quick nod as we waited for Doran's response. He stared at the ground with his eyebrows creased.

"Doran." She swatted his arm again and he snapped his eyes to hers. "You're not going to talk me out of this. Let's go."

He huffed in frustration, dropping from the tree. Delphia and I glanced at each other before following him down.

"I can only throw the blind in a five to six-foot radius, so you two will have to stay relatively close. If you step outside of that radius, you won't be hidden anymore." We nodded in understanding and stared at her, waiting for cover. "What?" she asked, looking from Doran to me. "Oh, we're already invisible. You can see within the blind, just not from the outside."

Taking a deep breath, we moved toward the encampment, anxiety churning in my stomach. As we neared it, a human passed us, and we collectively tensed. I stared at his face, a few feet from mine, but he seemed none the wiser. Releasing a shaky breath, we continued down the path through the tents. My feet sank into the muck, and I glanced back, wincing as our feet left fresh prints in the mud.

"They can see our footprints," I whispered. They both peeked back at the ground, and a suffocating blanket of tension settled over the group. "Try to step in footprints that are already there." They nodded, and we slowly made our way in silence.

We searched every pathway, every tent. There was no trace of General Starrin anywhere. I glanced at Delphia—sweat soaked her hairline, and her jaw clenched with effort. With a heavy sigh, I tapped them on the shoulder and jerked a thumb back to the tree line.

She held the blind until we reached the trees; when she released it, she dropped her hands to her knees, breathing heavily. Doran moved to her side and placed a hand on her back, his eyebrows pinched together in concern. She stood up, waving a hand at him.

"I'm fine," she panted, wiping her hair from her forehead. "I've just never covered so many people for so long before."

Doran shot me a hard look.

"Where is he?" I demanded, clenching my fist before running my hands through my hair, pacing. "It makes no sense. He's never been hard to spot before."

He has never been hard to spot before. I whipped back to Doran, eyes wide.

"He's not here." I stalked back to Doran. "He's not here. Why would he…" My heart stopped. "He knows."

The blood drained from Doran's face.

"There's no way. How could he possibly know?" he insisted, following behind me as I paced again, scorching a trail in the pine-covered ground.

My eyes darted around aimlessly, searching for answers that weren't there.

"It doesn't matter. That's the *only* possible reason he would sacrifice his daughter: he didn't want her anymore."

"Rogue."

I turned to see the gears turning behind his eyes.

"He's snuck a spy into Draig Hearth once already…"

My chest was tight. Too tight.

"He didn't just sneak in a spy. He snuck in an assassin," I uttered as my blood went cold. Icy panic speared through me.

"Go."

Snapping my wings out, I shot to the sky faster than I ever had before.

* * *

My muscles were screaming when I slammed into the courtyard, sending a cloud of dirt into the air around me. The startled shouts of guards were barely audible over the thundering in my ears. Sprinting up the steps, I flung the front doors open, and they slammed into the wall on either side.

I ascended the entryway steps two at a time, turning toward the keep's door just as Ara stumbled out, clutching at her side. We locked eyes, and a gasp of relief escaped her. I ran to her, catching her just as she staggered, and she grunted as my hand met something warm and wet.

Slowly dropping my eyes to her abdomen, I pulled my hand away to see blood soaking through her shirt.

No.

"Who did this? Iaso! Guards! Get Iaso! Now!"

She gazed up at me, placing a palm on my cheek. Her hand was cold, much too cold.

It's too cold.

Too cold.

My head shook of its own volition, my throat burning.

"Ara, hey. Stay with me." My hands trembled as I lowered us to the ground, cradling her in my lap, my vision blurring. "Please, Ara. Please."

Please.

Please.

Her face was pale, her lips not rosy like they always were. She was too calm.

I can't breathe. My chest was too heavy, rising and falling too quickly.

"You'll be okay. Iaso will save you. Do not leave me just yet, Ara. Do not—" My chest burned. *I can't breathe.* "I need-I need—"

CHAPTER TWENTY ONE

I needed her like I needed oxygen, and now, I was losing both.

"Breathe," she commanded, her voice strained. "I'm fine, Rogue. It's all right," she whispered, repeating my own words back to me. Her hand fell from my cheek, and a choked sound broke from my lips.

"No," I said, lifting her hand back to my cheek, holding it there. "No, you cannot leave me here. Ara, please. I-I—"

Her eyes slid closed as she fell limp in my hold.

A guttural roar tore from my throat, and then I felt it.

Her bond to me, drifting away.

Her body was here, but she, her soul, was not. It felt as though she were floating into an unreachable void, somewhere I could not protect her, could not save her, teetering on the edge of eternity.

Choking on a scream, I scooped up her lifeless body and ran to Iaso's chambers. I kicked her door open, shattering the door handle, and she jumped as I entered.

"What happened?" She rushed to me, guiding us to her surgery table.

"I-I don't know. I didn't get here fast enough," I said, my breath hitching. As I laid Ara on the bed, Iaso touched her throat with two fingers.

"She has a pulse."

Relief like I had never felt washed over me, and I gasped painfully as my lungs suddenly decided to work again. She pulled out a needle, pricked Ara's arm, and brought the drop of blood to her mouth, licking it off.

"Oh, Rogue. She... There's poison."

The brief respite I had been granted was ripped from beneath my feet. My head spun, and I gripped the edge of the table, begging for something to steady.

"What do we do?"

"I know the remedy, but it will take time, and she has already lost so much blood..." She glanced down at Ara's face, smoothing back her sweat-slicked hair. My grip tightened on the table, turning my knuckles white. "I don't think—"

"Take mine."

"Rogue—"

"Take it. Give her my blood. Save her, Iaso," I ordered, my face tight. "Please."

She stared at me and nodded, running behind the wall of her surgery. I leaned over Ara and placed my palm on her cheek.

"We will save you," I whispered. A tear dripped onto her face, and I wiped it away with my thumb.

Iaso returned, and I sat in the chair by Ara's side. She connected a tubular plant to the end of a needle, repeating the same process on the other side. Grabbing my arm, she set my wrist on the table and hesitated, the needle at the crease of my elbow.

"I can't promise this will work."

"It has to."

It has to.

My eyes stayed on Ara while Iaso pushed the needle into my arm.

It has to.

Iaso grabbed the other needle and inserted it into Ara's arm. Her golden eyes lit the room as she silently commanded it to pull the blood from me and into Ara. The tube slowly stained red as the blood filtered through, and I released a shaky breath.

CHAPTER TWENTY ONE

"You'll have to stay like this for a while," she said. "Until her color comes back, at least."

"As long as it takes."

Chapter Twenty Two

Rogue

Just as the rays of sunrise illuminated the surgery, I jerked awake, frantically searching Ara's face for any development, good or bad, but there was none. She was still unconscious.

I carefully pulled her shirt back, cringing as it stuck to her skin with crusted blood. The wound hadn't closed and my stomach twisted at the sight. My hand shook as I slowly pulled her shirt back down, covering her. With one final look at her face, I rose to my feet, leaving her side in search of Iaso. I found her strolling through the greenhouse, bending over to check her rosebuds.

"She's stable for now, and the antidote will be ready by the end of the day," she said as she stood, dusting her hands on her apron. "For now, take your shoes off and join me, child."

Sighing, not willing to argue, I tugged my boots off and joined her as we strolled down the aisle, the soil warm and soft beneath my bare feet.

"She's going to be all right. I can feel it," she assured me, looping her elbow through mine. The morning sun beamed

CHAPTER TWENTY TWO

through the glass roof, warming the room, and steam swirled up from the damp ground.

"I hope so," I whispered. *More than hoped. Needed.*

Still, even her reassurance did nothing to settle the nauseating worry—nothing would until Ara opened her eyes. So, we walked in silence, wading through her sea of plants.

After a little while, I worked up the courage to leave Ara with Iaso, and I left in search of the guards who had been ordered to search Ara's chambers. What they had to say, however, shocked me. They had found the assassin waiting in Ara's chambers, crumpled on the floor with the bloody knife and a shattered teacup. I almost didn't believe it to be true, but they claimed she admitted it herself, surrendering to the guards without a fight.

The second the words left their mouths, I turned on my heel and stormed to the dungeon, my fire thrashing beneath my skin, angry at its confines. I threw open the steel doors to the dungeon, barely noticing as they slammed against the stone walls. The guards at the stand jumped, snapping to attention.

"Where is she?" My words were clipped, harsh.

"Last cell on the left, sire."

I stalked to the cell and looked through the bars, my lip pulling up in disgust as I stared at Thana's sleeping face. She was chained by her wrists, standing, slumped at the shoulders. While she'd only been imprisoned for a night, she was already disheveled and dirty, a bruise forming on her swollen cheek. I unlocked the door, the click echoing through the room, the steel groaning as it slid open.

She woke, confused, and her eyes darted to me, gasping as I crossed the small cell.

"Explain," I demanded. Thana was the only lady's maid who had remained with my family. She was my mother's, and I had trusted her, which is why I assigned her to Ara in the first place. The betrayal was like a knife to the gut, wrenching an anger deep within me. At her. At myself.

Once again, Ara was hurt because of my decisions.

Guilt burrowed deep in my chest, fueling my inextinguishable rage.

I gripped her throat when she didn't respond, images of an unconscious Ara flashing through my mind.

"Explain, or I will start ripping your organs from your body, one at a time until you are nothing but a bloody heap on the floor," I threatened. She shook in fear, cringing away from my face. I tightened my grip before releasing her, and she coughed, regaining her breath.

"Please…" She choked out. "I-I—"

I ripped a knife from my belt and held it to her throat, my patience wearing thin.

"Evander!" She was sobbing now, her entire body trembling.

I'd expected it, but halfway hoped I was wrong. I turned away, running a hand through my hair. Ara was going to be devastated.

"Is Ara… Is she dead?"

I whipped my head to her, and smoke rose around us as my feet singed the hay on the floor.

"No, thankfully." I stepped closer, stopping inches from her face. "If she does die, however, you will die along with her, and it will not be quick. You will suffer the most excruciating death I can imagine." I reached up, and she screamed, sobbing harder, as I dug my thumb into the bruise along her cheek.

CHAPTER TWENTY TWO

"It will be much, *much* worse than this."

I didn't have the patience to interrogate her at the moment; I was fuming, literally and figuratively, and if I stayed for a minute longer, listening to her incessant sobs while Ara lay unconscious *because* of her, I was going to explode. So, I retreated, locking the door behind me, her cries echoing down the hallway as I left.

"Keep her here," I ordered, and the guards gave a quick nod.

I returned to the surgery to find Alden and Iaso at Ara's side. I nodded in greeting before glancing at Ara and wincing. Her torn shirt was still caked in dried blood, pulled back to reveal the wound on her side. Iaso applied a poultice, and Alden's shaky inhale was audible as she pulled her shirt back to down to cover it.

"Have you made any progress with the antidote?" I asked Iaso as she joined us and placed a hand on my shoulder. "Will it help to close her wound?

"It still needs to brew for a few more hours, but I had everything I needed. It won't be much longer now. Once she receives it, the wound should heal like normal." Alden and I simultaneously sighed a breath of relief, and she gave my shoulder a light squeeze. "All will be well soon, my child."

She returned to her seat and continued grinding tea leaves, filling the room with a floral aroma.

"Will Doran and Delphia be returning soon?" Alden asked.

I nodded. "Within a day or two."

With Ara's attempted assassination, their return hadn't even crossed my mind. I rubbed the back of my neck, guilt pricking at me. I'd left them there, albeit for good reasons, but it still made their journey home much harder. While it wasn't an incredibly long trek, they would have to cross the border mountains on foot, and that was difficult in itself.

They would also be passing by Nautia if they went the traditional route, the town Alden and his mate hailed from. It was a coastal town, tucked away within the mountains, hidden from Auryna.

I peeked at Alden to find him still focused on Ara, placing a hand on hers.

"When was the last time you visited Nautia?"

"It's been a very long time. Too long," he said, almost whispering. "Not since Ara died."

"Your mate's name was Ara, too?"

A ghost of a smile painted his lips.

"Yes. I'm assuming you know Vaelor was my son, with all your constant eavesdropping." He gave me a flat look before returning his gaze to Ara. "When he told me of Elora's pregnancy, he said if it was a girl, he wanted to name her after his mother."

His eyes brimmed with tears as he gripped Ara's hand with both of his.

"I didn't know he'd told Elora, or that she'd named her Ara until I met her that first night. I recognized her right away, you know. She looks so much like her mother, but those eyes... Those are Vaelor's, as they are mine." He leaned down and kissed her hand. "She is my blood and all I have left of my family."

Iaso stood, placing a hand on his back. "We will save her."

Alden nodded, wiping a tear from his cheek. "I never thought I'd get to meet her, not in this lifetime. She's so much like him."

"Yes, she is," she said with a sad smile. "She has his compassion."

CHAPTER TWENTY TWO

Alden smiled, laughing lightly as another tear fell. "She does, and her mother's wits and stubbornness. Vaelor always did say she had the brains between the two."

They both laughed at the memory, and an ache formed in my chest.

Nobody had happy memories of my parents—I certainly didn't. It broke my heart to hear what my father took from Ara, the chance to grow up with parents like that. So kind, so in love.

I had no idea what that looked like. I had never seen it, and now, neither would Ara.

I sunk into the chair as I listened to them share their stories, grief heavy on my chest.

* * *

The antidote was done.

Alden and I huddled around Ara as Iaso slid a hand behind her head, placing the small vial to her lips. She tilted it back, pouring its contents into Ara's mouth before laying her head back down.

"Now what?"

"Now, we wait. We have to give it time, and I'm not sure how long it might take," she said, carrying the vial back to her workbench. Alden and I anxiously waited, hovering over Ara before we resigned, sitting back down. Alden wrung his hands in his lap as he always did.

"Doran and Delphia should be through the mountains by now," I said, and he glanced up, grateful for the distraction.

"Yes, they should—"

Suddenly, Ara inhaled sharply, jolting up and coughing

before grunting and grabbing her side. We both jumped up, rushing to her side, and she looked at us in confusion, her gaze lingering on me for a moment.

"What…" Her face crumpled. "Thana."

Every emotion played out on her face: sadness, betrayal, hurt. Watching it reignited my rage at Thana, and I could barely control the smoke threatening to roll off my body in waves.

I will kill her.

"I need to talk to her." She swung her legs over the bed, attempting to stand before we could warn her against it. She staggered, gasping as her hand flew to her side, and Alden caught her by the elbow, steadying her.

"You have not healed at all, Ara. You lost a lot of blood, and the poison weakened you. I don't think walking, much less going to the dungeon, is a good idea," Iaso said, gently urging her back to the bed.

Ara's face whipped to mine.

"The dungeon? You're holding Thana in the dungeon?"

"She tried to kill you, Ara," I said only to immediately regret it as her eyes dropped to the floor.

"She was my friend," she whispered.

Dead. Thana is as good as dead.

"I'll take you to her," I voiced, stepping closer and wrapping my arm around her. Iaso shot me a disapproving look but released her as Ara glanced up at me, surprised.

"Thank you." A tear escaped the corner of her eye, and I wiped it away with my thumb.

Always.

* * *

CHAPTER TWENTY TWO

I led her slowly to the dungeon, supporting most of her weight, wishing there was more I could say. I should apologize for not being here. I should tell her why I wasn't. There were so many words I needed to say, *wanted* to say, but none would come—save the ones she needed to hear before we entered.

"Ara…" I murmured as we neared the steel doors. She glanced up at me with innocent gray eyes, and I swallowed hard, hating Thana, Evander, the world, for making me hurt her like I knew this would. "Thana did what she did because she was forced to…by Evander."

She went still in my grasp.

"No, he wouldn't do that. Why would he?" she said, shaking her head like denying it would make it any less true. She started to pull from my grasp, and I gripped her tighter.

"That's the only thing Thana told me, and I don't think she was lying."

She averted her gaze as she bit her lip. I gripped her chin lightly, and she didn't resist as I turned her face back to me, finding her eyes red and brimming with tears.

I will burn them all.

"Are you sure you want to do this? We don't have to. This can wait."

She shook her head, wiping her face with both hands.

"No, I need to know why—why she, why *he* would do this. Not knowing will eat me alive."

I nodded, understanding all too well, and guided her through the doors to Thana's cell.

"Ara? Oh, Goddess, I am so sorry. I never wanted to hurt—"

I looked to Ara expectantly, stunned to find she had seemingly steeled herself during our short walk to Thana.

"Stop," Ara commanded, holding up a hand, her eyes shut tight. Taking a deep breath, she returned her eyes to Thana. "Tell me why. Tell me everything."

"I-I don't know where to begin. Evander, he has my family," she said, choking on another Goddess-forsaken sob. It grated my nerves; if anyone had the right to cry, it was Ara, but she didn't. Instead, Ara tilted her head to the side, her brows drawing together as she listened.

"Why should we believe you?" I snapped.

Ara glimpsed up at me, something akin to shock registering on her face.

"I have no tangible proof, but I can tell you things. I have been his spy for…years. He kidnapped my family and me while I was visiting them four years ago. When he discovered I was a lady's maid here, he kept my family hostage."

Four years ago.

"Four years ago?"

She cast her eyes to the floor.

"Yes, four years ago," she whispered.

"Then, you…" I stilled, unable to say what we both knew to be true. My mind was blank, numb, unable to feel rage, betrayal, or even gratitude. There was nothing as I stared at her, processing what this meant.

Ara looked between the two of us, clearly confused. "What? What is it?"

Thana never looked up from the ground as she spoke. "I murdered Adrastus."

That snapped me out of it. I lunged forward, wrapping my hand around her throat, choking off her breath.

"How dare you—"

"Rogue!" Ara grabbed at my shoulder, attempting to pull me

CHAPTER TWENTY TWO

off Thana. I glanced back at her, her face twisted in disbelief, eyes wide, shocked. I turned to her, my arm still outstretched with my hand firmly around Thana's throat.

"Have you forgotten who I am, Ara? The vicious King of Ravaryn, the son of Adrastus? She just admitted to being a spy in my home—not to mention, she tried to *kill* you." My eyes turned back to Thana, blinded with rage. "My mate," I seethed.

Thana quivered, her hands jerking against the restraint as I tightened my grip.

Ara placed a palm on my cheek and pulled my face back to her.

"You are not him," she whispered. Her other hand grabbed my wrist and pulled gently. I held her gaze for a moment before releasing Thana, and she dropped her head, coughing.

Ara turned to face Thana, but my eyes remained on her, unable to look away. No one had ever said that to me before, as if they were all lying in wait for the moment I would snap and become him. Goddess knows even I was waiting for that moment, but she wasn't.

She didn't see him.

She saw me.

I blinked rapidly before reaching down to wrap my arm around Ara again, supporting her weight.

"Why would he order you to kill me?"

"He knows what you are, who you are. That's all I know," Thana replied, a tear streaking down her face.

"How?" Ara looked astonished, and I could have sworn I felt her begin to crumble in my arms. "Did you tell him?"

"No! No, I didn't. I would never. I swear," Thana said, shaking her head.

"Then how..." Ara trailed off, suddenly hyperventilating. Her eyes darted to me before she took off at a sprint back the way we came, clutching her side.

"Ara!" I rushed after her.

"No. No. No," she repeated as she ran down the hall, leaving a trail of blood dripping behind her.

"Ara, wait! What is it?"

Alden was entering the library just as we were, and Ara collided chest to chest with him, gripping his arms frantically.

"Can other people see the letters once the intended person has found them?"

My heart dropped.

"Yes, why? What..." Alden asked, his face falling.

"We need to send a letter right now," she urged, pulling his arm as they rushed to the fireplace. Alden handed her a piece of paper and a quill, and she quickly dropped to the table, scribbling a note before handing it to Alden.

He folded it, lit the fire, and tossed it in. We waited anxiously, my heart thundering, begging, praying that it would burn, but it didn't. It remained untouched. After an agonizingly long minute, the fire went out, leaving nothing but the note.

Alden and I shared a pained look.

"What does that mean?" she asked, her voice strained as she looked from Alden to me and back. When we didn't respond, she screamed, "What does it mean?"

"The receiver...cannot receive it. There is no safe space, because... they are no longer..." He hesitated, his face scrunching. "Here. Alive."

She froze, staring at him in shock, and dropped her gaze to the floor, shaking her head.

"No, that's not true," she said, shaking her head more violently. "No."

"Ara," I murmured, stepping towards her.

"No!" She jerked out of my grasp. "Try again," she demanded, turning to Alden. He looked at me, and I nodded, but we both knew it wouldn't change. There was only ever one reason a letter wouldn't send through the flames.

When the letter didn't burn, she released an agonizing scream that struck my chest as painfully as a bolt of lightning before collapsing in on herself and crumpling to the ground. I lunged, catching her before she hit the floor, and pulled her into my lap. She gripped my shirt with both hands, screaming as her body wracked with sobs again.

"It's my fault. I killed her. I killed my mother," she wailed into my chest.

I brought my hand to the back of her head, cradling her against me.

"No, you didn't. Evander did," I whispered, attempting to soothe her, but she only sobbed harder. I inhaled sharply, my heart shattering for her, wishing I could take the pain from her. I understood this feeling all too well, and I would not let her live with that kind of weight on her shoulders. "This is not your fault."

"I sent her a letter. I laid it out plainly. If Thana wasn't the one to tell him, it's the only other way he would have found out. He found the letter *I* sent."

"Even if he did find it, it still wouldn't be your fault. Finding out you're part Fae, or that she loved one, is not an excuse for murder. It was his own cowardice. *His* cowardice. You didn't decide her fate—he did. The fault is his and his alone. Do you understand me? You cannot blame yourself for simply existing."

"I hate him," she whispered, weeping as she buried herself deeper into my chest.

I tightened my hold on her, sitting like that for hours while she cried. When there were no tears left, she remained firmly pressed into me, hiccuping from the force of her sobs until she eventually fell asleep in my arms. I gently lifted her, carrying her to my chambers, and laid her on the bed.

Grabbing the healing salve from my nightstand, I carefully rubbed it into her wound before I crawled in behind her and wrapped my arm around her waist, pulling her back into my chest.

Chapter Twenty Three

Ara

I stirred awake surrounded by warmth, noting the morning sunlight through closed eyes.

Taking a slow, deep breath, I cracked my eyes open and froze. This was not my room.

An arm tightened around my waist, pulling me back, and my breathing hitched before quickening. Looking down, I found Rogue's arm wrapped around me and a wing thrown over my hip, enveloping me in his warmth.

My eyes snapped open wide, swollen and irritated, reminding me of the night before.

Grief stole my breath as guilt sank its claws in, sinking into my bones and rooting itself in my soul. It felt as if my chest was caving in under the weight and pain as my shoulders slumped.

The sunlight in the room darkened as a storm rolled in.

My mother.

Her sweet face echoed throughout my mind, and I couldn't stop imagining it as Evander…as he killed her. Because of me.

I needed to move. To get out of here. To breathe.

Peeking over my shoulder, I made sure Rogue was still asleep and carefully removed his arm, sliding out from under his wing.

As I stood, my hand went to my side in anticipation, but there was no pain. Shocked, I lifted my shirt to find the wound already closed and scabbed over. Someone must have applied the healing salve after I fell asleep. I glanced at the nightstand, noting the small container, the same one Rogue had used in the Cursed Wood.

Clenching my jaw, I moved toward the door but paused at the edge of the bed, glancing back and studying him for a moment. Part of me wanted to wake him so I wouldn't be alone, but the other part of me—the deep, guilt-ridden, disgusted part of myself—wanted to leave and hide and never face anyone again, never speak to anyone of anything again.

He sighed, rolling onto his back. My breath caught in my throat, but he remained asleep. My gaze lingered on his bare chest, tracing the scar that stretched across his abdomen.

Orphans. We're orphans, both raised by men who wished us dead.

My eyes burned with tears as heavy rain released from the clouds, filling the room with a dull roar.

I knew if I woke him, he would hold me and assure me it wasn't my fault. He would wipe my tears and try to make me feel less alone, less burdened.

How odd it was. My stranger turned kidnapper turned...

I jerked my face away and strode to the door on numb legs.

Stepping out of his room, I closed the door quietly behind me and stared into the hallway, unsure of where to go. I had spent my entire time here preparing to return home to my mother, and now, she was gone. My father hated me. No...Evander, not my father.

He killed her. He tried to kill me.

I have nowhere to go. No one to go to.

My head dipped to my trembling hands as they knotted into the hair at my temples, attempting to control my spiraling thoughts. The sorrow weighed on my chest, so tight, so heavy, I couldn't breathe anymore. I was tired of breathing, tired of having to force the breath into my lungs for so long, through so much pain. I cried out and dropped to my knees on the stone floor, curling in on myself.

No one.

Nowhere.

No one.

I wrapped my arms around my torso, holding myself together as best I could, as if I could stop my heart from breaking into pieces on the floor. A sob escaped me, followed by another and another, echoing down the hall. It was never-ending, the grief. It was an ocean, sucking me under and threatening to drown me.

Then, strong arms wrapped around me, lifting and carrying me back into the room. Rogue kicked the door shut behind us and walked to the chair by the window where he cradled me in his lap with a hand on my back, just as he had the night before in the library.

I almost allowed myself to settle into him, but I wasn't ready.

I wasn't ready to be soothed and forgiven. I wasn't ready to forgive myself for her death, as he thought I should. I jerked out of his grasp and stood. Staggering away, I avoided his gaze, shaking my head—too overwhelmed, too heavy, too guilty.

Guilty.

"Don't," I uttered as he stood, stepping closer. I made a beeline for the door, but he stepped in front of me, solid as stone.

"You are not leaving," he commanded.

My eyes snapped to his as a renewed rage burned in my chest. I tried to step around him and he matched it, blocking my way.

"You cannot order me around like you do the rest of your people," I spat at him, shoving his chest. "I *am* leaving!"

"No. You are not." He crossed his arms over his chest, glaring down at me. My teeth clenched, cheeks flushing with anger.

"You think just because you bit me like an animal, you own me? You don't. I am *not* your mate. Your possession. You cannot order me to stay here."

I shoved at him again.

"I am no one's possession."

And again, tears spilling down my cheeks.

"I belong to no one."

And again.

"I have no one."

He caught my hands that time, wrapping one hand around the back of my head and pulling me into his chest. I melted into him, unraveling as his scent enveloped me.

"Me. You have me."

My breath hitched, and I pulled back, searching his face. He looked genuine, and a small part of me wanted to believe him.

But I didn't.

CHAPTER TWENTY THREE

"You can be angry. Hell, you should be, but you'll be angry here. With me. Take it out on me. Take out every ugly, suffocating emotion on me, because I am not letting you go out there to shoulder this alone." He brought his hands to my cheeks. "You are *not* alone, Ara."

My mouth fell open at his words, lips quivering, but I couldn't let go of the rage. If I did, all that would be left was agony and guilt and overwhelming devastation. I couldn't go back to that. Not right now.

"Tell me what you need, Ara. Tell me what I can do," he urged, searching my eyes.

"I-I don't know," I stammered, shaking my head. "I don't know. I—" My palms found my forehead, and I scrunched my eyes closed. "I don't know."

It was too much. My thoughts were spiraling, the emotion suffocating, and together, they created a whirlwind within me. My head. My chest. My heart. It was chaos—out of control, painful chaos.

I dropped my hands, opening my eyes to meet his. He held my gaze before my eyes dropped to his mouth.

"Control," I said.

For once in my life, I need control.

Not wanting to think for one more second, I grabbed his face and pulled it down to mine, crashing my mouth to his. He tensed in my grip before groaning into my mouth, his hands moving to my waist, sliding down and pulling me against him. I could feel him hardening, and I shoved my hand into his trousers, wrapping it around him.

Breaking from his mouth, I dropped to my knees, looking at him through my lashes as I undid his belt.

"Ara, you don't have to—"

"I don't *have* to do anything." I unbuttoned his trousers, and his hardened length sprung free. My hand wrapped around him, and he inhaled sharply. His heated gaze burned into me as he watched my hand stroke him. "I want to."

He stopped fighting me then, nodding as I leaned forward, licking him from base to tip, tasting the bead of saltiness. He groaned, and a thrill of satisfaction shot through me at the look on his face, as his self-control crumbled beneath my touch. I took him into my mouth, sucking down as much of him as I could before gagging and pulling back.

"It's okay, pretty girl. You can take it," he purred, knotting his hand in my hair. He slowly pushed my head forward, and I relaxed my jaw, reveling in the taste of him, surrendering to his movement. He hit the back of my throat and pulled back out, repeating until he started to slide down my throat. My eyes watered at his depth but never left his face. "You're doing so well, Ara. Look at you. So perfect."

Pride swelled in my chest at his words. I moaned around him, and he hummed at the feel.

"So *mine*."

He increased the pace, bobbing my head on him, and I reached a hand down between my legs, circling my clit, but he grinned and jerked himself from my mouth. He dropped to his knees in front of me and ran a thumb over my swollen lips.

"Beautiful," he whispered as he pulled me forward, bringing his mouth to mine in a smoldering kiss. I returned it with reckless abandon, and he wrapped his hands under my backside, lifting and carrying me to the nearby table, setting me on the edge.

"You want control?" His grin was dark, promising, stoking

CHAPTER TWENTY THREE

the ever-growing fire within me.

"Yes," I breathed, and he pulled my shirt off over my head.

"Then consider me entirely at your mercy, little storm."

My heart skipped a beat at that name. *Did he know I dreamt of it?*

The thought didn't last as he slid a hand between my breasts, pushing me down to the table. I followed his hand back, reclining and lifting my hips as he pulled off my trousers, tossing them to the side. He grabbed one ankle, lifting it to his mouth as he planted hot kisses up my leg—my calf, my knee, my inner thigh, inching painstakingly slowly to the place I wanted his mouth most. As he neared my core, he dropped my leg to lift my other, and I groaned in frustration.

"Patience," he purred, kissing up my inner thigh before sinking to his knees and throwing my legs over his shoulders.

I gasped as he slid his tongue into me, thrusting before pulling back and licking to the apex of my thighs. He hummed into my clit, and I arched off the table, silently begging for more: more friction, more him, just *more*.

He brought a hand up, holding me down to the table as he feasted, and I exploded within minutes, sparks dancing across my vision. I started to sit up to grab him and pull him on top of me when he stopped me, returning his hand to my sternum.

"You're not done yet." He gently pushed me back down to the table.

"Wha—"

Without warning, he thrust two fingers into my core, curling them against my most sensitive spot, and I fell back to the table with a moan. He brought his mouth back down, licking and swirling until I was on the edge, about to tumble over again.

Suddenly, he stood, and I whimpered as his mouth left me. He slowly pulled his fingers out before entering me again as he undid his trousers with his other hand, dropping them to the ground.

"Don't worry. I would never leave you so needy." He slid his hand from me, using it to slick himself. "I want you to come apart around my cock this time."

He crawled above me, bracing a hand by my head as he lined up against my entrance. I wiggled, urging him forward, but he didn't budge; he merely grinned—a devilish grin I wanted to kiss and slap and *ride.* "Say it. Tell me what you want, little storm."

"I want you," I begged without a second thought. He turned his ear to me, smirking. *Yes, I want to slap that smirk off his damned face.* "Inside me. Rogue, please."

He slammed into me, sheathing himself completely, and we groaned in unison.

"*So* perfect," he whispered, kissing the pulsing hollow at the base of my neck. He pulled out and thrust back in, biting his mark on my skin, and I screamed. "So. Fucking. Mine."

He brought his hand to my throat, squeezing lightly as he hammered into me. I wrapped my legs around his back and brought my hands to his shoulders, doing everything I could to hold onto his punishing pace. It was brutal and blissful all at once.

Perfect.

I moaned his name as I exploded again, clenching around him and digging my nails into his back.

"Scream my name, little storm. Let everyone know who I belong to."

Mine, something whispered in the back of my mind, and I bit at his shoulder. A deep growl reverberated through his chest, and he thrust into me one final time, filling me. I slid my fingers along the base of one wing as he slumped on top of me, leaning into my touch before gripping my chin and jerking my eyes back to him.

"If you keep doing that, I may never let you leave this room again."

He leaned down, sliding his lips along mine in a whisper of a kiss before he pulled out. Sliding his hands under my thighs, he carried me back to his bed, crawling in behind me. Warm and sated, I lulled off into a deep, dreamless sleep before my thoughts could snap me back to reality.

* * *

A few hours later, we still hadn't left his chambers. Seated at his small table, we were playing some kind of board game I was unfamiliar with, and he beat me every time.

My leg bounced restlessly as he studied the board, deciding his next move.

"If you insist on doing that, at least let me give your legs a reason to shake," he teased with a lopsided grin, his eyes never leaving the board. My leg halted.

"We need to talk to Thana again," I blurted out, and his eyes snapped to me.

"Why? She can rot down there, for all I care."

"Why? What do you mean, why? Because she was forced to do it, and she didn't even succeed—"

"Thankfully," he added. "But we don't know what else she'll do, or if she'll try again. She cannot be trusted." He paused, swallowing hard. "How can you have forgiven her so easily? She tried to *kill you*, Ara."

I dropped my eyes with a sigh. "You don't think I know that, Rogue? I haven't forgiven her, not entirely, but... I just don't blame her." I raised my eyes back to him. "If I could've saved my mother by doing the same, I...I think I would've."

His brows furrowed as he nodded slowly.

"Besides, there are so many questions we haven't asked," I continued. "Like how does she communicate with him? Through the fire? And is he waiting for her response? What if he kills her family if she doesn't respond?" I flinched at the thought of yet another death and a wave of grief settled over me. "Look, if you don't want to go, fine. I am, so you can either let me go alone or you can join. Those are your only two options."

He hesitated, a muscle ticking in his jaw.

"Fine, but don't believe everything she says." He rose to his feet and walked to the door. "Well? Let's go."

I hopped up and jogged to his side.

* * *

Once in her cell, I gasped as a hand flew to my mouth, horrified. She was pale, her eye mottled with deepening bruises, blood dripping down her forearms where the metal cuffs bit into her skin.

"Release her," I demanded, staggering towards her. My hands hovered above the shackles, and her head lifted to me, startling awake.

"No." Rogue crossed his arms over his chest, his eyes never leaving Thana.

CHAPTER TWENTY THREE

"Yes! Look at her. She's wasting away."

"No. She made an attempt on your life, and she will suffer. Whether that's here in the dungeon or in death, you choose, Ara. What should you have me do?" he asked, lethally calm.

I started to argue when something behind him caught my attention: a set of keys hanging on a hook.

"Let her live," I uttered and turned back to Thana, stifling a small smile of victory. I would be back as soon as he released me. I could do that much.

Feeling Rogue's suspicious gaze on my back, I took another step toward Thana, taking a deep breath. "Thana, can you talk with me?"

"What is it you wish to know?" she rasped.

"What were your orders once you killed me?"

Her face blanched, her eyes bulging as she jerked against the restraints.

"Oh Goddess, I was supposed to send him a note telling him it was done. If he…if he doesn't receive confirmation, he'll kill my family. Please." Her eyes darted from me to Rogue, pleading. "Please. Let me do that much."

"You are not leaving here," Rogue declared.

Thana choked on a sob, her eyes wide and brimming with tears.

"I will do it for you. Tell me what to say," I blurted.

He gripped me by the arm, pulling me away from her. "Ara—"

"If you will not allow her to save her family, then I will do it for her," I spat at him, and he tensed, clenching his jaw. He studied me for a moment, and I held my chin high, meeting his stare. "I've already lost my mother. I will not allow another person to die because of me."

His face softened.

"Fine," he said, turning towards Thana. "But you will tell us *exactly* what to say to convince him. If anything happens to Ara, I will be back to fulfill my promise."

She nodded quickly, and my gaze lingered on him, surprised. *Promise?*

"Write *she is asleep*," she said, and my eyes snapped back to her. "That's it. Nothing else, nothing more. He gave clear instructions."

Rogue scoffed, but my blood froze, my mouth falling slack.

"She is asleep? That's it? Are you serious? Ara, you can't possibly believe this, can you?"

My gaze locked on Thana, blurred with tears, and it felt as if time had stopped. I couldn't look away, couldn't will my eyes to move—terrified that if I looked away, if I moved at all, the emotion welling in my chest would crush me. I couldn't, so I pushed it down, frozen, looking without really seeing.

She is asleep.

When I was born, my father gifted me with a puppy, a gray wolfhound named Willow. She was barely a few weeks older than me, and from the moment I could walk, we were inseparable; we went everywhere together. She was my best friend at a time when I had none, and I loved her like family. On my twelfth birthday, a year before the war started, I ran outside to see my father carrying her limp body into the backyard, shielding her from view.

"She is just asleep, darling," he told me, but I knew she wasn't.

She is asleep.
My father tried to kill me.
He wanted me dead.

CHAPTER TWENTY THREE

I believed it the first time Thana told me. I believed it when the note didn't burn, proving my mother's death. I believed it, and yet... This somehow confirmed it, set it in my bones, and rewrote my life. I squeezed my eyes shut as every happy memory I had of him flashed before me, shattering and turning gray, twisting and distorting until he was unrecognizable.

I took a deep breath, stifling the emotion as I exhaled.

"She's telling the truth," I muttered, my voice unnaturally flat. "Release her. It wasn't her fault."

"Ara..." Rogue began, but I couldn't hear. I didn't want to.

I turned, my gaze following my body, just as out of focus as my mind. I continued out of the dungeon, and he followed close behind, shadowing me. When we passed by the guard stand, I vaguely heard him give the orders, but I didn't listen as I continued through the doorway.

My feet led me through the castle, up the winding stairs, and down the hallway, stopping at Vaelor's door.

"These were Vaelor's chambers," Rogue said behind me, his voice distant.

I turned the knob and entered through the door without giving him a response. Rogue halted at the doorway as I entered. As soon as I stepped across the threshold, the fireplace lit, warming the room. I walked to the desk, pulling out paper and a quill. Dipping the quill in a small jar of ink, I slowly pulled it out and scribbled the words. Stalking over to Rogue, I grabbed his wrist and pulled him into the room, shoving the note into his hand.

"Send it," I commanded, and he gave a quick nod. As he sent it, my eyes followed the ebb and flow of the flames, imagining Evander finding the note, relieved to know I was dead. Happy, even. I swallowed hard as my throat tightened, and I sat in the chair, raising my eyes to the painting above the fireplace.

I just stared. I was numb. Everything was numb.

Rogue sat in the chair adjacent to mine and followed my gaze to the painting.

"I've never been in here before," he whispered. "It just... didn't feel right."

My eyes didn't leave my parents' faces. I couldn't look away.

King Vaelor was my father. He would've been kind.

He would've made my mother happy.

He wouldn't have killed her.

He wouldn't have tried to kill me like my father.

Evander. Not my father.

Not my father.

Not my father.

As my thoughts spiraled, the spark of anger became a violent inferno of rage. My hand gripped the chair, turning my knuckles white as I stared at my mother's face.

My dead mother's face.

I had been so *blind* my entire life. Evander had us so thoroughly under his thumb, I couldn't even think for myself—doing what I was told when I was told. I had been so convinced he was the only one who could protect us, that we needed his protection, when in reality, what we needed protection from was him.

"I hate him," I declared for the second time. My nails sank into the fabric of the chair, tearing little crescent-shaped holes. "We need to do something. He needs to be stopped."

Rogue sighed heavily. "I need to tell you why I was gone the past few days."

For the first time since we'd arrived, I turned to face him,

CHAPTER TWENTY THREE

meeting his gaze.

"We arranged an ambush of sorts to assassinate Evander. He agreed to meet us at a place called the Marsh for the handover, which is why I left you here. I'd planned to assassinate him, but he never showed. That's when I realized he knew. That would've been the only reason he wouldn't go through with the handover."

My gaze returned to the fire when he finished. Under normal circumstances, I would've been outraged by Rogue's attempt—behind my back, no less—but I couldn't bring myself to care. Every emotion I was feeling right now was pointed straight at Evander, a burning spear of fury, hurt, and hatred, aimed and ready to be plunged deep into his chest.

"Why did he send his men, then?"

"What?" Rogue asked, confused.

"Why did he send his men if he wasn't going through with the handover? Why not just not show up?" I asked again. Rogue paused for a moment and swore.

"That bastard must've been planning an ambush, too. We left before the meeting time because I..." He paused, clearing his throat. "I feared he might have sent someone after you since he knew I wouldn't be here, the same way he snuck someone in to kill my father."

"I don't know why saving me was worth leaving Doran and Delphia there," I replied. "Why am I still even here? If you can't use me as ransom, why am I—"

He gripped my chin, ripping my face toward him.

"I said you aren't leaving me, and I meant it. Whether you like it or not, you *are* my mate. You also happen to be the daughter of Auryna's general with a newly found vengeance, and I know you have relevant information in that pretty little head of yours, just waiting to be told."

My blood boiled as I held his gaze, my chest rising and falling quickly, before jerking my chin out of his grasp.

"Good to know I still have a purpose as a captive."

An angry muscle ticked in his jaw.

"Have you not been given the freedom to roam? Freedom to talk to whoever you want, read whatever book you want? Have you not been fed, dressed, fucked? Do you think others talk to me the way you do?" He leaned down, bracing a hand on each armrest. His face was mere inches from mine, but I refused to yield. "If you were just a captive, Ara, you would be locked in the dungeon." He lowered his mouth to my ear, his breath sending goosebumps across my skin. "Although, I would love to see you in chains if that's where you'd rather be. Just say the word."

I turned my face away, and he chuckled, stepping back.

"I just can't leave. Got it."

Hurt flashed behind his eyes, and I kept my face blank as guilt bit at me.

"Where would you go, Ara? Tell me. Where would you go? Make your way to Blackburn? To another Fae village where you know no one? To Auryna? With your pointed ears and out-of-control magic?"

I dropped my gaze to the floor. He was right, of course, but there it was, the reminder that I had no one. Before the hurt could sink in, though, I focused on the rage, letting it consume me, guard me.

Anything was better than the hurt.

Without thinking, I reached into my boot, ripped the dagger from its sheath, and hurled it at his smug face. He sidestepped it at the last minute and released a surprised laugh as the blade

CHAPTER TWENTY THREE

embedded in the wooden windowsill behind him.

Snapping his face back to me, he rapidly closed the distance between us. His hand wrapped around my throat as he pulled me up from the chair and led me across the room before he turned me around, so my back was flush against his chest.

We faced the mirror, his burning gaze locked on mine in our reflection.

"You're going to have to do better than that if you want to kill me, little storm. I thought you would've learned that by now." He tsked, harshly biting down on the mate mark. My eyes slid closed at the feeling, and I arched into his touch. "Look how your body reacts to me."

I cracked my eyes open to see my hands gripping his thighs of their own accord. His gaze dipped down my form, soaking in my reaction to him, and the sight set my body aflame. At the hint of my arousal, his pupils blew wide, and he inhaled deeply at my neck.

"Your fight is useless when you crave me this much." He slid a hand down my stomach, his fingers splayed, pulling me tighter against him as he ground into me. "You ache for me, just as I do for you."

He tightened his grip, momentarily choking off my breath before releasing me, and I stepped away from him, grinding my teeth.

"I only told you because I felt like you should know," he said tightly, turning and sitting back in the chair.

Taking a deep breath, I returned to my own chair, and my gaze snagged on the desk behind him. Everything I'd discovered while he was gone came crashing back to me, crushing the anger.

"There's something I need to tell you too," I admitted with

a sigh.

Rogue leaned forward with his elbows on his knees, eyebrows pulling together.

"I've been here before, after we…you know, before you left." My cheeks reddened, and he smirked. "I didn't know whose room it was at first until I saw the crest on the bed. Alden had explained what that symbol was before, so I recognized it."

He nodded, urging me to continue.

"Well, I found his desk and there were some journals inside, one of them detailing his power and some parts of his reign. Towards the end, he started to mention a draig."

The smirk slid from his face.

"He wrote that they found a maid from Adrastus' estate, and she explained why he was attacking the nearby towns, that he was looking for his mate…so he could pass on his shifting ability."

His gaze dropped to his hands knotted in his lap, and guilt fluttered in my chest.

"That's not it, though. He…"

Rogue glanced up with pained eyes, and I hesitated, the words caught in my throat.

"He what?"

"He fathered a son before you with another Fae."

Rogue's mouth fell slack before he blinked rapidly, shaking his head.

"No, someone would've known. There would've been talk," he insisted. "Let me see the journal. Where is it?"

"It's in my chambers, but before you read it, you should know…someone did know. Two people, actually: Alden and some man named Ewan. It says that Vaelor ordered them to never speak a word of it to anyone, for the child's safety."

"For the child's safety?" He scoffed, running a hand along the scar on his neck. "Of course."

I winced at his words as he stood and strode to the door, smoke trailing behind him.

Chapter Twenty Four

Ara

Following behind Rogue, I expected him to go straight to my chambers, but he veered left instead, entering the library.

My heart rate spiked.

He marched into Alden's office and slowed as he entered, stopping just before his desk. Alden's gaze bounced from Rogue to me.

Rogue eyed him, his head tilted to the side.

"Alden, tell me. Do I have a brother?" Rogue asked, his voice abnormally calm. Alden went completely still. "Well?"

"I—" His eyes flashed to me and back to Rogue before he closed the tome on his desk and stood, wringing his hands in front of him. "I don't know for sure if I'm being honest. Around fifty years ago, a rumor surfaced from a lady's maid that the reason behind Adrastus' violence was because he wanted to find his mate, breed her, and pass on his dragon shift."

Rogue flinched, and my heart sank. For a moment, I wanted to comfort him, as he had for me, but it was a brief moment, and I remained where I was.

"She said he'd been searching for a decade and was becoming increasingly infuriated, so he went village to village, forcing people to reveal their daughters and destroying homes when they wouldn't."

Rogue's mouth was tight as his eyes dropped.

"This all started because he supposedly sired a child who was born without wings, and when she birthed him… Adrastus exploded, obliterating the nursery along with half the castle. He sent the mother and babe away with no money and no place to go, and she was never heard of or seen again. We were never given a name or even her description, so when the child faded into obscurity, I assumed it was false. I wish I could tell you more, but I don't even really believe it to be true, which is why I never thought to tell you," Alden finished, his eyes full of pity.

Rogue sighed loudly and plopped down in a chair, shoulders slouched as he ran a hand through his hair.

"Well, if he *is* out there, he has nothing to fear from me. He needs to know that," Rogue uttered, lifting his gaze back to Alden. I couldn't pull my eyes away from him as he spoke, my lips falling slack. "At first light, I'll send a few messengers out to spread the word. Although, I'm sure they'll think I've gone mad, considering no one even knew he existed."

A small seed of respect bloomed in my chest at his words, and I found myself nodding absentmindedly. The act was so unlike what Adrastus would've done that I almost felt bad for ever having compared the two. Having an older brother with blood ties to the throne was a threat to his claim, and yet, he would rather him live his life without fear than eliminate the competition.

"I'll also have Doran spread the word through his men when he returns. That should cover a good bit of ground in and of itself," he added, and the mention of Doran pulled me from my thoughts.

"Shouldn't they have returned already?" I asked.

"Yes, and I'm starting to get concerned. The trek from the Marsh shouldn't be taking this long." He paused, his brows furrowing before he stood to grab a paper and quill. "I'll send a letter, just to make sure they're all right."

Rogue scribbled the note and tossed it into the small fire in Alden's study. It burned, disappearing within seconds—which was good, of course, but I couldn't stop the small twinge in my chest. The letter burned away as fast as it entered the flames, the way it should have when we tried to send one to my mother.

"Now we wait, I guess."

Alden nodded. "Do you need anything else from me? Any more questions? I don't know much I can answer, but I will do my best."

Rogue brought his hand to his chin, resting his elbow on the armrest of the chair. "Where did he send them, do you know?"

"We just know it was south, below his old estate, closer to the border towns, but I don't think he would still be there. Most of them have evacuated, seeking safe haven from the attacks."

Rogue slid a hand over his face with a sigh. "That does make pinpointing him much harder. Fifty years ago, you're sure?"

"Yes, from what we were told. The woman said the birth started his search, as he was unaware it took a mated pair

CHAPTER TWENTY FOUR

to pass on power like that. It would've been roughly ten to eleven years before you were born, if everything she said was truthful and accurate."

Wait.

My head snapped to Rogue, and I studied his face. "You're thirty-nine?"

He paused, half smiling, before bursting out in laughter.

"You don't look any older than me."

"Everything you've heard, everything you've learned, and that's what shocks you?" Rogue wiped his eyes as Alden began chuckling, and I gaped at them both. "Ara, do you know how old Alden is? How old Iaso is?"

I shook my head, shifting my gaze to Alden's face.

"Well, you know Fae don't age like humans. We age at a similar speed until puberty, and then it slows from there. I'm almost 800 years old, and I have looked like this for about a hundred years, I would say," Alden said, suppressing a smile.

My eyes bulged.

"Iaso is well over 1200," Rogue added.

My face snapped back to him, and I must have looked dumbfounded, because it set off another round of laughter. "Then why does she look so much younger? She looks our age," I asked, turning back to Alden.

"She takes a special tea she creates to stay youthful, and I'm sure she'll outlive us all. She's offered it to me a time or two, but I quite like the look of age. It reminds me of how far I've come."

My mind could not wrap around the fact that they were *that* old. *1200 years?* Iaso would have seen the building of Draig Hearth, which is incredible, but also unbelievable. Yet, I believed them entirely.

I glanced down at Rogue, grinning at me with his chin propped on his hand.

Young. We are so young.

"I'm only twenty-six," I uttered.

He sat up to close the distance between us, resting his elbows on his knees, his grin shifting to a soft smile.

"Yes, I know," he replied, patting my thigh with his hand. My eyes dropped to the subtle movement, and my cheeks flamed. As Rogue took a deep breath and turned back to Alden, I took a step away from him. "I'll tell the messengers a rough age and general location of birth. At least that narrows it down a little."

Alden nodded as Rogue turned to leave, but I hesitated, opening my mouth to speak just as the fire spit out a folded note. It drifted until it reached Rogue, and he snatched it from midair, quickly opening it to read its contents.

"They're not far. He said they decided to check in with local villages along the way and see how people were faring. They should be back tomorrow."

Alden nodded in response, and Rogue stepped out of the study as I remained behind.

"I'm sorry, Alden. I found Vaelor's chambers and the journals inside. Once I read that bit, I just felt like Rogue should know first, before I talked to anyone else."

Alden smiled softly. "No, don't apologize. You did the right thing. That was something we should've discussed a long time ago, and...I'm glad you found his room and the journals. He would've wanted you to have them, I think."

I offered him a light smile and turned to follow Rogue. As we left, my eyes snagged on the fireplace, reminding me of the note we sent to Evander, the confirmation of my death he so happily awaited.

My stomach knotted, and I blinked rapidly, forcing myself to look away.

As we strolled down the main hallway, I bit the inside of my cheek. "What do you think he'll do when he finds out I'm not actually dead?"

"I think he'll be long dead before he ever finds out," Rogue declared, his voice laced with restraint. "I've always planned on ending his miserable life for what he's done to my people, but now… Now, my desire to cleave his head from his shoulders is stronger than ever." An angry muscle ticked in his jaw.

Once we reached the fork, leading to either my room or his, he stopped to look at me.

"Which will it be? Are we staying in yours or mine?"

I tilted my head to the side. "We?"

"Yes, we. Everything is still so…fresh. I wouldn't want you getting too lonely without me," he teased, but it didn't quite reach his eyes.

"Mine," I answered, realizing he needed company, too—anything to avoid what lurks alongside loneliness.

He stifled a smile and led the way to my room. Once we entered, my heart sank a little, half expecting to see Thana reading in a chair as I had so many times before.

"Where is Thana now? She has been released, right?"

He nodded. "She was released from the dungeon, but she's still being kept under guard in her own room."

I released a breath of relief. "Thank you."

Tension rolled off my shoulders, and I made a mental note to visit her as soon as I could.

"You're welcome," he uttered, looking about the room with

furrowed brows. "I'm sorry I locked you in here."

"I was terrified when those guards threw me in here, and I was *so angry* at you. I-I was mad at myself, too. It was foolish of me to trust you so easily, to believe you when you said you wouldn't." I paused, feeling uncomfortably vulnerable under his intense gaze. "But I appreciated you sending Thana with the note. I don't think I would've survived being trapped in here otherwise."

I couldn't tell him it was all right, that I forgave him. He had kidnapped me, and that single event changed the trajectory of my entire life.

I wanted it to be okay, but it wasn't. *I* wasn't. I had barely been able to breathe as things piled up—surprising me, devastating me, rewriting my life and everything I thought I knew.

Yet, there was still a small part of me that recognized if he hadn't kidnapped me, I would still be in Auryna. I'd still be unhappy with life and full of empty dreams, probably married to Finn by now and moved into his home, where he would've expected me to take on the duties of a wife, a mother.

But at least my mother would be alive.

And that was why guilt bit at me every second of every day, lying in wait in the back of my mind, because while Rogue insisted it wasn't my fault, it was.

He may have been the one to kidnap me, but I, quite literally, ran into his arms.

He did what he did for the safety of his people. I did what I did in selfishness, because I stupidly wanted a small taste of freedom, to decide something for myself.

My heart wrenched in my chest, and I turned my face to the fire before he could see the agony in my eyes. He crossed

CHAPTER TWENTY FOUR

the room, sitting in the chair adjacent to mine. There we sat in silence until well after sunset, both lost in our thoughts.

I started to nod off when Rogue muttered, "I wish it had been me."

I lifted my head to look at him. His gaze was still locked on the fire, the flickering orange reflected in his dark eyes.

"What do you mean?" I whispered.

"I wish it had been me that was sent away."

My breath hitched slightly, quietly, as a lump formed in my throat.

"What a pair we are," I mumbled, lying my head back down on my elbow.

"Indeed. What a broken pair."

* * *

As we exited the stairwell the next morning, Doran and Delphia entered through the front doors.

"Well, long time, no see," Rogue shouted, a wide grin splitting his face as he quickly descended the stairs.

Delphia ran to me, and I froze as she threw her arms around my shoulders.

"I am *so* happy to see you're still alive! Although, I wouldn't think Rogue would let you go that easily," she teased with a laugh. "It's good to see you again."

"I'm glad to see you are well," Doran said with a smile, dipping his head in greeting.

"So, tell us about the people. How are they doing?" Rogue asked, and the mood shifted, the light tone draining from the room.

"It seems there haven't been any attacks since Ara's kidnapping, which is good news, of course, but..." He paused, sighing. "It seems they've amassed an army along the border. On *our* side of the border, in the abandoned border towns."

Rogue's mouth set in a tight line, and I vaguely heard his knuckles crack as Doran continued.

"They've been there for a few days at least, but they haven't moved forward yet."

"How much time do we have?" Rogue asked, his words quick and clipped.

"If they were to mobilize tomorrow, it would take a few weeks to move that many men all the way *here*, maybe two or three, but—"

"They would pass through too many towns on the way. We need to start recruiting *now*," Rogue finished for him, striding towards the front door. Doran didn't move. "Assemble your commanders immediately. We need to call a—"

"Rogue, wait. There's one more thing." Doran took a quick breath, lifting his eyes as Rogue stopped in his tracks. "There has been word that a person has been born with the gift of manipulation."

The color drained from Rogue's face, and my heart raced at the look on their faces, the hesitation.

"What does that mean?" I asked, glancing between the three of them. Rogue's eyes didn't leave Doran's.

It was Delphia who responded. "Someone with the magic to manipulate can do exactly that: manipulate people's minds. They can warp anything and everything that the mind perceives. A manipulator can drop seeds, little thoughts, into your mind, and you will wholeheartedly believe they are your own. By doing this, they can convince anyone of just about anything."

CHAPTER TWENTY FOUR

"It was thought the bloodline for that kind of magic was smothered a long time ago, as it's extremely dangerous to anyone around them," Doran added.

My hand rubbed my chest, willing my heart to slow down. "And one is alive? In Ravaryn?"

"If the stories are to be believed," Doran replied as his eyes cut back to Rogue.

"There's no way. There hasn't been one born in at least a century. Maybe two," Rogue said. "Do you believe the rumors?"

"I spoke with a man who claims to have met him. Whether he can be trusted or not, I don't know, but he had a sketch of him, which he made me pay highly for," Doran huffed, pulling out the page from his satchel. "He said his name was Adonis, but he had no family name."

Adonis? That's eerily similar to—

My thoughts came to a screeching halt as I caught a glimpse of the sketch. My heart thundered in my ears, and I staggered back, my breaths coming out too quick, too shallow. Rogue's eyebrows pulled together in concern, and he stepped toward me with an outstretched hand, but I shook my head, taking another step back.

"That is *not* him. That's impossible. It's impossible. The man is confused." My words came out in a rush, my voice shaking.

"Do you know him?" Rogue asked, raising the sketch to my view.

"That man"—my voice cracked as I pointed a finger at him—"is King Adon of Auryna."

All three faces fell simultaneously before their eyes darted to the sketch, examining it.

"Are you sure?" Doran asked. "That would be... For a Fae to become king of the human kingdom... That would be..."

"Impressive, for one," Rogue interrupted. "For him to be able to manipulate that many people into thinking he was human... How did he even become king? What happened to the last one?"

Their gazes snapped to me.

"He handed over the crown about twenty years ago, peacefully..." My mouth went slack. "Oh, dear Goddess. He handed it over willingly, claiming he was tired, and he chose Adon as his predecessor, even over his own daughter."

Rogue looked to Doran, who nodded. "That has to be him, then. I don't see why else a king would hand over his kingdom, especially to someone outside of his own family."

Rogue didn't seem entirely convinced. "But how could he convince so many people that he was human? Surely, it would exhaust his magic to hold a glamour over himself constantly."

"Actually," I said, taking a deep breath and stepping closer. "He doesn't see anyone. Ever. Just his inner circle, which includes Evander. The only reason I know what he looks like is because he occasionally came to dinner at our estate."

"That makes sense." Rogue nodded slowly. "When I was in Auryna, I couldn't find a single person who had spoken to him, not even a servant. If he keeps his circle tight, he can keep them thoroughly controlled without having to work on several people at once. But Ara, that would mean—"

"That he was controlling Evander," I finished for him, the knowledge hitting me in the gut.

I didn't know what to think or how to feel. A small part of me hoped that Adon was responsible for his hatred of the Fae, but even so, it would change nothing. It was still his hands that killed my mother, his orders that tried to kill me. I couldn't separate the two, and besides, it wouldn't make sense for—

"Why would a Fae be giving orders to attack Ravaryn?" I finished my thought aloud.

"That makes no sense at all. I have no idea why he would go against his own kind. Are you sure that this drawing is of King Adon?" Rogue asked.

I took the sketch from his hand and studied the face. The man had short black hair with a narrow face, pale skin, and dark eyes. It was definitely Adon. There was no mistaking him.

"Yes. He's younger here, but that's definitely King Adon. He looks the same, minus the pointed ears, and maybe a few years older."

"Well, this complicates things," Delphia said. "It makes no sense for him to attack Ravaryn. How could someone hate their own people so much?"

"We need to tell Alden. See what he says," Rogue said.

* * *

We found Alden in the library, rearranging shelves near the front. He glanced up from his work, and Rogue explained everything we had learned in excruciating detail. With each word Rogue spoke, Alden's mouth fell open farther, his arms falling to his sides with a book in each hand.

"Did you... Did you just say a manipulator? A living, breathing manipulator?"

Doran nodded curtly, and Alden turned his gaze to me.

"And he's ruling Auryna?"

I nodded, and Alden took a shaky breath, setting the books down on a table. "This is not good."

"We know, but what are we supposed to do?" Delphia asked, tossing her hands in the air.

Alden shook his head, his face still turned down to the table. "There has only ever been one bloodline with that magic, and the last remaining member died over seventy years ago. This should be impossible," he rasped. "I need to research their history. Someone had to have been missed." He chuckled but it was halfhearted, like the mere thought was exhausting, before he ran a hand down his face with a forced sigh. "I don't know how useful I'll be, though. I've been researching your dream, Ara, and I have yet to learn anything useful."

I dropped my eyes at the mention of it, cheeks reddening. I hadn't told anyone of it besides Alden. He glanced up, noted my reaction, and apologized.

"What dream?" Doran asked.

"It was a nightmare, sort of. It was dark, and I could barely see anything other than a storm overhead. The sky was trying to tell me something, I knew it was, but I couldn't understand, and that's when a bolt of lightning shot from the sky, touching down right in front of me. Instead of just flashing, it stayed until I reached my hand out to it. When I touched it, a warmth enveloped me, and I felt...safe."

"The odd thing, though," Alden added, "is that Vaelor had the same dream before his magic presented itself. It was exactly the same, every detail. I've been trying to research its meaning, to find a connection, but I haven't found anything."

"You are chosen." Delphia whipped her head to me in disbelief. "Dreams are a sign from the Goddess. I guess that explains why her magic is so powerful," she said to Alden.

"What? Where did you hear that?" Doran gawked at his sister.

"That is a well-known understanding." She rolled her eyes.

"Yes, I figured as much, but I've been trying to find more concrete evidence. Perhaps an account of this happening before," Alden sighed, defeated.

I glimpsed at Rogue, only to find him staring at me, his face unreadable.

"Back to the situation at hand," I uttered. "What do we do about King Adon?"

"I don't think there is anything we can do about him right now," Doran said. "We need to focus on one problem at a time, and right now, that is the army lying in wait."

Rogue faced me, sighing as he sat back in a chair.

"After so many years under Adrastus, our people were burnt out with fear and anticipation. Then there was the war, and we just… We lost too many. We were overwhelmed and completely outnumbered. After his death and the end of the war—or so we thought—I just wanted to grant my people a respite. A moment to breathe." He paused, releasing a sad chuckle. "Of course, that didn't happen. The attacks began shortly after, but we didn't have the strength to return to war, so we focused on moving people out."

Doran planted a hand on Rogue's shoulder. "We were doing what we could, brother."

"Well, with all of that being said, we don't have the numbers we need." Rogue brushed him off as he stood again and began pacing.

"First, we need to divide the commanders and assign areas. Doran, I'll leave it to you to give assignments, but we need to cover as much ground as possible, as soon as possible, and I need you to go to Blackburn. That town is full of pissed off warriors chomping at the bit to return to war, so a good amount of them should join the cause. Ara and I will go to Nautia," he said as he looked at me, and I nodded. "Once we return, you'll be in charge of honing their fighting skills, Doran. Just make sure they can hold their own when the time comes. We leave tomorrow at first light."

Doran dipped his head in response and left in search of his men. After we bid Alden farewell, Rogue, Delphia, and I strolled through the library.

"So where is Thana? I would like to catch up with her after so many years apart," Delphia asked excitedly, but her face fell at our hesitation.

"Delphia, she was the one who attempted to assassinate Ara," Rogue said.

She shook her head, furrowing her eyebrows.

"No, she would never..." She glanced at me. "She did that?" She gasped, bringing a shaky hand to her mouth. She dropped her eyes to the floor, bracing herself on a nearby bookshelf. "Is she dead, then?"

"No," I said quickly, placing a hand on her shoulder. She glanced up at me, her eyes pained, and my heart hurt for her. "No, she's not. It's...complicated. I'll let her explain it to you."

"Oh, thank Goddess." She inhaled sharply. "But she hurt you? Attempted to kill you?"

I dropped my hand along with my eyes and nodded as I stepped back into Rogue.

"Am I allowed to see her?" she asked, her face tight but hopeful.

Both of us turned to Rogue, and he sighed.

CHAPTER TWENTY FOUR

"The room is under guard, so as long as you remain in her room, I don't see the harm," he said.

As she turned to leave, I stepped to follow behind her, but Rogue wrapped an arm around my waist, snatching me back to him.

"Where do you think you're going?" he whispered into my ear, sending chills along my skin.

"To see Thana?"

"Give them time first," he whispered. "There's history there, and it's been a long time since they've seen each other."

I stifled a smile as I remembered the way Thana blushed at Delphia's compliment.

"Thank you for stopping me," I said, wiggling against his grasp in an attempt to free myself.

"Mmm, this reminds me of our first night. The way you writhed against me—although, I don't think you're trying nearly as hard this time. Do you remember?" He slid his hand down my hip, setting my skin on fire in its wake. My heart jolted as heat pooled in my core, and he inhaled at my neck.

He lowered his hand, skimming along the waistband of my pants, pulling a gasp from my lips. I relaxed into his grip, letting my head fall back onto his shoulder.

"I do love when you surrender to me, little storm," he whispered into my ear, and I whimpered.

He withdrew his hand, releasing me with a chuckle. I gritted my teeth as I faced the wall for a moment, fuming, before turning and offering him a saccharine smile. I prowled closer, and his eyes widened ever so slightly before he regained his composure.

I closed the distance between us, letting my fingers trail

along the top of his trousers, over his hip, up his abdomen. My hand glided over his chest, and I could feel his heart racing beneath my palm. I continued upward until my hand found the harsh line of his jaw. He was frozen beneath my touch, barely daring to breathe.

I pulled his face closer and lifted up onto my toes to graze my lips along his, smirking.

"Such a good boy," I purred against his mouth before I released him, laughing as I spun on my heel. I left him there without another word.

Chapter Twenty Five

Rogue

My jaw was on the floor, stunned, as she walked away, hips swaying. She had never returned my teasing, and she had completely bewitched me with a simple touch. Stifling a smile, I adjusted myself and followed behind her.

When I entered her chambers, Ara was already standing at her dresser with a drawer pulled open. She glanced over her shoulder and rolled her eyes when she saw me.

"I thought I might've actually shaken you off this time."

I chuckled, closing the distance. Bracing an arm on either side of her, I leaned down, gliding my lips over the curve of her neck in the way that always sent goosebumps over her skin.

"You won't lose me that easily. I thought you would've learned that by now," I teased, nipping at the mate mark. Reaching my hand around her, I closed the drawer and opened it again, pulling out a navy piece of silk that could barely be considered a nightgown. Her cheeks flamed as she snatched it from me.

"There is no way, in any hell, I'm ever putting that on," she rasped, shoving it back inside the drawer.

Oh, you will. I smirked, and the redness in her cheeks deepened.

I pushed off the dresser, resisting the delicious scent of her arousal, and plopped down on her bed with my hands behind my head. She glared before turning back to the dresser to pull out more clothes.

"Pack some for me, will you?" I said, closing my eyes, and she scoffed. "Unless you'd prefer me unclothed. If that's the case, all you'd have to do is ask. I'll happily oblige." I chuckled, peeking one eye open at her.

She was furiously shoving whatever clothes the dresser gave her into the bag, and I stifled a laugh—an actual laugh, for at least the third time today. I couldn't remember the last time I had something, someone, to laugh with. I took a deep breath against the rising warmth in my chest and started to doze off.

"I'm going to see Thana," she declared from the edge of the bed, pulling me from sleep.

Every part of me wanted to tell her no, to order her to stay away from that treacherous, lying attempted assassin. She shouldn't be trusted.

"All right, I'll be here," was all I said, throwing my arm back over my eyes to cover the worried crease between my eyebrows.

"All right? You're not going to fight me?"

"Do you want a fight, Ara?"

"No, I just—" She paused. "Never mind. I'll be back later."

The door clicked shut, and I stared after her as worry bit at me—for more than just her visit to Thana.

CHAPTER TWENTY FIVE

* * *

I walked through the castle the next morning, the hallways bustling with soldiers preparing to leave for their respective villages. I could hear Doran barking orders in the bailey, but I hadn't seen Ara or Delphia yet. By the time I had awoken, Ara was already gone, along with the bag.

I was searching for her when Delphia found me in the library, grabbing my arm and tugging me into a secluded corner. I gaped at her when she threw her blind over us.

"I need to talk to you," she whispered.

I resisted the urge to roll my eyes. "I gathered that. What is it?"

"Promise me you will not tell Doran."

My brows furrowed. "Delphia, I don't—"

"Just until we're gone. Then you can tell him if you wish, but not until we're already gone."

"We? Gone where?"

"Thana and I are going to rescue her family. It's the only way to protect them and everyone here, by freeing her from his grasp."

"Delph—"

"I can help her," she cut in. "No one else's power is more suited to a rescue mission than mine. It's been almost five years since she's seen her family and Goddess knows how long it will be before he releases them, if ever. No one can help her more than me, Rogue. We have to go."

I dropped my gaze to the floor, rubbing a hand on the back of my neck, considering her words. She was right, of course. She was the only one who could sneak them in and out completely unseen, but Doran...

"Doran will be furious at both of us." I eyed her cautiously.

"I know, but we can't just leave her family there to rot."

I nodded. Even if they weren't Thana's family, they were Fae.

"I know," I muttered. "If there are other Fae there, and you can get them out *safely,* bring them as well. Bring them all home."

"Yes, my King." She smirked, dipping into a faint curtsy.

"And be careful," I ordered, my voice low, serious.

The smirk slid from her face.

"Always." She nodded once before she dropped the blind and rushed from the library.

Sighing, I strolled to Alden's study, knowing he would already be awake and working.

"Ara and I will be going to Nautia today," I said as I entered.

He looked up from his book, his glasses at the end of his nose. "I know. I heard."

"Anyone you want to send a message to?"

"I do believe Ewan, an old friend of Vaelor's, is living there. If you can find him, he will join the cause. Well," he chuckled, "knowing him, he'll probably find you two first."

"Ewan? Ara mentioned his name. He knew of my sibling, didn't he?" My heart raced at the prospect.

"Yes, he was the one who questioned the lady's maid, so he may be able to give her description," he said, bringing a hand to his chin.

"I'll find him," I vowed, turning to leave. "I'll keep you posted on any progress we make."

As I walked back through the entryway, there was still no sign of Ara, so I exited through the front, spotting Doran still with his men in the bailey.

CHAPTER TWENTY FIVE

"Have you seen Ara?" I shouted to him.

He jerked his chin to the side of the castle. "She went around the side early this morning before sunrise."

I strolled around the castle and hopped onto the ledge with the help of my wings, landing silently at the top. That's when I saw Ara, sitting on the edge with her arms wrapped around her knees—a black silhouette against the vibrant pink and orange of sunrise.

I had never really cared about the weather before, but now, clear skies meant everything to me, and I was grateful to see another calm morning.

She startled as I joined her on the ledge, sitting beside her.

"This is the only place I've ever seen the sky so openly before," she whispered as if scared to disturb the peace.

I glanced at her sidelong, taking in the soft curve of her face.

"Draig Hearth does have the best views," I replied, turning back to the sea.

"Yes, it does."

A small smile pulled at my lips at her agreement, and we sat in silence, admiring the sun as it peeked over the horizon.

"When I lived in Auryna, I used to read...for more than just the stories, for the escape," she whispered, and I froze. "I never thought I'd see anything past my small village if I'm being honest, but the books allowed me to journey far, far away, to live a thousand different, exciting lives." She tightened her grip on her legs, resting her chin on her knee. Her next words were barely audible, just a whisper on her breath. "I don't know when reading became less of an escape and more of a...just because I *want* to." She took a shaky breath. "I don't *have* to anymore."

A sad smile twitched on her lips. As I opened my mouth to respond, Doran shouted from below, and she jumped, whipping her face to me. Her eyes were wide as she averted her gaze.

"Time to go!"

I could've wrung his neck in that very moment, but I suppressed it from showing on my face as I stood, offering my hand to her. She stared at it for a moment before cautiously lifting her hand to mine, and my fingers closed around hers as I pulled her up.

"Thanks," she muttered as she slid her hand from mine, walking to the ledge. Before she could climb down, I swooped her into my arms and leaped down. "What are you doing?" she screamed, wrapping her arms around my neck.

"Just helping out where I can," I said, grinning as I set her softly on her feet.

"I could've gotten myself down," she muttered, dusting her pants off.

"You're a decent climber, but that would've taken longer."

Her head tilted to the side in confusion.

"How do you…" She gasped, her eyes widening. "You watched me climb that vine in Auryna, too, didn't you?"

"It was quite the sight." I winked as I walked past her. "Come on, let's go before Doran leaves us here. We'll be taking the same route until we split ways down south at the fork."

* * *

We split from Doran's group about an hour before we made it to the woodland that surrounded Nautia, and Ara tensed as we neared it.

"This one isn't like the Cursed Wood," I said as we entered the forest and were swallowed by green.

The trees were thick with age and their sweet-scented foliage created a dense canopy overhead. Sunlight poured through the gaps, creating beams that illuminated the forest floor and our narrow trail, lined with ferns and emerald-green underbrush. Lively birdsong rang from somewhere in the distance, filling the forest with its lighthearted melody. Peeking over my shoulder, I smiled as Ara visibly relaxed, tilting her face to look at the trees, her lips parted in awe.

"No, it's nothing like the Cursed Wood," she breathed. "Nothing like any wood I've ever seen."

"According to legend, this forest was blessed by the Goddess."

"I believe it," she mumbled.

"Me too," I whispered. "We aren't far from Nautia now."

"What is it like? I know Alden and Ara are from there, right?"

"Yes, they were. Nautia is a beautiful coastal town, sitting on a peninsula surrounded by the sea. It's almost unreachable from the border, so it hasn't been affected in the same way as the other villages."

"What about the people? I know the majority of those from Blackburn are warriors and fire workers, so what about Nautia?"

I stifled a smile. "Been reading up on Ravaryn, hmm?"

Her cheeks tinted pink. "Yes, and? Would you rather me not?" she asked sarcastically.

"No. By all means, feel free. Actually, I prefer that you do. Ravaryn's people are just as diverse as the magic here," I said.

"The majority of Nautia have magic related to water, hence, being so close to the sea. Some can move water, some can turn into water entirely, and then there are those like Ara, your grandmother, who could pull the rain from the clouds."

"But she wasn't a Storm Bringer?"

"No." I shook my head. "That title is reserved for those who can form the storms and call to the electricity it creates, the rain and lightning together. It's extremely rare. Besides Vaelor, there has only ever been one other recorded Storm Bringer, but that was a millennium or two ago."

"Ah," was all she said.

"That was one of the reasons Vaelor was king. Don't get me wrong, he deserved the title because he was fair and kind, so I'm told, but he was also blessed."

She didn't respond that time, so we continued in silence.

As we neared Nautia, the ground became softer in some areas, indicating wetland. When a small trail split off from the main, I halted the cohort, jumping down from my horse. Ara hesitated when I offered my hand, but she took it cautiously and dismounted. Keeping her hand grasped tightly in mine, I led her down the footpath too small for a horse.

"Where are we going?" she asked from behind me.

I didn't respond, grinning ear to ear.

As we strolled, the ground became covered in thick, green moss and small round stepping stones replaced the dirt path. We continued, stepping from stone to stone until they led us to a shallow pool of crystal-clear water. She paused, glancing at me, and I nodded, tugging her forward. We stepped into the cool water together, lit green with the moss underneath.

Once we reached the end of the trail, it opened into a small clearing, and golden sunshine washed over us, pulling an

CHAPTER TWENTY FIVE

audible gasp from her lips.

It was the kind of wetland only found in these woods. Through the water, wildflowers sprouted, painting the clearing in a rainbow of pastel colors that swayed in the breeze. We carefully trod through the blooms as the breeze wafted their scent all around us.

The scent reminded me so much of Ara, it almost knocked me off my feet. *This.* This is what she smelled like: happiness and warmth and wet and wildflowers. I halted and inhaled deeply as she strolled to the small, grassy knoll in the center.

I followed behind her and once we reached the top, she turned to sit, pulling her knees to her chest. The hint of a smile danced along her lips as I plopped down beside her, leaning back on my hands, splaying my wings behind me.

"Worth the stop?" I asked and she glanced sidelong at me.

"Definitely worth it," she replied, returning my smile—a *genuine* smile. My heart skipped a beat, and I swallowed hard, turning my eyes to the field.

"Thank you," she whispered.

"You're welcome."

We sat, listening to the leaves bristling in the wind and the birdsong from the trees.

"I don't know why I told you what I did earlier. I'm almost embarrassed, but—" She hesitated, and I didn't dare look at her. "But I really, truly never thought I'd leave there. It was a terrifying thought—being shackled down to a place that drains you so, to people who don't see you, don't know you. This"—she waved a hand—"is so much more than I ever expected to see, especially when Evander tried to give my hand in marriage. I don't know if you know that, but he tried to force me into a marriage with my childhood friend. Now *that* would've really shackled me." She released a sad laugh.

My fingers gripped the ground, digging into the soil as anger shot through me, closely followed by jealousy.

I'd been so close to leaving Auryna, so close to missing her. That one night, that one small last-ditch decision, changed everything. Without that, she would've been married off, and this would've never happened. Never existed. My heart twisted at the mere thought.

Then I remembered who she was talking about, and anxiety churned in my gut.

"His name was Finley. He was my only friend—well, I thought he was a friend—and he was the only person my father let me leave the estate with. In retrospect, it should've been obvious that he was going to hand me over, but I had been so blindsided, so... hurt."

I glimpsed at her to catch her staring out over the blooms, lost in her memories as she absentmindedly twirled a blade of grass in her fingers.

"I guess I don't have to worry about that anymore, though." Her hand found the point of her ear. "I do wonder what Evander has told the town. Maybe they think I died in some tragic accident, or maybe they all just think I'm locked away in the manor, wasting away."

I stared down at the ground, my heart aching for her.

"The—" I started, but she jumped, turning away as she wiped her cheek, and I hesitated before continuing, "The discontentment you felt there was probably due, in part at least, to the curse placed on your Fae side. When a Fae's connection to their magic is severed, their life is left...lacking. They never feel truly comfortable or happy. They're never satisfied. That's why I—" I stopped mid-sentence.

CHAPTER TWENTY FIVE

"Why what?" she asked.

I closed my eyes, silently kicking myself.

"That's why I ordered Alden not to tell you of Vaelor. That curse, it should've been unbreakable. You were going to live a life of discontentment, and I thought if you didn't know, it would make the burden a little less intolerable," I explained, finally opening my eyes to look at her.

Her face was slack, her eyes brimming with tears.

"I have been so angry at you for that, for keeping it from me, and you were just trying to what? Protect me?" she whispered, processing it aloud.

I cringed and jerked to my feet, needing this conversation to be over.

"Yes."

I extended a hand to her, and she took it, her expression unreadable as I hoisted her up before quickly dropping her hand and stepping down into the water.

"You should also know that even if you had returned, you most likely wouldn't have married Finley," I said without turning around.

"Why is that?" she called out.

"Because I burned his farm and house to the ground."

I heard her stop, and I continued forward, avoiding her reaction. Her anger. Her disgust.

But when she burst out laughing, I whipped my head around in disbelief.

"You—" She wheezed. "You burnt down his farm?" She laughed again, wiping tears from her eyes. "You know what? Good." I gawked at her as she slid past me, patting my arm. "Serves him right for trying to force my hand."

I snapped my mouth closed, my eyes wide as she strolled

along, reaching a hand down to run her fingers through the blooms.

This woman…

"You coming?"

"Yep. Right behind you."

We entered the treeline along the stepping stones when she spoke again.

"So, you'll know where I am for the rest of my life?"

"Uh—" The question caught me off guard, snapping me back from my thoughts. "Yes."

"What does that mean exactly?" She paused and before I could answer, she continued. "If I were to take off right now, would you know where I was as I ran, or would it just be easier to track me?"

I stifled a smile. "Up for a game of cat and mouse, little storm?"

"No," she replied quickly—too quickly—and I couldn't help but laugh.

"No, I wouldn't know exactly where you were per se. It would be more like…a beacon calling me to you. I can feel you in relation to me," I described. "It's hard to explain."

"Oh," she breathed.

We were about halfway back to the cohort when we made it to the dirt footpath and the trees became dense again. Something flickered in my peripheral vision, but when I turned to look, I didn't see anything. Nothing unwelcome ever happened in these woods, but an uneasiness still settled in my gut.

I turned forward, keeping my eyes on Ara and our surroundings, when another flicker caught my attention. I stopped this time, studying the forest, but again, saw nothing

CHAPTER TWENTY FIVE

out of the ordinary.

Just as Ara turned to face me, thousands of butterflies released from the trees and she froze. Her eyes followed as they fluttered about, blurring the forest in a brilliance of orange, but I couldn't pull my eyes away from her. Her face lit with awe, and she gasped as a butterfly landed on her cheek, slowly opening and closing its wings.

She brought her gaze to me, smiling faintly, then returned her eyes to the butterfly as it fluttered away.

The sight sucked the breath from my chest, and I took a half step back, needing something. Space. Air. Anything.

Thirty-nine years. Thirty-nine years of darkness and rage and hurt. I didn't know what this was, but it wasn't that.

"It's beautiful," she whispered, her eyes following their movement.

"Yes, quite beautiful," I whispered back, my eyes never leaving her.

Once most of them had settled or fled, we returned to our men in silence. It wasn't long before we exited the forest and Nautia came into view from atop the hill.

"Wow."

"I know," I replied, trotting forward.

From this view, we could see the entire town and its surrounding sea. The buildings were varying shades of blue, green, and white, the worn cobblestone streets lined with lampposts lit with the same never-ending fire as Blackburn, except these lights were hung by strands, leading from one post to the next, welcoming its guests.

The sun was setting now, the air warm and humid with the smell of sea salt drifting on the breeze. The sound of children laughing, faint music, and waves lapping at a distant shore filled the streets, creating the melody of Nautia.

This town was happy. Safe. Untouched by humankind.

I hid my wings behind a glamour as we entered the town, but people still stopped to stare and whisper, children grinning before they ran back to their parents with the news of new arrivals. I led us to a tavern, and we dismounted, tying our horses to the posts. I hadn't brought many men—around ten—but even the sight of that many newcomers ceased all chatter as we entered.

"Welcome to the Sopping Sailor," the bartender said, glancing up from the several drinks he was pouring. With that, the rest of the customers relaxed and the hum of chatter resumed.

"Come on, let's go settle in first," I whispered, leading us to the back. "No need to rile anyone up just yet."

We sat at an old, rickety wooden table while my men spread out, most of them sitting at the bar.

"What's the plan?" Ara asked, glancing around the room.

"Well, I'll address them, tell them who I am, of the situation, and hopefully, they'll want to join us," I explained. "But...this town. This is where Vaelor was born and raised. They knew him, grew up with him, and they hated my father, so it's only a guessing game whether they'll hate me, too. I only hope I can convince them to join."

"What about me? What's my role?"

I turned to her, raising one eyebrow.

"What do you mean? This isn't your fight. I brought you to keep you safe, but I don't expect anything of you."

Hurt flashed behind her eyes as she leaned in to angrily whisper, "Not my fight? Not *my* fight? Is my father not the former King Vaelor? Do I not have pointed ears like the rest of you? Did Evander not try to kill me too? Before I even knew I was part Fae, this became my fight when I saw the people of Ravaryn. The mothers. The children playing in the streets. Thana. Iaso. Alden... You. None of them deserve this. I can't just stand by while they're brutally attacked."

My chest swelled with pride as she spoke. *Her fight.*

She whipped her head forward, her mouth set in a tight line.

"Now tell me. What. Is. My. Role?" she said, biting at each word.

My heart beat once. Twice.

I couldn't hide my smile.

"Well, I hadn't thought of that. I'm not sure yet," I replied.

She huffed, jerking to her feet before marching to the bar and taking a seat next to one of my soldiers.

She took on Ravaryn's fight as her own, willingly. She wanted to fight for Ravaryn. My people. Our people, if she considered herself one of us.

It seems I've underestimated you, little storm. That will not happen again.

Chapter Twenty Six

Ara

That arrogant bastard.

I flagged down the bartender and he sat a large mug of mead in front of me. I stared at it for a moment., reminded of Livvy. The thought pulled at my heartstrings, but I brushed it away, turning the mug up to down its contents.

I slammed it on the bar and the soldiers cheered, clapping me on the back.

"Well, look at that! She drinks!"

I cocked a smile at them before peeking over my shoulder at Rogue, only to find his red eyes burning into me. I whipped my head forward as a fresh wave of irritation washed over me.

He genuinely thought I'd just willingly come along for the ride. No purpose. No role.

The irritation grew to anger, and my blood boiled as I seethed, tightening my grip on the wooden handle. I felt it then—the sparks. They flickered at my fingertips and danced along my irises. I tensed before releasing the mug, but my heart thundered as I saw the blackened handprint burned into it.

My eyes darted around the bar and landed on the bartender. His mouth was slack as we locked eyes. He was staring. He saw.

My throat tightened with panic. I blinked rapidly, averting my gaze, but as I started to rise from the stool, he sat another mug in front of me, dipped his chin, and silently walked away with the other. I took it slowly, stunned.

Hours passed while I sat at the bar, eavesdropping.

As a group of men steadily got louder, the tavern quieted to listen, and I spun on the stool to face them.

"Their king is pushing against the border," one man said.

My heart skipped a beat. *They're speaking of Auryna. Convenient timing, I suppose.*

"The greedy bastard wants to claim the land as his own. That's what it seems like, clearing towns of the Fae either by slaughter or running them out of their homes," another man angrily spat, and several agreed.

"And where is the spineless King Rogue? Hiding in his dead father's shadow? He hasn't lifted a finger to stop them," a pale, stubby man said.

My eyes snapped to Rogue, deathly still as he listened.

"What would you have him do?" I asked, shocking even myself. Every pair of eyes snapped to me, including Rogue's. "Should he sacrifice the men he has to an army three times its size?"

All eyes shifted back to him, and his cheeks tinted pink.

"I would prefer it if he didn't hide in Draig Hearth while his people took the brunt," he muttered, and several men around him nodded.

"Is that what I'm doing, hmm?" Rogue replied, standing and dropping the glamour from his wings. The men tensed, the blood draining from their faces. "Please. Tell me how I can better myself for you." He stepped closer, shuffling his large wings behind him, his head cocked to the side.

They shifted back in their seats, cowering.

"That's why I've come. Auryna's troops are lining the border as we speak, and it's only a matter of time before they mobilize. I've granted Ravaryn three years to get what rest it can, but it's time. We can no longer allow Auryna to continue to attack and ravage *our* land. *Our* people. *Our* homes. We came to find men to join us sending those disgusting creatures back to their own land and off ours," he said. His passion was clear as day, written all over his face, in his words, in his stance.

The men hesitated, some shaking their heads.

"If their army is three times the size of ours, how will we ever stand a chance?" someone asked from the back of the room.

"Because we are the people of Ravaryn. We will band together and show them who *we* are. How powerful *we* are. They have taken too much, too many, and it's time we put an end to it. This is *our* land. *Our* home."

Some nodded in agreement, but the majority still hesitated.

"I will not pledge to you, the son of Adrastus, the son of the *murderer*. I will not betray Vaelor. I cannot. He was a friend to me and everyone else here," a woman said, gesturing to the room.

A muscle ticked in Rogue's jaw.

"This war is bigger than your allegiance to me or Vaelor," Rogue fumed as he glanced at me, holding his hand out. I

CHAPTER TWENTY SIX

stood cautiously, joining him by his side. "But if that is your concern, pledge your allegiance to her."

I whipped my face to him. "What are you doing?" I whispered harshly, feeling a blush creep up my neck.

"Giving you your role," he whispered back, his gaze intense. He turned back to the crowd and I gaped at him before snapping my mouth shut.

"Who is she? Why, in any hell, would we pledge to her?"

It was the bartender who spoke next. "Because she's the lost daughter of King Vaelor." He walked around the bar to stand in front of me, and I took a half step back, my brows furrowing.

"He didn't have a child," a man replied and several voices chimed in, agreeing.

"My name is Ewan, milady," he said, kneeling before me and bowing his head. "I was your father's general and friend, and now, I pledge my life and fealty to you, if you will have me."

Ewan. This is Ewan.

Words wouldn't form in my mouth as he knelt on one knee before me. I didn't know what to say, what to do, how to react, so I bent down to him, took his hand, and pulled him to stand.

"Thank you, Ewan. I accept," I said.

"My sword is yours to command," he declared with a smile, moving to my side and turning to face the crowd.

"I was there when Vaelor met his love, Elora. They did conceive a child, but when Adrastus murdered Vaelor, she had to flee for her own safety *and* the baby's." He glanced at me. "I never thought we would see your return, but I am beyond proud to meet you. Welcome home, princess."

My eyes watered at his words. *Home.* I swallowed hard and faced the crowd.

"How do you know that's his daughter?"

"Well, apart from just looking at her…" He glanced at me again, silently asking, and I nodded. "I believe she has his magic."

The crowd went into an uproar of denial.

"That's impossible!"

"King Vaelor was the Storm Bringer!"

"She cannot have that power."

Ewan and Rogue both turned to me, and the blood drained from my face as I realized they wanted me to demonstrate.

My mouth went dry. There were too many eyes. Too many expectations. Too much weight on my ability to control any part of my magic.

I can't control it. I never have.

I lifted a shaky hand, staring at it, begging it to do something—sparks, electricity, lightning, anything, but when nothing happened, the crowd began shouting again.

"She is *not* his daughter."

"This is no Storm Bringer."

"A pathetic attempt to trick us."

My heart raced as sweat formed along my spine. It was too loud. Too many eyes on me. I couldn't focus.

I squeezed my eyes shut, and Rogue grabbed my hand, rubbing his thumb along the back of it. I lifted my eyes to meet his, and he nodded in encouragement.

I took a shaky breath and closed my eyes again, blocking out the roar of the crowd.

Ravaryn needs this. I need this. For once, I will not let myself down.

CHAPTER TWENTY SIX

But nothing happened. My hands trembled and I took another slow breath, inhaling the scent of men and mead—wishing it was the scent of rain instead.

For once, I need control.

Then, the realization hit me like a ton of bricks.

If I cannot control it, maybe it doesn't want to be controlled. I knew I didn't. I had spent my entire life strictly under the thumb of someone else and I had wilted under it. Maybe my magic needed what I needed...

Release.

Choice.

Freedom.

Help me, I silently pleaded to the power seething inside me, to the sky above, to the energy surrounding me. I jerked my hand from Rogue's, snapping my eyes open just as I felt the surge and accepted it—accepted *all* of it.

Electricity lit my irises, sending energy racing down my spine to my fingertips. I held my face to the sky, closing my eyes, reveling in it as blue sparks illuminated the room, bouncing from finger to finger.

Outside, lightning cracked and thunder rumbled, shaking the building. The crowd gasped and went silent, grabbing onto whatever was closest as the roar of pounding rain filled the room.

The energy moved through me. Filled me. Healed me. Closed the gaps in my soul.

Finally.

Finally, we were one.

As it settled, I took another deep inhale, and it felt like I was taking my first real breath. It was clear and crisp and whole—satisfying.

It was satisfying.

Opening my eyes, I was met with the shocked faces of every person around me, including Rogue and Ewan. It was deathly silent, everyone frozen in place.

"The last Storm Bringer," someone breathed.

"The last Storm Bringer," Rogue echoed beside me, his eyes wide, smiling faintly in awe.

"I will stand with you, princess," a man said, closing the distance and kneeling in front of me.

"As will I," said another. And another. And another.

One after another, they all came forward until every person knelt on one knee, their heads bowed.

* * *

A few hours later, the heaviness in the room had dissipated as the mead flowed. I had spent the entire time listening to story after story of Vaelor, and my smile hadn't faltered since they began.

Every story was full of kindness, bravery, strength, and selflessness. I swelled with pride at every memory he had left on this town, but a small part of me was saddened, each story serving as a reminder that I would never experience that same kindness. I would never even get to meet him.

I lifted the mug to my lips, savoring the sweet honey as the man continued his story to the group I was sitting with.

"And there I was, a young lad of only eight with no wits in sight, thinking I could weather the storm and swim out to touch the rock as the older boys had done. Mind you, it was really storming now—rain, lightning, wind, you name it. I made it halfway when a riptide grabbed me. I fought it, but it was no use. I was a goner until Vaelor stalled the storm and jumped into the water to save me." He placed a hand on mine. "It's by his grace that I am here to tell you this story today."

Tears swam in the man's eyes, and I nodded, swallowing against the rising emotion.

"I will forever be grateful for your father. He was the bravest, kindest man this town ever knew."

"Aye!" The group cheered around us, raising their mugs in tribute. I smiled, lifting the mug and taking another sip.

Out of the corner of my eye, I could see Rogue at the table with his men. We hadn't spoken since the people pledged to the cause…to me.

My mind was still reeling. It didn't feel quite real, and it definitely didn't feel right. I didn't grow up here. I didn't even know Vaelor, and yet, these people were willing to follow me into battle just to honor his legacy.

I took another long drink from the mug, returning my focus to Rogue.

A man leaned across the table to say something unintelligible with a wide grin, and Rogue threw his head back in laughter. A smile pulled at my lips. I didn't think I'd ever heard him laugh like that. He caught my stare and turned his head in my direction, a lazy grin still painting his lips, and he winked at me before turning back to his men.

I released a soft laugh as butterflies took off in my gut, and I didn't know if it was the mead or something entirely worse. Lifting the mug to my lips, I downed the rest of its contents and walked to the bar, plopping down on a stool. As I approached, Ewan set another on the counter with a smile.

"I meant what I said, every word. My sword, and my life, are yours just as they were your father's."

"Thank you, Ewan," I replied. "I actually... Well, I found Vaelor's journals at Draig Hearth, and he mentioned you in them. I haven't read much yet, just the entries about Adrastus."

His eyes dropped to the bar, his hand running along the smooth wood.

"If I had known what Adrastus would go on to do, I would've killed him the first chance I got. Cut the head off the beast. But Vaelor...He believed every life could be saved. It will always be my biggest regret."

When he looked up again, I could see guilt in his eyes. I reached out, placing my hand on his and giving it a light squeeze, as Livvy had done so many times for me.

"None of that was your fault. You couldn't have known, Ewan. Don't let this weigh on you. From what I've heard, Vaelor wouldn't want that."

He gazed at me, swallowing hard. "I know you're right. He wouldn't, but it's still...hard. It will weigh on me for the rest of my days. But know this: I will *not* fail you."

"You didn't fail Vaelor, Ewan."

He nodded once and cleared his throat, dropping his gaze as he wiped the bar with a rag. "Well, I can say for certainty that you're just as compassionate as your parents. Your mother must be so proud. How is Elora?"

"Evander killed her a few days ago," I said as the numbness returned.

He snapped his head back to me, mouth open.

"I am...I am so sorry," he uttered as he pulled a decanter from under the bar and poured two shots of brown liquid into tiny glasses. He slid one to me and lifted the other. "To Vaelor. To Elora. To every kind soul taken too soon."

CHAPTER TWENTY SIX

I clenched my jaw, but it didn't stop the tear that slid down my cheek.

"To every kind soul," I echoed, lifting my glass and tossing the shot back. I embraced the burn, letting it chase away the hot lump in my throat.

As I set my glass back down, he filled it again. I lifted an eyebrow at him, and he chuckled.

"It's customary to take two—one for the life they lived and one for the afterlife to come."

I tipped it back and sputtered a little.

"That stuff is strong," I choked out.

He lifted his brows, nodding as he laughed. "It's rum from a local distillery. I would assume Fae rum is stronger than the whiskey in Auryna."

I grimaced, holding my hand over my mouth. "Oh, it definitely is."

Grabbing my mug, I stood from the bar stool and swayed, my head spinning. Rogue was there in a split second, wrapping an arm around my shoulders, chuckling in my ear.

"Oh, I'm fine," I said, swatting at his arm and pulling out of his grasp.

"Are you, little storm?" he said, stifling a smile before letting me go. Smirking over my shoulder at him, I took a step forward and ran straight into a table, knocking my hip on it. He started to laugh, but I held up a finger at him, glaring.

"Not a word."

I carefully stepped around the table to rejoin my group as he returned to his.

It may be the rum, but there was something about this place. These people. The warmth of their smiles and stories. The sound of waves crashing in the distance. Knowing Rogue was nearby.

It all felt safe. For the first time in Goddess knows how long, I felt myself exhale the tension I had been carrying for so long. For the first time, I felt at peace.

I sunk into the leather chair, losing myself in their stories. When I finally looked around an hour or so later, I glanced at Rogue just as a woman stepped closer to him, reaching a hand out to touch his shoulder.

I don't care.

I jerked my eyes away.

I told him he wasn't my mate. I told him I would never be his mate.

Sparks tickled my fingertips, burning spots into the mug handle, and as a distinctly female voice rang out above the chatter, I jerked to my feet. The men glanced up at me, pausing.

"I'm just going to step out for some air real quick," I explained, faking a smile that slid from my lips the moment I turned around. Stalking to the door, I left without another word.

I don't care. I don't.

I marched around the edge of the building, halfway expecting to see the pond from back home, but I was met with an ocean instead. I gasped at the sight; it was black and endless with small, calm waves lapping at the sand, the sky clear and moon full, reflecting off the water.

I took a half step forward when a hand grabbed my wrist. Expecting Rogue, I whirled around, only to be met with the face of a stranger instead. His beard was scraggly, surrounding a spine-chilling smile missing a few teeth. He looked at me with one eye, the other covered by a dirty

CHAPTER TWENTY SIX

patch, his broken gaze roaming over my form with such vile appreciation that it made nausea roll in my gut. When the breeze wafted his stench toward me, I had to force down a gag, but he only stepped closer. I jerked my arm free of his grasp, staggering back a few steps to put distance between us.

"So, you're the daughter of King Vaelor, eh?" He took another menacing step closer, and I took another step back. "I've never been with a princess."

My heart raced, my lip curling in disgust. "And you won't be tonight, either."

As I tried to stride past him, he grabbed me by the throat with shocking strength and slammed me into the wall. My mouth went dry as he choked my breath off, icy panic shooting through my veins.

"You bitch," he said, tightening his grip on my throat. Sweat broke out along my forehead as I clawed at his hand, my fingernails digging into his skin. "What makes you think you're so much better than me, eh?"

Just as my vision blurred, a thick hand wrapped around his own throat, and he released me with a bloodcurdling scream as flames licked at his neck. I fell forward, gasping, the smell of burning flesh filling my nose. The screaming ceased as Rogue choked off his airway, and the man's one eye bulged.

"Go," he ordered, lethally calm as smoke swirled around them. "Go inside, Ara."

I staggered to my feet and stumbled back around the corner, forcing myself not to look back as the raging fire cast my shadow in front of me. The screams resumed for a split second before stopping abruptly, and I clenched my fist, walking faster.

Chapter Twenty Seven

Ara

As I rounded the corner of the building, I stopped, bracing a hand on the wall while the other reached up to my throat.

"Fucking degenerate," Rogue seethed, his voice tight with rage as he strode around the corner, stopping mid-stride when he saw me. "Why would you come out here alone?"

My eyes snapped to him as anger pulsed through me.

"Oh, I don't know. I thought I'd give you and that woman some privacy," I spat back at him through clenched teeth.

His mouth fell open before snapping shut, and he quickly closed the distance between us, his fists clenched at his sides. I backed into the wall behind me as he neared, stopping just inches from me.

Thunder rumbled in the distance.

"That *woman* served in my father's army. She was expressing her desire to join the cause and return to the King's army. *And* she was impressed to see the blood of Vaelor and Adrastus working together for the benefit of the realm," he said, bracing a hand on either side of my head, dipping his face down to

CHAPTER TWENTY SEVEN

mine. He cocked his head to the side as a smirk slowly tipped up one corner of his mouth. "If I didn't know any better, I'd say you were jealous."

"I am *not* jealous."

He lowered a hand and gripped the side of my face, his little finger grazing my mate mark. He sighed as the smirk slid from his lips.

"You still don't know the entirety of what this means," he said in a low voice, his finger gliding across the mark again.

I waited for him to explain, but he released me, turning away. With a mind of its own, my hand reached out and snatched his arm, jerking him back to me. "Then tell me. For once, Rogue, *stop* being such a coward and tell me the fucking truth."

Lightning cracked in the distance as rain suddenly released from the clouds. His eyes rose to the sky, and he stiffened, dropping his eyes back to me.

I held my chin high, holding his gaze as the downpour soaked us both. A heartbeat passed, and he was on me again, pressing me back against the wall. The overhang of the building combined with the wall of rain cut us off from the rest of the world, the air thick with humidity, clinging to our already-soaked skin.

His hand gripped my cheek as his eyes locked with mine. "The truth, Ara? You want the truth?"

"Yes," I breathed.

He released a low, breathy laugh.

"There will never be another woman for me." He paused. "Ever."

I stilled at his words. "What…Why?"

"This"—his thumb slid down across the mark—"is a symbol

of… surrender. I know you believe that it was my claim upon you, but it wasn't. It never was. I bound my body and soul to you, little storm."

My heart skipped a beat.

"That cannot… That is not true," I whispered, shaking my head.

The crease between his eyebrows deepened as his lips curved into a sad smile.

"Unfortunately, it is." He brushed the hair from my face. "I will crave only you for the rest of my life."

Unfortunately. The word rang through me, suffocating any foolish hope that had arisen. My mouth tightened as I jerked my face from his hand and stepped away from him into the rain.

"Yes, how unfortunate for you. Shackled to me—"

He stepped from the overhang and grabbed my wrist, turning me back to him. Dark rain pelted us as we locked eyes and the tension felt as thick as the humidity.

"Shackled to you? That's what you think? That *I* am shackled to *you?*"

I nodded curtly, and he took the final step between us, cupping my face in both of his hands.

"Ara, you could not be more wrong. It is *I* who shackled *you,* and it is a regret that haunts me every day. Every day, I see the hurt I caused you, and I wish I could take it back. I wish I would've told you and courted you and convinced you to like me with pretty words and false promises, but I can't, and I know that. But I also know that it is more than this tiny, insignificant mark on your skin that binds me to you. It's *you.* All of you. Your strength and resilience. Your determination to endure no matter what fate throws at you. Your love of

CHAPTER TWENTY SEVEN

love and stories and hope. You are entirely the opposite of everything that I am, and I would *gladly* wear your shackles if it meant I could have you."

My mouth dropped open at his words, my eyes wide as they searched his face.

"I..." I hesitated, speechless.

He rested his forehead on mine.

"Don't worry, little storm. I never expected you to feel the same way," he said, releasing a sad, breathy laugh that broke me. "But there. That is the truth. All of it."

He pulled back, and his face looked pained as his thumb slid along my lower lip. His next words were barely a whisper. "If I'm fated to live a life of longing for someone who will never return my affection, I'm glad to long for someone so... worthy."

My throat burned, and I inhaled sharply, breathing in the scent of smoke and evergreen spice. Placing my palm on his cheek, I pulled back and studied his face—the face that had been burned into my memory the first night I ever saw it.

In the recesses of my mind, I knew it wasn't a matter of if I wanted him in return. That became glaringly obvious a long time ago. It was a matter of if I could allow myself to make the leap.

He studied my face in return as my thoughts warred.

I felt as if I was standing on a cliff with a choice. I could turn away and continue along the same path, well worn by broken dreamers but safe.

Or I could jump. It would be exhilarating and life-altering. It would set my soul on fire with the heat of passion, but would he catch me? Or would it end in us both crashing back down to a painful reality?

I want—I want—

I had always craved *more*, and now, it was staring me in the face, just waiting for my response. I licked my lips, and his eyes dropped down to them, following the motion before they darted back up to meet mine, the intensity in his gaze knocking the breath from my lungs, throwing me from the cliff.

"You. I want you," I rasped, and it wasn't the mate bond that forced the words from my lips.

His breath left him in a whoosh a second before every part of him crashed into me, his ravenous lips on mine, his hands knotted into my hair, pulling me closer, and I melted into him.

In that moment, cut off from the rest of the realm and surrounded by his warmth, I surrendered to him. To my wants. To my desires.

With that came the unabashed rush of freedom.

It was at that very moment I realized I *had* freedom, and tears pricked my eyes.

He was my choice to make, and I chose him.

The air was electrified as I threw my arms around his neck and wrapped my legs around his waist. He groaned into my mouth, and the kiss deepened, breathless and desperate and soul-shattering.

It was more than lust.

He walked me back under the overhang, and as soon as my back hit the wall, we were shedding clothes. Soaked and starved, we couldn't pull them off fast enough.

"I wish I could see you," I whispered as we dropped the last bit of clothing.

With the solid sheet of rain, it was too dark to see each

CHAPTER TWENTY SEVEN

other, but I could feel him. My hands roamed his body, feeling along his abdomen, his scar, over his shoulder. He was hard, all tanned skin over solid muscle, but completely malleable under my touch.

He groaned as I grazed the base of one wing and my exploration was over. He roughly grabbed my hips, pulling me away from the wall just enough that I was flush with him.

His hands slid along my hips, my waist, my breasts, touching every part of me as his mouth devoured mine.

My breath hitched as the tip of each wing glided up my calves, inching higher and higher until they reached the crease of my hips and lowered again. The feeling was foreign and tantalizing. *Delicious.*

It was a tease that set me on edge, and my breaths quickened as the need for him consumed me.

Then, his wings surrounded us entirely. I was enveloped in *him*.

If the overhang cut us off from the rest of the world, the cocoon of his wings *created* our own world, one of dark bliss and ecstasy and sensory overload.

As he dipped a finger into me on the same breath that his tongue pushed into my mouth, I was lost to him.

It was all I could do to stand. He pulled his finger out slowly, just to re-enter with two more, and I moaned as my head fell back.

He grinned as he tilted his ear to my mouth, reveling in the sound of my moans as he quickened his pace. The sight was devilish and wicked, and it went straight to my core. I needed *more.*

I wrapped my arms around his neck, pulling him down to me. "I need more. I need you."

As the words left my mouth, he pulled his fingers from me and slowly slid them along my behind, over my hip, and up my abdomen between my breasts, leaving a trail of my own arousal.

"Look how wet you are for me, little storm."

For once, my cheeks didn't blush at his words, my mind and body too preoccupied and desperate to care.

"No blush this time? Pity," he purred, tilting my chin up with his wet hand.

My lips parted. It was pitch black, and I couldn't see his face, even as close as he was. "Can you—"

He ran a thumb along my lower lip, and my words caught in my throat.

"Yes, I can see you and you look exquisite. Beautifully soaked and in need of your *mate*." He dragged out the last word before bringing his mouth down to mine in a soft kiss.

His hands slid down my waist and under my thighs to lift me, and I wrapped my legs around him as he lined himself at my entrance. A loud moan tore from my lips as he slid in, and he groaned in my ear as he lifted and lowered me back on him.

Perfect.

As I adjusted to him, he quickened his pace until I was just one scream after another, blocked by his wings and the torrential downpour.

It felt so *right*. So right, it almost brought tears to my eyes that I ever fought this in the first place.

He dropped his wings, and goosebumps spread over my skin at the exposure to the outside air. He backed me into the wall, bracing me against it as he lifted both of my legs above his shoulders.

My eyes went wide, and he grinned at me again, a smirk that told me he knew—we both knew—he was about to destroy me for any other man, as if he hadn't already.

Bracing one hand by my head and gripping my hip with the other, he eased out and met my eyes. "Hold on, little storm."

I tightened my grip around him and then he thrust, hitting deeper than he ever had before. Stars spotted my vision as he pounded into me mercilessly.

Did I think it was perfect before? No, this. *This is... There are no words.*

It was almost too much, the pleasure blinding.

Just when I thought I could take no more, the sparks in my vision exploded, and I came around him. It was powerful, wave after wave of destruction, wrecking me to my very core.

He increased his pace, prolonging the feeling until he slammed into me one final time. A roar tore from his throat as he finished, and he dropped his forehead to mine.

We were a tangle of limbs and sweat and breathlessness—beautiful chaos that came together to *finally* find a moment of peace.

* * *

We re-entered the tavern in silence, our hands mere inches from each other as we walked, the space between us diminishing with each hesitant step. His little finger grazed mine, and my heart skipped a beat.

How odd it was to be so on edge by his nearness when just moments ago, we were *much* closer.

Rogue glanced down at me, his fingers lightly intertwining with mine before Ewan noticed us.

"Well, welcome back," Ewan said, glancing up and then back down to the bar as he wiped it with a rag.

I started to pull my hand away when Rogue slid his hand into mine, holding it tightly as he turned his face to Ewan.

"So, you are Ewan, then?" Rogue asked.

Ewan threw the rag over his shoulder and rested his hand on the bar as we strolled over. "Yep, that'd be me. And you're Rogue, the son of Adrastus?" Ewan said without malice, just curiosity.

"Yep." Rogue nodded, mirroring Ewan's informality. "Speaking of...we recently discovered Adrastus fathered a son before me."

Ewan shifted on his feet as he ran a hand over the scruff along his jaw. "Ah, I forgot about that. We never heard anything more about it. To be honest, I wasn't even sure the woman I spoke with was being truthful."

"So, it was you, then? Who spoke with the lady's maid?"

"Yes, it was me," he said. "Why? Have you heard anything more?"

Rogue shook his head. "No, but I was hoping to find him. I want him to know he has nothing to fear from me. Living this long in hiding, in fear, is long enough."

Ewan eyed him carefully, nodding lightly.

"Well, I never got his name or the name of the mother, but I can tell you she escaped south, closer to the border. That's all she told me out of fear for the child's safety."

Rogue sighed, rubbing his forehead with his hand. "Well, thank you anyway. If you can, spread the word. Even if he doesn't reveal himself, the message will reach him eventually. I'm sure it won't take long to spread once the people learn of a second son."

CHAPTER TWENTY SEVEN

"Will do," Ewan replied. "If you and your men need a place to stay, there's an inn next door. I'm sure the innkeeper still has some rooms available."

"Thank you," we said in unison as we turned to leave.

"Is…" He started, leaning over the bar with one final question. "Are Iaso and Alden still at Draig Hearth by chance?"

I stopped, giving him a light smile. "Yes, they're still there."

Ewan returned my smile, dipping his chin in farewell as a newfound hopefulness lit his eyes.

With that, we exited the tavern, Rogue's men in tow behind us.

* * *

As it turns out, the inn only had three rooms left.

Rogue tossed two keys to his men and grabbed my hand, leading us to the last as my heart thundered in my chest.

As we passed by a small bar area, he dipped over, grabbing a decanter without missing a beat, and I stifled a laugh. We reached our room, and he held the door open with an outstretched hand.

One bed.

I swallowed hard. *Why did this feel so different from the castle? So…intimate.*

Even as I thought it over, I knew why. We had admitted our desire—genuine desire that went below the skin, below the bond. So many weeks of fighting and hating and bickering, all leading to this night. This moment. Now, the air around us had shifted, heavy with something I couldn't quite understand.

The door clicked shut behind me and I tensed, my heart racing. Rogue turned the lock, and the sound of his footsteps nearing closer set me on edge. My breaths were shallow as I turned to face him, but he glided past me, pulling his shirt off and hanging it over the bed frame.

Water dripped from his hair, and my eyes followed a droplet as it rolled down his back between his wings. He reached up to tie his sopping hair in a knot.

"I know you're wet, Ara," he said without turning around, and I jumped. "Your clothes, little storm."

I glanced down. My shirt was soaked through, clinging to my skin as my chest rose and fell quickly. Grabbing the hem with shaky hands, I pulled it overhead and laid it beside his. With my back to Rogue, I unbuttoned and slid my trousers down, feeling his gaze on me as I laid them out on the floor.

With a deep breath, I turned to him. He was completely unclothed, just as I was, and my lips parted in a small gasp. It was the first time I had seen him truly naked.

My eyes roamed over his face. The sharp line of his jaw. The hair piled atop his head, dripping beads of water down his scarred neck. The powerful, wine-red wings hanging behind him, shifting under my gaze.

Another drop of water dripped from his hair, and my eyes followed as it rolled down his neck, gliding down his tanned skin. I was mesmerized, entranced, as it led my eyes lower. It continued down his chest, down his abdomen, stopping just above his hips.

My breath hitched at the sight of him.

He was beautiful.

I returned my eyes to his to find them blazing, his gaze intense. He took a slow step toward me, and my pulse jumped in my throat. Hesitantly, as if scared I would turn and run, he closed the distance between us. He lifted his hand, pausing for a heartbeat before touching his palm to my cheek.

The nervousness left my body in an instant.

My eyes closed at his touch, at the warmth that radiated from his palm. His other hand slid around my waist, pulling me into him, and his warmth engulfed me. His hand angled my face up to him, and my eyes opened to meet his stare.

"I have waited so long for someone like you," he whispered.

"A mate?"

"No…" He paused. "Not just a mate."

He leaned down, lightly pressing his lips to mine, and I sighed into him. My hand slid into his hair, pulling his knot loose again, then wound around his neck, pulling him closer.

He groaned into my mouth, slipping his hands behind my thighs to lift me. On instinct, I wrapped my legs around his waist, and he walked us to the bed, easing me down, bracing himself on one hand.

"It's about time we made it to a bed," I said, and he laughed against my mouth—a deep, genuine laugh that pulled a smile to my lips. I whimpered as his mouth left mine, and he gently kissed his way down my jaw, my neck, to his mark.

My chest swelled at the tenderness, and I moaned as he slid into me with a groan.

"Perfect," he whispered, returning his palm to my cheek and resting his forehead on mine. "*So* perfect."

***

The moon peaked as Rogue pulled two chairs in front of the fireplace, lit it, and sat down in one. I joined him, reveling in the warmth that immediately filled the room.

"How does your magic work?" I asked.

"It...feels like an extension of myself, like an extra limb. I just command it as I would an arm," he explained, holding his palm up so small flames could dance along his fingers.

"Is it linked to your emotions too? Like mine?"

He turned back to the fire, dropping his hand. "Yes, but usually only if I'm angry or...upset."

I stared at the fireplace, picking at my fingernails as I remembered the day I told him I would never be his mate, the way the room had filled with smoke and flames as I left.

"Is it always fire or smoke when your emotions take control?"

"No." He grinned, chuckling. "There have been a few times recently where I've just warmed the room by a few degrees, but that's not out of anger."

He winked, and I flushed as the memory of breakfast flashed in my mind, the way Thana had rushed from the room, as if she could feel the heat too.

Oh, Goddess. The redness in my cheeks burned brighter.

"Ah," I breathed, tearing my gaze from his.

"You did great in the tavern, by the way," he uttered. "It was more than great. It was... incredible. I have never seen a Storm Bringer use their magic before. It was powerful."

"I wouldn't call myself that," I replied, my brows furrowing.

"A Storm Bringer?"

That or powerful, I thought as he turned to me.

"Ara, I promise you, no one else alive can do what you did in there. No one else can call to the storms and its lightning like that. Your magic...it's magnificent. You should be proud." He gripped my chin, forcing my eyes to him. "I know I am, just to be by your side."

My lips parted, and he lowered his face, gliding his lips along mine.

"In any way you'll have me."

He released my chin, sitting back in his chair as I blinked rapidly, turning to the fire without a response.

"How did you manage to control it?"

"I didn't actually," I said. He glanced sidelong at me. "I just...asked it. For help."

"You asked?" he said incredulously, and I nodded. "Well, it definitely worked, however you did it."

"I guess so."

The demonstration convinced the people, I know, but in that moment...it was more than just convincing them of my identity, of our cause. That moment felt like coming home, like taking a breath for the first time. It was becoming who I was meant to be, who I was always supposed to be, finally melding with the other half of myself.

I hadn't had a moment to think about it, but something had finally clicked into place. Even now, I could feel the pulse beneath my skin, and I knew if I wished it, it would materialize at my fingertips as flickering blue sparks.

It felt like Rogue had said. Powerful. Incredible. *Terrifying.*

It felt so right to be united, but an uneasiness still lingered in my gut as to *how* powerful it felt, almost like an unavoidable magnet calling to the energy humming around me.

But those people, they pledged to me. Not Rogue. Not the cause. Me.

And that was especially terrifying. Just the thought made my chest tight, heavy with expectation and anxiety. I closed my eyes and shifted uncomfortably in an attempt to ease the feeling.

Unfortunately, the uneasiness only grew as I thought about what was to come.

"Were you there during the Ten Year War?" I asked suddenly, the words rushing from my mouth.

"Yes."

"Me too," I replied and his face jerked towards me.

"You were there? How old were you?"

I picked absentmindedly at my fingernails, eyes locked on the flames—looking but not seeing.

"I was thirteen when it started."

His face fell as his hand covered his mouth.

"That's so young," he mumbled. "How long were you around it? Why were you there in the first place?"

"Evander. He dragged us along," I paused. "The entire time he was there, so was I."

Rogue stiffened. "He dragged you along? For what?"

"He claimed it was the only way to keep us safe."

He scoffed. "That's ridiculous. That war was brutal. It is something I will never forget and certainly no place for a teenager."

"I won't ever forget it either. The smell of blood. The sounds..." I swallowed hard at the memory, clenching my eyes shut. "I will never forget."

I won't. For as long as I live. That, I know.

"It still haunts me too," he said, barely louder than a whisper.

It should bother me that Rogue probably killed hundreds, maybe thousands, of human soldiers. It should, and yet, I couldn't help but question whether Auryna was ultimately responsible for the slaughter, if the Fae were ever really the aggressors at all.

CHAPTER TWENTY SEVEN

But I couldn't bring myself to ask, so I said nothing at all.

"I don't understand why he would think you would be safer with him," he continued. "By definition, the battlefield would be more dangerous than a guarded estate."

"I don't know, honestly," I replied. It wasn't something I typically thought about, much less talked about with anyone. "I guess it doesn't really make much sense."

"No, it doesn't. If anything, he put you *more* in harm's way."

"Yeah, that's how it felt too. We didn't stay with him during battle, but he would place us in the nurses' tent. That's essentially where I spent those ten years, seeing every wounded and dying soldier brought in. It's where I first saw the effects of Fae magic." I glanced up to find him listening intently, his dark eyes glued to me.

"It was gruesome. I remember vowing to myself that I would never return to the border, never set foot in Ravaryn, never see another Fae again." I chuckled, dropping my eyes. "How ironic."

"Looking back, my mother was never afraid. Not really—just concerned, worried, tense. She always assisted the nurses while I did the small things, like fetching water or supplies, helping where I could. She was never shaken by anything she saw, unlike me."

"You were a teenager, Ara." He shook his head, his brows furrowing over pained eyes. "I would be more concerned if you weren't."

"It's followed me. It always comes back when I'm reminded. The sound of an army or the overwhelming smell of blood—it always thrusts me back. It's like I'm back there. My heart races, and sometimes I can't breathe, can't focus." I closed my eyes, placing a hand on my chest. "The only thing that brings me back is a technique my mother taught me. She always told me to focus on three things that I could actually see, hear, or feel that reminded me of calm. Anything steady, peaceful, undisturbed."

He released a breathy laugh, and I whipped my head to him, my cheeks flushing.

"No, it's not you. That technique… 'Things that remind you of calm.' Those are Alden's words exactly. He calls it grounding, the act of bringing our head and soul back to the soil beneath us and rooting ourselves in the world we're actually in, not the one that torments us."

My lips parted as my eyes stung. *Of course.*

The only reason I could imagine Alden telling her that was to get her through the death of Vaelor as he helped her escape. Even while he was grieving the loss of his only child, he managed to help my mother.

My breath left me in a whoosh, choking and suffocating, as the hole in my chest reopened, the overwhelming ache that returned every time I remembered she was gone.

I brought my knees up to my chest, wrapping my arms around them, as I closed in on myself, trying to remember how to breathe. How anyone could get through this, I didn't know. It was all too much, the never-ending sea of grief that tormented me constantly, threatening to drown me every time I was reminded of my mother. Of her past. Of the father I never got to know. Of the one who raised me.

It was torturous—discovering bits and pieces of myself as they revealed themselves in the most agonizing ways.

I scrunched my eyes, dropping my face to my knees, and vaguely heard Rogue stand and step towards me. He knelt in front of me, softly placing a hand on each shin.

CHAPTER TWENTY SEVEN

"Things that remind you of calm," he whispered, and I sucked in a shaky breath.

Calm.

The warmth of the fire.

The pain was deafening, and I squeezed my legs tighter.

"Calm," he whispered again.

"Calm," I echoed, my voice cracking.

The warmth of the fire.

The sound of waves crashing on the shore.

I took a deep breath, peeking over my knees at him. His face was downcast, giving me privacy.

His chest rose and fell slowly, so I matched my breaths to his.

This. You.

"I'm all right," I managed. At the same moment, the clouds parted, allowing moonlight to shine through the window once again, lighting the room with its pale glow.

He lifted his eyes, the silver moonlight illuminating his silhouette as he rose to his feet and pressed his forehead to mine. Warmth blossomed in my chest, chasing away the panic.

We were *very* different now than we were just hours ago.

It felt as though the air around us had cleared while simultaneously igniting some unseen ember that grew hotter with each passing minute, casting him in an entirely new light.

Taking a deep breath, the scent of evergreen spice and smoke filled my lungs. His scent. I embraced it, settled with it, as my heart rate slowed back to normal.

He pulled back slowly, glancing out the window.

"It's getting late and we have to be up early," he said,

extending a hand to me. "Ready for bed?"

I nodded, sliding my hand into his. He stared at it for a moment, running his thumb along the back of my hand before pulling me into his chest and wrapping an arm around me.

"I have to be honest," he whispered, a light smile dancing along his lips. "This is not how I saw this trip going."

I laughed, pushing against his chest until he released me.

"I promise you, I didn't see this"—I gestured a hand between us— "happening either."

He smirked and grabbed my wrist, yanking me back to him.

"Oh, I saw *this* coming," he said as he lowered his face to my neck, running his tongue along my ear. "Just not this soon."

I shivered at his words, and he chuckled, running a fingertip along my spine, still bare.

"Although, I'm certainly not complaining," he purred, walking me back to the bed. Once my knees hit the mattress, he kissed me lightly on the lips before scooping me up and tossing me on the bed. "Now go to sleep. We have an early morning."

I couldn't stop the laugh that escaped me, and he beamed as he climbed in behind me, wrapping an arm around my waist to pull me against him. He draped a wing over us, and I relaxed into him, the feeling of warmth and safety lulling me to sleep.

Chapter Twenty Eight

Rogue

The skies were clear as we neared Draig Hearth with every able-bodied man from Nautia, and I couldn't contain my smile.

I was happy, for the first time in my life. Amid everything that was happening and everything that was to come, I was unapologetically happy. The feeling was ridiculous and foreign, but incredible and entirely due to the woman who rode beside me.

I glanced at Ara for what seemed like the thousandth time. She was holding her face to the sun, swaying as she rode her dapple-gray horse with her eyes closed. A smile tugged at the corner of my mouth, and I turned my face to the sun with her, reveling in the warmth and smell of wildflowers.

We entered through the gates and stopped just inside the bailey. I swung off my horse and offered a hand to her, the same hand she had denied so many times, but this time, she smiled down at me—a soft, breathtaking smile—and took my hand.

Just as her feet hit the ground, Doran and his men entered

the bailey with what looked like every man and woman from Blackburn, and I took a deep breath as relief and pride flooded me.

Ravaryn was coming together.

We will stand a chance.

Taking Ara's hand, we met Doran as he dropped from his horse, and his eyes went straight to our interlocked hands, a broad grin stretching across his face.

"About damn time," he said, clapping me on the back.

I laughed nonchalantly as if we had just come together by happenstance. As if she wasn't the single greatest thing that had ever happened to me.

"Any word on the troops at the border?"

"No, nothing yet, but my spies are watching carefully. They are still there for now, but I highly doubt they'll be staying much longer."

I nodded in response, eyeing our growing army.

"We need to begin training as soon as possible," he continued. "I would assume most of the warriors from Blackburn to Canyon will already be ready for battle, but I think the people from Nautia may be a little rusty. They've remained untouched by the humans, so they haven't prepared or trained as much as the rest of the kingdom."

"I agree. Give them the day to set up their encampment, but we start at sunrise. That includes you." I nudged Ara with an elbow. "Weapons with Doran and magic with Alden."

"And what about you?" she asked, cocking an eyebrow.

Leaning down to her ear, I whispered low enough for only her to hear. "Oh, I have other lessons in mind for you and me, little storm."

Her breath caught as her cheeks flushed violently, and the

sweet scent of her arousal met my nose. Chuckling, I pulled back as she cleared her throat.

"Yes, I need to get back into a routine," she said to Doran as he stifled a smile. "When I was in Auryna, I trained with swords and daggers every, but I obviously haven't since I arrived."

"Don't worry," Doran replied, patting her on the shoulder. "We'll get you back to tip-top shape in no time."

She swatted his arm away, scoffing.

"I haven't been here that long. I still managed to beat him the last time we were in a sparring circle," she said, hooking a thumb at me.

"I don't think the same tactics will work on the others," I said, not bothering to whisper anymore. "Or, on second thought…" I continued, letting my eyes lazily graze down her body, "Maybe, they would."

Her eyes were as round as saucers, and the flush in her cheeks deepened.

Goddess, I love that.

"Well, that's my cue," Doran replied, turning on his heel to rejoin his men.

"I'm going to go see Alden and Thana. I'll meet with you later, all right?" Ara said as she turned to leave.

My face fell.

"Ara…" I stared after Doran. "Thana isn't here. Neither is Delphia."

"Where are they?" she asked cautiously.

"They left to rescue Thana's family."

She clenched her jaw, glaring at me with furious eyes before glancing at Doran.

"How could you not tell me? Does Doran know?" She

stepped closer, her voice barely above a whisper.

"Delphia made me promise not to tell Doran, and then, with everything... No, he doesn't know yet," I whispered in return, grabbing her hand and tugging her toward the door. "But they should be in Auryna by now. Come on. We need to send a letter."

She nodded curtly, fuming as she followed.

As I turned towards her chambers, her eyebrows pulled together. "Why—"

"Alden doesn't know either."

She sighed audibly, and I bit at the inside of my cheek, silently kicking myself for not telling her sooner.

Once we were in her chambers, she pulled paper from her nightstand and handed it to me. I quickly scribed the note to Delphia and tossed it into the flames.

"It shouldn't take long for her to respond," I assured her.

She strolled to the window, peeking out over the water. "I missed the view."

"Me too," I replied, joining her by the window. Standing behind her, I wrapped my arms around her waist and rested my chin on her head.

"Please, no more secrets." Her words were tight.

"No more secrets," I echoed, and I meant it. With every fiber of my being, I meant it.

The fire sputtered, and we both jerked toward it to see a note floating from it. She jogged to catch it and quickly unfolded it, her eyes darting across the page. The crease between her eyebrows deepened before she handed me the note.

"They're alive, thank the Goddess. They just arrived at the castle. They're scoping the area."

CHAPTER TWENTY EIGHT

"They'll be all right," I said as she nodded, but the crease between her brows didn't ease. I lifted a hand and rubbed my thumb between her brows, gently smoothing the worry line. "If anyone can get them in and out, it's Delphia."

"Yeah," she replied, sitting in a chair as she chewed on her bottom lip. I strolled around behind her and massaged her shoulders, kneading into the tight knots.

I was worried too, the Goddess knew I was, but I was managing it, and I sure as hell wouldn't let Ara see it when she was already so worried. I trusted Delphia, so I was leaving it in her hands. She was right when she said it could be no one else.

She will get them in and out, I reassured myself.

"Try not to worry about them. With most of the soldiers heading our way, I would say they're safer than us right now," I said with a halfhearted chuckle.

She gave me a flat look, and I exhaled slowly.

"Now that we know they're alive and well, I, unfortunately, have to break the news to Doran that they're gone. Protective big brother is not going to be happy."

As I descended the entryway steps into the bailey, I sighed against the tightness in my chest, spotting Doran just outside the gates. Anxiety churned in my gut as I closed the distance between us.

He nodded as I neared him, dismissing the men he was speaking with.

"Done with Ara so soon?" he asked with a lopsided grin.

I didn't respond, and his smile fell.

"What is it?"

"Delphia."

His spine stiffened.

"She's in Auryna with Thana, rescuing her family."

"Wha— How could she be so reckless? She told me she was going to stay behind with Thana *here,* at Draig Hearth. When did you find out? We must go help her." The words rushed from his mouth as he strode to the gates.

"No, Doran," I replied and his face snapped back to me with confusion. "We're not. I talked to her before she left. She asked for my permission, and I gave it."

His mouth fell open before twisting into a snarl. He stalked back to me, his fists clenched at his sides as he stopped directly in front of me. Clenching his jaw, he shook his head slightly, reared back, and clocked me in the jaw.

"How the hell could you let them leave like that and not tell me?" he shouted. "You *know* how much she means to me, everything we've been through!"

I stood, rubbing my jaw.

"Doran, there are Fae down there, being held captive and probably tortured. Delphia is the *only* one who can get them in and out undetected. You know this! She has the power to be exceptional, yet you never allow her to be."

"I'm protecting her as I always have!"

"She doesn't need protection anymore, Doran."

A muscle ticked in his jaw, the silence between us feeling louder than any words could have. He shook his head and turned away, striding back to the front gates.

Guilt tugged at me, and I dropped my head to my hand, rubbing my temples. She needed the freedom to put her magic to good use, to make decisions on her own, but Doran was still my best friend—my only friend—and it was not my place to stand between them.

With a deep sigh, I snapped my wings out and shot to

CHAPTER TWENTY EIGHT

the sky to coast over the sea, salty air clinging to my skin, welcoming me home.

I stayed out awhile, releasing the tension and reveling in the feeling before I landed on a ledge and headed to the library. Alden was in his study, reading a small book when I entered. He peeked over his glasses at me.

"Oh, good, you're back," he said, standing and ushering me to the book. "You'll never believe what I found. Well, firstly, how did the recruitment go? Were you all successful?"

"Yes, more than we could've hoped." I strolled to his desk, tilting my head to get a better look at the book. "The encampment being set up outside the gates is extensive."

He nodded. "How was Nautia?"

"Beautiful as ever, and every able-bodied person joined the cause." I peeked up at him to see a hopeful grin spread across his face. "For Ara's sake."

"So they know her identity, then?"

At my nod, he dropped his gaze to the desk, his smile deepening into one of pride.

"Well, back to what I was saying. You'll never believe what I found in the oldest recesses of the library: a journal with entries from the first Storm Bringer. It's so ancient, it barely stays together."

My eyes bulged, and I rushed around the desk to look at the decrepit book. "What have you learned?"

"The dream. He had it too, every detail exactly the same. So, it's not a coincidence," he replied. "And from his account, Vaelor barely touched the tip of their abilities."

I cocked my head, frowning. "What do you mean?"

"Well, this one... He could do so much more. Not only could he call the lightning to himself, which Vaelor clearly did as well, but he could call *all* the energy to himself."

"All the energy...?"

His fingers tapped my chest. "All the energy," he echoed.

"So he—"

"He could pull the life force from anyone, anything. Storms. Animals. Nature. People." His eyebrows pulled together, wringing his hands in front of him. "That's not all... With the ability to control all the energy that pulses within the realm, he could control *anything.* Theoretically, she could manipulate someone's body, move them as she wished, if she controlled the energy that flowed through their muscles, their hearts."

"Is that not something your people can do as well?"

"No. Much like your magic, ours is an extension of ourselves, so we can only use what is already inside us, not take from others, but from what I've read in this journal, his magic is not like that." He paused, returning to his desk. "He speaks of it like a separate entity, part of himself, but more like the other half. Not another limb."

My heart raced as the dots connected.

She asked it.

"While we were in Nautia, Ara created a storm on purpose. When we were in the tavern, the people didn't want to join us, so I revealed who she was. Of course, they didn't believe me until she demonstrated—and she did. She shook the tavern with her storm."

A stunned smile pulled at Alden's lips.

"But afterward, when I asked how she managed to control it, she said she didn't. She said she asked it."

"Asked?"

"Yeah, *asked.*"

CHAPTER TWENTY EIGHT

"Well, I guess that confirms that then. I'll talk to her. We will have to train, try to practice these skills because if she accidentally sucks the energy out of anything, anyone…"

I nodded, running a hand through my hair. It would be catastrophic for her.

"We can't let that happen. She said she feels like she has some control over it now, so hopefully, training will help bridge the remaining gaps." Sighing, I walked back around the desk and plopped down. "On a lighter note, we met Ewan. He was bartending at a tavern and he pledged his life to Ara. They all did, actually. They pledged to *her*, Alden."

Pride swelled in my chest at the memory, and Alden dropped his face again, grinning ear to ear.

"You should have seen her. She was incredible."

"I wish I could've," he said. "Vaelor would've been so proud, and a much better teacher than me, but I will do my best to help her."

"And just one more thing you should know…"

As I explained the Doran, Delphia, and Thana situation, his mouth fell open.

"Did he do that?" he said, gesturing to my already bruising chin.

"Yes," I said flatly.

"Well, I'm not surprised about that." He tilted his head to get a better look and chuckled. "I am surprised, however, that he didn't do more damage. Have you heard from them?"

"Yes, they're just outside the castle. She's going to send more updates as they scope the area."

He nodded. "May the Goddess be with them."

"May she strike down any who wishes them harm. May she bathe them in triumph," I finished for him on the way out.

***

Sitting on one of the logs around the fire pit, I was surrounded by the familiar chatter of soldiers—telling stories, laughing, boasting.

The moon was full, lighting the camp, the air tranquil. Considering what was to come, everything was relatively calm, including myself, and that had never been a word I'd used to describe myself.

Staring up at the castle, I spotted Ara's window. Warm firelight flooded from it, indicating she was inside. A faint glimpse of her silhouette blotted out the light as she walked by the window, unintentionally calling me forward. With a smile, I pushed off my knees to my feet as the need to be closer to her tugged at me.

Just as I stepped in Ara's direction, though, a note flittered out of the fire, and I caught it as it drifted on the breeze.

> *Ro,*
>
> *Firstly, we're still alive and well.*
>
> *Secondly, we found the dungeon and there are at least two dozen Fae here. We will get them out to safety, I have no doubt, but there are also a few humans being kept here. Should we rescue them as well—if they want to come, that is?*
>
> *-D*

Two dozen Fae. Two dozen of my people were being held

captive, tortured, and starved.

My blood boiled. The grass at my feet singed as the bonfire doubled in size, causing the men to jump and stumble back. After grabbing a quill from a nearby tent, I jerked back down to the log, turning the paper over to reply.

> D,
> Yes. Save all who wish to be saved.
> Also, Doran is angry. Please write to him (I said please, but that's an order).
> -Ro

Satisfied with my note, I folded it, tossed it into the fire, and continued through the sea of tents back to the castle.

Every commander had arrived with their recruits by nightfall and the encampment was large—just walking from end to end took well over an hour. We estimated over a thousand men had joined us.

Since I had become king, there had not been a single minute in which I'd felt proud of anything I'd accomplished. I had always been grasping at straws, trying to mend the broken pieces my father left behind.

But this.

The open display of our people's love for Ravaryn. The loyalty to each other. The unwavering selflessness.

They all had come to defend the other, steadfast at each other's backs.

It inspired me, galvanized me.

In this moment, I was proud.

I took a deep breath as a hopeful smile pulled at my lips.

"Sire?" a soldier asked hesitantly behind me and I turned to see him bow his head.

"No need for formalities. Call me Rogue," I said.

He nodded, smiling.

"Very well. My name is Alex. I was picked up by Commander Lee in Canyon."

"It's nice to meet you, Alex."

"It's nice to meet you too, Sire." He paused, rubbing his palms on his thighs in nervousness. "I... Well, I wanted to speak to you about your brother. I heard the message that you were seeking him."

I leaned forward with a renewed interest.

"Do you know him?" I asked. "Have you met him?"

"Yes, I knew a man who claimed to be your half-brother several years ago, probably close to twenty years ago now. I didn't really believe him at the time. I honestly thought he was jesting, but now...after hearing about your search and seeing you"—he gestured up and down at me—"you look pretty similar. He was a bit thinner, and his eyes weren't quite as red, but I can see the relation."

My heart was thundering in my chest as hopefulness, albeit fearful hope, rushed through me.

Just then, another note appeared in my fist.

Unfolding it while still looking at him, I asked, "What was his name? Do you remember?"

I glanced down at the note at the same moment he responded.

"His name was Adonis."

CHAPTER TWENTY EIGHT

Rogue, he's your brother. The king. It's him.

Chapter Twenty Nine

Ara

Alden and I had been on the island all morning. As we sat down for lunch, we talked through everything that had occurred in Nautia again.

"Ewan was your father's closest friend. I knew he would pledge himself to you if he ever got the chance to meet you," Alden said, taking a bite of his sandwich.

"We didn't get to speak much, but we did talk a little," I replied, reliving our toast to my parents. "He seems genuine."

"He is. He's a good friend to have at your side and an even better warrior to have at your back, honest and loyal. I'll have to find him when we return. It's been so long since I've seen him."

I nodded, taking another bite before asking, "Speaking of finding people, did you see Rogue this morning? I haven't seen him since we arrived yesterday."

He glanced sidelong at me, stifling a smile. "No, I haven't, but that is normal with everything going on. I'm sure he's working with Doran and the commanders. Well, maybe not Doran so much, all things considered."

CHAPTER TWENTY NINE

I pursed my lips. "Ah, he told me he was going to speak with him about Delphia."

"He did. He came to see me afterward, a nice bruise setting in," Alden said with a laugh as he peeked at me. "I've heard you two are…together. Is that true?"

My cheeks flushed furiously, and I averted my gaze.

"It's nothing to be embarrassed about, Ara. We all expected it at some point, if I'm being honest." He shrugged his shoulders, taking another bite. "But since you clearly don't want to talk about it, we can get back to speaking of your power."

He had explained everything he'd found in the book in explicit detail—the ability to manipulate and absorb the energy around me—and it was terrifying to hear. Not because I was learning of what I could possibly do, but because I already knew I could. I could feel the ability hovering just under my skin.

When Rogue broke the curse, I felt something, a tingling, a current, moving throughout the realm. I knew it was there, that it was calling to me, but I couldn't quite grasp it, not in its entirety.

Now, however, I was acutely aware of the energy surrounding me in every waking moment. Even here, it was everywhere, in every breath of wind, every blade of grass, every heartbeat. I could feel the storm miles off the coast and the lightning racing through the clouds.

I knew I could take it if I truly wanted. Hearing Alden say it only confirmed it, made it real, and *that* was terrifying.

"What would happen if I absorbed someone's energy?" I asked, bracing myself for what I knew he would say.

"You would pull the life force from their body. Their heart

would stop beating the moment the energy left."

My heart sank into my stomach.

"But that's why we will train and practice. You won't do that, not unless you intend to. Once you master your magic, it will become second nature, I promise."

I nodded—for his reassurance or my own, I didn't know, but I could *not* kill someone due to my own lack of self-control. *I would not,* I assured myself, but my stomach still rolled with dread.

Alden stood and held a hand, yanking me to my feet. "Let's get back to it, then."

Once we stepped back into Vaelor's circle, his power washed over me. His memory was here, the magic he had cultivated here leaving its mark in the soil, and I could feel it mingling with mine.

"All right, let's try moving the leaf again."

I had spent the entire morning trying to get this one damn leaf to hover, just an inch.

The closest I got was wiggling it, but even then, Alden had rushed over to clap me on the back. It was more irritating than anything, like a tease, but the frustration from this morning had dwindled out over lunch.

I closed my eyes, took a deep breath, and planted my feet. I had attempted to control it in the way Alden explained, but that clearly wasn't working.

It never had, and I suddenly felt foolish for thinking it would this time.

My magic isn't another muscle or limb. I'm not going to be able to pick the leaf up like I would with a hand.

I looked down to see leaves scattered all around my feet. Zeroing in on one, I focused on the minute amount of energy holding it together, listening to its hum.

I latched onto it and tugged, and it responded immediately, lifting from the ground.

An excited gasp escaped me.

That was it.

I had spent all morning focusing on the leaf, but that's not what I had control over.

It was the energy.

My eyes darted around before closing to focus on the feel of everything. I could feel the soft hum all around me, just as I always did, but this time, I called to it.

"Ara," Alden whispered.

My eyes flew open. It had listened.

Every leaf on the island hovered, floating and swirling about in the breeze. I dropped them with a relieved laugh and they drifted down like leaves in autumn.

"That was incredible," he said, grinning ear to ear. "How did you manage that?"

"I just listened."

I returned his smile, finally feeling a small flutter of hope.

* * *

The sun was setting by the time we stepped back onto the boat to return to the castle.

"Any chance you'll let me sleep longer than sunrise tomorrow?"

"Nope, not even a little one," Alden replied as he steered out to sea.

"Didn't think so," I laughed.

The sky lit the sea on fire, reflecting the deep oranges

and reds. Just as the last bit of light disappeared behind the horizon, something snatched me from the boat, tearing a scream from my throat.

Not something.

Someone.

"Rogue!" I swatted at his arm.

Alden shouted as Rogue shot to the sky. "Next time, give a warning, will you? I'm too old to be this close to a heart attack."

"Next time," he hollered down with a grin. "Miss me?"

"Not at all," I said, wrapping an arm around his neck, and his smile widened.

We continued upwards until I could see the horizon in every direction, which was beautiful, but the sudden awareness of how high we were had me tightening my grip on him.

"Scared of heights, huh?"

"Well, I don't think I've ever been high enough to think about it, but um, I might be."

"You'll get used to it."

I doubted it. "Where are we going, anyway? Why did you grab me? I could've just met you back at the castle."

"I was out, and I realized you've never flown with me. Awake, at least." He paused, shaking his head as he shrugged his shoulders. "I just wanted to show you."

I glanced up at him, and my eyes snagged on the stars behind him. I had never been this high, yes, but that also meant I had never been this close to the sky before, and I suddenly had the urge to feel a cloud.

My heart skipped a beat at the prospect.

Looking past him, I imagined soft clouds. As we flew, they

started to form, thick but light, blocking our view of anything else. Rogue slowed, releasing a stunned laugh.

"Did you do this?" He glanced around in wonder.

"Yes," I whispered. Reaching my hand out, it ran through the cool, pale mist as we moved forward, and the haze swirled at my fingertips.

"Incredible," he breathed.

My heart fluttered, and the clouds dissipated as my cheeks tinted pink. We flew in silence for a while, admiring the view. I could see everything, including the border mountains on the edge of the horizon.

Sighing at the reminder of what was to come, I turned my eyes to Draig Hearth. In the darkness, firelight flowed from the open windows, deepening the shadows of the dark vines crawling along the castle's side. It was eerie but beautiful.

"I need to tell you something," he said. The lightness was gone from his voice, and it snapped me from my thoughts. "I received a letter from Delphia last night. That's why I didn't return to your chambers."

I tensed in his grasp.

"They're alive, and they found the prisoners. They plan to get them out tonight," he declared. "That's not it, though."

He paused and the anxiety in my chest doubled.

"What is it, Rogue?"

"She saw King Adon and...he is my brother. A soldier I spoke to last night confirmed it. He said he knew my brother twenty-odd years ago, and his name was Adonis."

My mouth fell open as the gravity of his words set in. I hadn't seen the similarities between the two at first, but now that we knew, it was glaringly obvious. The same dark hair, red-brown eyes hidden under glamour, the height. It was all similar.

My heart broke for Rogue. Every attack. Every murder. Every innocent soul taken too soon. All of it was ordered by his own brother with the help of Evander. The realization weighed on my chest along with every other horrendous deed he had ever committed.

My eyes closed against the tears as I tightened my hold around his neck.

"I'm so sorry," was all I could manage.

"I just don't know why." His voice shook, and I forced myself not to look up at him. "His own people. Why would he order the death of his own people?"

I shook my head. "I don't know."

"I... If he is doing this because... I won't be able to live with myself if he's doing this because of me, if he's...jealous in some twisted, sick way that our father kept me and not him. I cannot bear every cruel, merciless, pointless murder being my fault."

I turned my face to him. "Don't say that. This is not your fault."

He continued to stare forward, but his throat bobbed as he swallowed. "I..." He tightened his grip around me.

I reached up, placing a palm on his cheek to turn his face to me. "Just as you told me, you cannot blame yourself for simply existing. You have done *nothing* to him to warrant such brutality. There is nothing you *could've* done to warrant this. This war is rooted in his own lacking character, not yours."

He blinked rapidly, inhaling a shaky breath.

"I hope you're right," he sighed, landing on the ledge outside the castle. He set me on my feet and paused, staring at me.

CHAPTER TWENTY NINE

"Wha—"

He stepped forward and wrapped his arms around me in a tight hug, his cheek pressed to the top of my head. I wound my arms around his waist and held him just as tightly, wishing I could take away his pain. All of it. Every traumatic moment he didn't deserve.

"Thank you." He released me and stepped away. "I still have to tell everyone else and Doran... Well, we haven't spoken since he gave me this." He gestured to his chin. "He's been working with his commanders since well before sunrise."

He held the door open for me, and we entered his chambers.

"We don't know when the army will mobilize, so they're working as quickly as possible to make sure everyone is ready."

"And the army—they're at the northern tip by where you had your camp?"

"Yes." He nodded. "It's the closest and fastest way into Ravaryn from the Capitol."

"Why is there an army this time? Why not more small attacks? I could understand if Evander was still pushing to get me back, but...he thinks I'm dead."

"He's starting another war. I wouldn't be surprised if they're using your 'death' as the spark."

As we walked, my thoughts clung to Evander.

The difference between him before the Ten Year War and now was stark, black and white. Before, he was caring and kind, a good father who radiated warmth. Then, he dragged us along to the war, putting us in danger. It was completely out of character.

Now, none of those words could be used to describe him. *I don't understand—*

Then it hit me, and my feet halted, my mouth falling open. "I can't believe I haven't thought of this before. King Adon is the manipulator."

Rogue stopped walking and turned back to me, his eyebrows pulled together in confusion. "Yes..."

My thoughts and heart were racing in tandem as everything clicked into place.

After the war, his entire identity shifted and centered around his role as general. He became harsh and distant, only focused on his duties and orders. The ideal general.

He didn't seem like the same person...because he wasn't.

"We both said it made no sense for Evander to bring my mother and me with him from battle to battle, right?"

He nodded slowly, still unsure.

"Because a man wouldn't want his wife and daughter in danger...but what if it wasn't his thought at all?"

"It was Adon's," he breathed, and I nodded, meeting his gaze.

We rushed to the library, passing Doran on the way. Rogue grabbed him by the sleeve without saying a word and dragged him to the library with us, where we found Alden and Iaso sitting in the chairs under the window.

"Good, you're all here," Rogue said. "We need to talk."

We pulled chairs over to theirs and explained everything.

It was Doran who spoke first. "So Adon, the manipulator, is your brother?"

"Yes," Rogue answered.

"Adon became king six or seven years before the war started, and over the ten years of war, Evander became a completely different person. Everything he believed in changed. It had to have been Adon messing with his mind. He became the ideal general, I suppose."

Doran sighed, bracing his hands on his knees. "It would be the most logical scenario. He's already convinced everyone he's human, so it makes sense he would go one step further and align them with his motives."

"So, how do we undo it?" I asked, looking at Rogue. When he didn't respond, I turned to Alden, then Iaso. "We can undo it, right?"

Iaso reached out, placing a hand on mine. "Child, magic like this, it weaves itself into the mind. Evander wouldn't have realized the thoughts weren't his at first, but over time, the thoughts become so rooted, so deep within the mind…it changes the person. They begin to think like that on their own, without outside help. It's been too long, the lies and commands too complicated and interwoven. There's nothing we can do now."

The little flame of hope that had sparked flickered out.

"So Adon might've not even been the reason he tried to kill me? It was him?"

Everyone was silent, pity almost palatable in the air.

Of course.

I shifted, pulling my hand from Iaso's. "So, what do we do next?"

"Ara…" Rogue whispered.

"I don't want comfort. I want to know what we're doing next."

Rogue dipped his chin, and just as he opened his mouth to speak, he froze. His eyes dropped to his hand as it opened slowly, revealing a crumpled piece of paper.

"Open it," Doran demanded. "It could be Delphia."

Rogue unfolded and read it before handing it to Doran.

"The army has mobilized."

* * *

We made it to the Cursed Wood the following night, just as the moon peaked in the sky, and set up camp along the base of a tall cliff.

As soon as we received the letter, Doran and Rogue left for the encampment. Under their direction, it was torn down and packed in record time. We left an hour before sunrise and traveled throughout the day and half the night, breaking only when necessary.

"How close do you think the army is?" I asked, dismounting my horse and stretching out stiff limbs.

"They'll be crossing through by morning," Doran said, his voice clipped. As he joined his commanders, I turned to Rogue.

"We plan to let them cross through the forest and ambush them as they break through," he said as he led our horses to a nearby tree and tied the reins to it.

I chewed on my lip as we walked. It was a good plan, sacrificing them to the creatures of the forest. Gruesome but effective.

"At least the slicers will work in our favor this time," I replied. "It seems fitting. A repayment of blood to the land they've massacred."

He eyed the forest, his spine rod stiff. "Exactly," he said with a finality that sent goosebumps over my skin.

Whatever happened tomorrow would change the realm. For the better or worse? I didn't know, and the lingering question sent a spike of panic through me.

CHAPTER TWENTY NINE

I glanced at the forest, and a chill went down my spine. Eyeing the tree line, I couldn't see any creatures in the darkness, but I could feel them lingering, watching, the pulse of energy in their heart beats. They were there, waiting.

"I'm going to speak with Doran and the commanders for a while," he declared before he stepped into me, wrapping a hand around the back of my neck. Resting his forehead on mine, he took a breath and released me. "I'll find you soon, all right?"

I nodded as he left. Glancing at the forest one more time, I turned and strolled in the opposite direction to the base of the cliff. It was tall and jagged with foliage peeking over the edge. For a moment, I considered climbing it to get a better view of our surroundings, but I decided against it and sat at the base.

With not much else to look at, my gaze fell upon the men. They were unpacking and preparing, most of them passing flasks of whiskey or rum around. Several fire pits were lit, each with a group of men sitting around it.

The sight resembled the Ten Year War so much, it was unsettling.

Surprisingly, the flashbacks hadn't returned—not yet. That would come with the flowing rivers of red that always followed war, the sounds of swords and screams and death.

I clenched my fists and scrunched my eyes, reclining my head back onto the cliff face.

Lowering my hands to the ground, I laid my palms flat and splayed my fingers into the cool grass, letting it pull me back down and slow my racing heart.

I sat like that for a moment, taking deep breaths when I felt the tickle of energy at my fingertips. Hesitantly, I let my magic reach out and follow it, gasping when I realized it was the collective energy of the men before me. It was moving its way through the ground to me.

Pushing out farther, I continued until I reached the tree line and paused. It felt different—dark and twisted. The energy was slower, the humming deeper. It was ominous, edging dangerously close to what I imagine death would feel like if there was an energy to it.

Pushing forward, I felt the slicers, moving in groups.

There was also something else nearby, something large and powerful.

I snapped my eyes open, searching the woods, but it was still pitch black. Goosebumps pricked my skin as it continued moving through the forest.

While we couldn't see it, it could see us. That much I knew.

Taking a deep breath, I urged my magic farther, past the forest. I didn't feel anything at first, but miles from the forest, there was a wisp, a movement just out of my grasp. For me to have felt anything from this distance, the amount of energy would have to be massive.

It had to be the army.

I swallowed hard, staring into the forest as if I would miraculously see anything.

"What are you looking for?" Rogue asked, and I jumped.

"Nothing, I...I can feel the army. They're still a few miles away, but they're nearing the forest."

Rogue's face was tight as he turned to the tree line. "They'll stop to rest before crossing. With the absence of light, the forest is impassable at night." He chuckled lightly, sitting beside me. "Hell, even during the day, it's hard to pass through."

CHAPTER TWENTY NINE

I nodded in response and pulled my knees to my chest.

"You know you don't have to be here, right?" he whispered, and I turned to him. "I know how... haunting the last war was. I don't want you to have to go through that again." He paused, sighing before lifting his eyes to me. "I just want you to know you have the choice. No one is forcing you to stay, fight, or even witness what is coming."

The choice.

He was offering me the choice.

The man who had kidnapped me and held me hostage, delivering me freedom.

Fate did have a sense of irony, but I was grateful for it, nonetheless.

I laid my head on his shoulder and glanced at the men, recognizing several from Nautia. The same men who stood by Vaelor, believed in him, now believed in me, pledged to me.

"No..." I shook my head. "No, I need to be here."

It wasn't a need out of obligation. It was more than that. It was a need to stand at their backs, just as they were at mine. A need based in earning and returning loyalty. A need to prove to them that their pledge meant something to me because it did.

They deemed me worthy, and I would *be* worthy for them.

Not only that, but this is where Vaelor and Elora would be, if given the chance—fighting for those who needed it, against those who would threaten to dismantle everything they worked for.

While they couldn't be here, I could. I would.

I felt him nod as he settled an arm around my shoulders. "We'll be ready."

Chapter Thirty

Ara

I woke before Rogue, a knot of uneasiness forming in my gut. Carefully sliding away from him, I strolled to the edge of the cliff and sat with my feet dangling.

A tiny beacon of yellow light lit on the horizon beyond the forest, shifting the black sky to indigo. My hands gripped the ledge as the sun slowly peeked its head out, and red flames devoured the sky, lighting it a vibrant, violent red.

A frown twisted my mouth as an old saying wormed its way into my mind.

Red sky at night, warrior's delight. Red sky in the morning, warrior's warning.

My heart sank to join the knot in my gut.

Death was coming.

***

CHAPTER THIRTY

Rogue

Ara was sitting on the ledge, her silhouette illuminated by the vermilion sky in front of her.

I desperately wished she had left when I gave her the choice. An overwhelming dread bit at me as I watched her. The air was crisp as birds chirped in the distance, the soft breeze blowing her hair, and it all felt wrong. It was too calm, in stark contrast to the whirlwind of anxiety in my chest.

It had taken everything I had to not leave her in Draig Hearth, and then in Blackburn, in every town we passed through. Even now, I resisted the urge to fly her somewhere safer, somewhere far away from here.

I wanted to offer her the choice. She deserved that, as we all did.

Still, the thought of her so close to battle, standing in the midst of death, was tearing me apart from the inside out.

* * *

Ara

Rogue joined me on the ledge, just as the troops came into view, still hours away, just a speck in the distance on the other side of the Cursed Wood.

"Do you think they know what they're walking into?" I whispered. "In the forest, I mean."

"You didn't, so I wouldn't think so." He wrapped an arm around my shoulders and pulled me into him.

"How long do you think it'll take them to cross through?"

"Well, it takes us maybe two hours, but we know the way, what to avoid. I don't imagine they'll make it through that fast."

I nodded, biting the inside of my cheek.

"We should eat. Let's go down and sit with Doran. I need to talk to him, anyway." We stood and I yelped as he scooped me up. "Hold on," he warned with a devilish grin.

I started to respond when he turned his back to the cliff and fell backward, free-falling. I gasped, wrapping my arms around his neck as a scream caught in my throat. Just before we hit the ground, he snapped his wings out and we coasted a few feet before landing.

"Rogue!" I shouted, my cheeks flushed. He chuckled, wrapping a hand around the back of my neck as he kissed the top of my head. I placed my hands on his chest, giving a light shove. "Please, let's not do that again."

"Since you said please." He smiled and took my hand, leading me to where they were serving rations.

Doran was already there, sitting on a log. He looked up at us and immediately dropped his eyes back to his bowl. Feeling the tension between them, I stepped toward the man serving food to give them privacy.

"Good morning," I said as he poured a scoop of porridge into a bowl and handed it to me.

"Morning to ya, lass," he said with a warm smile that was missing a tooth.

Turning around, I found Rogue and Doran firmly engaged in conversation, so I took my bowl and wandered the camp, eating as I went. It wasn't long before I spotted Ewan exiting his tent.

"Ewan!" I shouted as I jogged over.

CHAPTER THIRTY

"Ara. Nice to see you again."

"Likewise," I replied. "Did you get a chance to speak with Alden before we left? Have you seen Iaso?"

"Alden, yes, and I actually rode by Iaso for most of the way. It was nice to hear her voice again." His cheeks tinted pink as he ran a hand along the back of his neck.

I stifled a smile. "You and Iaso were good friends, then? When Vaelor was king?"

His eyes darted to me, seeing straight through my thinly veiled question.

"Yes. We were friends." The blush in his cheeks deepened, and I grinned. "But back to Alden—we didn't get to speak long. I'll have to catch up with him when we return."

Return.

The smile slid from my lips.

"And we *will* return," he assured.

We wandered for some time with no direction, strolling through the endless sea of tents.

"Have you eaten yet?" I asked, holding up my empty bowl.

"Yes, I ate early this morning." He glanced at me sidelong and his mouth tilted into a mischievous grin. "Since we have some time, you up for a quick round of sparring?"

"Always," I replied, returning his smile.

From the weaponry rack, he grabbed two swords and tossed one to me. I caught it by the hilt and gave it a quick spin at the wrist, slicing it through the air. His eyes lit at the subtle challenge, and he drew a circle in the dirt. Stepping into it, we faced each other, and adrenaline shot through my veins.

"Good luck," he said, his voice light with amusement. I took my stance, and he charged, swinging the sword.

We continued, round after round, for hours. The sun had revealed itself, cutting through the fog, and the early summer heat was nearly stifling under the beating sun.

We paused, catching our breath, and I couldn't hide the smile on my face as I wiped the sweat from my forehead. We had drawn a crowd now. They cheered and placed bets, happy to have a distraction when there was nothing to do but wait.

I smirked as he stepped back into the circle, and we began the dance again.

"For someone so young, you're quite good at this."

"For someone so old, you're pretty good yourself," I replied and the crowd erupted in laughter, including Ewan.

"I'll show you pretty good," he challenged as he stepped closer, swinging his sword.

I blocked, and the swords clanged on impact. Our faces were a mere foot from each other, our swords creating an X between us. I winked, stepped back, and spun, swinging low. He laughed as he blocked and counter-swung. Blocked.

He spun in the opposite direction, slicing through the air. Blocked.

With our swords locked into each other, I kneed him in the thigh, and he dropped to one knee, chuckling. I hit his hand with the pommel of my sword, and he dropped his with a clatter.

Half the crowd cheered and clapped, the other half groaning as they handed over lost money.

I extended a hand to Ewan, and respect shone in his eyes as he took it.

* * *

Rogue

"I hope you can forgive me, Doran. You are my oldest friend."

He nodded, his eyes still focused on the stick he was twirling in his fingers.

"She wrote to me, telling me she pretty much cornered you on our way out that morning."

I released a quick laugh, and he smiled faintly.

"I mean, I wouldn't say cornered…but that sounds about right. You know how she can be. Once she's decided, there's no changing her mind."

"That's for damn sure," he sighed, tossing the stick onto the ground. "I've spent our *entire* lives protecting her from harm. I took the brunt for the both of us, so she didn't have to." He paused. "We were only twelve when our parents died, Rogue. We were kids. With nowhere to go, we lived in the shadows of alleyways. Everything we had, I stole—food, clothes, shoes. After all that, I just wanted her to have a nice, quiet, *safe* life somewhere away from this. She deserves that much…but I'm starting to realize she doesn't want it."

Another reason we got along so well—we both understood the weight of growing up in darkness.

"No, Delphia craves adventure. Purpose."

Not unlike you and me, I wanted to add. *Not unlike Ara.*

"Her and Ara are a lot alike in that regard," he said, glancing up at me.

"They'll be fast friends," I said, nodding. "Forgive me?"

He sighed and clapped me on the shoulder with a lopsided grin. "My king, do I have any choice?"

"When you put it that way… No. No, you do not," I replied, but relief flooded me at his words. I needed us to go into battle with clear heads, and we couldn't do that with tension hanging over us like a suffocating blanket.

We stood just as a loud cheer rang out across the encampment. We glanced at each other, eyebrows raised, and strode in the direction of the sound.

As we neared, I found Ara in a sparring circle, glistening with sweat. She reached a hand down to Ewan who was on one knee and disarmed, his sword lying at his feet. I cocked my head to the side as I stepped closer.

"No one was going to tell us that a sparring ring was set up?" I called out, and the crowd whipped their faces to us, falling silent. Ara glanced up, a cocky grin painting her face as a bead of sweat rolled down her neck. She was relaxed for once, in her element.

Goddess, she is the most delicious creature I have ever seen.

I shucked my overshirt off, tossing it on a nearby post. "Got one more round in you?"

Her smile grew devilish as she wiped her forehead with the back of her hand and dropped to one knee. I started to rush to her, but I stopped when I realized what she was doing.

She dropped her face to the ground, laying her hand flat, spreading her fingers through the grass. When she snapped her face back up, her irises crackled with lightning, and the grass around her hand wilted and died as she sucked the life force from it, replenishing her own.

Every man and woman from Nautia flew into a frenzy.

"Our Storm Bringer!" A man from Nautia shouted, and the men from every other village froze. Their eyes were fixed on Ara, seeing her for what she was—who she was—for the first time.

Ara rose slowly, meeting my eyes, as I stepped into the

CHAPTER THIRTY

ring, and every person in the crowd watched with renewed interest. But just as my foot crossed the line, screaming rang out from the forest, and the crowd went silent as their attention snapped to the tree line.

"Prepare," I ordered, and they scattered.

I glanced at Ara. The blood had drained from her face.

She closed her eyes, the cords in her neck popping with restraint. A heartbeat passed, and she clenched her fists, her head tilting to the side as the screaming continued.

I closed the final step between us and took her hands in mine. She opened her eyes, and I could see the internal struggle playing out.

Forgive me. I scooped her up in one swift motion and thrust into the sky.

"What are you doing?" she shouted.

I landed on the edge of the cliff, meeting her eyes.

"I'm sorry," was all I said.

"Sorry for wha—"

I fell backward, my eyes never leaving hers, as every emotion played out on her face. Realization. Anger. Betrayal. She rushed toward the edge, leaning over to watch as I fell.

"Rogue! Do not leave me here! Bring me back down!" Her fists were clenched at her sides and I averted my gaze.

Guilt ate at me, crawling up my throat and choking off my breath, but I couldn't leave her down here to struggle through flashbacks within the swarms of men and swords. I couldn't. I could survive with her hating me, but I couldn't survive her death.

Clenching my jaw, I landed by Doran and drew my sword.

He spoke without looking away from the tree line. "Did you just—"

"Yep."

He nodded. "That was a bold move."

"Yep."

He nodded again and left it at that.

Facing the tree line, we waited, every muscle taut in violent anticipation.

* * *

Ara

My chest heaved as Rogue landed by Doran.

How dare he? The people from Nautia—*my* people—were here to stand by *me*, and yet, I was up here, safe, while they were on the ground, prepared to lay down their lives to safeguard their people. Just as I was.

My blood boiled at his refusal to look in my direction.

Then the screaming resumed, and my mind cleared of any rational thought, spiraling me into chaotic darkness. My hands cupped over my ears to muffle the sounds, replaced by my thundering heartbeat. Sweat broke out along my spine.

Things that remind me of calm.

Calm.

I frantically searched for something calmer than me, anything, but the only sounds were that of death. My eyes were glued to the tree line; there was no avoiding it.

I was losing grip. I couldn't pull my eyes away, couldn't turn away.

My vision tunneled.

A hand gently rested on my shoulder, and warmth flowed

CHAPTER THIRTY

from it. A choked sob escaped me as I turned to meet Iaso's golden eyes.

"It's okay, child," she whispered, pulling me into a hug. "It's okay. You're going to be okay."

I inhaled a shaky breath and then another and another. My heart rate slowed, my chest opening up to accept air again.

Opening my eyes again, I looked over Iaso's shoulder to see a dainty, orange butterfly floating towards me. *Calm.* I forced my eyes to follow it as it fluttered about. Hesitantly, I reached a finger out, and it landed lightly, slowly opening and closing its wings.

This reminded me of calm, the simplicity of it. She had no worries, no concerns, but at the same time, we had the same purpose—to survive.

"We're not so different, you and I," I whispered, and she stilled, before lifting back into the air and drifting away. My eyes followed her as she flew over the cliff edge and movement caught my eye.

Humans.

They exited the tree line, staggering and bleeding. Their faces fell at the sheer number of Fae.

It was starting.

Clenching my fists and forcing myself to breathe, I walked to the edge of the cliff.

After the first few stumbled out, hundreds began charging from the trees. Thousands. More than we could have expected. More than we had.

The clash of swords rang through the air, and I gritted my teeth as a man rushed at Rogue.

* * *

Rogue

There were too many.

My eyes darted to Doran. He was engaged with three men at once, slicing and dodging. My eyes shot to the rest of my men. They were all occupied, but hundreds more were still pouring from the trees.

Snapping my wings out, I shot to the sky and positioned myself at the tree line. My fire raged and thrashed against the confines of my skin, and with a focused breath, I freed it.

It roared and raced down to meet the ground.

On impact, the men let out blood-curdling screams, the same screams of my innocent people.

Anger pulsed through my veins, and I urged it harder, hotter. The screaming stopped abruptly, a dozen blackened corpses dropping to the scorched ground all at once.

But I could only burn what I could focus on, and there were too many still charging from the tree line.

Too many.

Blood stained the soil as men dropped like flies—humans and Fae alike.

Bile rose in the back of my throat at the sight.

I turned my attention back to the tree line.

Burn.

My vision tinted red as heat and rage consumed me.

Burn.

* * *

CHAPTER THIRTY

Ara

Blood.

Blood everywhere.

I blinked rapidly and tore my eyes from the growing pools.

Rogue was in the sky, blazing every human that exited from the tree line, but there were already so many.

I paced, biting my nails as my heart pounded in my chest.

"I have to do something. I have to do something."

I looked to the forest.

"I have to *do* something."

Closing my eyes, I searched, and that's when I felt it.

The beast. The massive source of power prowling through the trees.

I narrowed in, listening for the pulse of its heart, the energy of its mind, its life force. I called to it, and it stilled, listening.

Come.

It took a half step in our direction, and I clenched my teeth with effort.

Come. I tugged at its life force, and it took off at a sprint toward the battlefield. Sweat broke out along my forehead as I held its lifeline with every bit of control I had.

My eyes snapped open as it neared the tree line and slowed.

A loud thump shook the ground.

The soldiers stilled and looked back at the trees as horrified screams erupted from the men still in the forest.

The trees swayed.

Another thump.

Thump.

My jaw went slack as the largest creature I had ever seen emerged from the woods.

It looked feline, but not. Its skin was black as night, sleek like oil, and it was armored with iridescent scales. Long canines protruded from his mouth, just under the black pits that served as eyes. They absorbed the light, creating a soulless abyss in each socket.

It prowled towards the men, its shoulders slinking with each step. Shadows billowed from its skin, shrouding it in constant darkness.

Every man froze with terror.

It halted at the edge of the field and raised its head to me, meeting my eyes.

I gave a single nod and it lunged.

* * *

Rogue

My heart stopped as a colossal creature of the night stepped from the tree line.

It must've smelled blood.

Just as I readied to incinerate it, it raised its eyes to Ara.

The blood drained from my face.

I snapped my eyes to Ara, but she was already meeting its gaze. Fiercely. Proudly.

My jaw fell slack as pride swelled in my chest. *Incredible.*

It was asking her permission.

An incredible force of nature.

I glanced down at Doran as he looked up at me, and we locked eyes, stunned. She nodded to the creature, and it pounced, ripping through human after human, flinging their bodies to the side as it went.

They began screaming and running, straight into Fae territory.

* * *

Ara

I glanced up at Rogue to find his eyes already on me. He gave me a fierce smile with a nod of approval before returning his attention to the field.

Dropping my gaze, I found Ewan engaged on all sides but successfully warding them off with a vicious grin.

I shifted to Doran. He was locked in a fight with a large man, easily a foot taller than him. I bit my lip, tensing as he swung and dodged, stepping back as the man gained ground. I inhaled sharply as Doran spun, slicing through the man's thigh, and the human dropped to the ground. Doran slit his throat and turned to the next human.

Movement beyond him caught my attention.

Evander.

He stalked furiously to Doran from behind, sword in hand.

"Doran!" I shouted, but nobody heard me. "Doran!"

It was too loud.

Nobody heard me.

"Doran!" I screamed.

It was too late.

Doran froze, lowering his eyes to see the sword protruding from his chest.

A piercing scream sounded from the center of the field as

Delphia materialized, her eyes locked on Doran as he fell to the ground.

I choked on a sob as she screamed again—a shattered, heartbroken scream.

Her face twisted in agony, and she disappeared again.

Then, there was a flash of red hair, and my heart skipped a beat.

Red hair.

I followed it to see Finley, just as he locked eyes with me. His face fell before twisting into anger or disgust—I couldn't tell.

My breath caught in my throat, and I stumbled back from the ledge. My eyes shot to Rogue, but his were glued to the lifeless body of his only friend.

I dropped my gaze back to Finley. He was studying me, his head cocked to the side. Time slowed as he lifted his face to Rogue, making the connection. He angrily tore the bow from his back and docked a thick arrow.

"Rogue..." I whispered. "Rogue!"

Finley pulled the arrow back, aiming.

"Rogue!" I screamed with every ounce of my soul.

His eyes snapped to me just as an arrow struck him in the heart, slipping straight through a small gap in his armor.

A silent scream stuck in my throat as I fell to my knees. He mouthed some words to me, but I couldn't make them out. With one final flap of his wings, he stilled and fell.

I felt it, the life leaving his body, his presence being pulled from the mate mark at my neck, leaving me.

He tumbled end over end, and by the time he hit the ground, it was gone.

There was no pulse.

No energy.
No life.
No life.
No life.
My vision blackened as those two words echoed endlessly in my skull.

Agony ripped through me, and I screamed, shredding my throat.

The sky cleaved in two as a long streak of lightning cracked across the sky just before it went dark, blotting out the sun as rain beat down from the clouds.

Wind whipped all around me as I crumpled to the ground, folding in on myself.

A tunnel of wind and rain formed around me as screaming filled my ears.

It was overwhelming.

The pain.

Take me with you, I silently pleaded to Rogue. Although, I knew he couldn't hear me. He would never hear me again.

Take me with you.

Take me with you.

Electricity hummed and popped around me, my hair standing on end. I threw my head back and a guttural scream ripped from my chest.

I screamed at the sky, who saw everything and did nothing.

Rain pelted my face as murderous lightning rippled across the black clouds and I shot my hand to the sky.

Lightning struck me, pulling me into its embrace.

For a moment, I could breathe.

For a moment, I could forget.

For a moment, I hovered between my realm and the realm

that was just energy, that just observed.

I opened my eyes to find another pair of gray eyes staring back at me, older with smile wrinkles in the corners. They were strained as a whisper surrounded me.

Go.

I almost wanted to stay, to spare myself from the impending devastation that awaited me, but they needed me.

He needed me.

Lightning struck the ground near Rogue's body and dropped me. I staggered to my feet and ran to him, tears pouring down my cheeks, washed away by the rain.

I slowed as I neared him and dropped to my knees, my hands trembling as they hovered over him.

"Please, Rogue. Please." My hands gripped his arm as my head fell to his shoulder. I scrunched my eyes, staving off the sobs tightening my throat. "I-I—"

I need you.

Sitting up, I carefully pulled the arrow from his chest, wincing at the sound before I tossed it aside.

"You are not leaving me," I managed, shaking my head and delicately placing my hands on either side of his chest. "You are *not* leaving me."

My power thrummed beneath the skin, nearly vibrating, and I closed my eyes, releasing it. It flowed willingly into his body and the broken skin over his chest glowed a faint blue. I tried to visualize it stopping the bleeding, closing the wounds. Mending him. Healing him. Reviving him.

Still no heartbeat. A shaky cry escaped me.

I pushed into his chest harder, begging it to work, but the exhaustion was setting in, and I was losing my grasp on consciousness. My shoulders slumped as my arms shook, but

CHAPTER THIRTY

I forced it to continue. My vision tunneled to him, blackening at the edges.

The wound at his chest slowly closed, the skin rippling with blue light as it mended. The blood sizzled, evaporating into smoke, and I released a breath and paused, waiting.

He didn't move.

I ripped the rest of his soaked shirt off in a frenzy.

There was no wound, the blood gone, but there was still no pulse.

"No," I cried as I cupped his face, kissing his forehead, his cheeks, his closed eyes. "No, no, no."

I sat back on my heels as my thoughts spiraled. "I-I need more."

More energy.

More power.

My hand shot to the sky again, but when the lightning struck this time, I held, screaming as I fed from it, absorbed it. The crackling intensity burned into my palm, splitting the skin down my forearm, revealing a silver light instead of blood.

My hand shook. My whole body shook with exhaustion and the overload of power, but I clenched my jaw and braced myself as I stared at Rogue's pale face. Every muscle in my body strained, but I continued.

I took everything the sky offered me.

I will save you, even if it kills me.

Just when it felt like I would explode, the bolt disappeared, and I slammed my palm into his chest. Bolts of silver lightning erupted in every direction across his skin.

"Start his heart," I commanded. My vision darkened, and I swayed. "Start. His. Heart!"

Every ounce of power drained from my body into him, and my arms collapsed. I slumped on top of him, weak and utterly consumed. Turning my head, I pressed my ear to his chest.

Thump.

I froze.

Thump, thump.

Thick arms wrapped around me, and I gasped, a fresh wave of tears falling as I struggled to sit up, meeting the warm red eyes staring back at me.

"Little storm," he rasped as he reached a hand up to wipe the tears from my cheek with his thumb. My hand reached to cover his, and I pulled it down to my mouth, kissing his palm.

"I—"

The word stuck in my throat as pain laced my abdomen.

I slowly looked down to see the head of an arrow protruding from my stomach. Rogue roared behind me as I turned in the direction of the archer.

I gasped, choking on pain. Evander was standing across the field, a bow in his hands.

Why...

Suddenly, a shimmering started above his shoulder, and my mouth fell open as Delphia's vengeful face faded into existence behind him, the icy face of death incarnate replaced her once cheerful one.

She leaned down to his ear, and his eyes bulged as she whispered something unintelligible. A sword thrust through his chest. He heaved, falling to his knees.

When his eyes lifted and returned to my face, he was… confused.

Recognition crossed his features as he looked at me, and

CHAPTER THIRTY

he smiled faintly before his eyes dropped to the arrow and pool of blood soaking the ground beneath me. Pain and guilt twisted his face as his mouth fell open in a silent scream, a shaky hand reaching towards me.

A final tear slid from my eye.

The last thing I saw was Delphia's dagger as it sliced Evander's throat.

Chapter Thirty One

Three Days Later...

Rogue

A ra and I sat in my chambers, quietly watching the rain fall when a note floated from the fireplace. I caught it as it drifted on the breeze and unfolded it.

> *Rogue,*
>
> *We have arrived in Blackburn. Upon your request, the innkeeper has granted us rooms and warm meals. Everyone is fine. Tired, but fine.*
>
> *Have you heard from Delphia? She never returned to us, and I'm starting to worry. Please let me know if you hear anything from her.*
>
> *See you soon,*
> *Thana*

I handed the note to Ara and rested my chin on my hand. Delphia had disappeared with Doran's body a few moments

CHAPTER THIRTY ONE

after she killed Evander. We hadn't heard from her since, despite having written to her multiple times. The letters burned, so she was alive, just not replying, and I think that hurt Thana more than she let on.

Doran's death was something I tried not to think about, not yet. It left a gap in my world where he should be, and with it came a lingering cold that his warmth had always filled. He unknowingly saved me from the wretched depths of my father, and it killed me to know I couldn't save him in return.

I swallowed hard, shifting my attention to Ara.

She sighed, placing the note on the side table with her now-scarred arm. My eyes lingered on it, studying the marks that remained from where her skin had split.

The energy she had consumed to save me had permanently left its mark in the shape of silver lightning bolts stretching from the center of her palm up to her elbow, wrapping around her arm.

She had almost sacrificed herself to save me, and the thought twisted my gut.

And then Evander. *Fucking Evander.* When she collapsed in my arms—for the second time since I'd met her—panic clouded my every thought, worse than the first time, but once again, Iaso was able to save her and close the wounds from the arrow.

I had never known more gratitude than I did in that moment.

Losing her now, after everything, would have destroyed me, torn my heart from my chest and laid it bare for the disaster that would've followed.

But she was safe. For now.

Iaso was also able to close the gaping wounds along her

arm within a day or two, but the scar remained as a testament to Ara's selflessness, to her strength.

My force of nature.

Reaching out a hand, I caught hers and pulled her into my lap, lifting her palm to kiss it gently.

"Thank you," I whispered for the thousandth time. "I will never be able to express how grateful I am for you, and not just because you saved me."

She laid her head on my chest, gazing out the window. "It's not over yet. Adonis won't stop at this."

"I don't want to think about that just yet. Let us have this moment if only to catch our breath."

She nodded and I wrapped my arms around her, resting my chin on her head.

"When I was in the air, I knew I was about to die. I felt it," I whispered and she stilled.

"I felt it too," she uttered under her breath.

Tightening my grip on her, I continued, "In that moment, there was so much I wanted to tell you, and the thought of never getting to say any of it to you... It would have been my biggest regret." My chest was tight with the weight of the words I wanted to say, and I prayed she couldn't feel my heart pounding beneath her. "I don't want you to live another day, or Goddess forbid die, without knowing that I...I love you."

I had never said those words aloud. To anyone. Ever.

My cheeks flamed, and when she didn't immediately respond, my muscles itched to move. To hide. To escape the vulnerability.

She slowly lifted her head, and her eyes brimmed with tears. "I love you, too, Rogue," she whispered, nodding.

I released a breath of relief as warmth and happiness

filled me, expanding my chest. This was a feeling I would never grow tired of. It was addictive and intoxicating and delicious—everything that she was, wound up in a feeling that consumed me.

She consumed me, and I would gladly burn in her fire for eternity.

"Without you, little storm, I would still be lost in a world of darkness," I uttered, cupping her face to bring her mouth to mine.

She moaned into me, and the sound went straight to my cock. She shifted to straddle me in the chair, and I hardened beneath her as she ground her hips.

She tugged at my shirt, and the buttons popped off as she yanked at it, baring my abdomen. I grinned against her mouth as she undid the buttons of my trousers and freed me, groaning as she wrapped her hand around me.

She hiked her dress up, exposing her bare sex.

I love that. *Such a good girl, always ready for me.*

My hands gripped her hips as she slid down, impaling herself on me with a moan I wanted burned into my mind forever.

* * *

Ara

Grabbing the back of the chair for leverage, I lifted myself and dropped back down, taking all of him. My head fell back at the feel of him, and I ground my hips, pulling another moan from my lips.

"You feel so good, little storm." He knotted his fingers in my hair and jerked my eyes back to him. "But you will look at me while you take your pleasure."

My breath caught, and I nodded, his hand still entwined in my hair. Holding his gaze, I lifted myself and lowered again painfully slowly. I repeated, teasing him, and a smirk danced along my lips as he clenched his jaw with restraint.

"Such a tease," he groaned with a breathy laugh. Gripping my hip with his other hand, he held me in place as he thrust into me, hitting deep. A smile tugged at one side of his mouth, and he pulled out to slam into me again, slow but powerful, leaving me on edge.

"Rogue," I pleaded.

He thrust again, and I melted into moan after moan.

"My sweet girl," he said, driving into me harder this time, and a loud, breathy scream tore from my throat. He pulled me forward until my breasts were pressed against his chest to whisper in my ear, "Chase your release, little storm."

I ground my hips, moaning into his neck before lifting and dropping myself onto him. I repeated the motion, again and again, increasing my pace and lowering my hand to circle my clit, my breath matching my pace.

"That's it," he groaned. "Just like that."

The praise barreled through me, sending me over the edge. As I neared my climax, my face buried in his neck, and I drowned in his scent.

Then, I felt it.

The need to *finally* claim what was mine.

My tongue trailed along his neck to his ear, and he groaned as I nipped and sucked, grazing my way back down to the connection at his shoulder.

CHAPTER THIRTY ONE

As I rode him faster, I kissed the spot, and his breath caught.
Mine.
I bit, breaking the skin. My sparks licked at the wound, and he gripped my hips tighter. There would undoubtedly be bruises in the shape of his fingers, and the image only drove me harder.

"Yes," he hissed as his head fell back.

The taste of him hit my tongue, and I was delirious, drunk on the taste of him.

My mate.
Mine.

Then, everything shifted, and I understood.

I understood everything. The surrender. The deep, soul-craving longing.

Bound. I was bound to him. Body and soul.
Entirely his.

"This is what it was like for you?" I asked, tears blurring my vision as I cupped his face and kissed him again and again.

The idea that he'd spent every waking moment between that night and the one in Nautia fighting this—this heart-shattering desire—broke me.

"Never again," I whispered. Tears slid down my cheeks, wetting his.

"I would've waited forever," he whispered back in understanding as he took control of my movements. I wrapped my arms around his neck and surrendered.

He lifted me enough to move and pounded into me. Between the feel of him and the mate bond, I was drowning in pleasure. I would happily spend the rest of my days right here, doing exactly this.

Just as he slammed me down and filled me, he stilled, his

eyebrows pulling together. He brought his hand to the bite mark and pulled it away, examining it.

"What is it?"

"I don't know. It kind of burns," he grunted.

I stepped off and he gripped the armrest, his knuckles white. Jerking to his feet, he stalked to the mirror and examined the mark, but it looked just as mine had.

"Are you okay? Did I do it wrong?" I edged closer to him.

"No, it's not you," he said, his voice strained as he faced me. Scrunching his eyes, he reached up, clawing at the back of his neck. "My skin. It's on fire. It feels like it's being ripped from my body."

He released a pained groan that twisted into an agonizing scream. Smoke billowed from him in every direction, instantly filling the room. He ripped his shirt off, removing the friction, and doubled over in pain with his arms wrapped around his abdomen.

The position revealed his back to me.

The blood drained from my face.

The skin along his spine between his wings had split to reveal large, red-black scales.

He screamed again, and his eyes snapped to me.

Glowing red, slitted eyes.

A Letter

Dear Reader,

While I wish I could send this through the flames to you, this will just have to do.

Thank you *so* much for reading and taking the time to meet Rogue and Ara.

I never thought I'd get to this point, much less have others reading my work, and I don't think it will ever feel less terrifying, releasing a book to the world. To scrutiny. But it has been an incredible journey getting to tell their story. Rogue and Ara, my sweet babies, have become so special to me and their story deserved to be told.

I hope you loved them as much as I did. <3

With all the love in my little writer heart,
　JD Linton

PS. Book 2 is the works. **The Last Draig** will be coming in 2023.

About the Author

JD Linton is the Amazon Best-Selling debut author of The Last Storm.

She is married to her high school sweetheart and a mother of one. She enjoys reading and writing spicy fantasy romance, and as with most writing mamas, she's also a midnight writer—up all day with her real baby and up all night with her fictional babies.

When not writing, you can find her reading, making a million tiktoks, or at the park with her son.

She is currently working on her debut series and is so excited to see where it leads. Writing has truly changed her life and she's even more thankful for the incredible community it brought with it.

Made in United States
Troutdale, OR
10/04/2024